Then Came Heaven

Then Came Heaven

LaVyrle Spencer

G. P. Putnam's Sons

New York

G. P. Putnam's Sons
Publishers Since 1838
a member of
Penguin Putnam Inc.
200 Madison Avenue
New York, NY 10016

Library of Congress Cataloging-in-Publication Data

Spencer, LaVyrle.
Then came heaven / LaVyrle Spencer.
p.   cm.
ISBN 0-399-14369-6 (acid-free paper)
I. Title.
PS3569.P4534T49   1997
813'.54—dc21   97-36715 CIP

Printed in the United States of America

1   3   5   7   9   10   8   6   4   2

This book is printed on acid-free paper. ♾

Book design by Jennifer Ann Daddio

pled their world and mine when I was little, I have indiscriminately dropped the names of real people into this book. Many of them are now dead; some are not. Not one of them spoke the lines I made them speak, or knew a nun named Sister Regina, for she did not exist.

But Sister Dora did. And still does. She taught me first and second grades, and I include her as a character with thanks for her send-off that made me love school for the rest of my life. Sister Marl, grades three and four, helped me remember those wonderful school days. She is still a nun today, and a gentle, sweet lady.

My mom was so much like Krystyna. It was she who set hair for pin money, and made all our clothes, and sent my sister and me off to school looking like "little dolls" (her words). My dad wasn't the school janitor, but he did make the furniture and cabinets in our yellow brick house, along with our playhouse, and his workshop out back. He did put in a bathroom for my mom, and it was she who painted the cabinets pink. She hung the washer on the light string for us, too.

Our home had an open-door policy and a coffeepot always on the woodstove. Friends didn't knock. They walked in and poured a cup.

On a cloudy autumn day in 1996 I walked back into St. Joseph's parochial school to check some detail for this book. It was midmorning. A school day. The building was absolutely deserted, the big doors unlocked, classroom doors thrown open the way doors were left when I was a child. All the kids were next door in the church: it was Grandparents' Day. I walked over and slipped in, and there they were, performing some pretty little song for their grandpas and grandmas, and I thought how little it had changed. Still a pretty good place to raise kids.

The house where the nuns lived is gone, along with the beautiful altars that were there in the fifties. But the grottoes are still there, and my yellow brick house, too. Though it now houses the *Browerville Blade* newspaper, the bathroom cupboards are still pink!

It has been fun going back, a trip down memory lane for me, and so too, perhaps, for many of my readers who were raised in little towns like mine, particularly those steeped in the Catholic tradition.

Author's Note

❧

A songwriter once said of hometowns that when you're young you want to get away and when you're old you want to go back. Browerville, the setting of this book, is my hometown. I left it at age nine, but I went back to the area when I was in my forties and built a log cabin close enough to town that I could drive past my old house now and then, walk into my old church and school, buy Polish sausage at the meat market, and remember what I now realize was a growing-up that set me off on very much the right foot. I had family love, a safe little town where everybody knew everybody else, and the grounding of church and parochial school where tradition created a strong sense of security.

It's not so surprising, then, that when I wrote my first book, I set it in Browerville. And perhaps it's not so surprising that now, as I write my last, I once again return to Browerville.

This story is a work of fiction. But in memory of my mom and dad and the folks who peo-

In loving memory of my mother and father,

Jennie & Louie Kulick

Thank you to all the people who helped me during the writing of this book:

Virginia & Bill McDonald

Sister Marl Gapinski, my third/fourth-grade teacher

Al Case, retired Northern Pacific engineer

Mary Gaida Brown, family friend and keeper of memoirs

Joan Gaida Schmitz, family friend

Jim Lucas, son of St. Joseph's janitor, Eli Lucas

Jean Poplinski, my dear aunt

who passed away before this book could be published

Fred Poplinski, my cousin who remembered so much

Mike Poplinski, my cousin who didn't remember much

but got me stood in the corner one time for running in the halls

Sister Ruth at St. Benedict's Archives

Sister Mary Kraft at the Sisters of St. Joseph of Carondolet Archives

This, then, is my last book. I am retiring, but leaving my many loyal readers with a glimpse of my early life, and with a thank-you for every single copy you bought and every single letter you sent. It has been a grand twenty-one years.

—*L. S.*
April 22, 1997
Stillwater, Minnesota

Then Came Heaven

$\mathcal{O}ne$

~⚬~

Thursday, September 7, 1950

$\mathcal{C}$yril Case was making the daily run from
St. Cloud to Cass Lake, sitting up high on
his box seat in engine number two-eighty-two.
Beside him, his fireman, Merle Ficker, rode with
one arm out the window, his striped denim cap
pushed clean back so the bill pointed skyward. It
was a beautiful morning, sunny, the heavens deep
blue, farmers out in their fields taking in the last
of their crops, most harvesting with tractors,
though down around Sauk Center they'd seen
one working with a team. They'd passed a country school a couple miles back where the kids, out
for recess, waved from the playground, and their
teacher—a slim young thing in a yellow dress—
had stopped gathering wildflowers, shaded her
eyes with an arm and fanned her handful of
black-eyed Susans over her head as she watched
them pass. It was days like this that made driving
a train the best job in the world—green woods,

gold fields and the smell of fresh-cut alfalfa blowing straight through the cab. And beneath the men the *shuug-a-shuug-a* of the steam engine hauling smooth down the tracks.

Cy and Merle were having another one of their friendly disagreements about politics.

"Well, sure," Merle was saying, "I voted for Truman, but I didn't think he'd send our boys to Korea!"

"What else you gonna do?" Cy replied. "Those Communists go in and start bombing Seoul. Can't let 'em get by with that, can we?"

"Well, maybe not, but you ain't got a nineteen-year-old son and I do! Now Truman goes and extends the draft till next year. Hell, I don't want Rodney to get called up. I just don't like how things are going." Merle pointed. "Whistlepost up ahead."

"I see it. And don't worry, MacArthur'll probably clean 'em up before Rodney gets any draft notice."

Up ahead on the right, the arm of the white marker shone clear against the pure blue sky. Cy reached up and pulled the rope above his left shoulder. The steam whistle battered their ears in a long wail: two longs, a short and a long—the warning for a public crossing.

The whistlepost flashed past and the long wail ended, leaving them in comparative quiet.

"So," Cy continued, "I suppose your boy's gonna go to work for the railroad if he doesn't get . . ." He stiffened and stared up the track. "Sweet Jesus, he ain't gonna make it!"

A car had turned off of Highway 71 and came shooting from the left, trailing a dust cloud, trying to beat the train to the crossing.

For one heartbeat the men stared, then Cy shouted, "Car on the crossing! Plug it!"

Merle jumped and hit the air brakes.

Cy grabbed the Johnson bar and squeezed for dear life. With his other hand he hauled on the steam whistle. Machinery ground into reverse and the brakes grabbed. From the engine through the entire train line, everything locked in a deafening screech. Steam hissed as if the door of hell had opened. The smell of hot, oily metal wafted forth like Satan's own perfume. The couplers, in progression, drummed like heavy artillery from the engine clear back to the caboose while the two old *rails*, with fifty-three years' experience between them, felt it in the seat of their pants: forward propulsion combined with a hundred tons of drag, something a railroad man hopes he'll never feel.

"Hold on, Merle, we're gonna hit 'em!" Cy bellowed above the din.

"Jesus, Mary, Joseph," Merle chanted under his breath as the train skated and shrieked, and the puny car raced toward its destiny.

At thirty yards they knew for sure.

At twenty they braced.

At ten they saw the driver.

Dear God, it's a woman, Cy said. Or thought. Or prayed.

Then they collided.

Sound exploded and glass flew. Metal crunched as the gray forty-nine Ford wrapped around the cowcatcher. Together they cannonballed down the tracks, the ruptured car folded over the metal grid, chunks of it dragging along half-severed, tearing up earth, bruising railroad ties, strewing wreckage for hundreds of yards. Pieces of the car eventually broke free and bounced along the flinty ballast of the rail bed with a sound like a brass band before tumbling to rest in the weeds. Throughout it all some compressed piece of the automobile played the tracks in an unending shriek— metal on metal—like a hundred violins out of tune. Dust! They'd never seen so much dust. It billowed up on impact, a brown, stinky cloud of it, momentarily blinding Cy and Merle as they rode along haplessly above the discordant serenade. The smell of petroleum oozed up, and sparks sizzled off the steel tracks, setting small fires in gasoline drips that flared briefly, then blew out as the train passed over them.

Slower . . . slower . . . slower . . . two terrified railroad men rode it out, one maintaining a death grip on the Johnson bar that had long since thrown the gears into reverse, the other still hauling on the air brakes that had locked up the wheels more than a quarter-mile back.

Slower . . . slower . . . all those tons of steel took forever to decelerate while the two big-eyed men listened to the fading squeal that dissolved into a whine . . .

Then a whimper . . .

Then silence . . .

Cy and Merle sat rigid as a pair of connecting rods, exchanging a shocked, silent stare. Their faces were as white and round and readable as the pressure gauges on the boilerhead. Number two-eighty-two had carried the Ford a good half a mile down the railroad tracks and sat now calmly chuffing, like a big old contented whale coming up for air.

Outside, something small fell—glass maybe, with a soft tinkle.

Merle finally found his voice. It came out as tight and hissing as the air brakes. "No way that woman's gonna be alive."

"Let's go!" Cy barked.

They scrambled from the cab, bellies to the ladder, free-sliding down the grab rails. From the caboose, twenty cars back, the conductor and a brakeman came running—two bouncing dots in the distance—shouting, "What happened?" A second brakeman stayed behind, already igniting a fusee that started spewing red smoke into the gentle September morning, mixing the stink of sulphur with the sweetness of the fresh-cut alfalfa.

Running along beside the locomotive, Cy yelled, "Look there, the engine's hardly damaged." The lifting lever on the drawbar was a little scraped up, and a couple of grab bars were marred, but when the two men rounded the snout of the engine, they halted dead in their tracks.

It was a sickening sight, that car riding thin on the pilot as if it had been flattened for a junkyard. The coupler at the front of the cowcatcher had actually pierced the metal of the automobile and protruded like a shining silver eye. Some broken glass remained in the driver's-side window, jagged as lightning.

Cy moved close and peered in.

She was brown-haired. Young. Pretty. Or had been. Wearing a nice little blue flowered housedress. Surrounded by broken fruit jars. He closed his mind to the rest and reached in to see if she was still alive.

After nearly a minute, he withdrew his hand and stood on a crosstie facing Merle.

"I think she's dead."

"You sure?"

"No pulse that I can feel."

Merle remained as colorless as whey. His lips moved silently, but not a sound came out. Cy could see he'd have to take charge here.

"We're gonna need a jack to get her out of there," he told Merle. "You better run to the highway and flag down a car. Tell 'em to run to Browerville and get help . . ." Merle was already hustling off at an ungainly trot. ". . . and have 'em call the sheriff in Long Prairie!"

At that moment the conductor and brakeman reached Cy, panting.

"He dead?" one of them asked.

"She. It's a woman."

"Oh my God." The conductor had a huge florid face that hung in soft folds from his cheekbones. He glanced at the wreck, then back at Cy. "She dead?"

"I think so. Couldn't feel any pulse."

They stood motionless, absorbing the shock while Cy, the engineer whose job it was to take command in emergencies, took control of the situation.

"Better get that other fusee out," he told the brakeman.

"Yeah, sure thing." The brakeman headed up the track to the north, waving a red flag as he went, to set out the warning for any southbound trains. A mile he would go before igniting the flare, while the other brakeman walked a mile off the rear of the train and did the same thing.

Left alone with Cy, the conductor said, "There's fruit jars all along the tracks. What do you suppose she was doing with all those fruit jars?"

The two men gazed back along the tracks at the shimmers of sunlight glancing off the pieces of broken glass.

"Probably some farmer's wife with a big garden," Cy replied.

Reaction to the tragedy only now began setting in, delayed like the sting that follows a slap. Cy felt it deep in his vitals, a terrible trembling that traveled to his extremities and brought a faint nausea as he stood at the head of the train with a dead woman caught in the twisted wreckage of her gray automobile.

"Her license plate is gone. The back one anyway. I'll see if the front one is there." The conductor walked further around the train, but came back long-faced. "Gone too. Want me to walk back along the tracks and see if I can find it?"

"She's got a purse," Cy said, dully. "I saw it under one of her . . ." He quit talking and swallowed hard.

"Want me to get it, Cy?"

"No, that's . . . that's all right. I will."

Cy steeled himself and returned to the wreckage while a herd of lethargic holsteins, chewing their cuds, watched from inside a nearby fence. The soft morning wind, not yet tainted by the red sulphur from the faraway fusee, carried the faint scent of manure, not wholly unpleasant when mixed with the continuing aroma of cut alfalfa. In the distance, a silo pointed toward heaven, where the woman had probably gone. Nearer, over a copse of shiny green oaks, a flock of chattering starlings lifted and milled. One of the cows mooed, and the engine, its steam kept up according to railroad regulations—gave out an intermittent quiet chuff. All around, the bucolic countryside presented a picture of life as it should be while Cy retrieved the purse of the dead woman and wiped it off on the leg of his blue-and-white striped overalls.

Merle returned from the highway, short of breath, and reported, "Fellow from Eagle Bend, going that way, said he'd get word to the constable and sheriff soon as he hits Browerville. That her purse?"

They all looked down at it in Cy's oversized hands. It was a little wedge-shaped white plastic affair with hard sides. Its handle had been broken in the accident, and its jaws skewed so the metal clasp no longer worked.

Cy opened it and looked inside. He picked things out very gingerly, then set them back in with the greatest care: a clean white handkerchief, a rosary with blue glass beads, a pack of Sen-Sen. And a small black prayer book, which he examined more slowly. Stuck in its pages was a recipe for "Washday Pickles," written on the back of an envelope, with the word *Mother* in the upper right-hand corner. A name was written on the front of the envelope with its canceled three-cent stamp and its simple address of *Browerville, Minn.* The same name was written on the inside cover of the prayer book, and on a social-security card they found in a small pocketbook that also held some school pictures of two little girls, and a dollar bill plus eighteen cents in change.

Her name was Krystyna Olczak.

*E*verybody in Browerville knew Eddie Olczak. Everybody in Browerville liked him. He was about the eighth or ninth kid of Hedwig and Casimir Olczak, Polish immigrants from out east of town. Eighth or ninth they said because Hedy and Cass had fourteen, and when there are that many in one family the order can get a little jumbled. Eddie lived half a block off Main Street, on the west side of the alley behind the Lee State Bank and the Quality Inn Cafe, in the oldest house in town. He had fixed it up real nice when he married that cute little Krystyna Pribil, whose folks farmed just off the Clarissa Highway out north of town. Richard and Mary Pribil had seven kids of their own, but everybody remembered Krystyna best because she had been the Todd County Dairy Princess the summer before she married Eddie.

The children around town knew Eddie because he was the janitor at St. Joseph's Catholic Church and had been for twelve years. He took care of the parochial school as well, so his tall thin figure was a familiar sight moving around the parish property, pushing dust mops, hauling milk bottles, ringing the church bells at all hours of the day and night. He had nieces and nephews all over the place, and occasionally on a Saturday or Sunday he'd prevail upon one of them to ring the Angelus for him at noon or six P.M. In truth, weekends meant little to Eddie; he had no such thing as a day off. He worked seven days a week, for there was never a morning without Mass, and when there was Mass, Eddie was there to ring the bells, most often attending the service himself. He lived a scant block and half from church, so when the Angelus needed ringing, he ran to church and rang it.

The bells of St. Joseph's pretty much regulated the activities of the entire town, for nearly everybody in Browerville was Catholic. Folks who passed through often said how amazing it was that a little burg like that, with only eight hundred people, boasted not just one Catholic church, but *two!* There was St. Peter's, of course, at the south end of town, but St. Joe's had been there first and was Polish, whereas St. Pete's was an offshoot started by a bunch of disgruntled Germans who'd argued about parish debts and objected to the use of the Polish language in liturgy, then marched off to the other end of town with the attitude, *to hell with all you Polaks, we'll build our own!*

And they did.

But St. Peter's lacked the commanding presence of St. Joseph's with its grandiose neo-baroque structure, onion-shaped minarets, Corinthian columns and five splendid altars. Neither had it the surrounding grounds with the impressive statuary and grotto that tourists came to see. Nor the *real* pipe organ whose full diapason trembled the rafters on Christmas Eve. Nor the clock tower, visible up and down the length of Main Street. Nor the cupola with *three* bells that regimented everyone's days.

And nobody was more regimented than Eddie.

At 7:30 each weekday morning he rang what was simply referred to as *the first bell:* six monotone *clangs* to give everyone a half-hour warning that church would soon start. At 8:00 A.M. he rang all three bells in unison to start Mass. At precisely noon he was there to toll the Angelus—twelve peals on a single bell that stopped all of downtown for lunch and reminded the very pious to pause and recite the Angelus prayer. During summer vacation every kid in town knew that when he heard the noon Angelus ring he had five minutes to get home to dinner or he'd be in *big trouble!* And at the end of each workday, though Eddie himself was usually home by five-thirty, he ran back to church at six P.M. to ring the evening Angelus that sat the entire town down to supper. On Sunday mornings when both High and

Low Mass were celebrated, he rang one additional time; then again for Sunday Vespers. And on Saturday evenings, for the rosary and Benediction, he was there, too, before the service.

Bells were required at special times of the year as well: during Lent whenever the Stations of the Cross were prayed, plus at all requiem Masses and funerals. It was also Polish Catholic tradition that whenever somebody died, the death toll announced it to the entire town, ringing once for each year the person had lived.

Given all this ringing, and the requirement that sometimes a minute of silence had to pass between each pull on the rope, Eddie had grown not only regimented, but patient as well.

Working around the children had taught him an even deeper form of patience. They spilled milk in the lunchroom, dropped chalky erasers on the floor, licked the frost off the windowpanes in the winter, clomped in with mud on their shoes in the spring, stuck their forbidden bubble gum beneath their desks and wiped their boogers on the undersides of the fold-up seats whenever they forgot their hankies. Worst of all, right after summer vacation, when all the floors were gleaming with a fresh coat of varnish, they worked their feet like windshield wipers underneath their desks and scratched it all up again.

But Eddie didn't care. He loved the children. And this year he had both of his own in Sister Regina's room—Anne in the fourth grade and Lucy in the third. He had seen them outside at morning recess a little while ago, playing drop-the-hanky on the rolling green playground that climbed to the west behind the convent. Sister Regina had been out there with them, playing too, her black veils luffing in the autumn breeze.

They were back inside now, the drift of their childish voices no longer floating across the pleasant morning as Eddie did autumn cleanup around the grounds. Instead he listened to the whirr of the feed mill from across town. It ran all day long at this time of year, grinding the grain that the farmers hauled in as they harvested. Eddie liked the smell of it, dusty and oaty; reminded him of the granary on the farm when he was a boy.

The town was busy. There were other sounds as well: from Wenzel's lumberyard, a half block away, came the intermittent *bzzzz* of an electric saw slicing through a piece of lumber, and occasionally the rumble of the big silver milk trucks returning to the milk plant with full loads, their horns bleating for admittance. Now and then the southwest wind would carry the metallic *pang-pang* of hammers from the two blacksmith's shops—Sam Berczyk's on Main Street, and Frank Plotnik's right across the street from Eddie's own house.

Some might disdain his town because it was small and backward, clinging to a lot of old-country customs, but Eddie knew every person in it, every sound lifting from it, and who made that sound. He was a contented man as he loaded a wheelbarrow with tools and pushed it over to the fishpond in Father Kuzdek's front yard to clean out the concrete basin that had grown green with algae over the summer. It was an immense yard, situated on the south of the church, with the rectory set well back from the street and fronted by a veritable parkland covering an entire half block. The statue of the Blessed Virgin Mary stood in a stone grotto near the street, a rose bed at her feet and a screen of lush green pines behind her. The long sidewalk to Father's house was flanked by great shade trees, intermittent flower beds and rock gardens, all of this surrounded by a fence substantial enough to stand till Judgment Day. The fence, of stone piers and black iron rails, set off the grounds beautifully, but it went clear around three sides of the church property and made for a lot of hand clipping when Eddie mowed the lawns. Sometimes though, the Knights of Columbus helped him mow and trim. They had done so last Saturday, the same loyal workhorses showing up as they always did.

Eddie was on his knees at the fishpond when he was surprised to see one of those workhorses, Conrad Kaluza, coming up Father's sidewalk. Con had hair as black as ink and whiskers to match, dark even after a fresh shave. He owned a little music store on Main Street and always wore nice trousers and a white shirt open at the throat.

Eddie sat back on his heels, pulled off his dirty gloves and waited.

"Well, Con, what the heck are you doing up here at this time of day? Come to help me clean out this slimy fishpond?"

Con stepped off the sidewalk and crossed the grass. He looked pale and shaken.

"Hey, Con, you don't look so good. What's . . ."

Con squatted down on one heel in the shade beside the pond. Eddie noticed the muscles around his mouth quivering and his whiskers blacker than ever against his white face.

"What's the matter, Con?"

"Eddie, I'm afraid I got some bad news. There's, ah . . ." Con paused and cleared his throat. "There's been an accident."

Eddie tensed and looked southward, toward his house. His backside lifted off his heels. "Krystyna . . ."

" 'Fraid so," Con said.

"She okay, Con?"

Con cleared his throat again and dragged in a deep breath.

"I'm . . . I'm afraid not, Eddie."

"Well, what's . . ."

"A train hit her car at the crossing out by her folks' place."

"Jezus, Maria." Eddie said in Polish—*Yezhush, Maree-uh*—and made the sign of the cross. It took a while before he could make himself ask, "How bad is it?"

When Con failed to reply, Eddie shouted, "She's alive, isn't she, Con!" He gripped Con's arms, repeating, "Con, she's alive! She's just hurt, isn't she?"

Con's mouth worked and the rims of his eyelids got bright red. When he spoke his voice sounded wheezy and unnatural.

"This is the hardest thing I ever had to say to anybody."

"Oh God, Con, no."

"She's dead, Eddie. May her soul rest in peace."

Eddie's hands convulsed on Con's arms. "No . . ." His face contorted and he began rocking forward and backward in tiny pulsing beats. "She can't be. She's . . . she's . . ." Eddie looked north toward his in-laws. "She's out at her ma's house canning pickles. She said she was . . . she and her ma were . . . oh, Con, no, Jesus, no . . . not Krystyna!"

Eddie started weeping and Con caught him when he crumpled. Over at Wenzel's the saw started up. It sang a while and stopped, leaving only the sound of Eddie's sobbing.

"Not my Krystyna," he wailed. "Not my Krystyna . . ."

Con waited awhile, then urged, "Come on, Eddie, let's go tell Father, and he'll say a prayer with you . . ."

Eddie let himself be hauled to his feet, but turned as if to head toward the school building on the far side of the church. "The girls . . ."

"Not now, Eddie. Plenty of time to tell them later. Let's go see Father first, okay?"

Father Kuzdek answered the door himself, a massive, balding Polish man with a neck and shoulders like a draft horse. He was in his early forties with glasses like President Truman's, their wire bows denting the sides of his round pink face. He wore his black cassock most of the time and had it on today as he opened the door of his glassed-in porch and saw who was on his step.

"Con, Eddie . . . what's wrong?"

"There's been an accident, Father," Con told him.

"Come in."

While they moved inside, Con explained, "It's Krystyna . . . she . . . her car . . . it was hit by the train."

Father went as still as if riddled by two hundred ten volts. Eddie had worked for the parish for twelve years. Father's concern for him went far beyond that of a priest for a parishioner. *"Kyrie, eleison,"* he whispered in Latin. *Lord, have mercy.* "Is she dead?"

Con could do no more than nod.

Father Kuzdek's breath left him like air escaping a ruptured tire. Rocking back on both heels he closed his eyes and lifted his face, as if begging divine sustenance. *"Erue, Domine, animam ejus."* *Deliver her soul, O Lord,* he prayed in an undertone, then caught Eddie around the shoulders with one beefy arm.

"Ah, Eddie, Eddie . . . what a tragedy. This is terrible. So young, your Krystyna, and such a good woman."

They took some time for their emotions to swell, then Father made a cross in the air over Eddie's head and murmured in Latin. He laid both of his huge hands right on Eddie's head and went on praying, ending in English, "The Lord bless you in this time of travail. May He guide you and keep you during the difficult days ahead." After making another cross in the air, Father dropped his hands to Eddie's shoulders and said, "I ask you to remember, my son, that it's not ours to question why and when the Lord chooses to take those we love. He has His reasons, Eddie."

Eddie, still weeping, bobbed his head, facing the floor.

Father dropped his hands and asked Con, "How long ago?"

"Less than an hour."

"Where?"

"The junction of County Road Eighty-nine and Highway Seventy-one, north of town."

"I'll get my things."

Father Kuzdek came back wearing his black biretta, carrying a small leather case containing his holy oils. They followed him to his garage, a small, separate building crowding close to the north side of his house and the rear of the church. He backed out his black Buick, and Eddie got in the front, Con in the back.

The Reverend Anastasius T. Kuzdek commanded the driver's seat the way he commanded the respect of the town, for though Browerville had a mayor, its undisputed leader was this priest. In an area of the state where the vein of old-world Catholicism ran deep, none ran deeper than in Father Kuzdek's parish. Legends were told about the man, about the time neither family members nor the local constable could break up a fight between two drunken brothers-in-law at a family reunion. But when Father Kuzdek was called in, he grabbed the pair in his beefy hands, conked their noggins together as if they were little more than two poolballs, and ended the fist-fight on the spot. When he stood in the pulpit and announced, "The convent needs wood," firewood appeared like Our Lady appeared at Fatima, miraculously delivered into the nuns' yard already dried and split. When he ordered school closed on the feast day of St. Anastasius, his patron saint, there was no school and no complaint from the Archdiocese. Some bigwigs in St. Paul once decided that Highway 71 should be rerouted to bypass Browerville, taking along with it the frequent tourists who stopped to see St. Joseph's, both the church and the grounds, and drop their money in the offerings box and spend more of it at the businesses in town. Kuzdek took on the Minnesota State Highway Department and won. Highway 71 still cut smack through downtown, creating its main street and running right past the front steps of St. Joseph's Church.

Father turned left onto the highway now. When he said, driving his Buick toward the scene of the accident, "Let us pray . . ." they did.

They spotted the red warning cloud from the fusee long before they saw the train itself. By now the cloud had stretched and drifted clear across the highway, stinging the air with its acrid sulphur fumes. The train, one of the little local freights, was only about twenty cars long, carrying hardware, grain, machinery, mail—hardly a deadly cargo, only the trappings of the ordinary lives lived in this peaceful rural area. They passed the caboose—even it had cleared the crossing—and paralleled the train until they saw, up ahead, on the shoulder of the highway, a gathering of vehicles: Constable Cecil Monnie's Chevrolet, a truck from Leo Reamer's D-X station, the sheriff's car and Iten & Heid's hearse. Browerville was too small to have a hospital, so when the need arose, Ed Iten used his hearse as an ambulance.

As Father slowed down, Eddie stared. "It pushed her all this way?" he said, dazed. Then he saw his car, flattened and ripped and peeled off of the locomotive in sections. Beside the train a body was laid out on a stretcher.

He left the Buick and stumbled through hip-high grass down a swale in the ditch, up the other side, with Father and Con close on his heels. The train was still steaming, its pressure kept up by Merle who would periodically climb up to read the gauges and throw another shovelful of coal into the firebox. The engine gave a hiccup, while across the tracks a herd of holsteins watched the goings-on from behind a barbed-wire fence. Nearer, the conductor, with his clipboard, stopped gathering accident data for the railroad company and stood in silent respect, watching the party of three arrive.

Never again would Eddie Olczak fear hell, for on that day, during those broken minutes while he knelt beside Krystyna's body, he experienced a hell so unfair, so unmerciful that nothing in this life or the next could hurt more.

"Oh, Krystyna, K . . . Krystyna, why . . . . . ."

Kneeling beside her, he wept as the souls in purgatory surely wept, to be set free from the pain and the loss. With his face contorted, he looked up at those standing above him and asked, repeatedly, "Why? Why?" But they could only touch his shoulder and stand by mutely. "How am I g . . . going to tell my little girls? What will they d . . . do without her? What will any of us d . . . do without her?" They didn't know what to say, but stood by, feeling the shock of mortality come to stun them, too, as Eddie looked down at his dead wife. He took the collar of her dress between his fingers. "Sh . . . she made the . . . this dress." He looked up at them again, fixing on the pitiful fact. "D . . . did you know th . . . that? She m . . . made this dress hers . . . self." He touched it, bloody as it was, while Father Kuzdek kissed and donned his stole and dropped to one knee to pray.

"*In nomine Patris . . .*"

Eddie listened to the murmuring of Father's voice as he administered Extreme Unction, the same voice that had prayed their wedding Mass and baptized their children. He watched Father's oversized thumb anoint his wife's forehead with oils and make the sign of the cross on her ravaged skin.

Krystyna's parents came, and her sister Irene, and they clung to Eddie in a forlorn, weeping band, and fell to their knees on the cinders, keening and rocking while Eddie repeated the same thing over and over. "Sh . . . she was on her way out to your house c . . . can pickles with you . . . that's all she was g . . . going to do, Mary. That's where sh . . . she should be right n . . . now. She should b . . . be at your h . . . house." And they stared through their tears at the wreckage of the fruit jars strewn along the railroad tracks, reflecting the noon sun like waves on a lake, imagining her loading them in the car a couple of hours ago, thinking she'd be returning home that night with all of the jars filled.

When they'd had time for weeping, Father gave a blessing to Mary, Richard and Irene, and the stretcher was borne through the ditch to the hearse, trailed by the bereaved. When the doors of the hearse closed, Mary asked her son-in-law, "Have you told Anne and Lucy yet?"

"Not yet." The thought started Eddie crying again, dully, and Krystyna's father clamped an arm around his shoulders.

"Do you want us with you when you do?" Mary asked, since Richard found himself still unable to speak.

"I . . . I don't know."

"We'll come with you, Eddie," Irene put in. "You know we'll come with you if you want."

"I don't know," he repeated with an exhausted sigh, looking around as if the holsteins in the field could provide an answer. "I think . . ." His gaze went back to Krystyna's family. "I think it's s . . . something I got to do alone. But you'll come over to the school with me, won't you? I mean, I don't know wh . . . what's going to happen after. What do we . . ." He stopped, unversed in the mechanics of death's aftermath, his mind refusing to function for the moment.

Father Kuzdek stepped in and said, "Come, Eddie. We'll tell the children together, you and I, and then you and Mary and Richard and Irene can all take them home."

"Yes," Eddie agreed, grateful to have someone tell him what to do next. "Yes, thank you, Father."

The little group dispersed to the various cars, a new dread spreading through them. For they all knew that as difficult as the last hour had been, the next one would be even worse, telling the children.

Two

❦

Sister Regina rang the brass handbell and
waited beside the west door for the children to come in from recess. They came barreling down off the hilly playground and gathered
on the narrow sidewalk that connected the
schoolhouse with the convent, a stone's throw
away. Double file they lined up, the same obedient ones doing so quickly while the usual trou-
blemakers jostled and aggravated. She waited
patiently until all of them were in rank and file
before leading the way inside. The hall was narrow and shadowy after the stark sunlight of the
playground. Some children detoured to the bathrooms while Sister went on ahead and placed the
brass bell on one end of the parapet where it remained while not in use—and woe to the student
who touched it without permission! She waited
beside the drinking fountain outside her room,
her hands hidden inside her sleeves, monitoring
their return to classes.

St. Joseph's Parochial School was laid out

symmetrically, with three rooms on either side of a central gymnasium, divided from it by a thick parapet topped with square columns that created a hall on either side. Each hall had two classrooms holding two grades apiece. At the northwest corner was the lunchroom; at the southwest corner the flower room, where the nuns raised plants for the altar.

At the east end the gym gave onto a storage room with a full bank of windows, but the folding doors were usually kept closed so the gymnasium remained gloomy. At the opposite end was a stage with an ancient canvas curtain sporting a tableau of a Venetian canal and gondolas rendered by some long-ago artist in the dull, monochromatic hues of rutabagas. Countless piano recitals had been held on that stage, for musical training was so vital a part of the curriculum at St. Joseph's that the gymnasium had been named Paderewski Hall, in honor of Poland's most famous composer.

That afternoon, as the third- and fourth-graders finished up in the bathroom, Paderewski Hall was dusky, as usual, the stage curtain lowered, the fold-aside storeroom doors closing off the rich east light from the gym.

Sister Regina held her classroom door open for the last straggler who tested her patience by continuing to guzzle water at the hall fountain.

"That's enough, Michael. Come along."

He took three more gulps, then swiped his face with the back of a hand as she swept him inside her room with the closing door.

She clapped her hands twice, then left them folded. "All right, boys and girls, let's stand and begin our afternoon lessons with a prayer."

Michael Poplinski jabbed his buddy Jimmy Lucas on his way down the aisle, feinted to avoid the retaliatory punch, then put on a burst of speed and skidded to a halt beside his desk. Sister waited with her hands folded while the shuffling subsided and the room grew quiet.

"In the name of the Father, and of the Son and of the Holy Ghost . . ." Thirty-five children made the sign of the cross with her and began the afternoon as they always did, with a prayer. When it ended, they took their seats with a sound like a flock of geese landing, while Sister walked around her desk to face them. She was a tall, thin woman with pale skin and kind hazel eyes. Her eyebrows were the light brown of summer cornsilk and her lips as prettily curved as the top of an apple. Even when she was displeased, her expression never grew grim, nor did her lips lose their forgiving lift. When she spoke, her voice was filled with patience and quietude.

"Third-graders, you're going to work on your spelling." Her two rows of third-graders occupied the right half of the room nearest the south windows. Every girl wore a dress. Some of the boys wore overalls with striped T-shirts, others wore corduroy pants and cowboy shirts. "The list of words is on the blackboard, and I want you to write them once on a paper of your own—has everyone got a tablet?" Fourteen children tipped sideways to search for their tablets. "Tear off one page, please." Fourteen sheets were ripped off fourteen tablets before the children tipped sideways again and stuffed their tablets away. Finally it was quiet and Sister Regina continued. "After you've written the whole list of words, use them again to fill in the blanks on this worksheet." She passed out the worksheets and got the third-graders busy, then went to the left side of the room to work with the fourth-graders on their arithmetic tables. She had brought a basket of oranges into the room to demonstrate addition and subtraction: three oranges plus two oranges equals five oranges. She gathered her twenty-one fourth-graders around her desk so they could all see the oranges and the corresponding flash cards.

At close range, it was obvious that the children had played hard in the hot sun at noon recess. The smell of their sweaty heads reminded her of the dogs they used to have on the farm who would follow her dad and brothers through the snow when they went to feed the stock, then come back inside and lie on the kitchen floor by the woodstove to warm and dry.

Still lecturing, Sister Regina maneuvered herself to the bank of south windows and raised three of them, letting the fresh air waft in, then pulled down the green roller shades above. The bright autumn afternoon light continued streaming in below the shades as she returned to her desk, where the arithmetic lesson continued.

She was still there shuffling oranges when someone knocked on the door. The interruption signaled a swell of chatter, and she shushed the children as she moved to answer.

In the hall Father Kuzdek stood with Eddie Olczak.

"Good afternoon, Father. Good afternoon, Mr. Olczak." She could tell immediately something was terribly wrong.

"Sister, I'm sorry to interrupt your class," Father said. "Could you shut the door please?" Father was recognizably distraught and Eddie had been crying. When the door closed Father said, "We've brought some very bad news, Sister. There's been a horrible accident. Eddie's wife was killed by a train this morning."

Sister Regina gasped softly and her hand flew to her lips. "Oh no." She made the sign of the cross, then broke a cardinal rule by touching a layman. "Oh, Mr. Olczak," she whispered, laying a hand on his sleeve, "I'm so sorry." Horror had sent her heart clubbing at the thought of those two little girls in the classroom behind her and this hardworking and gentle man with whom they were all so familiar. Why them, she thought as she retracted her hand and knotted it tightly with the other against her black-clad chest. "Oh, my goodness, not your lovely young wife. What . . . what happened?" She looked to Father for an answer.

"She was driving," he replied, having trouble controlling his own emotions. "It appears that she was, ah . . ." He swallowed and bumped his glasses up to clear his teary eyes. ". . . she was trying to beat the train to the crossing on her way out to her folks' house."

Sister felt the shock rush through her, prickling her skin and making her skull tingle. Of all the women in the parish, Krystyna Olczak was the one the nuns relied on the most for help. One of the most cheerful, pleasant ladies in town. "Oh, dear me, this is so terrible."

Eddie tried to speak, but his voice was choked. "I have to . . ." He had to clear his throat and start again. "I have to tell the girls."

"Yes, of course," Sister whispered, but she made no move to return to the classroom and get them. Fully realizing his daughters must be told, she found herself reluctant to open the door and watch their happiness be shattered. They were such lovely children, Mr. Olczak's girls—carefree, polite, above-average students with Krystyna's sweet disposition, who never caused problems in the classroom or on the playground. They were children who were fussed over at home, clothed in pretty dresses that their mother made herself and kept starched and ironed to perfection. Many days Anne and Lucy came across the school grounds holding hands, their hair fixed in ringlets or French braids, their shoes polished and their hot-lunch money tied into the corners of their cloth handkerchiefs. Some days they went home for noon dinner, across the brow of the green playground, one block down the alley to their house, always returning well in time for the bell that ended noon recess, never late. Sometimes Sister Regina could tell that their hair had been neatened, their barrettes tightened and the bows on the backs of their dresses retied when they returned. Their mother had taken pride in her children, sending them off looking like little Shirley Temples, and when the Olczack family walked into church together on Sundays, everybody watched them and smiled.

But now she was dead. How unthinkable.

Poor little children, Sister thought. Poor Mr. Olczak.

Eddie Olczak was a simple, diligent, easygoing man whom Sister Regina had never heard criticized for anything. He had worked as the church janitor since before she came here four years ago, and everyone rather took his presence for granted. Tens of times a week she heard people say, *Ask Eddie*, or (if it was a nun speaking) *Ask Mr. Olczak*. Whatever anyone requested, he provided without complaint. He didn't talk much, just went about his duties with the tenacity and tirelessness of a draft horse, keeping out of people's way, but always there when he was needed.

It felt peculiar to see this man cry, to see him needing help when it was always he who was sought for help.

Yet here he was, standing in the hall weeping, with Father's arm around his shoulders. He was dressed as always, in a worn blue chambray shirt and striped overalls that his good wife had washed and ironed for him. He swiped his eyes and tried to summon the fortitude to have his children brought into the hall.

"I . . . I'll be all right," he managed in a cracked voice, drawing a red hanky from his back pocket. "I've . . ." He cleared his throat and blew his nose. "I've just . . . just got to get through this, that's all."

Father was cleaning his glasses—Father often cleaned his glasses when he was out of his depth—and replaced them on his head one bow at a time, letting the springy earpieces grab him behind the ears. When they were firmly in place, he pushed on the nosepiece and said, "Please get the children, Sister."

Give me strength, O Lord, she prayed, turning back into her classroom to carry out the hardest assignment she had ever been given.

The room had grown noisy in her absence. The fourth-graders were still gathered around the oranges at her desk. She clapped her hands twice and sent them back to their desks, all but Anne Olczack to whom she said, "Please wait here, Anne, by my desk."

"Should I put the oranges back in the basket, Sister?" Anne offered. She was a thoughtful child, taught to be helpful by both of her parents, always eager to please in any way she could.

"Yes, Anne, thank you."

Anne had pretty blue eyes and brown hair parted in the middle today and drawn back with matching barrettes. Her dress was green and brown plaid with a white collar and a ruffle that formed a V in the front. Sister Regina touched her on the shoulder and felt a welling inside such as she'd never experienced before, made up of empathy and love for this child who had blithely bid her mother goodbye this morning with absolute trust that she'd be there at home waiting at the end of the school day.

Who would be there for her and Lucy from now on?

Halfway down the aisle closest to the windows, Lucy was laboring over her spelling words, gripping her pencil and concentrating so hard that the tip of her tongue was showing. Lucy resembled her older sister, but with a smattering of freckles and one dimple in her left cheek. Teachers were not supposed to have favorites, but Sister Regina couldn't help favoring the Olczak children. It wasn't only that they were pretty as pansies, but that they showered their inveterate sweetness indiscriminately on their classmates and on each other.

Anne, the older, mothered and protected her younger sister. Last year when one of the big boys, a seventh-grader, had knocked Lucy down, Anne

ran halfway across the playground and gave him what-for, and told him that
Jesus was disappointed in him, and if it happened again she'd march straight
to Father Kuzdek's house and report him. What made Anne Olczak different from the other big sisters was that she'd have done it.

Lucy, the younger, reflected the care she received from Anne by demon-
strating it with others in her class. Yesterday, when her classmate Jimmy
Plotnik had cried because he'd put glue on the wrong side of his construction paper, she had patted his shoulder and said, "Don't cry, Jimmy, that's
the way we learn is by our mistakes."

Lucy was dressed today in a starched yellow dress with bubble-shaped
sleeves, biting her tongue and forming her oversized spelling words with the
concentration of one who believes the only way to make it to heaven is to
do exactly as she is told.

Sister Regina stopped beside Lucy and leaned down to whisper, "Lucy,
your father is here to talk to you and your sister. Will you come out into
the hall with me?"

Lucy looked up and took a beat to register this interruption, for even
though her father was there every day of the week, this was unusual.

"Daddy?"

"Yes. He wants to talk to you."

Lucy flashed a smile totally bereft of concern.

"Yes, S'ster," she whispered and, with an air of importance, laid her yellow pencil in the groove at the top of her desk, then slid from her seat and
led the way to the door. Sister Regina opened it and followed the children
out into the hall, her heart heavy with dread for them and for their poor,
grief-stricken father who waited. She wondered what was proper, to linger
nearby or to return to her room and give them privacy. The children—she
sensed—liked her and might possibly feel comforted by her presence. As
for herself, the thought of returning to her classes at this moment was in-
supportable. She was still so stricken that she needed time to compose herself.

Anne and Lucy, unsuspecting innocents, smiled and said, "Hi, Daddy!"
going to him as if he'd come to take them out of school early on some lark.

Eddie dropped to one knee and opened his arms. "Hi, angels." His little girls hove against him and hugged his neck while his throat worked and his face reflected torture. Sister Regina watched the children go up on tiptoe in their brand-new brown shoes, bought for the start of the school year. She watched their daddy's arms go around their waists and crush the bows on the sashes that their mommy had tied for the last time ever, that morning before they left for school. He kissed their foreheads hard and clung to their small bodies while Sister pressed the edge of her folded hands against her lips and told herself she must not cry. A line from the Scriptures went through her mind: *Suffer the little children to come unto me,* and she committed a venial sin by questioning God's wisdom in taking their mother. Why a good and young woman like that? Why not someone older who'd lived a full life? Why Krystyna Olczak when she was needed here by her family?

Eddie sat back on his heels and looked into his children's faces. "Anne... Lucy... there's something that Daddy's got to tell you."

They saw his tears and sobered.

"Daddy, what's wrong?" Anne asked, her hand on his shoulder.

"Well, honey . . ." Against her small back his open hand looked immense. Stained and callused, it covered the plaid cloth of her dress while he cleared his throat, trying to make himself say the words that would alter their lives forever. "Jesus has decided to . . . to take your mommy to heaven."

Anne stared at him silently. Her mouth tightened slightly.

Lucy said matter-of-factly, "No, Mommy's at Grandma's making pickles. She said that's where she was going today."

Eddie forged on. "No, sweetheart, she's not. She . . . well, she wanted to go there, and she *started* to go there, but she never made it."

"She *din't?*" Lucy's eyes got wide with bemusement, still no fear. "But how come?"

Eddie knew Anne would grasp the truth before Lucy, so he looked into her eyes when he said it. "A train hit her car at the railroad crossing, and Mommy died." The last words were uttered in a ragged whisper.

Anne's mouth grew more and more stubborn while she considered her father's words. Her concept of death came largely from attending requiem Masses. She and her sister, like many children in the parish, had been impressed into the children's choir which sang at funerals. But the solemn Latin words and the distant coffin so far below the choir loft left little understanding of what death really meant. Now, for the first time, its true meaning was beginning to dawn on Anne, and with it came denial.

"She did not!" Anne spouted angrily. "She's at Grandma's! I know she's at Grandma's!" She looked up at Father Kuzdek, the ultimate authority figure at St. Joseph's, a man who would set things straight. "My mommy didn't die, did she, Father? Tell my daddy that it's not true! She's making pickles at my grandma's!"

Father Kuzdek struggled to lower his considerable bulk down on one knee. His cassock puddled on the floor around the child's feet as he placed his hands on her shoulders and put his round pink face close to hers. His spectacles had bifocals and he had to lower his chin to peer above them. "We don't know why Jesus took your mommy, Anne, but it's true. She's in heaven now with the angels, and what you have to remember is that she'll always be there looking out for you, your own special guardian angel who loved you and took care of you while she was here on earth. Only now she'll keep doing the same thing from heaven."

Anne stared into the priest's eyes. Her chin remained stubborn, but it had begun to quiver. This time when she spoke it was in a whisper, much less certain.

"My mommy can't be dead because she's got to take care of us here. She was gonna make potato dumplings for supper because they're my favorites."

Little Lucy, mystified, glanced from her sister to the priest and back again, trying to figure out what all this meant.

In a tiny voice, she asked, "Isn't Mommy going to make dumplings, Annie?"

But Annie wheeled and flung herself against her father who was still kneeling, burying her face against his shoulder.

Unsure of what she should be feeling, Lucy asked timidly, "What's wrong with Annie, Daddy?"

Sister Regina had begun crying, her young, smooth, unlined face remaining serene while tears ran down her cheeks and wet the starched white wimple beneath her chin. She knew not for whom she felt the more pity, this father or his children. Though she had never longed for secular liberties, she suddenly wished for the freedom to open her arms and embrace them, the father included. But it was not done, of course. *The Rule of Benedict*, the book by which nuns lived, forbade physical contact with the secular. Thus, she stood in silent prayer, asking for strength for herself and the Olczaks, who clung together, two of them weeping, the third—Lucy—sending perplexed glances over her daddy's shaking shoulder at the priest and nun, as if asking their intercession for this enigma she didn't understand.

Father Kuzdek drew Sister Regina aside and said, "Under the circumstances, Sister, I think we should excuse classes for the remainder of the day."

"Yes, Father."

"I'll speak to your students first."

"Yes, Father."

They left the Olczaks in the hall and entered her classroom, where some disorder had naturally taken over. Father's appearance immediately silenced the children and sent them scuttling for their seats. He stood centered before them while Sister Regina remained near the door at the front of the room, her wrists overlapped inside the copious black sleeves of her habit.

"Good afternoon, children," he said.

"Good afternoon, Father," they chorused in a singsong, joining their hands on their desktops, transfixed as if God himself had entered the room.

He had a habit, when he lectured them, of clasping his hands at his spine and rocking back on his heels. When he did so, his high-topped black shoes would squeak. They squeaked now as he rocked repeatedly, lifting his face to the ceiling while composing both his words and his emotions.

"Boys and girls . . ." he began, then studied the hardwood floor where a streak of sunlight turned the boards the yellow of honey. While he went on searching for the exact words, absolute silence filled the room. "You all know what death is now, don't you? We've taught you about dying, and how important it is to be in a state of grace when you die. We never know when we're going to die, do we?" He went on, incorporating a catechism lesson into what he had to tell them. When he finally divulged that Lucy and Anne's mother had died today, Sister Regina sensed the change in them. The fourth-graders understood more fully. Some of them contorted their faces, lifting eyebrows, biting lower lips, expressing their dismay wordlessly. Others stared at Father Kuzdek, disbelieving. Best friends exchanged glances laced with fear or fascination. The best friend of Anne Olczak, Janice Goligowski, lowered her head onto her arms and kept it there.

Father gave them time to acclimate to the news, continuing his lecture for several minutes, then announcing that school would be closing for the remainder of the day and they'd all be going home as soon as the school buses could be recalled. He ended, as always, with a prayer.

"In the name of the Father . . ."

Sister Regina made the sign of the cross and folded her hands, but while her lips formed the words her mind was on the Olczaks, out in the hall, wondering how they would get along without the woman who had been the linchpin of their family, who had fed and clothed and loved them and kept their home the happy, thriving place it had been. Those sweet, well-adjusted children, she thought—let them not change. And their unassuming, hardworking father—let him persevere.

The prayer ended and Father asked the children to be quiet and obedient while he and Sister Regina left the room. He told her he would go himself to call Gus Drong and get the buses here as soon as possible. He asked Sister to go to the other three classrooms and inform the other nuns that school was being dismissed and why.

Returning to the hall, Sister was not at all surprised to find that two of Eddie's brothers and their wives had already heard the news and had arrived, along with some older nieces and nephews and one of Krystyna's sisters, Irene Pribil, who was weeping copiously in Eddie's arms. Krystyna's parents were there, too, hugging their grandchildren and weeping. Browerville was so small that it took no time at all for the word to spread that

27

one of its young had died tragically. Up and down Main Street and from farm to farm, the news traveled like a prairie fire, in many cases without even the benefit of a telephone. Krystyna Olczak was especially well loved by the women of the town, for she took in sewing and gave home permanents in her kitchen to earn pin money. She was a member of the Sacred Heart Society and the Third Order of St. Francis, and volunteered to set up the booths for the church bazaars and to decorate the outside altars for the feast of Corpus Christi. She contributed pies and cakes for bake sales and drove the nuns to Long Prairie when they needed their eyes checked, and took carloads of children out to Horseshoe Lake in the summer to swim, and in general, brought a dazzle of energy and willingness to all the works of charity she performed for so many. She was to the town's society what Eddie was to St. Joseph's: the one you could always call on to do more than her share.

It was no surprise that the crowd began to grow even before Eddie could get his children out of the school building. They continued arriving in the dimness of Paderewski Hall, hugging him, weeping with him, gulping back tears as the women knelt before Eddie's children and tried to console them, and the men offered to finish Eddie's daily work for him—sweep the classrooms, wash the blackboards, take in the flag and lock up the building.

It was Eddie's brother Sylvester who said, "Nobody's rung the death toll yet. You take the kids home, Eddie, and I'll do it."

Eddie—dry-eyed now, but trembling visibly—replied, "No, Sylvester, I want to do it myself."

Father Kuzdek was back by this time and interjected, "Eddie, Eddie, why put yourself through it? Let Sylvester do it."

Eddie stepped back and raised his hands as if pushing open a heavy door. "No, sir! No, Father! She was my wife and now she's gone and I've rung that bell for everybody that's died for the last twelve years, and now I'm going to ring it for her. I got to, see? 'Cause what would she think, my Krystyna, seeing . . . seeing someone else ringing the bell for her? She'd think, why, where's Eddie? How come he's letting Sylvester ring that death bell? And I thank you, Sylvester, for offering, but this . . ." Eddie's voice broke. ". . . this is my job."

The crowd in the shadowy hall remained silent. Eddie's children stood one against each of his legs, with their temples on his ribs and his hands on their shoulders. Lucy, who hadn't sucked her thumb since she was three, had it buried to the knuckle in her mouth.

"I'd appreciate it, though, if you'd take Anne and Lucy home. That's what I'd like you to do, all of you . . . take the girls home."

Some doubtful glances were exchanged. Some feet shifted. Some voices murmured reluctant agreement.

"All right, Eddie," Sylvester said, gripping Eddie's arm. "If you're sure."

"I'm sure."

"All right, then." Sylvester dropped his hand. "You want me to wait out on the church steps for you?"

"No . . . no, you go along with the rest. I'll walk home when I'm done. Girls," he said, dropping down to one knee, "you go with Uncle Sylvester and Grandma and everybody, and I'll be there in a little bit, okay?"

"All right, Daddy," Anne said obediently, "but I have to get my sweater first."

"Me, too," added Lucy.

Sister Regina was back in her room, preparing her children to leave, leading them in a final prayer of the day when the door opened and Lucy and Anne came in.

The prayer stopped and the room fell silent.

Anne said, "We have to get our sweaters."

"Yeah, we have to get our sweaters," repeated Lucy.

The two girls walked sedately as they'd been taught—no running in the schoolhouse—to their desks and got their sweaters from the backs of their seats. Their classmates stared at them in mute fascination, unsure of what was expected of them. Lucy's eyes met those of her friend Janice, but neither said a word.

On their way back to the door, Lucy stopped before her teacher, looked up and crooked her finger. Sister Regina leaned down so Lucy could whisper in her ear. "My mommy died, that's why we have to go home."

Anne nudged her and whispered, "Come on, Lucy, let's go."

Sister Regina thought surely her heart would explode into a hundred shards at the words of this child who still did not understand the import of today's tragedy. Again she wanted to put her arms around her—around both children—and comfort them, and thereby comfort herself as well.

But Holy Rule forbade it.

Instead, she could only say, "I shall pray for you both."

Somehow, today, the promise of mere prayer felt inadequate.

*E*verybody faded away and left Eddie, as he wished.

Lucy and Anne went off with his brothers Sylvester and Romaine, and their wives Marjorie and Rose, and the rest of the relatives.

The school buses came and the students were dismissed.

Father Kuzdek went over to the church to burn a vigil light and pray for Krystyna's soul.

The nuns retreated to the convent next door.

Alone at last, Eddie stood in the gloom of Paderewski Hall, laden with a frightful emptiness that hurt in much the same way as a hunger pang. It pressed up high and sharp in his midsection, just below his breastbone. There had been moments since receiving the news of Krystyna's death that he'd felt disassociated from what was happening, as if he were awakening from a bad scare to discover it was really a nightmare after all, and everything was all right.

But it wasn't all right.

Krystyna was dead, and it would never be all right again.

He remained alone for several minutes, relieved the others were gone so he could feel miserable without them looking on. Tears leaked down his cheeks, but he hadn't the energy to wipe them away. Instead, he buried his hands in his deep overalls pockets, glancing around the hall from force of habit, making sure everything was tidy at day's end—storeroom doors closed, classroom doors opened, no lights on anywhere, the bell on the parapet, a slip of sun shooting in from the flower room on the sunniest corner of the building. So much easier to think of common everyday responsibilities than of this huge and stultifying thing he was being forced to accept. So much easier to stay here than go next door and start ringing that bell. He sighed once, but it ended in a shudder.

Better get over to church and get it done.

He urged his feet to start moving toward the double doors at the end of the first-grade hall. The doors were constructed of wood below and small glass panes above. He noted that the lowest row of windowpanes needed washing; he'd do that tomorrow. Then he realized he probably wouldn't be here tomorrow. He'd be home, preparing for Krystyna's funeral. Once again the thought brought a quick flash of unreality, as if somebody had mixed up the messages he was receiving.

Outside all was silent. Not a bird chirped. Not a car moved past on the highway out front. Even the saws at Wenzel's had stopped, as if the entire town were observing silence in honor of Krystyna.

He walked next door to the church, across the skinny blacktop driveway that separated it from the school, and up the eighteen sandstone steps that rose to the majestic edifice above. It had occupied so much of his life, this church; it somehow seemed fitting it should require him now when death stepped in.

He entered through one of the center doors. It closed behind him, sealing him into the vestibule with its stuffy silent smell that he'd known since before he was baptized. It was the smell of aged wood and snuffed candles and of old-country traditions brought here by his Polish immigrant grandparents and the grandparents of his peers before the turn of the century. A pair of ornate holy water fonts, shaped like acanthus leaves, flanked the doors to the nave, pedestals so tall that as a child he'd had to reach above his head to touch the water.

He reached down now, wet his fingertips and crossed himself without registering the words that accompanied the motions. His mind was elsewhere, in a vale of sorrow so sheer it made him wish he'd been in the car with Krystyna, that he was with her now in heaven instead of here, preparing to ring her death bell.

The bell ropes hung to his left, beside a radiator, three of them, suspended from an ornate tower one hundred and fifty-two feet above his head. He knew which rope was which by its length and the number of knots, and chose the one that played the lowest most morose note. The rope was thick as a cow's tail, worn smooth and oiled by his hands over these last twelve years.

It took a surprising amount of effort to swing an inert bell that large, and a modicum of experience to haul on the rope just hard enough to make it ring once. But Eddie had done it so many times it was second nature to him.

Today, however, when his hands gripped the rope, nothing happened. Only his fists closing around the sisal.

I can do this, he thought, *I can do this. I will do it for Krystyna.*

His grip tightened.

His shoulders rounded.

His eyes stung.

Bonng.

The bell tolled once . . . for the first year of her life—born on the bed in her parents' bedroom out on the farm where they still lived, raised in the Polish Catholic tradition, baptized in this very church.

He waited a full minute, the longest minute of his life, while pictures of her flashed before him, a spectrum of pictures, from photographs of her as a child to imagined pictures of her last few seconds of life before the train hit the car. Oh, Krystyna, why did you do it? Why did you try to beat that train? If only I had been with you, I would have said, *Stop, wait, you can't make it!*

Bonng.

The bell tolled again . . . for the second year of her life—when she was photographed on the back of a draft horse so broad her legs stuck out like a dragonfly's wings. That was long before Eddie Olczak knew her, or loved her, or kissed her, or stood in this church and spoke vows with her or became the father of her children.

Bonnng . . . for the third year when . . .

Surely this was all a mistake. Surely when he finished and walked home Krystyna would be there, the same as always, wearing an apron, standing at the kitchen table, setting some woman's hair in pin curls. She would flash him a smile as he entered, and say, "Well, look who's here. It's my Eddie spaghetti." (Or sometimes she'd say Eddie confetti, or Eddie my steady, or whatever rhyming word came to her mind that day.) And he'd pour a cup of coffee, and lean against the kitchen cabinets and watch while she worked, and visit with the women, and wonder what Krystyna was saving up for this time. Twenty-five cents she earned for each head she set. Fifty cents for giving a Toni home permanent, which took her four full hours to do. She loved pretty clothes, and jewelry, loved to go dancing on Saturday nights over to the Clarissa Ballroom or out to the Knotty Pine Coliseum. Sometimes she bought perfume and lipstick from the Avon lady. Most often though, she spent her money on yard goods to sew clothes for herself and the kids.

But no more. No more.

Bonnng.

Oh, Krystyna, Krystyna, why were you taken so soon? How can I go on without you? How can I face that house at the end of every day, and who'll be there for the children?

Bonnng.

Twenty-seven times he rang that bell. Twenty-seven minutes it took him to tell the town she was gone, while he remained dry-eyed and stoic in the face of duty. And then, at the end, according to custom, he grasped all three ropes at once, sending up a glorious tintinnabulation of rejoicing— *life everlasting, amen!*—and it was then, as he rang the bells in unison, that Eddie finally broke. Surrounded by the deafening sound, his tears came all at once, and with them anger and condemnation. He hauled on those ropes as if to punish them, or himself, or to curse a fate too cruel to be borne, sometimes hauling so hard that the weight of the bells pulled his boots several inches off the floor, weeping and howling out his sorrow and rage where only God and Krystyna could see him, while above his head the bells poured forth a celebration of her arrival in heaven.

Three

～✦～

$\mathcal{E}$ ddie might have thought all the nuns went to the convent after the school buses left, but Sister Regina did not. She returned to her room and remained alone, listening to the soft weeping in the hall, the voices fading away, and his footsteps leaving the building. She had over-heard the conversation and knew Mr. Olczak was going over to the church to ring his own wife's death knell. In the quiet of the schoolroom she waited for it to begin. The sound of the first bell, and the picture of him ringing it, drove her to her knees in profound sympathy.

It was there Mother Agnes found her, with her back to the door, her forehead on her sleeve and her sleeve on the edge of the desk.

"Sister Regina?"

She lifted her head and discreetly wiped her eyes before turning, still kneeling, to face her su-perior.

"Yes, Reverend Mother?"

Mother Agnes was in her late fifties with a

prominent chin, ruddy complexion, and pale blue eyes that appeared huge and watery behind thick glasses. "Have you forgotten Matins and Lauds?"

"No, Mother. I haven't."

"Ah," Mother Agnes said, then stood thoughtfully for a moment. "We waited for you."

"I'm sorry, Reverend Mother, I . . ." A truly obedient nun would have followed her superior without a word, and this is what Mother Agnes expected. But Sister Regina felt as if she would suffocate if she had to kneel in the tiny chapel at the convent with seven other nuns praying Matins and Lauds, when she was having trouble drawing a steady breath without bursting into tears.

The death bell rang again, a lugubrious clong that seemed to reverberate forever.

"I beg your indulgence, Mother Agnes. I wish to stay here awhile, in the school. I feel that I need some time alone." Permission was needed for everything that differed from commonality within the religious community. Matins and Lauds were the ultimate example of commonality: universal prayers being sent up by every religious the world over at the same time of day. One did not ask to be alone to pray Matins and Lauds when your community was doing it together. To do so was to break your vow of obedience.

She knew immediately Mother Agnes was not pleased. Her watery blue eyes might hold a degree of understanding, but her mind was as fixed as the polar star: she had been a member of the Order of St. Benedict much longer than Sister Regina, and she understood the value of giving up *self* in order to serve God. Sister Regina had not fully learned how to give up *self*.

"It's the children, isn't it?" Mother Agnes asked.

"Yes, Mother, it is." Sister Regina rose and faced her superior.

"You aren't forgetting what Holy Rule says?" Mother Agnes referred to *The Rule of Benedict* by its common name.

"No, Mother, I'm not." Holy Rule said familiarity with the secular was to be avoided.

"At times such as these, when one feels compelled to offer sympathy, it would be easy to become too familiar." Given the attraction the Olczak girls held for Sister Regina—of which Mother Agnes was fully cognizant—the situation bore watching.

"They're so young to lose their mother."

"Yes, they are, but your concern for them would be better directed toward prayer than grief, and the sublimation of your own sorrow toward the greater glory of God."

Sister Regina felt a flutter of resentment that surprised her. She'd had Anne in her third-grade class last year and had tried very hard not to favor her, but within her black habit beat a very human heart that could not help being warmed by the child. Now this year, not only did she have Anne again in fourth grade, but along came little Lucy, equally beguiling, and Sister Regina felt herself drawn to her in the same way. To see them—her favorites out of her entire two classes—lose their mother, who also had been a favorite layperson, was the most traumatic thing Sister Regina had experienced since taking her vows. To be told she should sublimate her feelings, which were overwhelming at the moment, brought her such a piercing wish to rebel that she felt it best to keep silent.

Both nuns knew all of this as Mother Agnes waited in the doorway and the death bell sounded again. Furthermore, they both knew that Sister Regina had taken vows of poverty, chastity *and obedience*, and that of the three, obedience had always been the most difficult for Sister Regina to swallow. Mother Agnes was subtly reminding her of that vow. But Sister Regina was, at times, willful, and this, too, was against Holy Rule. Being obedient meant subjugating oneself to the will of God, renouncing the vanity of self-concerns so that only Godlike thoughts could flow within one, and the movement of grace could be felt within the soul. Sister Regina had tried to accept this. She had struggled to find inner peace, to spend time in contemplative prayer so as to reach that quiet place within, where she could feel herself in communion with God. But she was not sure she had ever succeeded. Furthermore, she could not understand how subduing her grief today could do her soul or those of the Olczak children any good. What she wanted to do was weep for them, and do it alone.

Mother Agnes, however, had other ideas.

"We must be watchful of worldly cares, Sister, lest they creep in and distract us from our one true purpose, which is to esteem a perfect union with God."

"Yes, Mother."

Mother Agnes paused momentarily to let her message sink in. "So you'll return to the convent for meditation?" Meditation always followed Matins and Lauds.

"Yes, Mother."

"Very well, then . . ." Sister Regina knelt to receive Mother Superior's blessing, then the two of them left the schoolroom together. While they trod the silent hall in their high-topped black shoes, the death bell rang again and Sister Agnes said, "Remember, Sister Regina, we must not question God's will."

"Yes, Mother."

As they left the yellow brick schoolhouse Sister Regina worked very hard to quell her resentment, to humble herself in God's eyes and accept Mother Superior's admonition. She focused all her thoughts on obedience and willed all worldly distractions out of her mind to let obedience flow in, and with it godliness. The two nuns walked side by side to the square white clapboard house a mere thirty feet away. It sat to the west of the school building and was shaded by a pair of elms half again as high as the three-story structure. They climbed a set of stone steps and entered via the back door, into an immaculate kitchen that smelled of freshly baked bread. The room had a single wall of built-in cupboards, a cast-iron wood range on one wall and in the center of the room an oversized worktable with a built-in bin that held fifty pounds of flour. Mr. Olczak filled it for them whenever it got empty, often with flour that his wife had bought and donated to the nuns.

Sister Ignatius, the cook, and Sister Cecelia, the housekeeper, were nowhere to be seen. The house was as silent as a cave.

They passed into the central hall that divided the house in half with a long strip of linoleum flooring that shone from a recent waxing, past the doors of the community room and two empty music rooms with their pianos closed for the day, up the hardwood steps to the second story, past the row of closed bedroom doors, to the tiny chapel in the northwest corner.

Inside the chapel six nuns knelt on six prie-dieux. Two other prie-dieux waited, empty. Mother Agnes knelt on one, Sister Regina on the other. Not a word was spoken. Not a head turned. Not a veil fluttered in the absolute stillness of the chapel. At the rear of the room an organ without an organist hunkered in the shadows. At the front, above a miniature altar, a pair of candles burned at the foot of an alabaster crucifix. The light from a pair of north-facing windows was muted by stretched brown lace that tinted the chapel the dim rusty hue of tea.

Neither the elbow rests nor the kneelers of the prie-dieux were padded. Sister Regina knelt on the unforgiving oak and felt it telegraph a pain clear up to her hip joints. She offered it up for the faithful departed, welcoming the discomfort for the betterment of her soul, and in the hope that she might more gracefully fulfill the vows she had taken. One of those was the vow of poverty: austerity and a lack of creature comforts, presently padded kneelers, were part of that poverty. She accepted this the way she accepted the sky being blue and the chapel being darkened: as part of her life as a Benedictine nun, and after eleven years since entering the postulate, she no longer thought of the softness of the furniture at home, or the luxury of drinking all the warm milk she wanted straight from the cow, or the greater luxury of occasionally staying in bed until midmorning. She folded her hands, closed her eyes and bowed her head like her sisters.

Meditation had begun.

Meditation happened twice a day, in the morning before breakfast, and in the afternoon, immediately following Matins and Lauds. It was a time in which it was possible to get closest to God, but to do that one had to grow empty of *self* and full of His divine love.

It was while Sister Regina was attempting to empty herself of *self* that the three church bells began pealing in unison, signifying the beginning of life everlasting for Krystyna Olczak. At their celebratory note, Sister

Regina's head came up and her eyes opened. It was he ringing them, Mr. Olczak—but, oh, how could he bear it? They should not have let him; one of his brothers should have wrested the job from him and sent him away without subjecting him to this most dolorous duty. Oh my, how heartbreaking for a man who obviously loved his wife the way Mr. Olczak did, to *celebrate* her death. She pictured him, toiling at the ropes, and became filled with a mild form of outrage on his behalf, the second time that anger had menaced her that day. Once again she tried to free herself of it by reciting Holy Rule. Holy Rule said anger robbed you of sublimity and thereby held grace from flowing freely through you.

But she found it difficult to eradicate anger from her thoughts today. It felt good, and just, and deserved!

She spent the rest of meditation doing exactly what Reverend Mother had warned her not to do, questioning the why and wherefore of Krystyna Olczak's death. She longed, during her moments of doubt, to discuss it with her grandmother Rosella, who'd had such a profound influence on her as a child. Grandma Rosella Potlocki had been the most deeply religious person the young Regina Potlocki had ever known. Grandma never questioned God's will, as Sister Regina was doing now. It was Grandma Rosella who had been unshakably certain that it was God's will young Regina become a nun.

There had been a moment, watching the Olczak girls collecting their sweaters, leaving with their aunts and uncles and grandparents and cousins, that Sister Regina had wished she, too, could be folded into the wings of her family, just for this one day. But she had given up all temporal ties to family when she'd taken her vows. Holy Rule allowed home visits only once every five years. Her *family* was now her religious community, namely these seven other nuns who lived, worked and prayed together in this convent and in the school and church next door.

She opened her eyes and examined them as discreetly as possible without stirring.

Sister Dora, who taught first and second grades, the most animated and happy of them all. She was the perfect choice for introducing children to their first year of school, for she respected them and was a gifted teacher. Although Holy Rule forbade special friendships within a community, Sister Dora was Sister Regina's favorite.

Sister Mary Charles, grades five and six, a tyrant who elicited satisfaction out of whipping the naughty children with a strip of rubber floor tile in the flower room. Sister Regina thought that what Sister Mary Charles needed was for someone to bend *her* over the lowest bench beside the gloxinias and wail the tar out of her backside one time, and see if she might change her ways.

Sister Gregory, the piano teacher, fat as a Yorkshire on market day, who declined dessert every night under the pretext of offering it up, then nipped at it after it was placed before her until it was gone. Sometimes she stayed behind and ate the unfinished desserts of the others while helping clear the table.

Sister Samuel, the organist, who was pitifully cross-eyed and plagued by hay fever. Sister Samuel sneezed on everything and didn't always cover her mouth.

Sister Ignatius, the cook, who was very old, very arthritic and very lovable. She had been here longer than any of them. Years ago she had taught, and stayed on after her classroom days ended, retiring to the kitchen, where she sometimes fell asleep next to the worktable with a paring knife in her hand. She had wangled the birth dates out of all the nuns and insisted on baking birthday cakes for them even though Holy Rule said they were to celebrate the birthdays of their patron saints, rather than their own. Sister Ignatius would have done very well being somebody's grandmother.

Sister Cecilia, the housekeeper, was an inveterate busybody who felt it her province to tell Mother Agnes anything that she discovered or overheard within the community, claiming that the spiritual well-being of one affected the spiritual well-being of all. Sister Cecilia thought that because she had once visited the Vatican she was irreproachable, but she was an unmitigated busybody, and Sister Regina was getting tired of forgiving her for it.

Sister Agnes, their superior and principal, taught seventh and eighth grades. Sister Agnes was very much in cahoots with Sister Cecilia in monitoring the consciences of the other nuns rather than letting them monitor their own. She was a stickler for Holy Rule and the Constitution of their order. She could quote both books verbatim and was more unbending than a superior perhaps ought to be.

They were all meditating in silence, each of them having been helped by Mr. Olczak hundreds of times, encountering him repeatedly each day, knowing him perhaps better than they knew any other man, knowing both of his children, and having relied upon their mother for her charity on many occasions.

Were none of them grieved more by her death than they'd been grieved by any death in this parish, ever? Could they truly divorce themselves from caring about the aftereffects of this tragedy on that family? Well, Sister Regina could not. To do so, she felt, would be a mockery of what this habit stood for.

O Father, forgive my faithlessness, for only in You can I find eternal joy, only in accepting Your will can I . . . can I . . . can I what?

A fold of her habit was caught under her right knee. She rocked the knee and intensified the pain, offering it up as penance for her wayward thoughts, seeking selflessness, finding instead that her mind was filled with images of Anne and Lucy and their father. Had he gone home to them now? To that yellow brick house that could be seen from the main corner of town, where his family and Krystyna's had undoubtedly gathered? Would he cry in his bed tonight without her? Would the children? What was it like to love someone that way and lose them?

Sister Regina was surprised when meditation ended. She couldn't believe thirty minutes had passed, but Mother Agnes rose and led the silent departure from the chapel, the line of women descending the steps in single file and gathering in the refectory at their accustomed places. They began with grace, led by Sister Gregory, their prayer leader this week. She called for a special blessing on the soul of Krystyna Olczak and on her family. Then their simple supper began—beef stew tonight, served over boiled noodles with a side dish of pickled beets, grown in their own garden and pickled by Sister Ignatius, and fresh white bread, baked by her that afternoon.

Sister Samuel said, "It's very sad about Krystyna Olczak. We will miss her."

Sister Cecilia said, "She bought us our last fifty-pound sack of flour and had Mr. Olczak empty it into the bin. She was a generous woman, the kind you'd like to see live a long life."

"Never missed a church bazaar or a bake sale," Sister Ignatius added.

Reverend Mother spoke up. "Though we'll all miss Mrs. Olczak, we must not question the Lord's will in taking her."

Sister Regina said, "Why not?" And seven forks stopped in midair.

Sister Regina knew immediately she should have held her tongue. Poor Sister Samuel was staring so hard it looked as if her crossed eyes might switch sockets.

The opportunity was too juicy for Sister Cecilia to resist. "Even though you have both of her children in your room, Sister, you know what Holy Rule says."

"But this was a special friend. Mr. Olczak's wife. Someone who took special care to . . . to . . . to see to our needs." Sister Dora nudged her under the table, but she persisted. "Tell me, Sister Cecilia, didn't she give you a ride to Long Prairie the last time you needed your teeth fixed?"

"Yes, she did. But that doesn't mean I would question—"

"I believe . . ." Mother Agnes stepped in, nipping this exchange in the bud, ". . . that at evening prayer we'll say a Litany for the Faithful Departed."

And so the talk about Krystyna was silenced and Sister Mary Charles brought up an article in the *St. Cloud Visitor*, the weekly diocesan newspaper, regarding a proposed decency rating for movies. While the talk revolved around the benefit such a rating would have for the schoolchildren, the meal proceeded as usual. Sister Samuel sneezed on the bowl of stew, rubbed her nose with her hanky afterward and tucked it out of sight up her sleeve. Sister Cecilia left the table and went to get desserts. Sister Gregory held up a hand, refusing her apple cobbler, which the old cook put before her anyway. When the meal ended, Gregory's dish was as empty as everyone else's.

Each member of the community was assigned a charge—a duty—each week, by Mother Agnes. Those whose charge was dishwashing this week went off to do them and help Sister Ignatius clean up the kitchen. Afterward they joined the others for evening recreation in the main-floor community room. Recreation time was part of their unwavering schedule. It lasted sixty minutes and everybody was required to be there. Each nun had a drawer on the north wall of the community room, and from the drawers came crocheting, knitting, letter-writing gear and books. Sister Dora read from a volume about the life of Saint Theresa, the Little Flower, while everyone worked on whatever they liked. Though conversation was allowed, little of it flowed, for Sister Dora had been *assigned* her reading by Reverend Mother, and it filled the hour of recreation time fully.

At 7:30 everyone left the community room and went upstairs to their own rooms, where they spent an hour and a half preparing the next day's lessons. Sister Regina used part of that time to read Matins and Lauds, which she'd neglected earlier in the day.

At nine o'clock a soft bell rang, and they gathered once again in chapel to chant the Divine Office and end with evening prayers, tonight the litany that Mother Agnes had designated. Then Sister Samuel played the organ while they all sang *Stabat Mater.*

After evening chapel the nuns retired to their rooms, locked in Nocturnal Silence which would last until 6:30 A.M., when everyone gathered in the chapel to meditate and chant the Divine Office from their Breviaries once again.

Sister Regina's cell was a duplicate of everyone else's, a narrow room with a single cot, desk, chair, lamp, window and crucifix. No bathroom, no clock and only a tiny closet in which hung two extra sets of clothing and a mirror no larger than a saucer, by which she could pin her veil in place or pick an eyelash out of her eye, should one fall in. The mirror was used for little else, for vanity had been forsaken along with all other worldliness when she took her vows.

She untied her guimpe in back and removed it along with the wimple—headband and veil intact—hanging them on a metal coat hanger bent especially to accommodate them. Next came the sleevelets and the loose scapular, followed by the cincture—the belt—with its three knots signifying the three vows she'd taken. From the pocket of her habit she took a black rosary and laid it on her desk before hanging up the long black dress. Sitting on her bed, she removed her shoes, black stockings and white garter belt, then donned a white nightgown from her closet, and sat down quietly to wait for the click of the bathroom door, signifying that Sister Cecelia was done.

Full baths were taken once a week, on Saturdays, for anything more would be considered wasting water, and wasting anything defied their vow of poverty. Practicing poverty had never bothered Sister Regina in the least. She sponged quickly, reaching underneath her commodious nightgown without glimpsing more than her feet. The last time she had seen her body she was sixteen, taking her own private vow of chastity long before she pronounced her final vows, for even then she had known that Grandma Potlocki was right, and she would enter the postulate as soon as she graduated from high school.

Communal living had never bothered Sister Regina except during bathroom time, for as a child she had been a dreamer, and it was during those long stretches in the outhouse on the farm that she had done her best dreaming. There, with the door propped open facing the woods, she had whiled away hours until her mother had called from the house, "Regina! Time to do dishes! You get in here now and quit hiding in that toilet!"

Eight women on a strict schedule in a house with one bathroom left little time for any of them to lollygag behind a locked door.

Sister Regina switched off the light, slipped from the room and met Sister Dora going in. The urge to whisper pushed Sister Regina's tongue against her teeth. She wanted to talk about Krystyna's death, and the children's loss, and Mr. Olczak's ringing the death bell himself, and of her own sorrow and misgivings, which were growing and growing as the night wore on. But Nocturnal Silence had already begun, so she passed her friend in the hall without uttering a syllable and entered her cell with a silent closing of the door.

At ten P.M. when the last bell sounded for lights out, she lay in the dark with her arms locked over the covers, stretching the blanket binding so tightly against her breasts she hoped it would relieve the ache within. But it relieved nothing. Instead, all the pain and sadness she had so dutifully sublimated came bursting forth in a rash of weeping. It surprised from her a single loud sob before she could cover her mouth and turn her face into the pillow. And while it started out as grief for the Olczaks it permutated into something altogether different, for at sometime while she cried, she realized she was doing so for her growing dissatisfactions over this life she had chosen. She'd thought Benedictine communal life would mean strength and support and a constant sense of peace within. A strifeless valley of serenity where sacrifice and prayer and hard work would bring an inner happiness leaving nothing more wanting. Instead, it meant silence when communication was called for, withdrawal when it was sympathy that was needed, and a Litany for the Faithful Departed when it was tears that were needed.

With the greatest of sorrow Sister Regina admitted that her religious community had let her down today.

Four

❦

When Eddie Olczak got home, his house was overrun with family, both his and Krystyna's. Nine of his brothers and sisters still lived in the area, and five of Krystyna's as well. Most of them were in his kitchen and living room, along with assorted spouses, nieces and nephews, and, of course, both sets of parents. So many people were there, in fact, that his little four-room house couldn't hold them all. Some had overflowed onto the side porch and yard.

The family members had been counting the chimes of the death toll, knowing Eddie was ringing it himself, and were watching for him to appear. Sometimes he came down the alley from the north, sometimes he walked the block and a half along Main Street, around the corner of John Gaida's store, then half a block over to his place. Today he came around the corner of the store and crossed the street kitty-corner. They were waiting, and moved toward him as he came up alongside the pair of overgrown box-elder trees in his front yard.

Their loving arms, reaching to comfort him, opened the floodgates again, and they shared tears as he was passed from brother to sister, father to mother.

Facing his parents was worst of all. He found them in his crowded living room and went to his mother first. She was a short, stubby woman with tightly curled graying hair that always seemed to smell like the foods she cooked. Her body was softening with age, and with each passing year it seemed to settle more and more into the shape of a pickle crock. Her face was always red, in the summer from gardening; in the winter from the heat of the kitchen range. He'd outgrown her by so much that now when they hugged, he had to dip his head to kiss her hair.

"*Mommo,*" he said, in Polish, as their arms went around each other.

"Oh, Eddie . . . my boy . . . my precious boy . . ." They did their weeping, and hugging, then he turned to his dad.

"*Poppo,*" he got out, then his dad's powerful arms were around him, strong farmer's arms with splayed hands as tough as harness leather, hauling him close. "She's gone, Poppo, she's gone."

"I know, son . . . I know . . ." Cass Olczak was not an articulate man, but a loving one just the same. He could only hold his boy and suffer with him, and hope Eddie understood that he'd do anything to take the pain away if he could, would take it solely unto himself if he could spare any one of his kids any kind of suffering. Cass had come straight from the fields in his striped bib overalls and smelled dusty and sweaty, with overtones of the barn. He was a thick man, a little shorter than Eddie, built low to the ground like the Cossacks from whom he'd descended. His brown wavy hair was beginning to recede, and he had ears the size of a toddler's foot, with large velvety lobes. Eddie's Grandma Olczak had always said you could gauge a man's intelligence by the size of his ears, so Eddie had always known his dad was one of the smartest men around. Cass had taught all his boys everything they knew about crops and engines and animals and carpentry and the thousand unforeseen repairs a farmer has to face in a year of running a farm. But most important, he'd taught them how to love a woman— not the showy kind of love that could mask a hollow core, but the faithful, undecorous kind that stood by, no matter what, with few words and fewer arguments, but a constancy that was immutable. Above all, Cass and Hedy's children knew security, because through all the toil of birthing fourteen kids, and walking the floor with them when they were sick, and putting food on the table for them when they weren't, and worrying where the money would come from for the oldest one's shoes, and how the bills would get paid during the years when the crops were lean—through all this they loved each other, and those kids knew it.

Cass, a man of few words, had once told Eddie, "You only marry once. Pick her right and treat her right and you'll be happy." It was as close to philosophizing as Cass had ever come, but Eddie had followed his father's advice.

They both knew this as they drew apart and Cass asked, "Why didn't you let one of your brothers ring that bell?"

"I couldn't, Poppo. Krystyna would've wanted me to ring it."

Cass had his hand folded over Eddie's collarbone, and squeezed it so hard he broke a couple of blood vessels. But Eddie was as honed and hard as his old man and hardly noticed.

"She was like one of our own, your Krystyna."

"I know, Poppo."

They were still standing that way, struggling to think of something to say, when Irene Pribil came up, asking in a shy, retiring way, "Have you eaten anything, Eddie?"

"No, I'm not hungry, Irene."

His mother said, "We should make coffee though."

"Yes," Irene added, "and there's cake."

Where the cake came from so fast, Eddie couldn't guess, but he wasn't surprised: these women thought food was the antidote to any crisis. They brewed egg coffee and before the first cake could be cut another arrived from a neighbor woman, Mrs. Berczyk. It was followed by other foods from other neighbors—a platter of deviled eggs, a roaster full of sliced roast beef and gravy, some pork chops over scalloped potatoes, fresh-baked buns and poppy-seed coffee cake, potato salad and sliced tomatoes from somebody's garden. Near closing time, Mr. Kuntz from the bakery brought over the last of his bismarcks and glazed doughnuts that hadn't been sold that day. Pete Plotnik came from the back door of his meat market across the alley and brought three rings of Polish sausage. The women warmed them and laid the foods out on the kitchen table that Eddie had made for Krystyna as a wedding gift. He had painted it white and she had trimmed the backs of the four matching chairs with fruit decals she had bought at Lloyd Berg's hardware store. They had figured that whenever they had more children he'd make more chairs in his little workshop in the backyard.

But there would be only these two little girls, the ones upon whom, at that very moment, the women were forcing plates of food, and who sat down dutifully on the front porch with a bunch of their cousins at a miniature table and chairs that their daddy had also made.

Lucy ate only a piece of cake.

Anne ate nothing.

One of her cousins, a girl a few years older than Anne, stood beside her chair with an arm around the younger girl's shoulder, patting her on the shoulder the way she'd seen the aunts do, while Anne stared at her food in silence.

Adults sat on the porch rails with plates on their knees, and on the wide porch steps, and inside the tiny living room on the piano stool and the overstuffed maroon horsehair sofa, and even out in the yard on the wooden platform surrounding the pump that wasn't used anymore.

Afterward, the women washed dishes, and the men stayed with Eddie, who asked six of them to act as pallbearers—three of his brothers and three of Krystyna's. The women hung up the dishtowels on the clothesline out back, and the air grew chill as the stars came out. The younger children started playing Starlight Moonlight, but were stopped by their mothers, jerked sharply by their arms, and scolded for their insensitivity. The older ones got sheepish and the young ones pouted, not clearly understanding what they'd done wrong.

The hovering departures began.

Eddie's mother said, "Why don't you bring the girls and come out to the farm tonight? Sleep there."

"No, Mommo, we'll stay here. I feel closer to her here. You understand, don't you?"

"Of course I do. But it'll be worse here, won't it?"

"If it gets too bad, I'll run over to Romaine's house and wake him up." Romaine lived a short sprint away, across the alley, through the vacant lot, across Main Street and around the corner from the creamery.

"Well, if you're sure . . ."

"I'm sure, Mommo. I promise we'll come out to the farm whenever we get lonesome."

"All right, then. Well . . ." She didn't know what else to offer. "I'll pray the rosary for her then." She pronounced it *rozhary.*

"Thank you, Mommo."

The four parents, plus Krystyna's sister, Irene, who had ridden with her folks, and Romaine and his wife, Rose, were the last ones remaining. Irene commandeered Eddie's arm and clung to it as the group moved toward the two cars parked at the boulevard. Eddie could feel Irene trembling as she clamped her elbow firmly around his, as if to steady herself. The tremors came from deep within her, and he understood what she was going through. She was two years older than Krystyna. The two of them had been closest. She had stood up for Eddie and Krystyna at their wedding, and because Irene had never married and still lived with her folks, she spent a lot of time here at the house. They had done everything together, Krystyna and Irene— given each other permanents, danced the polka together at the Saturday-night dances, made matching dresses, cut recipes out of *The Farmer* magazine, dyed curtains with Rit when their bedrooms needed sprucing up, and confided secrets.

What Irene was feeling was what Eddie would be feeling if it were Romaine who'd died.

When all the parents had gotten in the cars, Irene gave Eddie the last hug. It was meant to be a short one, but in the middle of it she let loose a sob and said, muffled against his clothes, "Oh God, Eddie . . ." She wept against his shoulder and he held her head fast, from behind as they rocked some, knowing that out of these two vast families, nobody would miss Krystyna more than the two of them. Husband. Sister and best friend.

"I don't know what to do," she said.

"Neither do I, Irene. Go on, I guess."

She cried a while longer until she had calmed somewhat. Finally, withdrawing from his arms and turning toward the car, she said, "Anything you need, you let me know."

"I will."

She climbed into the backseat of her dad's '38 Plymouth and Romaine shut the door. The cars pulled away and left Eddie standing on the boulevard with his daughters and Romaine and Rose, who had sent their brood home under the care of their oldest.

Romaine said, "You want me to stay awhile, Eddie?"

"Yeah, I'd like that, Romaine."

"The girls need baths," Rose said. "Why don't I take them inside and fill the tub?"

Eddie dropped a heavy hand on Rose's shoulder. "Thanks, Rose." To his children, he added, "Daddy will be right here. You go with Auntie Rose and she'll bring you down when your pajamas are on." He watched them go, exhausted and listless, following every order they were given because their emotions, like everyone else's, were in chaos.

Then Eddie and Romaine sat down on the porch step in the gathering dark. The night was quiet. From behind them the living-room ceiling fixture threw a patch of light across the porch floor and outlined their shapes in shadow across the sidewalk and grass. A couple of late crickets sang in the astilbe bushes at the base of the house. Across the alley, at the Quality Inn, Hub Ringwalski shut out the lights, closed his back door, and locked up for the night. They listened to his footsteps heading for his car, which was parked by the power pole out back. He started the engine and backed into the alley, left the car running and got out to step over the low double-railed wooden fence that separated Eddie's yard from the alley. Hub crossed the grass, bent down and took Eddie by the back of the neck and said nothing for a long time. Then he uttered in a choked whisper, "So sorry . . ." and went back to his car.

When Hub was gone, Eddie said, "What'm I gonna do, Romaine? What'm I gonna do?"

"Keep working at the church, I guess. Take care of the girls the best you can. The women will help you with them, and you'll get through it one day at a time."

"How do I go in there to that bed?"

"You can sure come to our house tonight," Romaine offered. "We'll find room for the three of you someplace."

"I'd still have to face it though, wouldn't I? Tomorrow night or the night after that."

"Yup. You still would."

They heard the sound of the bath in progress, and Rose talking quietly to the girls in the upstairs bathroom that Eddie had put in for Krystyna only a little over a year ago. Such a short time she'd had to enjoy it.

"You know what, Romaine?"

"What?"

"From the first time I saw Krystyna I knew I was going to marry her. It was at a wedding dance out at Knotty Pine, and I asked Poppo who that girl was and where she lived and if they went to St. Joe's. I found out right away that I was seven years older than her, but I made up my mind I'd wait for her. Then when she was fourteen I asked her out for the first time and I couldn't believe her folks let her go. But it was like they knew I was the one for her, and there was nothing they could do but let her go. They never uttered a peep, just said to have her home by ten, and I did. And we had to *walk*, too! Clear over to Clarissa to the dance, because I didn't have no car. But she didn't complain. Ah, she never complained. When she got old enough to wear high heels, if we had to walk, she just put on her low shoes and carried her high heels, and off we went dancing. Matter of fact, I think the first pair of high heels she wore she borrowed from Irene." He paused for a moment, then added, "I feel bad for Irene. She's really going to miss her."

Romaine knew all this, but he let Eddie talk.

Soon Eddie said, a little more animated, "Hey, Romaine, remember that time when you were dating Irene and the four of us drove your Model-T down the railroad tracks?"

Romaine laughed. "Lucky that damn car didn't bust an axle."

"Oh, we had some times, didn't we?"

"Sure did."

"And we picked up that huge snapping turtle out by Thunder Lake and put him in the car to make turtle soup with, and the girls screamed and climbed in the front seat with us."

"Boy, did that old turtle stink!"

"Those women about went crazy."

"I don't think we ever did make that soup."

"Nope . . . never did."

Eddie smiled into the dark. Soon his smile faded and he covered his face with both hands. Romaine flopped a brotherly arm around him and massaged his shoulder.

"I don't know how to cook," Eddie said, battling a new round of despair. "How'm I supposed to do my job and come home and fix supper for them, and wash and iron their dresses like she did, and fix their hair in pin curls and comb it fancy and do all that stuff? Hell, I got to be at church to stoke the furnace before Mass in the winter, and shovel the steps and ring the bells at seven-thirty and eight, and that's just when they should be getting up and getting ready for school. How can I be in two places at once?"

"We'll work it out, Eddie, don't worry, we'll work it out. All of us can help you for a while till we figure out what to do."

Eddie sighed and dug his fingertips into his eyes. Suddenly he squared his shoulders and exclaimed, "Hoo!" blowing the word out as if to fortify himself to go on without further tears. "I don't know, Romaine . . . I don't know."

The children came to the door behind them and Lucy said, "Daddy, we're all ready for bed now. Are you coming in?"

He turned and saw Rose standing behind them, folding their wet towels over her arm. *Laundry,* he thought, *how am I supposed to manage doing laundry after I get home at night?* Like all the other housewives, Krystyna had spent every Monday morning, the entire morning, washing in the wringer washer and hanging the clothes on the line, then a good hour folding things in the late afternoon and some more time dampening the stuff that needed ironing. Ironing itself took hours and hours on Tuesdays. Hell, Eddie had never handled an iron in his life. Boys didn't need to learn how. His mother and sisters had done the ironing at home, while he and his brothers helped in the fields. Now ironing, too, would fall to him.

"Daddy?" Lucy repeated, her voice small and lost.

"I'm coming in now, dumpling." The pet name reminded him of the dumplings Krystyna had planned to make them for supper tonight, but he pushed the thought from his head and went inside. The reminders would be everywhere for a long, long while, and he must not give in to weeping every time they surfaced.

After Romaine and Rose went home he closed the doors against the night chill and turned to find the girls hovering a footstep away, looking up at him as if fearing he, too, would disappear from their lives. "Girls . . ." he said, and dropped down to their level. They moved into his open arms the way floodwaters move into riverbanks, pushing and burrowing and eroding his substructure. What to say to them, how to fill this immense void, how to be strong for them when he felt annihilated. He couldn't offer any of the usual platitudes—Do you want to color? How about a cookie?—they didn't want color crayons or cookies. What they wanted was their mother, and he couldn't bring her back.

"I was thinking . . ." He struggled to think of a diversion for his children, then extemporized. ". . . you don't have to go to school tomorrow if

you don't want to. Maybe you'd like to go out to Grandpa and Grandma Olczak's for a while."

"We want to stay with you," Lucy said, clinging.

"Well, Daddy's going to have some things to do." Picking out cemetery
plots and coffins.

"I don't want to go to Grandma's. I want to stay with you!" She started
to cry.

"All right. All right." He'd handle it tomorrow.

He picked them up and carried them into the kitchen, where the
women had obliterated any dear little remainders Krystyna might have left
behind this morning—her coffee cup in the sink, the pot with the grounds
on the cold stove, the last dishtowel she'd touched, her chair maybe angled
out from the table as if she'd just risen. Whatever domestic traces she'd
walked away from when she left for her mother's, the women had unwit-
tingly bulldozed with their kitchen fervor. Momentarily he resented it, then
immediately felt guilty; after all they'd meant well and he *had* been grateful
to have them here.

He snapped out the bright fluorescent light and carried the girls upstairs, pausing at the bottom for Lucy to pull the string that dropped clear
down from the light in the upstairs hall ceiling, and was weighted with a
metal washer at the bottom. Krystyna had tied that string on for them
when they grew old enough to go up to bed by themselves.

His house was very small, only a kitchen, living room and a little entry
hall downstairs; two bedrooms upstairs, plus the bathroom he'd made out
of a closet. At the top of the steps he passed the door to the girls' bedroom
and asked, "How would you like to sleep in Daddy's bed tonight?"

Another night they would have squealed, "Yes! Yes!"

Tonight Anne nodded her head without speaking a word, and Lucy
asked somberly, "Will we sleep with you all the time from now on?"

"No," he answered. "Just for the time being."

He stood them on the bed Krystyna's folks had given them for a wedding present. It was made of tubular tin that chimed as the mattress took
the girls' weight. A reading light was clamped onto the headboard; Krystyna

had put it there. He turned it on and pulled down the covers that she had washed last Monday and put on the bed fresh off the line, the way she loved to do. "Get in and I'll be here in a minute, soon as I get washed up, okay?"

He left them sitting on the bed staring after him as he went into the bathroom and closed the door.

Krystyna's nightie was hanging on the back of it. Her face powder had left a dusting around the faucets on the sink that she had chosen when he'd converted the room last year. Her toothbrush hung on the chrome-and-glass holder along with the other three. He'd installed some cupboards for towels and blankets, and she'd painted them pink, and had crocheted a pink-and-white doily for the top of the toilet tank. On the doily sat a bottle of her Avon perfume. He lifted it and read the label. *Forever Spring.* He opened it and smelled it, and dropped down to sit on the closed lid of the toilet with the bottle in one hand, the cap in the other, his head hanging so his tears dropped straight as a plumb line from his eyelids to the pink rug between his boots. A tornado of weeping swirled out of him suddenly, and he opened his mouth and pointed his face toward the ceiling, suppressing the sound for his children's benefit. He cradled his ribs with both arms as his body was wracked with torment. He writhed, letting the misery inundate him, holding silent all the while lest his little girls carry away any memories that would haunt them further. And when he could contain it no longer, he got up and ran the tub water full force to cover the sound, and muffled his sobs in a towel that was hanging on a rack and still smelled of Krystyna's dusting powder.

Later, when the worst had passed, he washed his face and hung up his soiled overalls over her nightgown as if it were he lying over her for the last time, and shut out the bathroom light and went in to the girls, dressed in his boxer shorts and undershirt.

Anne was sitting up in the middle of the bed, wide-eyed and motionless, the way she'd been so much of the time since it happened. Lucy was curled up on a pillow, awake, sucking her thumb. She popped up the minute he came out, as if to stop him should he try to go somewhere else in the house.

"We want you to sleep in the middle, Daddy," Anne said.

So he got in between them, his head on the crack between the two pillows, and got them both snuggled up at his sides with their freshly washed hair close by for kissing. Oh, how she had fixed their hair, so many different ways. On Saturday nights she set it in pin curls for Sunday Mass. Plaited it in French braids when it was long enough. Gave them Toni's a couple of times a year. Fussing with white ribbons and veils for the various feast days when they had to march in processions at church. How could a daddy learn to do all that? And when would he have time?

He reached up and switched off the bed lamp.

"Uh-oh, we left the hall light on. Will you turn it off, Annie?" She was closest to the outside.

"No," she answered stubbornly, curling on her side and presenting her spine. "I don't want to. Mommy always let us leave it on as long as we wanted to!"

But that was when Mommy put them to bed first, then came back downstairs to spend the rest of the evening with him. He climbed over Anne and went out to the hall to pull on the string. At the bottom of the stairs the washer bumped against the wall. He returned to bed and got between them and felt them move as close as they could against his sides.

Above the bed a high window faced east. Beside it a door with another window gave onto the railed roof of the downstairs porch. Moonlight flooded in over the linoleum floor and across the flowered chenille bedspread that Krystyna had saved her hair-setting money for. He remembered the first night they'd slept beneath the new spread, a little over a year ago, and how they'd made love and giggled softly afterward with their heads covered, so they wouldn't wake up the girls.

Lucy sat up in the moonlight and said, "Daddy, isn't Mommy really coming home anymore?"

He smoothed her silky hair and said, "No, baby, she's not."

"Mary Jean says that they're gonna bury Mommy in the ground." Mary Jean was her cousin, a sixth-grader, one of Romaine's girls. "Are they really, Daddy?"

"Well, sort of, honey, but it's not really Mommy, because she's already gone to heaven."

Lucy put her thumb in her mouth and considered for a full minute, sitting still as a stuffed doll. Then she began to cry. Anne, meanwhile, remained coiled up in a pinwheel of hurt with her backside to her daddy and her tears wetting the sheets on her mother's side of the bed.

Five

⤜❧⤛

The town knew when a body lay in repose because the purple neon light above the door of Iten & Heid's Funeral Home would be turned on. For the next four days the light glowed for Krystyna Olczak. The door was never locked. Mourners could visit Krystyna at any hour of the day or night, and almost everybody in Browerville did. People often went in alone, to kneel in the long, narrow wine-hued room among the stinging smell of carnations, and pray the rosary for her. Or they went to church and prayed the rosary in the evening, led by Father Kuzdek. They lit vigil lights and had Masses said for her, and the women made sure Eddie didn't run out of food, while the men made sure his janitorial duties were taken care of at St. Joseph's. Since Eddie was the one who usually dug the graves at St. Joseph's Cemetery, his brothers saw to that job for him. Eddie, as honest as the day was long, offered to pay them the usual fifteen dollars for the work, but they made him put his money back in his pocket and took him uptown for a beer, which Eddie couldn't finish. The beer, like all the other good things in Eddie's life, had lost its appeal without Krystyna.

Eddie went to the funeral home to sit beside her casket two or three times a day. With everyone taking care of his chores for him, he had too much time on his hands. Even the girls seemed to be gone a lot, sometimes out to one of the farms, other times at their cousins' houses around town. He had only to cross the vacant lot and Main Street to get to the door with the purple light above it. Inside, looking down at her peaceful face, at her hands folded around the blue beads of her own rosary, he tried to understand why God had taken her, but could not. Sometimes he would touch her cold cheek and worry about the children seeing her dead, but what could he do? She would be buried on Monday, and before the service everyone would gather here for the closing of the casket.

Eddie happened to be there alone on Saturday when the thumblatch on the door behind him clicked, the afternoon light momentarily flooded the maroon gloom, then the door closed once again. He remained as he was, seated, facing the casket, lost in reflection when Sister Dora and Sister Regina approached his side.

He rose immediately and whispered, "Good afternoon, sisters."

"Good afternoon, Mr. Olczak," they whispered in unison. They looked like bookends, their veils spread precisely to the tips of their shoulders, their hands tucked into their sleeves.

"It's so good of you to come."

"Your wife was as close to a saint as it's possible to be on this earth," Sister Dora said.

"She was a good woman, yes."

"How are the children doing?" Sister Regina inquired.

"Not so good, not so bad. It's hard to tell yet. They won't sleep in their room alone and Anne has to have the light on. They're out at my folks' today. You know how they love it out at the farm."

"Yes, Lucy has told me many times how she loves it, and so has Anne. They are very dear children, Mr. Olczack."

"Thank you, Sister."

"The schoolroom seemed so sad without them yesterday."

"Yeah, I suppose it did. The rest of the kids, they all kind of feel it too, I suppose."

"And how about you, Mr. Olczack?"

"Me? Oh, well . . ." His gaze moved toward the casket and tears gathered in his eyes. "It'll take time."

"I've been praying for you," Sister Regina whispered.

"Thank you, Sister."

The two nuns stepped back in unison. They had a way of nodding almost imperceptibly in deference to whomever they were addressing, and of moving in so smooth a fashion it appeared they were on wheels. Their angelic mien left an afterglow, a warmth that melted the sharp edges off Eddie's sadness as they went to the casket and stood looking down at Krystyna. Though a velvet-padded prie-dieu was provided, they made the sign of the cross, then stood motionless with their hands folded, fingers pointing straight to heaven. From the back they again looked identical— same height, same outline of the same black clothing. Through Sister Regina's veil Eddie could see the vigil light that burned in a red glass sconce on the wall. The thin black fabric dimmed its glow as the nuns stood silent, praying. Sister Regina reached into the folds of her habit, found a white handkerchief and dried her eyes, then tucked the hanky away and refolded her hands.

The nuns' presence brought Eddie a measure of ease. It always had. Working among them at the church and the school, he'd often thought that their tranquillity somehow seeped into him and calmed him, too, for even during the most demanding days, when it seemed Eddie was needed in three places at once—and such days were many when a person worked around children—he remained unruffled.

After several minutes, the nuns turned in unison and moved several feet away from the coffin, where they knelt on the carpeted floor and took out their rosaries.

Eddie knelt, too, keeping a respectful distance, and closed his eyes and let his mind drift in prayer. Their presence beside him momentarily salved his wounded heart and wiped away his terrible suffering.

Many minutes later the nuns put away their rosaries and got to their feet. The faint rustle of their clothing opened Eddie's eyes and he said the sign of the cross and got up, too.

"Thank you, sisters, for coming. She liked all of you," he said quietly.

"We'll miss her very much," Sister Regina said.

"Oh, I know. Everybody's going to miss her."

Sister Regina could see how grief had ravaged his face. The skin beneath his eyes had turned violet, and his cheeks seemed to have sunk like a fallen cake. Lines that had been barely visible two days ago now cut deep grooves the shape of ice tongs beside his nose and mouth. Once again she felt the strong desire to comfort him with a touch, there, on his face, perhaps, to soothe it with her palm as she once soothed Grandma Rosella. The memory was vague, but Sister Regina knew it was the day they had buried Aunt Esther, who was Grandma Rosella's second-youngest daughter. She had died of pneumonia in the spring of the year Regina was ten years old. After the funeral Regina had been with a number of her cousins who had gathered around their grandmother while she stood somewhere quiet and peaceful, away from the hustle and bustle of the women who were preparing food to be served to the crowd. She remembered that there'd been an apple tree in bloom and most of the blossoms had fallen and lay in a drift of white on the grass, and that the sun had been behind them as they looked down a hill toward the east. Her grandma had sat down on the grass and sighed, surrounded by her grandchildren, and her eyes had held a sadness so grave that the ten-year-old Regina had never forgotten it. Grandma Rosella had spoken as if to the red barn and silo that were visible at the bottom of the hill. "She used to bring me little bouquets of violets and harebells that she found in the woods, and the stems would all be squashed from her little hand, and her hand would be green. She was the sweetest little girl you ever saw." It was then Regina had soothed her grandmother's soft, fuzzy cheek and said, "Don't be sad, Grandma. She's with God now."

The emotions that had run through her then ran through her now as she looked into the sorrowful eyes of Eddie Olczak. But instead of touching his face she hid her hands deep within her sleeves as all nuns were expected to do in the presence of seculars, particularly men. She noted, however, that his eyes were brown—something she had never noticed before—and that he kept his usual respectful distance as they spoke. In terms of condolences, never had she wished mankind had more to offer at times like these than she did at this moment. She could only say what she'd said to her grandmother all those years ago.

"Try not to be sad, Mr. Olczak. She's with God now."

Her words, instead of consoling, brought his tears brimming. They spilled over the edge of his eyelids leaving a pair of shiny tracks that glowed molten, reflecting the light of the red wall sconces. He averted his head and nodded once as the tears fell and made two dark spots on the front of his plain blue shirt. She felt decimated to have made him feel worse.

"We shall have a Mass celebrated for the repose of her soul," she told him.

With his head still lowered he ran a knuckle beneath his nose and whispered, so thick and low she could barely hear, "Thank you, Sister."

The two nuns left the funeral home, squinting in the vivid autumnal sun that hurt their eyes. On their way back to the convent Sister Regina felt an overpowering frustration pushing up, up from deep inside. It came out of nowhere, catching her by surprise, like the sun after the dimness. It clutched at her throat and beat against her mind as she thought of Krystyna and the senselessness of her death. It wasn't exactly blame she felt toward God, more a vast disappointment in Him for His bad judgment in robbing Krystyna's family of her.

She finally asked Sister Dora, "Does Krystyna's death affect you more deeply than others have, Sister?"

"I think it does, yes."

Sister Regina sighed and looked at the clear blue sky. "I've been struggling to understand the why of all this."

"God has His reasons."

"But what good reason could there be for this?"

Sister Dora glanced over and said, "It's more than Krystyna's death, isn't it? I think you've been struggling with a number of things lately."

Sister Regina made no reply. Instead she sighed deeply and kept in perfect step with Sister Dora, a soft afternoon breeze billowing their veils while from someplace on the southwest side of town came the sound of life continuing. A dog barking, a car engine droning, the Zigan boys sawing firewood. The familiar *zz-zzing zz-zing* of their rig drifted through the quiet afternoon as each piece broke and left the sawblade.

"I've been praying for you, Sister," Sister Dora said. "I've asked the Holy Mother to intercede for you that you might be freed from this discontent you've been feeling."

"Discontent," Sister Regina repeated, as if the word rested heavy on her mind. "You're right. It's been growing for quite a while now."

"I fear for you, Sister," her companion said.

"Because I broke the rule of obedience by challenging Mother Superior at supper the other night?"

"There've been other things."

"Yes, there have. It seems like everything we do breaks one of our rules, and I'm tired of confessing what no longer seems wrong. Goodness, we're defying our Constitution right now just by discussing this!"

Their Constitution stated: *Words of complaint, severity and reproach are never addressed to one another. The confidential communication of rash judgments and feelings of discontent can disturb the peace and harmony of a religious community and should have no place among those who profess to be followers of Jesus Christ.* It was one of the rules under which Sister Regina had lately begun to chafe.

"Yes, I know. I shall ask for a penance at the Chapter of Faults next Friday."

"I don't wish to be the cause of your asking for a penance."

"Forgive me, Sister, but my penances are my concern."

"All right, then, haven't you ever asked yourself what good it does us to distance ourselves from everyone outside the religious community? If we're to perform acts of charity to the best of our ability, we need to be among the people. When I was restrained from physically comforting the Olczak children, I felt . . . I felt . . . well, I just didn't understand it at that moment. I'm not sure I've ever fully understood it."

"So you questioned Mother Agnes's authority."

"Not her authority. Only her judgment."

"But that's what our vow of obedience is about. Willingly submitting to the judgment of our superiors, and believing that it's through them that the will of God is manifested to us."

"And I still believe that . . . most of the time."

"And when you don't, that old demon self-will rears its head, right?"

"The vow of obedience has always given me the most trouble."

"I've known that for some time. I've watched you struggle with it."

"And lately I've become less tolerant of the, shall we say, personality quirks of some of the sisters. I thought . . ." Sister Regina searched the sky again. ". . . I thought when I entered the novitiate that life in the religious community would be absolutely devoid of turmoil. Submit to the rules, devote myself to a life of hard work, and prayer, and humility, and life would be one unbroken vale of inner peace. But it isn't turning out that way. It's . . ." Sister Regina shook her head.

"It's this particular time, the sadness, the feeling that you want to do more. But you mustn't let it undermine all you've aspired to. We all face doubts at one time or another. Place your trust in the Lord, and He'll give you the grace to understand the judgments of those who are in authority."

"Will He help me to understand the aggravation I feel lately with Sister Samuel when she sneezes on all our food at the table, then takes her handkerchief out *afterward?* Or with Sister Gregory, who deludes herself that she's offering up dessert? Or with Sister Mary Charles when she punishes the children with her strap?"

"I must confess, I grow angry with Sister Mary Charles, too."

They were approaching the church as Sister Dora said, "Goodness, we really are breaking Holy Rule, aren't we?"

"I shall have to ask Mother Superior for a penance next Friday, too."

"But on the other hand, R. B. admonishes us to *offer prudent admonitions and charitable counsel to our sisters,* and isn't that what I'm doing?" Sister Dora had quoted directly from the book and Sister Regina could have pointed to the exact page, for the frequent study of the Holy Rule and their Constitution was incorporated into their stringent schedule of prayer and reflection. This study was meant to reinforce the vows they had taken, but lately Sister Regina had come to view it as the way the Catholic Church chose to keep the nuns in line. These thoughts above all troubled her.

"Sister, do you think . . ." She found herself unable to go on. It was scary putting your doubts into words for the first time.

"Do I think . . ." Sister Dora urged.

"Nothing." They had reached the parish grounds and were walking up the narrow tarred driveway between the church and the school. "Thank you for your prayers and for your charitable counsel," Sister Regina said as a corner of the convent came into view. "I shall strive to do better."

They entered the convent through the kitchen door and found Sister Ignatius crimping the crusts on two apple pies. The room was redolent of bay leaf and onion from the chicken that was stewing on the stove. The sound of rudimentary piano music came from one of the music rooms as Sister Gregory gave a piano lesson, and Sister Regina felt her emotions shift into a comfort zone, for this was the familiar, and there was a great deal of comfort in the familiar. Even in the regimented words of greeting they spoke as they encountered the cook.

"Praise be to Jesus," the two said as they walked through the room.

"Amen," replied Sister Ignatius.

In the refectory, Sister Cecelia was setting the table for supper.

"Praise be to Jesus," they greeted her as they passed the open doorway.

"Amen," Sister Gregory replied, and they continued upstairs.

It was Saturday afternoon, which was considered free time. But Sister Regina's charge this month was to act as Sacristan, which meant keeping the sacristy clean and preparing it especially for Sunday Mass. In her room she found a straight pin and tacked her veil together in back, donned a clean white floor-length apron over her black habit and, since she'd be scrubbing, removed her elastic undersleeves.

She entered the church by the back door that led into Father's sacristy. It was connected to the altar boys' sacristy, on the opposite side of the sanctuary, by a passageway that curved around behind the main altar. Now in late afternoon the light in the passageway was the color of apple juice as the sun filtered through the amber panes of the leaded windows.

Crossing the sanctuary, Sister Regina genuflected, made the sign of the cross, and began her work. Father had finished Confessions, so all was still. She damp-mopped the floor, dusted the carvings on the altar, the priest's and servers' chairs against the left wall, the pulpit, the furniture that held Father's vestments, and the deep windowsills. She changed the altar cloth and put a crisply ironed corporal over the chalice. She made sure the chalice was filled with hosts from the small safe in Father's sacristy. She put new candles in the gold candlesticks and kept the old stubs to melt down for future use. She threw away some wilting gladioli from the altar and went over to the schoolhouse to get two potted yellow chrysanthemums from the flower room. When they were nicely balanced on the main altar she went to one of the side altars and put a lighted candle before the statue of the Blessed Virgin Mary—always part of the Saturday ritual. At the communion rail she hung a crisp new linen cloth edged with wide crocheted lace. And finally, she went to the twenty-gallon crock in Father's sacristy and filled a pitcher with holy water. She was replenishing the fonts in the front vestibule when the door opened and Eddie Olczak appeared. He was dressed as he'd been at the funeral home, in dark trousers and a plaid shirt instead of his workday overalls.

He stopped halfway inside when he saw her, then his hand went up to remove his felt dress hat.

"Oh, Sister," he said in surprise, and let the door close behind him. The vestibule turned dun in the scarce light from the two tiny leaded windows set high in the doors.

"Mr. Olczak, what are you doing here?" She had not expected to encounter him since his brothers had taken over his work.

"Well, you know . . . force of habit. Just wanted to make sure everything was okay over here. Tomorrow's Sunday."

"Your brothers have seen after everything. There's no need for you to worry about anything here. And I've taken care of the sacristy for Mass."

"Yes . . . well . . ." He glanced away, then at the holy-water font she'd been filling. "Excuse me," he uttered and reached over to dip his fingers in the font and make the sign of the cross, keeping a respectful distance from her.

She was immediately aware that she'd left her undersleeves in her room and her wrists were bare and that there were specific rules against this, especially with a secular of the opposite sex. Not only were her wrists bare, she was encumbered with a heavy pitcher of crockery so she could not hide her hands in her sleeves. But it would be sacrilegious to set the holy water on the floor.

Mr. Olczak was aware of none of her angst.

"Truth is," he said, "they've seen after everything so good that they left me with idle hands. With the kids out at my folks', the house is too empty, so I just thought . . ." He glanced at the bell ropes hanging straight and motionless, at the cold radiator, the clean floor of the vestibule and the rubber mat beneath their feet. At her again, then dropped his gaze. Holding his hat in both hands, fiddling with its brim, he said quietly, "You know, Sister, in one way you're lucky that you never got married. You'll never have to go through this."

"I am married," she reminded him gently. "To Jesus."

"And He'll never leave you, will he," Eddie said.

"Nor will He leave you. He is always with you."

He nodded thoughtfully, then said, "Sister, I'm worried."

It struck her that Holy Rule admonished her not to encourage familiarity through idle conversations with the secular, but once again the rule seemed harsh in light of his circumstances. He was a heartsore man in need, one who had been a Catholic all his life and had worked around nuns a long time. He understood the protocol required between them and could not have been more deferential to any of them had he been a monk, always nodding, or doffing his hat, and keeping the most respectable distance whenever in their presence. Holy Rule demanded that she put a quick end to this exchange, but she felt that to do so would be the most heartless thing she could do.

Christ would want me to hear him out today, she thought, and decided to stay. "About what?"

"The girls seeing Krystyna in the coffin." He withdrew and stood clear across the vestibule, near a door that led to the choir loft, backing up against the door frame. "They're so little, and they're going to remember it the rest of their lives. I don't want them to see her that way."

"Perhaps you should talk to Father about it."

"You're their teacher. You know them better than Father does. I thought maybe you'd know what I should do."

"Perhaps they could stay with their grandparents at the rear of the funeral home during the closing of the casket."

"And what about during the Requiem Mass?" The casket would be open then, too, right here in the vestibule before the service.

"Is Anne still denying that her mother is dead?"

"No. But she's grown so quiet. Doesn't talk, as if she's mad at somebody but she doesn't know who."

Sister grew quiet herself. She let the pitcher of holy water rest against her stomach. "That's how I feel sometimes."

"You, Sister?" His eyebrows lifted in surprise.

"It's not befitting for a nun, I know, but there've been moments when I've found myself overcome by . . . by . . ."

"Rage?" he supplied.

"Almost. And disillusionment."

Eddie was flabbergasted that she'd confide such a thing to him, equally as flabbergasted that she harbored such feelings, for in the years he'd known her he'd never seen her any way but serene.

"It'd be a sin to feel rage against God, though," he said.

"Yes, of course."

He thought for a moment, then asked, "So who do we feel it against?"

He stood with his back against a door frame while she stood beside the holy-water font, trying to figure it out.

"I don't know, Mr. Olczak," she admitted. "I don't know."

She realized she was breaking Holy Rule again, and said, "Well . . . I must get back to the convent."

*S*ister Regina was about thirty seconds shy of being late for Matins and Lauds. Mother Superior gave her a look of disapproval when she hurried into chapel short of breath from running to the convent from the back door of the church.

Within their own tiny chapel, with its feeling of refuge, she once again felt the angst of the day begin to slip away. Kneeling beside her sisters, in this place where she'd spent so many hours, falling into the familiar routine, she felt a reaffirmation that this was where she belonged. Their sweet soprano voices chanting in unison brought the assurance she so desired. During the Magnificat she felt transported, the Latin words flowing through her like fresh rain through dusty air, clearing and purifying.

During the thirty minutes of meditation, however, in the extreme silence of the airless chapel, all efforts to free her mind of temporal thoughts failed. The conversations with both Sister Dora and Mr. Olczack kept intruding, and by the time she went downstairs for supper she felt like an imposter in her habit. Surely a truly good nun would be able to achieve a union with God that would supersede all worldly thoughts.

But not she. Not she.

At supper Sister Gregory pushed her dish of apple pie aside, then nipped at it all through the meal until she'd eaten it all. Sister Samuel sneezed on everything in sight, and Sister Cecelia told Sister Agnes that she had seen Sister Regina leave the convent without her undersleeves on, and even though she was only going to clean the sacristy, it wasn't proper.

During community hour Sister Mary Charles, fulfilling her charge, read a chapter from their Constitution. Sister Regina did not know whether it was by chance or by order of their Reverend Mother that tonight's reading was the chapter on obedience.

Sister Mary Charles read:

Religious should have a great reverence for holy obedience and should strive earnestly to overcome every inclination to self-will.

On all occasions they should conform to the directions of their superior with a prompt, exact, and wholehearted response, and they should never censure the judgments of those who are in authority, believing that the will of God is manifested through them.

Sister Regina realized, upon hearing the rule read aloud, that not only since the death of Krystyna Olczak but for months before that she had broken her vow of obedience time and again. She had broken it by silently railing against the many constraints put upon her by Holy Rule and the Constitution. Even worse, she had begun assessing the methods used by the order to keep the nuns in line, and to consider them akin to brainwashing.

That night in her room, during the hour set aside for reflection, Sister Regina performed the required daily examen. Kneeling beside her bed, with her eyes closed and her hands folded, examining her conscience, she admitted that she had much for which to ask forgiveness, not only of God, but of her superior and her entire religious community as well.

Six

Irene Pribil awakened on the Monday of her sister's funeral in the same bedroom the two had shared as girls. It was a big south room with high ceilings and wide white woodwork in a farmhouse that had been built in 1880. The center of the floor was covered with linoleum—pink cabbage roses on a forest of green—that she dustmopped every Saturday during the regular weekly cleaning. Around the linoleum the edge of the floor was painted gray; she repainted it every April. The windows were hung with inexpensive white sheer panels that she helped her mother starch and hang on curtain stretchers every spring and every fall. Outside, east of the house, was the garden she helped her mother plant each spring and harvest each summer. And downstairs in the kitchen was the nickel-plated cast-iron stove, where they canned for weeks and weeks during the hottest part of the year. In the chicken coop beyond the garden was a flock of Plymouth Rock hens she'd raised in the brooder house and fattened all summer, and which she would soon sell to Louis Kulick at his produce in Browerville, earning herself enough cash to buy a few Christmas gifts for her folks and sisters and brothers and their kids. Ahead of her, as far as she could tell, were years and years of nothing but the same.

Irene had gone to country school through the eighth grade, like all the rest of her brothers and sisters. Then, just like they, she had gone to work—in Long Prairie, where she kept house for a family named Milka who owned the dry-goods store. Also like her sisters and brothers, she'd brought home her checks and given them to her parents, doing so without whining about it because it was expected of her.

Krystyna, too, got a job in Long Prairie, operating a mangle at the dry cleaners, and on weekends the two girls always managed to catch a ride home to the farm, and from there go with their brothers to one of the dance halls for a Saturday-night dance.

It was at the Clarissa Ballroom that they met the Olczak boys for the first time. There were so many of them that Irene couldn't keep all their names straight. But two she remembered: Romaine, because for a while he was sweet on her and gave her her first kiss. And Eddie, because from the first time she ever met him, she was sweet on him and wished more than anything that he *might* try to kiss her.

It had never happened.

Eddie had taken one look at Krystyna and gone blind to all others.

Never once, in all the years since, had Irene let Krystyna know how she felt about Eddie. Eddie either.

The job at Milka's ended when they sold the business and moved to Melrose. It was followed by others, always doing housework, always for meager wages, always returning to the farm on the weekends, until the spring of 1945, when her mother fell off a stepladder while painting the granary, broke her collarbone and suffered a severe concussion. Irene returned to the farm to help out while her mother recovered, and stayed.

She had always intended to leave, preferably by getting married, but with homegrown pork and beef and cream and butter plentiful, and the cooking rich, she had gotten quite fat. There were no young men asking her to the dances on Saturday nights anymore. And since the war ended, women tended to take care of their own homes, so housekeeping jobs were fewer and harder to find. With a limited education, Irene was ill prepared to live on her own and support herself. At home with her folks she had food, shelter, company and love, and she grew complacent with these.

But life there was lonely and steeped in routine. All of her siblings had left and gotten married, and they rather expected Irene to remain where she was, taking care of her parents, providing them with company as they grew older, and with help during the busy times of year.

Once, a couple of years ago, at a wedding dance where she'd gone with her parents, a fellow named Bryce Polavik from over near Philbrook had danced with her and driven her home. He'd even kissed her and asked her out the following Saturday. She had bought some yard goods and sewn herself a brand-new dress, and Krystyna had put a new Toni home permanent in her hair and shared her excitement, and Irene had even bought a new pair of high heels with cut-out toes for the occasion.

But at the end of the night, on the way home from a dance hall called Bink's, Bryce Polavik had pulled off the road onto a little trail leading into somebody's woods and had kissed Irene like a sex fiend, and tried to unhook her garters, and unsnap her brassiere. When she stopped him, he became insistent, and zipped down his trousers and forced her to touch his privates, and then he'd used his superior strength to subdue her and touch her between her legs, where nobody had ever touched her. When she'd continued to struggle and fight him off and beg, no, no, please no, it's a mortal sin, no, please, he had roughly thrust her aside, called her a stupid, fat cunt, and said she should be happy any guy at all would even want to screw somebody like her, and that it was likely the only time she'd ever get the chance, so don't come begging him when she changed her mind, because he'd never so much as look at her again. Then he backed out of the woods so fast the car lurched into the opposite ditch before he changed gears and tore off down the gravel road at such a breakneck pace he'd scared Irene even worse than earlier when he'd tried to force her to have intercourse. Her parents' driveway was nearly a quarter of a mile long, and he skidded to a halt at the end of it, reached across her and threw her door open. When she'd asked, "Aren't you going to drive me the rest of the way?" he'd said, "Get out, fatso. The walk will do you good. Might wear off a pound or two."

So Irene lived on at home, seeking social diversion primarily with Krystyna and Eddie, playing cards at their house, often eating supper there, talking gardening and sewing, loving their children while growing more and more afraid she'd have none of her own. She was the one who went to their house and took care of Krystyna for ten full days after each of the babies had been born. She had bottle-fed and burped them and changed many a dirty diaper. She made clothes for their dolls, taught them how to play jacks, bought them coloring books and took them out to the farm to spend overnights so that Eddie and Krystyna could have occasional nights alone. In spring she showed them where the best spreads of trilliums bloomed in Grandpa and Grandma Pribil's woods, and broke off fresh bloodroot and showed them how it *bled*. She took them to the barn and showed them the baby kittens, and let them help her cut out sugar cookies and slice rhubarb with a paring knife for the first time, folding their small hands around the knife handle and cautioning them on how to use it. At Halloween she helped Krystyna make their costumes and carve their pumpkins. At Christmas the gifts she bought them were nicer than those she bought for her other nieces and nephews. At bedtime, when she was at their house, they ran to her scrubbed and fresh in plissé pajamas and kissed Auntie Irene goodnight with the avid abandon they gave their own parents.

Only they were not hers.

Irene envied what Krystyna had with Eddie. She envied their beautiful children, their house, their marriage, and his unmistakable love for her. She envied her his easygoing manner, his calm appreciation of all she did, the way he'd walk home from St. Joseph's at any hour of the day, just to have a cup of coffee with her, then quietly draw her into the front hall away from the others to give her a goodbye kiss before going back to work. She envied Krystyna because Eddie was always doing things for her—improving the house in whatever way she asked, building things for her in his workshop, and for the children, too—their first high chair, doll furniture from Santa, a playhouse outfitted with a miniature table and chairs the perfect size for little bodies. When Krystyna asked him to put up a swing for the girls on one end of the clothesline pole, Eddie did it with a smile, then pushed his children on it, laughing with them. When Krystyna asked for a short white picket fence to surround her garden, he made it without a murmur of complaint, and the two of them painted it together, sitting on the front-porch steps while townspeople walked by and stopped to visit, and Krystyna would say, "Go on in and pour yourself a lemonade." Or a cup of coffee, or have a doughnut or a cookie, she'd say, because their house was always open, and people wandered in and out of it as if it were a restaurant. When Krystyna asked if Eddie wanted to go to a "hard-time dance," he put on the foolish costumes she contrived, made of onion sacks, and they went to Clarissa and won first prize, he shyly, she with the vibrance she brought to everything she did.

And once Krystyna had confided to Irene that Eddie had given her a bath. Filled the tub and picked her up and carried her to it and pressed her back until she was lying limp against the porcelain, and soaped her from head to foot and kissed her stomach, which was no longer tight and flat after stretching around two babies, and told her she was perfect. Perfect, mind you, Krystyna had said, when there were stretch marks bright and jagged as lightning running all across her stomach, and she couldn't fit into the straight dresses she'd worn before Anne was born, and her fingers were often stained and cracked from all the chemicals in the permanents she gave.

Over the years that Irene watched the young married couple together, she grew to love them both even more. Her love for Krystyna was so pure and rewarding it would never have occurred to her to let her sister know she loved Eddie. And her love for Eddie—well, it had grown into a golden glow that filled her like a perfect dawn whenever he was near. In Irene's eyes he was more than ideal. He was a god.

It was through Krystyna and Eddie that Irene had lived vicariously. Her joy at being with them and the children dulled the dread she carried at the prospect of life as an old maid. As long as they were there, their door and hearts open to her, Irene could escape to them and from the stunning mediocrity of her reality.

But now Krystyna was dead and there would be no more borrowing shoes, and giving each other permanents, and going to dances on Saturday nights. On the odd Wednesday or Sunday afternoon when the changelessness of life on the farm became suffocating, she could not drive into town and visit in Krystyna's kitchen. Who would she laugh with? Remember her days in Long Prairie with? Tease Mother and Dad with (for Krystyna had been the one who could always make them laugh)? Who would lift her above the drudgery to that plane of companionship she'd never shared with anyone else?

On the morning of Krystyna's funeral, Irene awakened and sat up in her childhood bed, feeling abject and targeted, as if some preeminent force had it in for her and was showing her how simple it was to remove every vestige of happiness from her life. Across from the foot of the bed a pair of tall, skinny windows nearly touched the white mopboards. Through them she could see the sun, persimmon orange, nesting above the row of scrub willows clear down beyond the south pasture. How dare the sun shine on the day of Krystyna's funeral? There should be rain, like there was in Irene's heart.

She rose with an effort and cocked a hand to her head, where a swift throb reminded her of how much crying she'd done in the last four days. Downstairs her mother was making sounds in the kitchen. Her father, she knew, was out cutting hay, catching a couple good hours before dressing for the funeral: death didn't halt the seasons, and though the saying had become cliché, it was true that a farmer had to make hay while the sun shone.

Irene shuffled downstairs, where she found her mother taking a cake out of the oven: there would be a dinner after the funeral at the Paderewski Hall with the ladies of the parish providing food, so even in her grief, Mary Pribil, like her husband, felt the demands of life pushing her from behind.

"Mama?" Irene said from the doorway.

Mary straightened with the cake pan in her hand and closed the oven door. She wore rimless eyeglasses over close-set eyes. Her thin gray hair was as short and curly as a Persian lamb coat. The broken collarbone she'd suffered had left her right shoulder sagging lower than her left, like an old, weathered wooden gravemarker that had once been a cross.

She set the cake pan on the cupboard and said, "Mornin', Reeny."

To her mother's back, Irene said, "I'm going to take the old truck and go in early and help Eddie get the girls dressed. Fix their hair the way Krystyna would have liked it, okay?"

Mary refused to turn around. She stood a moment with the butts of her hands resting on the edge of the wooden cabinet. Then she pulled up her apron and used a corner of it to wipe her eyes inside her glasses. "You do what you got to do. It ain't gonna be a easy day to get through, that's for sure."

Irene crossed the kitchen and kissed her mother on the side of her neck, and slipped her arms around Mary's thick middle and rocked her awhile. Then Mary patted the backs of Irene's hands and the younger woman left the room.

*T*he funeral was scheduled for eleven A.M. It was shortly after nine-thirty when Irene crossed Eddie's front porch and knocked on the door. Used to be she'd walk right in, because Eddie would be at work and Krystyna would be in the kitchen doing housework or setting somebody's hair.

Eddie answered the door with shaving cream on one side of his face, dressed in black gabardine trousers and a sleeveless ribbed undershirt with a U-neck.

"Irene," he said without his customary smile. Though he was a low-key man, he had a shy, lopsided smile with which he usually greeted people. Today he merely spoke her name as a flat, gleeless recognition.

"Hi, Eddie," she said as he opened the screendoor to let her in. "Sorry I interrupted your shaving."

He waved off her apology without a word.

"Pretty sad day, isn't it?" she said when he'd closed the inside door.

"Yuh," he managed while they both struggled with resurfacing emotions.

They stood in a shallow entry that stretched the width of the living room, separated from it by a wall with an archway flanked by two square white posts on set-in shelves that the children had called parapets, because that's what the nuns called the ones at school. To the right, against the end wall of the entry, Krystyna's treadle sewing machine stood with an unfinished project folded up on top of the boxy wooden cover. Off the left end of the entry a stairway led to the second story, from where the children's voices and running water could be heard.

"I thought I'd come over and fix the girls' hair and help them get dressed, the way Krystyna would have."

Eddie took a beat to register what she was offering and to accept the fact that Krystyna was gone and would never fuss over the girls again.

"That's nice, Irene. I appreciate that."

"I didn't think . . . I mean, I didn't know if you, how you'd . . . I mean who'd . . ."

"It's okay, Irene, I know what you mean. I hadn't got around to figuring that out yet, either."

"Then it's okay that I came over?"

"Sure. And you're right. Krystyna would have wanted them to be all dolled up." He tried for a smile, but *all dolled up* was Krystyna's expression, and the reminder only saddened Eddie and Irene the more.

"Well, listen, your face is drying. You go back and finish your shave and I'll go up and help them get dressed and make up their bed, how's that?"

He nodded despondently and headed upstairs. Halfway to the top he turned and said, "I wanted them to wear those little pink-and-white striped dresses, the last ones Krystyna made for them."

"Sure, Eddie."

At the top of the stairs, the hall doubled-back upon itself with a handrail overlooking the steps. The children's bedroom was situated there,

Eddie and Krystyna's down the hall. One had to walk through Eddie and Krystyna's room to reach the bathroom. The children came running through their parents' bedroom, dressed in their cotton underwear. Lucy was squealing, "Daddy, Daddy, look at us!" They had painted their faces with his shaving cream. "We're going to shave!"

"Auntie Irene is here," he said. "She's going to get you dressed and comb your hair real pretty."

Irene watched the children run to him, bearded in white, their bare heels pounding on the hall runner. He stopped them and turned them by the backs of their heads, pointing them back toward his room. "Now you come back in the bathroom with me and wash that shaving soap off so Auntie Irene can get you dressed."

They both peered around him, said, "Hi, Auntie Irene," then he herded them away.

She stood looking after them, filled with a sense of loss complicated by the realization that Krystyna was gone forever and Eddie was no longer married. The smell of his shaving soap lingered in the hall, and in her mind the image of his wiry arms and the hair on his chest behind the strappy undershirt. Through the open door of his room she could see the foot of his bed, still mussed. She had never, in her entire lifetime, had access to the smell of a man's shaving soap or the appearance of him or his tossed sheets in the morning, other than her father's and the middle-aged men she'd worked for. She found it dreadful that she should be observing Eddie's private morning routine at the expense of her sister's life, even more dreadful to discover that she was enjoying the pseudo-intimacy.

She went into the girls' room and made up their bed, picked up their dirty socks and pajamas from the floor and opened a tall chest of drawers that held their folded clothes. She and Krystyna had bought the chest at an auction sale when Krystyna was expecting Anne, and had painted it pastel green and put teddy bear decals on the fronts of the drawers. She straightened some stacks of undershirts and underpants and listened to Eddie and the girls. He was the gentlest, most loving father she had ever seen, and she felt she had the capability of being the same kind of mother. How perfect it would be if she could marry him and take care of him and the girls for the rest of her life.

Guilt swept down and smothered the idea. Krystyna wasn't even buried yet and here she was wishing to step into her place. Was this what was meant by *coveting?* She promised herself she would go to confession next Saturday and ask absolution from her sin.

She wiped a tear from her eye with a small folded undershirt, looked up and whispered, "Forgive me, Krystyna. I'm so sorry."

But she loved the children, and loved Eddie, and would fill in for Krystyna in a heartbeat, even if he never loved her back. And how could he love her, a fat, boring, farm woman who had none of Krystyna's vibrancy or verve?

The children, at least, loved her: of that much she was sure, and that would be enough for her if it ever came to that.

But it wouldn't, and she must never let Eddie know she'd had such thoughts, especially so soon after Krystyna died.

She dressed the girls in their full-skirted pink dresses with fluffy white petticoats underneath, and wide sashes that tied in the back. She found white anklets and let them buckle on their shiny black patent-leather shoes. Then she took them down to the kitchen and, in turn, stood them on the seat of a kitchen chair next to the sink where Eddie had made built-in cabinets with special triangular-shaped cupboards on either side of the window, with angled doors to make it easy for Krystyna to see the back of her hair when she was setting it and combing it. If Irene had thought of this last night, she would have come over then and set the girls' hair in pin curls the way Krystyna always did on Saturday night, in preparation for Sunday Mass. Lacking fresh curls, she parted their hair on the side, drew a little tail to the opposite side, secured it with a rubber band, then trimmed it with a wide pink ribbon which she carefully tied in a bow. She knew right where Krystyna kept the ribbons and the rubber bands and combs—all in the kitchen drawer where her other paraphernalia for giving permanents was also kept. The smell in the drawer—of ammonia and wave set and the rubber bands that hung on the permanent rollers, half decomposed from the strong chemicals—brought back so sharp a memory of Krystyna that Irene had to struggle once again to keep from crying.

The girls were all dressed and combed when Eddie came downstairs in his black suit, a crisply ironed white shirt (Krystyna had always taken such pains with his shirts) and striped tie, wearing his Knights of Columbus pin in his lapel. He reached the doorway just as one of his brothers rang the first bell at St. Joseph's, a reminder that in thirty minutes Krystyna's funeral Mass would begin. The sight of Eddie sent a billow of longing through Irene, a visceral reaction that rolled along and lifted in much the same manner as the wind over a field of tall, green grain. As with the grain when the wind has passed, she stood straight and waiting, hiding what lay underneath.

"Well, I guess it's time to go," Eddie said.

"I guess so."

"Guess we can walk over to the funeral home."

"I g . . . guess so."

"Folks'll be getting there by now."

She simply could not speak anymore, didn't know how he could.

"The girls look . . ." He had to stop and compose himself before going on. His voice got even quieter. "Girls look nice, Irene."

She touched them on the backs of their heads. "Go see your daddy," she whispered.

They crossed the kitchen solemnly and took their daddy's hands, and he thought that without those two small hands in his he might have sunk to the floor and refused to leave the house, refused to walk down the sidewalk and cross Main Street and see that precious face lying in the casket and watch the metal lid close over it forever.

But he did it, did what he must, clutching those two small hands and listening to the pat-a-pat of their patent leathers on the sidewalk while Irene followed behind. Reaching Main Street, he found that townspeople were funneling toward Iten & Heid's Funeral Home from all directions. Relatives, friends; by foot, by car; so many that the funeral home was packed and some had to pay their respects from the sidewalk outside.

What Eddie had faced the day of Krystyna's death he faced again, renewed weeping with each loved one he embraced, especially all four parents, and the sisters and brothers of both sides. In the end the decision about letting Anne and Lucy view Krystyna was decided when the girls balked and pulled away. They were beginning to cry when he left them with Irene at the rear of the funeral home and took his place up front. Father Kuzdek said prayers and performed the closing of the casket, replete with the sprinkling of holy water and the spreading of incense. The pallbearers bore the casket out to the hearse, and the lengthy procession of mourners walked the block and a half to St. Joseph's, Eddie once again holding his children's hands.

At eleven o'clock, when he climbed the church steps and followed the casket through the vestibule, he saw that it was his older brother Clayton ringing the bells today. *Bless you, Clayton, pulling on those ropes with tears streaming down your face, bless you and all my brothers for all you're doing to see me through this. What would I do without you?* All three bells pealed overhead, filling the vestibule with so much sound it reverberated inside Eddie's head as the children looked up at him and pressed close to his sides.

Inside the church, in the fourth and fifth rows, Sister Regina waited with her pupils. They sat and fidgeted. She knelt and prayed. There had been no eight o'clock Mass this morning. Instead, the entire student body was attending the Requiem Mass, and the children's choir would be singing.

It had been a terribly distressing morning for Sister Regina. When she'd tried opening the school day with a prayer, her voice had broken and she'd had to press her folded fingertips against her lips and begin again. She'd tried to concentrate on her teaching, but Anne and Lucy's empty seats stopped her eyes each time she scanned the room, and time and again she'd had to turn away from the children to hide the tears she couldn't stop from forming. She'd tried not to wish the school building had a clock in every room (her vow of poverty dictated that she be content with what she had) but after her fifth trip into the hall to check the clock out there, she'd begun accusing the parish board of miserliness rather than expedience in deciding the building needed only one clock in the gymnasium.

She'd been guilty of long stretches of preoccupation this morning and had been standing at the schoolroom window when the first bell rang half an hour ago, standing there staring out, filled with grief and imagining the Olczak family gathering at the funeral home, wishing she could be there with them, to comfort the children and draw comfort from them. There it was, that old self-indulgence again.

Now she was in church, sitting behind the three empty rows of pews reserved for the family, and even with her back to the door, she knew they were here at last. Distant light flooded in from the rear, meaning the double doors had been propped open as they always were for funerals.

She waited with a sorrowful yearning that surprised her, for the first glimpse of them. Sister Samuel played the organ very softly in a minor key. The whisper of Father's cassock and the squeak of his shoes reached her even before he did. The funeral procession finally passed by her pew: an altar boy leading the way carrying a crucifix on a long wooden pole; Father Kuzdek wearing black vestments and flanked by two altar boys; behind them the pallbearers, three of Krystyna's brothers, the rest all Olczaks, all thick, strapping fellows who looked out of place stuffed into suits and ties. And finally there was Mr. Olczak, holding a hand of each of his children, moving slowly, slowly. When Lucy came abreast of her teacher and classmates, she covertly signaled *hi* as she was shepherded along. Sister Regina's heart swelled with so much pity and love it caused a physical ache in her breast, and she felt persecuted at being unable to show it. Then the children moved past and she caught a glimpse of Mr. Olczak's lorn face as he directed them into a front pew.

The Mass began.

Eternal rest grant unto them, O Lord . . .

The children sang in hesitant Latin, the prayers for the dead were lengthy and Sister Regina's children grew fidgety, too young to understand the import of this Mass and its full impact on two of their classmates. She had to reach over the pew in front of her and nudge two of the boys who were beginning to leg and shoulder each other and instigate some sort of silent combat over territorial pew rights. The older schoolchildren received Communion while hers remained in their seats, too young yet to participate. When Mr. Olczak left his children to go up to the Communion rail, Lucy again turned around to make eye contact with those behind her. Sister could tell the little girl had been crying. When Mass ended, Father Kuzdek donned his black cope and prayed at the foot of the coffin, then circled it, sprinkling holy water and swinging the gold censer until the smell of the incense became so overpowering it burned Sister Regina's throat.

Then the service was over and the exit from church began, once again in procession, accompanied by the intermittent tolling of the single mournful bell which would continue until the hearse pulled away from the curb and headed for the cemetery. In the vestibule the coffin was opened so that those who knew and loved Krystyna could glimpse her one last time.

Sister Regina had no chance for a last glimpse. She and the other nuns took their pupils out a side door and back to school, where it was time for noon lunch and recess. But she could not eat, nor could she face the idea of romping on the playground while Krystyna Olczak was being buried. She wanted to be at the graveside, to say final prayers and *feel* the final goodbye. She needed the mingling just as Krystyna's friends and family did. But Holy Rule would not allow it, nor could her students be abandoned.

She found Mother Superior on her way to the refectory and asked permission to be excused from noon dinner and recess.

Mother Agnes said, "It's best to remain with the community as much as possible, even at times when you're troubled."

"Yes, Mother," she relied meekly.

After a moment's thought, Mother Agnes said, "Nevertheless, I give my permission. Please see that you're back in your classroom at one o'clock."

"Yes, Mother. Thank you. Praise be to Jesus."

"Amen."

Sister Regina went upstairs to the chapel. Her stomach growled and her knees hurt as she knelt on the hard prie-dieu, but she offered up her discomforts for the repose of the soul of Krystyna Olczak, and for herself that she might recapture the zeal she had once had for her vocation. She prayed that she might become more obedient, and open her heart to God more and to the plight of the Olczak family less. That she might embrace poverty and not wish for a clock in every classroom, and that she would stop airing her dissatisfactions with certain members of her religious community—especially discussing them with Sister Dora—and would accept each and every one of her sisters lovingly, no matter what their faults. But most fervently she prayed that she would stop thinking of Mr. Olczak so much, especially in the dark after lights out.

She prayed the long Miserere, and six Our Fathers and Hail Marys and Glory Be's, offering up these, too, for all the suffering of the world. And all the while she prayed, that single bell kept tolling once every thirty seconds, and each time it did it brought Mr. Olczak's face sharp and clear into her mind, until at last there was silence and she knew that everyone had left the church and the doors of the hearse had closed and borne Krystyna away to the cemetery.

Seven

❧

When the funeral was over they all said, "Oh, Eddie, come on out to the farm for a few days, come to our place, don't stay at the house alone"—his folks, her folks, his brothers and sisters. But Eddie had no desire to leave his house. Besides, what good would it do? It would only delay the inevitable loneliness. Nor had he any desire to put off going back to work. Idleness only made the time pass slower.

He asked his girls, "Anne, Lucy, do you want to stay home from school tomorrow? 'Cause you can if you want to. You can go out to Grandma Pribil's or out to Grandma Olczak's for a few days."

"Will you come, too?" Anne asked.

"No, sunshine. It's time for me to go back to work. I've been off for four days and that's long enough."

"Then I want to go home with you."

"Me, too," Lucy seconded.

Irene overheard and approached Eddie hesitantly. "What are you going to do with them in the morning when you have to ring the bells and be at church before they leave the house?"

"I don't know."

"I could come, Eddie . . . I could come any day, every day actually, and feed them breakfast and get them ready for school."

"Aw, no, Irene, that's asking too much."

"I wouldn't mind. I know how Krystyna took care of them and I can do the same. I know where their things are in the house, and how she set their hair and combed it, and what color hair ribbon goes with which dress—she set a lot of store by those things, Eddie, and I could do all of that. I'd be happy to."

"But you'd have to drive in from the farm every day."

"Four miles, what's that? And I can take Dad's old truck. He doesn't mind."

Anne peered up at her daddy and tugged on his hand. "Can she, Daddy?"

Irene added, "I even know what they like for breakfast—Coco-Wheats, real thin, cooked with milk instead of water. Who else knows their routine the way I do?"

Lucy repeated, "Can she, Daddy, pleeease?"

Eddie ignored the warning that sheered through his mind and disappeared with his sister-in-law's words. He was so tired. The funeral had been depleting, and he hadn't slept well for four nights, with the girls sleeping with him till he carried them to their own bed. Furthermore, he'd been wondering what to do about the kids being alone in the mornings. Physically and emotionally spent as he was, Eddie found it easy to accept Irene's solution.

"Well, all right, Irene. I won't be able to pay you much, but I'd—"

"Oh, for heaven's sake, don't be silly, Eddie. I wouldn't take one red cent if you begged me. These are my nieces and I love them. I loved Krystyna, too." She didn't say, *and I love you, too,* but she thought it, thought it with a catch in her heart as she examined his exhausted face and the eyes that had lost their sparkle.

He squeezed her arm, half on her sleeve, half on her bare skin, and said, "Thanks, Irene," sending shivers clear through her.

That night he filled the bathtub for the girls, laid out their clean night-clothes and let them bathe themselves. Lucy got into Krystyna's For-ever Spring talcum powder and, with the help of a fluffy white puff, managed to dust not only herself, but the entire bathroom. He had to wipe it down with a wet cloth, and the scent, when dampened, intensified as if Krystyna had walked into the room. The reminder of her was almost more than he could take.

When he finished cleaning up the bathroom, he found the girls in his bed. Anne was reading to Lucy from *Old Mother Westwind*: "Why Jimmy Skunk Wears Stripes." It was one of their favorite books, one Krystyna had read to them nearly every night. His heart took a turn as he looked at Anne and thought, *Oh, sweet little girl, you don't have to try to fill in for your mother.*

Relegating them to their own room, especially tonight, after their mother's funeral, seemed a heartless thing to do, yet he feared their be-coming too dependent and attached to him. Furthermore, he was so ex-hausted he needed to have his bed to himself. If he felt like crying he wanted privacy to do so. If he felt like getting up in the middle of the night and prowling around in the moonlight, he didn't want kids waking up.

"Listen, girls, tonight I think it's time you go back into your own room."

"Nooo!" Lucy wailed. "I like it in here!"

"We want to stay with you. I don't like it in there without Mommy."

"But Mommy didn't stay in there with you."

"But she always tucked us in."

"I'll come and tuck you in." Often in the past he had done this as well, but there were certain times of the day when they missed Krystyna more, and bedtime was the worst.

Anne's lower lip began trembling and two plump tears sprouted on her lower eyelids. "I want Mommy back," she said.

Lucy, forever parroting Anne, stuck out her lower lip and said, "I want Mommy back, too."

In the end he let them have their way because it was easier than watching them cry for Krystyna. They insisted on having him in the middle, and by the time they fell asleep their warm little bodies were crowding his, sticking as if slathered with wallpaper paste. He waited nearly half an hour to make sure they were slumbering soundly before carrying them to their own room.

Back in his bed, alone, he lay wide-eyed, exhausted but unable to sleep, considering the monumental change his life had undergone. Loneliness— that was constant. And indescribable. More consuming than first love had been with her. He rolled to his side and pressed his wrist into Krystyna's cool pillow, cursing himself for how smug he'd been in his satisfaction with life as it was before, humbled by the suddenness with which that smugness was snatched away. There were worries, too—a stack of dirty clothes in the bathroom hamper and nobody to wash and iron them; tomorrow night's supper and nobody to cook it; the girls coming home from school at four o'clock in the afternoon and nobody here to watch them till he got home, to have warm cookies waiting, and an admonition to change their clothes before going out to play. Could he leave them unattended every day for an hour and a half? They were only eight and nine years old—he didn't think so. He might be able to cook supper himself every night, but he couldn't accomplish much between five-thirty and six when he had to run back to church to ring the Angelus; so supposing he started cooking after that, it would be eight o'clock or later before the supper dishes were done. And after dishes he still had to see to their baths, and get them ready for bed, and read to them.

There were other worries, too. Anne would make her First Communion in the spring. That meant memorizing her catechism, which Krystyna had been helping her with, and special white dresses and veils, and long white stockings and white shoes. How would he do it? How could he do it all?

The truth was, he couldn't. Not without Irene.

Irene showed up at seven o'clock the next morning. He was only half-dressed and ran downstairs to answer the door with his shirttails flying. Irene was wearing makeup and wouldn't look him in the eye.

He left her downstairs building a fire in the kitchen range, and closed his bedroom door when he heard her coming up to awaken the girls.

By the time he finished getting dressed, made up his bed and went downstairs, she had cooked hot Coco-Wheats for the girls and oatmeal, coffee and toast for him. The table was set with a crisply ironed floral luncheon cloth, and his favorite oversized cup, cream and sugar were all set out, waiting. The girls were in their places, still in their pajamas, but their school shoes were lined up on the cabinet, freshly wiped off, and on top of each pair, a freshly laundered handkerchief. Beside each of their cereal bowls she had put one of their daily vitamin pills.

He came up short in the kitchen doorway, surveying the perfect duplication of Krystyna's morning routine, and suddenly it struck him what she was doing. He wanted to shout, *Get out! I'll do it myself! You're not Krystyna, so don't try to pretend to be!* But he needed her. And what if he was wrong? What if she was merely trying to cheer herself up by putting on makeup after five days of too much crying? What if she was only trying to get the girls through these first few days without their mother by presenting the illusion that things would go on as before? What if it was a great imposition for her to volunteer to come here every morning, and he jumped on her for something about which he was totally wrong? It would embarrass them both to the point where they'd probably never be able to look each other in the eye again.

When he stopped in the kitchen doorway, she looked over at him and flushed. "I uh . . . I think you like oatmeal . . . um, right?" she stammered, as if unsure of her footing.

"Uh . . . yes. Yes! Oatmeal's fine." He stepped into the room and pulled out his chair. "Thanks, Irene."

When he sat, she didn't, but stood near the kitchen sink, rubbing her hands together and watching him doctor up his coffee. He grew uneasy being watched, set down his cup and gave her a baffled look. "Aren't you eating anything?"

Her forearms flew up as if someone had pushed her from behind. "Oh, I ate at home."

"Oh," he said, unsure of how to deal with her. "Well . . ."

He began eating, feeling self-conscious when he'd never felt that way around her before.

"If you have a nickel for each of their school dinners, I'll tie them in their hankies."

"Oh . . . sure . . ." He cocked one hip and reached into his pants pocket, then handed her the coins. It was uncanny: the woman knew every single nuance of their morning routine.

Out of the blue, Lucy declared, "I want to eat noon dinner at home today. We're having creamed peas at school and I hate them and Sister Mary Charles always makes me eat them. She says the children in China are starving, so I have to clean up my plate."

Anne asked, "Where's China, Daddy?"

"On the other side of the world."

"Then how could they eat Lucy's creamed peas?"

Eddie caught Irene's eye and they both suppressed grins. "Sister Mary Charles is just trying to teach you not to waste food."

"I'm scared of her."

"There's no need to be scared of her."

"She gives the bad boys lickings in the flower room. I've heard them howling in there. She hits them with a rubber strap that she leaves laying on the fern stand. I've seen it! It's made out of floor tile."

"Well, be good, then she'll never use it on you."

Anne said, "I thought you said that we didn't have to be scared of her."

Eddie polished off his coffee, set down the cup and evaded the issue. "Got to go ring the first bell," he said, pushing up from the table.

"What about my creamed peas, Daddy?"

"I'm afraid you'll have to do your best to eat them because you have to eat noon dinner at school from now on."

"You mean *every* day?" Lucy's face scrunched up in dismay.

"I'm afraid so, dumpling."

It struck her that her mother wouldn't be there to fix it, and she looked at her aunt. "Can't Auntie Irene fix dinner for us?"

His glance veered to Irene, then he got busy making preparations to leave. "Auntie Irene has to go back home."

"Oh."

He hugged the girls, taking extra time today, kissing their thin necks that smelled like Forever Spring. How he hated leaving them in Irene's care, not because she wouldn't do a good job of getting them ready—unless he missed his guess, she'd do just as good a job as Krystyna—but because he was stepping into a new routine without Krystyna in it. He was striding forward with his life as he must, but each step he took made him feel as if he was betraying her by carrying on this farce of feigned normalcy.

Yet he didn't know what else to do.

Irene was dressing the children when the first bell rang at seven-thirty. At the sound of it, her hands fell still as she pictured Eddie in the church vestibule alone, hauling on the rope. Poor Eddie, she thought. Poor lonely Eddie.

She made sure the girls had brushed their teeth, washed their faces and behind their ears, then she fussed with their hair, and tied their sashes in back with big, perfect bows. When they were ready to walk out the door she handed them their hankies with the nickels tied into the corners, and gave them hugs and firm kisses on the cheek. "Would you like me to be here when you get back home from school?" she asked.

"Well . . . I guess so," Anne replied.

Lucy asked, "You mean you'd stay here all day?"

"No, I'm going back out to the farm as soon as I wash the breakfast dishes and slick up the house a little bit."

"Oh."

"But I can come back in at four o'clock when school is out, if you'd like."

Lucy deferred to her older sister.

Anne said, "We can be by ourselves for a little while. We're not babies."

"No, of course you're not. I just thought . . ." She patted Anne on the shoulder. "Well, in any case, I'll see you tomorrow morning. Take your sweaters now. There's a chill in the air."

A minute later the two little girls started out for school, each with a navy blue sweater over her dress, Anne dutifully taking Lucy's hand as they crossed the street and headed up the alley.

"Is Auntie Irene going to be our new mother?" Lucy asked as they walked up the twin worn tracks with the grass strip up the middle.

"How can she be our mother when she's our aunt?"

"I don't know." Lucy shrugged. "She's doing everything that Mommy did, so I just thought she was going to be."

"She's just our baby-sitter, that's all."

"Oh."

They continued up the alley, which was as familiar to them as their own yard. It ran behind the deep back lots of the businesses on Main Street—Myman's Ford, Sam Berczyk's blacksmith shop and Wangler's jewelry shop. Between the businesses were some empty lots, where Anne and Lucy had picnics on hot summer noons and played hide-and-seek with the neighborhood kids in the mosquitoey after-supper hours on sticky summer evenings, and where they often found things to explore—old grindstones knee-deep in quack grass; the skeletons of rusting farm machinery whose purposes they could not name; short stacks of lumber, which, when overturned, revealed fat pink angleworms that made good gifts for their dad who said he liked to go fishing, though he never seemed to find the time. There were sheds, too, holding old trucks that nobody ever seemed to drive, and chicken crates and cordwood piles and tilting outhouses with shovels and scythes leaning against them, and heavy steel chains and rusty automobile axles, and up behind Nauman's Plumbing, a creaky back door that was never locked, leading to a basement so full of salamanders that it made them shriek with fright and pound back up the steps every time they sneaked down there to shine a flashlight in the salamanders' eyes. Those eyes turned green as lime Popsicles when the light hit them, and were the most deliciously scary things in the entire world. Sometimes Brenda Nauman charged kids a penny to take them down and see.

On the other side of the alley, directly across from Anne and Lucy's house, was Frank Plotnik's blacksmith shop and the backyards of small houses with clotheslines and gardens and sheds. In a couple of those houses lived old women who were related to their grandparents, though neither Anne nor Lucy quite understood how.

At the end of the alley they came to a T with a street that had no name, and across the street, the fancy fence surrounding Father Kuzdek's house and the churchyard. They loved the churchyard. It was filled with life-sized statues carved in glistening white stone, and the fishpond where they sometimes came to drop bits of bread for the goldfish to eat. Every year on the feast of Corpus Christi they were dressed in white with veils on their heads, and they strewed peony petals before Father Kuzdek, who said Mass at four small altars that their mother had helped set up all around the lawns and decorate with flowers from her own garden.

Walking the perimeter of the churchyard, Lucy said, " 'Member when we got to dress all up and carry flowers for Father Kuzdek? What was that called again?"

"Kurpius Christi," Anne answered, mistakenly pronouncing a family name she'd heard around Browerville her whole life.

"Yeah, that's right. Kurpius Christi. Well, who's going to make our white dresses for that and for Easter and stuff?" The many occasions when church ceremony called for white dresses and veils had seemed like playing movie star to Lucy.

"I don't know. You'll probably wear my hand-me-down one from last year."

"I always have to wear your hand-me-downs," Lucy replied with a pout.

"You do not. Mommy made you lots of dresses of your own."

"I know, but she promised me that she'd make me a brand-new one for Easter, and I for sure don't want to wear your hand-me-down then. So who's gonna make it?"

"Well, I don't *know* who's gonna make it!" Anne was having difficulty keeping her lip from trembling, and the result was a spate of irritation.

Lucy halted, jerked her hand out of Anne's and abruptly started to cry. They happened to be smack in front of church, and she sat down on the bottom step and howled, openmouthed, without even covering her face. "I don't want Mommy to be dead! I want her to make my Easter dress! I'm goin' back home!"

She got up and would have run back the way they'd come, but Anne grabbed her hand. "You can't go back home. Nobody's there."

"Auntie Irene is there."

"She said she was going home."

Lucy stood in the middle of the sidewalk and bellowed, "I want my mommeeee!"

Anne, who wanted her mommy, too, was forced to act as consoler. She put her arms around Lucy and petted her hair the way their mother would have. "Come on, Lucy, we have to go to school. Let's go see Sister Regina and she'll know what to do. Where's your hanky? Here, get it out and blow your nose."

Sister Regina was writing on the blackboard when they came in: *September 12, Feast of the Most Holy Name of Mary.* For each day that celebrated a particular saint, she wrote the name of that saint on the board and taught the children about him or her. Some of her students had already arrived and were mingling around the desks when Sister heard the cloakroom door open and close and Lucy sniffling as the two sisters came into the schoolroom.

"Good morning, Sister," Anne said.

Lucy tried to say the same thing, but it came out choppy as she cried.

"Good morning, children. Oh, my goodness, Lucy, what is it?" Sister said sympathetically, setting down her chalk and turning to the children.

"She wants to go back home, but I told her Mommy isn't there."

Lucy stood dejectedly, rubbing her eyes, her words coming in jolts that were divided by residual sobs. "I w . . . want my m . . . mommy." Some of their classmates turned to watch in fascination.

"Come with me," Sister said, and reaching for both of their hands, led them through the cloakroom and into the flower room, away from the curious eyes of their classmates. Three tiers of varnished bleachers held plants of many varieties, and between two ferns Sister Mary Charles's rubber strap waited. The girls eyed it fearfully and nudged closer to Sister Regina, gripping her hands tighter. Along one wall a short section of bookshelves held the school "library," and against another a metal cot covered with an army blanket sufficed as a "nurse's office." Sister sat down on the cot and drew the children down beside her, tugging their hands against her black skirts until she felt them huddle against her, small and forlorn and trusting. In spite of the fact that Holy Rule disallowed it, she put her arms around them and drew them fast to her sides. Having had no children of her own, she'd rarely felt small bodies curl against her this way. Their shoulders reached the sides of her breasts which were bound firmly inside her habit, as if to deny the fact that she was female. The feel of the children gathered against her filled Sister Regina with an expansive rush of maternal love.

"Now what has made you cry on this beautiful new day?"

"She wants our mommy back."

"Oh, Lucy, dear, so do we all. But let me tell you something. When you came into my schoolroom a minute ago, do you know what I was writing on the blackboard? I was writing down what today's feast day is, just like I do every morning. And do you know what it is?"

Lucy, intrigued in spite of herself, looked up and wagged her head no, swiping the tears from beneath her eyes.

"Why, it's the feast of the Holy Name of Mary. That means that if we ask the Blessed Virgin to intercede for us for anything today, we have a good chance of getting it. I think we should ask Mary if your mother is happy in heaven? Shall we do that?"

"I guess so."

Continuing to hold the children tightly, Sister Regina shut her eyes and prayed aloud, "Dear Mary, most holy Virgin, mother of Jesus, who loved and cared for Him just as Krystyna loved and cared for her children, Anne and Lucy, we pray that you might ask our Lord to shed His grace on these two children who have a very special need of His help today. They wish to send a prayer that their mother's soul be happy and abiding with Jesus. They want her to know that they will do their very best to persevere here on earth."

Lucy whispered, "Sister?"

She looked down at the angelic face lifted to her. "Yes, Lucy?"

"What's a 'purse of ear'?"

"It means to do our best even when it's hard. For you and Anne it means that you'll go to school and continue to be the obedient children you've always been, and go to Mass every day, and help each other the way Anne helped you today. But just think, on the days when you wish you didn't have to do any of those things, you'll have special help not only from Jesus, but from your own Mother who lives in heaven with Him now."

"But how can she help me? Can she still make my Easter dress?"

"Well, no, she can't, Lucy, but she'll find a way for you to get one."

"She will?"

"Of course she will."

"How?"

"Well, your mommy's an angel now, and you heard what Father Kuzdek said. Angels find a way."

At the nun's reassurance, Lucy offered a quavering smile.

"Now, do you know what?" Sister brightened her voice and returned the smile. "The other children have arrived and it's time to line up and go to church for Mass. Your daddy will be ringing the bell in a minute and he'll be watching for you. Would you like to go see him?"

Lucy was already climbing down, drying her cheeks with the backs of her freckled hands when something unexpected happened. Anne, too, slipped to her feet and before Sister could rise, swung around and flung up her arms in a spontaneous hug. She caught the nun around the neck and clung, pulling her veil taut against her head, holding on tenaciously, her warm cheek against Sister's cool one. Within Sister Regina a bubble of joy burst and spread its goodness, as if the Angel Krystyna were, indeed, watching over all of them, giving them each a very precious gift in their newfound closeness. It was so unexpected, that hug, the kind of thing children do without compunction, the kind of thing a mother must get all the time and take for granted. But Sister Regina had never had such a hug before, and it incited her every maternal instinct, forcing it up into the light like a wildflower growing from the crevice of a rock.

For once in her life she forgot Holy Rule and hugged the child back.

As abruptly as it began, it ended, and Sister found herself following the children back to the classroom with a new, expansive feeling in her heart, as if someone had pumped its chambers full of the rarefied air of heaven.

What had passed in the flower room quite naturally brought thoughts of the children of her own that she'd given up by becoming a nun. Funny how little she'd thought of it back then. Throughout all the years when she was growing up she had never considered another path in life than that of becoming a nun. Her grandmother had begun putting the notion into her head when she was perhaps seven or eight years old, no older than Anne and Lucy were now. So young an age, in fact, that the idea of marriage and children had never had room to nurture and grow. The nuns who had taught her had furthered the notion of her entering the convent by assuring her that to become a religious was more rewarding, more noble, and more privileged than any other walk of life, and that she should feel very blessed that she'd had the calling to a vocation. God had chosen her.

Anyone could be a wife and mother, they intimated, but only the *Chosen* could enter a religious vocation.

But look what I've given up, she thought now.

She got the children into rank and file and led them to church. The bell was ringing as they mounted the steps and entered the vestibule. After taking holy water herself, she stood off to one side and watched as they all followed suit, making the sign of the cross, then folding their hands as they went inside to their customary pew. To her left, Mr. Olczak stopped ringing the bell when he saw his children heading toward him. He could see that

Lucy had been crying. She ran the last couple of steps and his face crimped tight—eyes, lips, jaws—as he bent on one knee and scooped her up. Holding her fiercely, he whispered at her ear.

Sister couldn't hear what they said to each other, nor what he and Anne said as he opened his other arm and included her in the embrace, but she found herself comparing the love that she, as a religious, felt for her God, to the love this father and his children felt for one another, and she was struck by an earth-shattering realization.

They were wrong, she thought. *They were all wrong. These are the Chosen ones. I was the one who left life behind.*

Eight

❧

Irene Pribil came right to the classroom door to collect Anne and Lucy at four o'clock when school was out. The students were lined up double-file ready to be marched out-doors as Irene arrived. The girls ran to their aunt gladly, and Sister smiled, relieved that they'd be cared for, for she'd been wondering. "It's so good of you to come for them, Irene."

"It's no trouble at all, Sister. They've always been my favorites."

Sister bid the Olczak girls goodbye, then ac-companied the rest of her pupils outside, half of them to be excused to walk home, the other half to be marched to their waiting buses.

They clambered on, noisy, disheveled, jostling, shouting in high-pitched voices, " 'Bye, Sister! 'Bye, Sister! See you tomorrow, Sister!" She watched them go with the relief that four o'clock always brought.

In the quiet after the buses pulled away, Sis-ter Regina idled a while before returning to the building. It was a sunny afternoon and the school grounds were pleasant with thick, manicured grass, branching sidewalks, and geraniums in the grotto where there was a statue of Jesus praying in the garden of Gethsemane. The grotto was set on elevated ground surrounded by rock terraces and aged pine trees. It was approached by natural stone steps. Moss roses and sedum grew among the rocks, spilling onto the path as Sister walked up to make a visit.

Before the statue she dipped down on one knee, looked up into the carved face of Jesus and said, "Watch over the Olczaks, Lord. They need you now."

Rising, she dusted some pine needles from her black skirts and paused, enjoying her freedom and the spicy smell of the pines whose lowest boughs were so wide they swept the ground. A faint breeze lifted her veil, and the sun felt warm on her shoulders, captured and held by the black cloth of her habit. From the north came the distant *ka-klunk, ka-klunk* of a mold making cement blocks at Borgert's Block Factory. From the east issued the hiss of air hoses as rail cars were disconnected and dropped off at the milk plant. Twin bleats sounded from an air horn as one of the shiny silver milk trucks came in from its farm route and honked for admittance into the plant. Even as Sister listened the sounds from the east ceased, and the town grew quieter. Only the faraway *ka-klunk, ka-klunk* continued, reassuring in its familiarity.

She sighed. Time to return to the schoolroom.

Inside the building all the classroom doors were open, pressed back against the walls, and she smiled in at Sister Dora as she passed the first- and second-grade room. The building was blessedly quiet. The water fountain had been left running and she leaned to take a cold drink, leaned very low, to the level of a first-grader, savoring water so icy that it hurt her teeth. Good as it was, she turned the fountain off, remembering her vow of poverty and that wasting even water was a sin.

In her own room the shades and windows were at half-mast, letting the low afternoon sun fold across the sills. At the front end of each row of desks a small pile of refuse waited, whisked there by the students—one from each row—who got down on hands and knees and ran a side-broom between the desk runners at the end of each day to save Mr. Olczak the trouble of doing so.

This was Sister Regina's favorite time of day. With the children gone, the room became her own. She went to the blackboard, rolled back her sleeve and began erasing when Mr. Olczak said from the doorway, "Afternoon, Sister."

Her heart leaped but her outward demeanor reflected only placidity as she turned and found him standing in the doorway holding a dust mop.

"Good afternoon, Mr. Olczak."

"How did my girls do today?" Beside him a rolling bucket held an assortment of cleaning supplies slung on its sides.

"It was a day of mixed emotions, I'm afraid."

"What happened?" He came in and began running the wide mop around the perimeter of the room, spreading the smell of dusting oil.

"This morning Lucy had a bad spell and wanted to go back home, but Anne brought her to me and we had a quiet talk away from the other children. Both of them seemed much calmer afterward."

He turned a corner and went along the back of the room. "If you want to know the truth, I worry about Anne more than I do about Lucy. She might seem like the stronger one, but underneath it all I think she'll miss her mother more than the little one."

"I guess it's natural, since she's known her longer and has more memories built up."

Eddie stopped in the far corner, the length of the room from Sister Regina. He stacked his hands on the end of the mop handle and planted his feet comfortably. "I'll tell you, Sister, I'm sure glad they have you. I could've used somebody to talk to this morning myself."

She knew she should not encourage personal talk, so offered a small smile instead and sat down at her desk.

He went around the third side of the room, then down one aisle and stopped at the rear again. Leaning over, he scraped something off the hardwood floor with his fingernail, then straightened and seemed to pause before saying what was on his mind. "Irene came in this morning," he told her. "She sort of . . . well, she sort of took over for Krystyna, if you know what I mean."

Sister merely nodded.

"Don't get me wrong," he hurried on. "I was glad to have her get the girls ready for school, but she . . . well she . . ."

Sister waited.

Eddie worried the tip of the mop handle with a thumb. "I kind of re-sented her being there, invading Krystyna's territory."

In her lifetime no adult man had ever confided in Sister this way. It was wholly unexpected, his choosing her as a confidante, and she felt somewhat rattled by his openness. Holy Rule was wildly waving its arms for her at-tention, but she ignored it. After all, his children were her students: what he had to say affected them, did it not?

"That's perfectly understandable."

"I guess that was pretty selfish of me, wasn't it?"

Their eyes met across the classroom. "I wouldn't worry about selfish-ness for a while if I were you, Mr. Olczak. Irene meant well, but she un-derstands how hard it is for you right now."

"She knew where everything was—you know what I mean?—like where Krystyna kept things, and all of a sudden I had this feeling like . . . like she was trying to *be* Krystyna. I didn't . . . well, I didn't like that very much."

Sister nodded again.

"Same thing the day Krystyna died," Eddie went on. "The women came in before I even got home and they cleaned up everything as if she was only in the other room, things I wish they would have left alone, the last things she touched. I wanted to storm in the kitchen and say *'Get out! Leave the coffeepot where she had it! And put back every bobby pin and crumb she left on the cab-inet, and the dishtowel just the way she folded it and the grocery list leaning against the can-isters and her empty coffee cup in the sink!'*" He grew visibly blue, his voice quiet as trickling water. "But they moved it all. They brought in their cake pans and their roasters and pushed things aside to put out food and I never did see how Krystyna had left the kitchen that day. I know they meant well, but they shouldn't have done that. They should have waited."

He was no longer looking at Sister. He was staring at the sunlight on the windowsill and battling tears. She could see his Adam's apple working, and his thumb bent motionless against the mop handle. From outside the *ka-klunk, ka-klunk* from the block factory sounded like a heart beating when you put your ear to someone's chest, and she imagined, for a moment, it was his heart, broken, and it was her ear on his chest searching for a way to heal it.

He sent her a look of appeal and asked, "Shouldn't they, Sister?"

"Y . . ." She tried to find her voice, which cracked. "Yes . . . they should have," she whispered, quelling the urge to approach and comfort him. Forbidden to do such a thing, she went on in the calmest voice she could muster. "But they simply didn't think. It's natural that you should want Krystyna's place to be inviolate, that you should want to . . . to move among her memories and find them untouched. All you can do is remember that the women, and Irene as well, only meant to help. Just don't waste your time feeling guilty about your reaction. I don't think God would find you uncharitable, Mr. Olczak. I think He would understand what you're going through."

She could see the tension ease from his shoulders. His hand loosened and slid lower on the mop handle. He shifted his feet.

"You know what, Sister? There's never been a time when I talked to you that I didn't feel better afterwards." He even managed a little smile for her benefit.

"Yes, well . . . that's . . ." She realized she was treading on forbidden ground and finished lamely, ". . . that's good, Mr. Olczak." In the kneehole of her desk she belatedly rolled down her right sleeve, discovering she had forgotten it all this while. She pulled a stack of fourth-grade spelling papers to the center of her desk and began correcting them as he resumed sweeping the aisles. Up and down, collecting the little stacks that the children had left at the front of the rows, picking up things with a big metal dustpan. After some time, he said, almost as if to himself, "Well, I'm glad the kids did good today anyway."

The room settled into silence. She ran a red pencil across a row of arithmetic sums, making an occasional check mark, while he emptied her garbage can and began washing the blackboards on the side of the room, then behind her. She recorded the grades in her grade book while the black-boards began drying in gray rainbows. He disappeared into the cloakroom to clean it while she looked up tomorrow's feast day and found there was none to post on the blackboard. Instead she wrote a new set of spelling words for the fourth-graders, and a simple prayer: *Holy Mary, mother mild, smile upon this little child. Amen.*

She was seated at her desk once again by the time he was finished with everything and pushed his rolling bucket to the doorway. He paused to read what she had written. "That's nice, Sister. Well, I'll see you tomorrow."

"Yes, goodbye, Mr. Olczak."

When he was gone she sat as still as the painting of the Blessed Virgin Mary that hung above the blackboards on the opposite wall. She looked up at the visage of the woman in the blue dress and white penumbra, all the while recognizing the rush of feelings and the stirring of blood caused by the man who'd just left the room. It was the kind of womanly response she had denied herself when she donned this habit. And it was forbidden.

She folded her hands—not a relaxed pairing with the fingers pointed up toward heaven, but a tense gripping with the fingers knit. Lowering her head to her knuckles, she closed her eyes. *Dear God,* she prayed, *help me to re-main pure of heart and immaculate of body like your blessed mother. Help me to maintain the vows I've taken and to resist these impulses toward worldliness. Let me be content in the life I've chosen, so that I may serve You always with pure heart and spirit, in Jesus' name I pray, Amen.*

*I*rene was still there when Eddie got home that day. He'd been expect-ing her to be, of course, since she'd shown up at school, announcing that she'd come for the girls and was taking them home.

When he walked into the house he could smell chicken stewing and coffee brewing. Irene was in the kitchen lifting fluffy white dumplings out of a kettle when he reached the doorway.

She looked at him. He looked at her.

She blushed. He frowned. His displeasure barely showed between his eyes, but she recognized it and felt her stomach quaver.

"Lucy wanted dumplings," she said, apologizing.

"Lucy always wants dumplings."

"Well, she said Krystyna was going to . . . she was . . ."

Her words trailed away and he walked past her, straight over to the sink to wash his hands. It was easier to say what had to be said with his back to her.

"Irene—"

She went to the back door and called through the screen to the girls in their playhouse, "Girls, time for you to come in and get washed up for supper!"

"Irene, I appreciate your help but—"

"No, listen . . . you don't need to say anymore. I was just going to get the food on the table, then I was going home. I wasn't going to stay, honest, Eddie."

He bent over and washed his face with his soapy hands to give himself time to think of how to handle this. When he turned, drying his face on a blue towel, she had withdrawn as far from him as she could get and was trying to put the last of the food on the table without infringing on his space. Though she tried to hide her tears, he saw them glimmer in her eyes. The sight of them made him feel small, so he relented.

"All I was going to say was that there's still food left over that people brought last week."

"It was old," she said, keeping her face averted. "I cleaned out the icebox and threw a lot of it away. I also washed all the roasters and casserole dishes and put everybody's names on them so you know who they belong to. If you want me to return them for you I—"

"No, Irene, you've done enough. I'll make sure they get back to everybody. Now listen, you've made this nice supper. You might as well stay and eat with us."

The girls came barging in.

"Are the dumplings ready?" Lucy bellowed.

"I'm hungry!" Anne declared.

The meal was laid out, steaming and smelling delicious, and though Irene gave the table a longing look, she did so backing away. "Ma's expecting me," she told Eddie. And to the children, "Girls, you be sure to wash up good before you sit down. Now come and give me a hug . . . bye-bye, honey. Bye-bye, dear." She hugged them both and scuttled away.

The girls dove for the sink and the bar of soap while Eddie followed Irene to the front door, feeling guilty as hell for resenting her kindness. He remembered Sister Regina's words. She only meant to help. Furthermore, she probably needed to be near him and the girls to handle her own immense grief.

She knew he'd come up behind her and paused, looking down at the screendoor spring. "You want me to come again in the morning, Eddie? 'Cause I don't have to if I bother you."

"Irene," he said, laying a heavy hand on her shoulder. Though he had not sighed, a sigh was implied. Neither of them spoke for a while. In the kitchen the kids quibbled about who'd get the first helping of dumplings.

"I only meant to help, Eddie. I didn't mean to . . . well, you know."

He squeezed her shoulder and let his hand drop. "I know, Irene."

She got brave and turned to face him. "What do you want me to do, then?"

This time he did sigh, and put his hands in his back overall pockets. "I guess I need your help, Irene," he admitted.

"Okay, then, should I come in the morning?"

Resigned, he answered, "Yes, if you don't mind."

She opened the door and said, "I'll be here."

He watched her hurry to her dad's truck, which was parked at the curb. She got in and drove away a little fast for Irene, and he realized just how much he had hurt her without intending to.

———

he meal she'd cooked was delicious. He couldn't tell the difference between her cooking and Krystyna's. They both made chicken and dumplings the way their mother did. He hurried the girls to finish eating and let Mrs. Plotnik next door know that they'd be outside playing with a bunch of the neighborhood kids while he ran over to church to ring the Angelus. When he got back home the dirty dishes were still on the table and the children were still playing Annie-I-Over over at the small white frame United Brethren church across the street from the Plotnik house. The U.B. church, as it was known in the neighborhood, had a steep roof like a tent, so they could see the ball rolling toward them clear from the peak, and it had a grassy yard good for running, and two outhouses with lattice screens around the doors, very convenient. So all the neighborhood kids would be outside playing until their parents called them in. Anne and Lucy were old enough to wash and dry the dishes for Eddie, but the sound of their care-free voices calling, "Pigtails!" softened his heart, so he let them go on playing and washed the dishes himself. Though Krystyna would never have let dishes drip dry in the sink, he had to cut corners wherever possible on the housework, so he left them to do just that.

By the time the kitchen was put back in order, it was time to call the girls in for their bath. It took three repeated calls and another fifteen minutes before they obeyed, coming in crumpled and winded, their cheeks rosy from exertion.

He filled the bathtub and left them with orders to stay out of their mother's dusting powder. A minute after he closed the bathroom door it opened again, and Anne came out in her underwear, bringing him a note. "Look at what I found on the clothes hamper, Daddy."

It was written in pencil, nearly illegible.

Eddie I tuk yor close home and washd them you can coom & get them tomorr they will be irned Aunt Katy.

Aunt Katy, he thought, drooping with gratitude, *bless your heart, old girl.*

"What does it say?" Anne wanted to know.

"Aunt Katy washed our dirty clothes."

He went into the bathroom and looked inside the hamper. It was empty except for the clothes the girls had worn today.

Aunt Katy Gaffke was his mother's sister, a great-aunt to his girls, though they found shirttail relations hard to categorize, so they had always referred to her as Grandma Gaffke. She lived around the corner from the U.B. church, up the hill and across the street, about a two-minute walk from Eddie's house. She'd been born in Poland, as had his mother, and had come to America with her parents when she was four. She spoke English with an accent and had never become proficient at writing it, but Eddie understood her message and the love behind her charitable deed.

The next day when he went to her house, he found his freshly ironed shirts hanging from her kitchen doorway, and Aunt Katy in a low armless rocker on her glassed-in porch, fast asleep. She'd been tearing strips of rags for making rag rugs, a common winter pastime for the old Polish women who sold them or donated them to church bazaars. Her lap, the floor and the rockers of the chair were so littered with strings that she looked like a bird in a nest.

He leaned down and touched her shoulder. "Aunt Katy?"

She jerked awake, tried to figure out where she was, looked up and mumbled, "Oh . . . hmm . . . must've drifted off." The corners of her mouth were shiny. She dried them with an edge of one speckled hand and boosted herself up straighter in the chair. "Well, Eddie, didn't hear you come in. Sit down, sit down."

He sat on her daybed which was covered with two of her homemade rag rugs that made the mattress nearly as hard as a church pew. It was late afternoon and the porch was on the shady side of the house. On a small crude blue-painted table in one corner were the coleus plants she'd taken in from her gardens and rooted for winter. Beyond the window martens were swooping around a fancy white birdhouse on a tall pole. Her cat was hunched up, watching them, on a concrete step that led from the porch door directly onto the grass, with no sidewalk between it and the street. He could look down the hill to his right and see his kids playing hopscotch on the sidewalk in front of the Plotnik house. He could look to his left and see the top of the school grounds about thirty yards away.

"I sure appreciate your washing and ironing our clothes, Aunt Katy."

She flapped a hand as if shooing a fly. "Gave me something to do."

"I didn't know how I was going to manage that. I'd like to pay you."

"You might like to, but you ain't goin' to."

"But—"

"Nossir."

"But if this town had a laundry I'd have to pay them."

"Nossir."

"You know, you're a stubborn old cuss when you want to be."

"Yessir. And what's more, I intend to keep on washin' 'em ever Monday when I wash m' own. Ain't hardly got enough of my own to make it worth while filling that washer anymore."

He got up and kissed her on the forehead, then sat back down. She smelled like homemade lye soap and fried Spam.

"How're them little girls doing?" she asked, looking down the hill at them.

"Irene comes in the morning and gets them ready for school."

"How 'bout in the afternoon?"

"Well, she's been coming then, too, but I think it's too much to ask of her."

"Tell 'em to come here."

"Oh, Aunt Katy . . ."

"No, you tell 'em to come here after school! They can play around here just as well as they can play around your house."

"Are you sure?"

"They'd be company. Days get pretty long since your Uncle Tony died. Besides, every housewife in the whole town knows Krystyna is gone. Your girls'll have more mothers keeping an eye on them than they want. And *you're* right over there at church. Shucks, if they need you, they can just run over there, can't they?"

"I guess so. 'Course, it won't be so easy in the winter."

"Then they can come here, like I said."

"Are you really sure, Aunt Katy?"

"They ain't learned to make rag rugs yet, have they?"

"No."

"Nor to crochet."

"No."

"Nor to embroider much."

"No."

"Well, they got to learn all three, ain't they? I'll keep their hands busy, you can bet on that."

She kept their hands busy all right. The next afternoon when Eddie walked into her house he found his daughters elbow deep in flour.

"We're making biscuits!" Lucy exclaimed. "Grandma Katy's letting us cut 'em out with this. See?" She held up a round cookie cutter.

"And she's already got pigs-in-the-blanket cooking!" Anne added. "She let us roll the meat up in the cabbage leaves, and put them in the roaster and I got to put the roaster in the oven!"

"You're staying for supper," Aunt Katy decreed.

And so a pattern was established. In the mornings Irene came before school, and in the afternoon Aunt Katy watched the girls after school. She fixed supper for all four of them and Eddie bought the groceries. She taught the girls to dry dishes for her, and on wash day Eddie would run over across the school grounds to her house sometime in the late morning and help her carry out her washtubs and empty them in the yard. On Saturdays, when he wasn't needed at church so frequently, he cleaned his own house. The girls learned to dust the furniture and beat the rugs. On Sundays they learned to fix their own hair the best they could, and he tied their sashes, and sometimes helped Lucy fasten her barrette in her hair. On school days at four o'clock Eddie need not worry.

It was a small, safe town, Browerville, and as Aunt Katy had pointed out, parents watched out for everybody's children, not just their own. Every adult in town knew not only the name of every kid in town, he knew the names of their dogs as well. A back door would open and a housewife would yell, "Rexy, get out of that flower bed!" or "Bunny, stop digging!" just as they might yell, "Anne, it's cold out there. Go home and get your jacket!" or "Lucy, you can get hurt on that woodpile! Get down off of there!" Doors were not locked—not Eddie's, not Grandma Gaffke's, not anyone's—so the girls could have walked into anyone's house and gotten whatever they needed. If they had fallen and needed a bandage, someone would put it on. If their wound had been more serious, they would have been led down to Dr. Lenarz's office. If they had been hungry and needed a snack, a cookie jar and glass of milk would have been offered. If they had grown sad and needed their mother, a pair of loving arms would be there to gather them in.

And so, just as the doors to Eddie and Krystyna Olczak's house had always been open to others, others' were now open to their children. The insurmountable logistics of being a working daddy without a mommy to look after his children were ironed out for Eddie by the simple charity that was taken as rote in this close-knit Catholic community.

Yes, his friends and neighbors and relatives took care of everything.

Everything but the loneliness.

Nine

❦

The Chapter of Faults was a forum for the nuns to express their sorrow for any misdeeds committed during the week. It was regulated by the Constitution of their order and was held every Friday evening in the community room, presided over by Mother Agnes.

On the Friday following Krystyna's funeral the entire community of nuns gathered after supper and Sister Agnes led them in the *Veni, Creator Spiritus*, followed by its versicle and prayer. From youngest to oldest, the nuns knelt before Mother Superior to accuse themselves of two or three exterior faults, ask for a penance from her, then return to their places. It wasn't Confession—only a priest could preside at Confession—but it felt the same afterward, a cleansing and renewal to start over and do better next week, bolstered by the loving if silent support of those who knew the demons with which each nun was doing battle.

As it turned out, Sister Regina was the

youngest one at St. Joseph's, so she knelt first. Sister Agnes sat on an armchair while the late sun settled behind the playground and the room's rutabaga walls faded to umber. In keeping with their vow of poverty, no one turned on a light yet, even as the shadows deepened.

Sister Regina bowed her head, giving herself a view of Sister Agnes's skirts and cracked black shoes.

"Reverend Mother," she murmured, "in the days since Krystyna Olczak died I have repeatedly questioned God's wisdom in taking her. My sorrow over her death and the plight of her children has at times taken the form of anger, and sometimes that anger has been directed at members of this community. At other times it has forced me away from my community to be alone, which I know is contrary to Holy Rule. I've also defied our Constitution by voicing my discontent about all of this to one of the other sisters. For this I ask a penance, Reverend Mother."

Reverend Mother touched Sister Regina's bowed head and said, "Pray the Rosary for the needs of the congregation, Sister."

"Yes, Reverend Mother."

When it was Sister Dora's turn to kneel before her superior, much to Sister Regina's surprise, she confessed almost verbatim what Sister Regina had confessed with the exception of seeking solitude. Reverend Mother also told her to pray the rosary for the needs of the congregation.

Each nun in turn knelt before her superior.

Sister Samuel confessed to impatience in handling a student who continually missed choir practice.

Sister Mary Charles said she had shouted at her students one day and also that she had wished for candy.

Sister Ignatius confessed to wasting time: she had fallen asleep one afternoon while polishing the silverware. (Sister Regina supposed she was not the only one trying to suppress her smile when she heard this, for Sister Ignatius confessed this nearly every week.)

Sister Gregory confessed to a violation of nocturnal silence and to having uncharitable thoughts about a parent of one of her students.

Sister Cecelia, the perpetual busybody who so energetically tried to keep everybody else in line, confessed to nothing.

The Chapter of Faults closed with the recitation of an Act of Contrition and an Our Father, Hail Mary, and Glory Be in honor of St. Joseph for the needs of the congregation.

When recreation time resumed the others visited, but Sister Regina did not. She occupied herself making small tablets out of leftover worksheets that had writing on one side, cutting them into fourths, punching holes and binding them with bits of yarn for her students to fill with autumn leaves. While she worked she berated herself for failing to confess another entire list of faults regarding Mr. Olczack. Had she not touched him the day his wife died? Wished to embrace him and his children the same day? And felt anger on his behalf when his family let him ring the death bells? And she'd encouraged idle conversation with him not only on one occasion, but on two. She had hugged his children in the flower room that one day before school—she could still feel the maternal response to them when she closed her eyes. Worst of all, she'd admitted to herself that the feelings she harbored for Mr. Olczak went far beyond those which any nun should be having for a secular, particularly for one of the opposite sex whom she encountered every day of the week. And even more particularly, one who had so recently lost his wife.

What would people think? More important, what would God think? And why was it that any infraction against the vow of chastity was the hardest to confess? Obedience and poverty, yes—these were vows of equal import: breach these and the words came tumbling out easily at the Chapter of Faults or at confession. But breach the vow of chastity and it became complicated by one's failure to confess it, after which it lay on the conscience heavier than ever.

Sister Regina decided that what she needed more than all else was silence and recollection to help her combat the incipient attraction she was feeling for Mr. Olczak. Silence and recollection—she'd been taught—were essential to the formation and preservation of the interior life and to a living awareness of the indwelling presence of God in the soul. She'd known this since she'd first entered the postulate. Put plainly and simply, she'd been talking too much.

She made up her mind she would try very hard from now on to talk less, think of Mr. Olczak less, and avoid being in his vicinity whenever possible.

After recreation ended she went to her room and prayed, prayed long and hard that she might rekindle the zeal she had once had for her vocation and dispense with all the unsisterly inclinations she'd been having. Night fell but, in keeping with her vow of poverty, she left the lamp off, kneeling on the hard floor in the dark and attempting to empty her mind of all worldly thought and achieve a true communion with God. For a while she thought she'd succeeded, but as her knees began aching she'd find herself searching for distraction beyond prayer, and more than once that distraction came in the image of Mr. Olczak stopping in the far corner of her room, stacking his hands on his mop handle and admitting that he resented his sister-in-law for invading Krystyna's territory. He had loved his wife the way Sister Regina imagined dreamy-eyed young girls hope to be loved by their husbands. She had never given herself the chance to be a dreamy-eyed young girl, for she had committed herself to being a nun from the time of her early teens. How odd that she'd never dreamed of boyfriends or husbands. It almost seemed abnormal now. But with Grandma Rosella whispering in one ear, and the nuns whispering in the other, what chance had she had?

Pray! she admonished herself. You are not *praying!*

And so she would start again.

"Virgin most clement, pray for me . . ."

She had been trained to espouse the highest ideals of the evangelical counsels—poverty, obedience and chastity—and she *wanted* to excel, to be a content, obedient, chaste nun. Truly she did! The idea of being anything else was terrifying, for she'd had the sanctuary of communal convent life throughout all her adult years. Its structure and ritual were so ingrained that the idea of living alone was as scary to her as divorce was to a married woman.

A clean heart create for me, O God, and a steadfast spirit renew within me.

But something had changed within her, and the perfection for which all nuns aspired, as delineated in their Constitution, seemed unattainable. Indeed, at times, it seemed egotistical to believe one *could* be perfect.

On Saturday she went to Confession. But she lumped all her Olczak-related sins into one statement. She told Father, "I've had unchaste thoughts."

On Saturday afternoon she was once again getting set to carry out her charge as sacristan, when she encountered not only Mr. Olczak but Anne and Lucy as well. He had brought them along with him in his green pickup, which he'd backed up into the driveway between the buildings just as she came out of the convent to head over to church.

When the girls saw her coming, they both burst into smiles and ran toward her.

"Sister Regina!" they both shouted.

"Hello, girls."

Lucy ran smack into her and hugged her skirts, hanging her head back to look up. Her hair was braided and untidy, and she was dressed in faded dungarees and a wrinkled white blouse with a ketchup stain on the front. She looked happy and adorable.

"How come you're wearing a apron?" Lucy asked.

"Because I'm going over to clean the church."

"But our daddy cleans the church, how come you got to?"

"I do more than clean. I make sure everything is ready for Father Kuzdek for Sunday Mass."

Mr. Olczak approached at that moment and paused in the balmy autumn day, wearing leather gloves and carrying a tall load of boxes stacked one upon another. His blue shirt was rolled up at the sleeves and the boxes reached the middle of his chest.

"Afternoon, Sister."

"Good afternoon, Mr. Olczak."

"Bowling leagues starting tonight." In the basement of the school building there were three alleys that he maintained along with everything else. "Got to get the candy case stocked and the pop coolers filled."

"Yeah, and guess what!" Lucy spouted. "He says if we help him load the cases we can each have a candy bar! I like Zagnut the best!"

Sister Regina had never tasted a Zagnut candy bar. As a youngster in a large farm family, opportunities and cash for buying candy were rare. As an adult nun, any money she received was turned over to Mother Superior to be put into a communal pot.

Out of nowhere, on this splendid fall afternoon, came a sense of having been cheated, and an innocent wish to taste a Zagnut.

"My, aren't you lucky?" she said to the child.

"Sounds like we're going to have a busy bowling season," Mr. Olczak remarked. "Alleys'll be in use five nights a week."

"Ah," she said, acknowledging his remark without encouraging more, and keeping her eyes chastely lowered. But what she saw were his bare forearms wrapped around that stack of candy cartons, the blue veins standing out like welting on a chair cushion. She wondered what it was like to have a man's arms around you at night, then lying wrist-up on the pillow beside you in the morning. To share a breakfast table with your life's mate and talk about your plans for the day; then supper at the end of the day when you were tired and fulfilled by work. To put a child to bed, and kiss her, and leave the door ajar as you tiptoed out together.

Guilt struck swiftly. "I must get over to church," she said, keeping her head averted and hurrying on.

He yelled after her, "Call me if there's anything you need over there."

She kept walking and replied, "Thank you, Mr. Olczak. I will."

When she got inside the church she put both hands to her face and found it hot, the image of his strong arms vivid and unsettling. She stood awhile in the cavernous coolness, alone and confused about what was happening to her. Had she chosen wrong? Had she wasted the best years of her life on a vocation for which she was not meant?

Fear struck and she hurried inside, kneeling to say a quick prayer of supplication.

Dear God, what is happening to me? Why do these thoughts persist and why can I not be happy here as I've always been before? Is this lust? It must be, for it is most powerful, and I need Your help to combat it. Reside in me, help me, strengthen me. I would not know how to live in any other life. Where would I go? What would I do? Help me, Heavenly Father.

September moved on and the leaves began to turn. Sister Regina's third-grade class made their colored leaf booklets, and Eddie Olczak emptied the window boxes at the convent and transferred all the geraniums from the outdoor urns into the church basement for winter storage.

Sister Regina's fourth-grade class began studying liturgical vestments and nuns' habits, cutting pictures of them out of catalogues and memorizing their names: it was time to begin encouraging a new generation of Catholic children to think of the priesthood and sisterhood as the most esteemed walk of life to which they could aspire.

At Eddie's house, his girls began "playing sister," cutting out bandeaux and guimpes of cardboard and draping them with Krystyna's silk scarves, and hanging rosaries around their necks. Up in their bedroom they played school, teaching imaginary students, begging for a toy blackboard so they could write on it "like Sister Regina did."

Father Kuzdek began preparing the fourth-graders for their First Communion in the spring, and Sister Mary Charles began feeling familiar enough with her new students to periodically whip the bad boys in the flower room.

As the weather cooled, Father announced at Sunday Mass that the nuns needed firewood, and a load appeared in their backyard, donated by some parishioner who owned a farm and offered the wood in place of his annual parish tithe.

Eddie spent the better part of one day throwing the wood down the metal chute into the storage room in the nuns' basement, then stacking it to the ceiling inside.

Sister Regina saw him at his work when she took the children out for recess. Anne yelled, "Hi, Daddy!" and he straightened and waved to her. Then he tipped his cap to Sister Regina and watched her go past with her black knit cape snugged around her shoulders. She felt his eyes following, but she told herself he was merely pausing for a breather; he'd have done the same if it had been old Sister Ignatius passing.

She took the children as far away from him as possible, clear up to the top of playground, where she organized a game of pump-pump-pull-away. But distance could not dull her awareness of the man working below, nor drown the rhythmic *klung-klung-klung* of the wood hitting the metal chute. The sound reverberated through the crisp autumn air, reminding her he was there. Sometimes she'd give in to temptation and glance down at his black-and-red-checked lumberman's jacket in the yard below as he loaded the wood that would keep her warm through the winter.

Then she said an Act of Contrition because she was wed to Christ, and such thoughts violated the vows she'd taken.

In early October Sister Ignatius got some dizzy spells and had to go into the hospital at Long Prairie for some tests. While she was gone Sister Cecelia, the housekeeper, tried to take up the slack and cook as well as clean, but it soon became apparent she could not handle both jobs. Mother Agnes ordered the entire community to help in the kitchen. She posted a schedule and gave them a special dispensation to skip chapel and pray their Divine Office whenever was convenient on the days when they helped out in the kitchen.

Sister Regina was helping Sister Cecelia cook supper one Tuesday afternoon when a knock sounded on the back door. Sister Cecelia was busy peeling potatoes and said, "Will you get that, Sister Regina?"

She opened the door to find Mr. Olczak standing on their stone stoop bearing a ten-gallon crock on his shoulder.

"Why, Mr. Olczak, what's this?" she said.

"I brought you your sauerkraut," he announced.

Sister Cecelia said, "Oh good, our sauerkraut," as he stepped inside. "I didn't think we'd be getting it this year. God bless you, Mr. Olczak, you're so good to us."

"Krystyna put it up for you just before she died. Fifty heads, same as always, and you can thank her folks for raising the cabbage. Where do you want it?"

"In the basement, if you don't mind," Sister Cecelia answered. "Sister Regina will turn on the lights for you."

Sister Regina went ahead, clear down the stairs into the musty, cool basement, and opened the rough wooden door into a room with fruit jars lining the shelves, all of them filled with freshly canned fruits and vegetables from their own garden. She pulled a string and turned on a dim ceiling light, then watched as he set the heavy crock on the concrete floor, handling it as if it weighed no more than a wastebasket full of crumpled paper. He made an arresting sight, strutting in beneath his burden and manhandling it into place, his head bare and his hair mussed by the autumn wind.

She looked away.

"I've got three more crocks in the back of the truck," he said, and headed out to get the next one, calling over his shoulder, "I've brought some clean boards to cover them if you've still got the rocks, Sister!"

While he was gone she searched through the storage room and found some good-sized rocks that Sister Ignatius had used to weight the boards on top of the crocks. "Sister Cecelia?" she called up the stairs, "can you throw down a rag so I can wipe the cobwebs off these rocks?"

In the minute the rag came sailing down and she put it to use.

When Eddie brought in the last of the crocks, he had four square scrubbed boards under his left arm.

"Can you take these, Sister?" he asked.

She took the boards and he set the crock down beside the others, pushing it over with a gritty scrape till it clinked into line against the cellar wall. "Krystyna, she'd be pleased how this batch turned out," he said, straightening and brushing off his palms. "It's good this year. Crunchy. She said she was making the brine just a little less sour." He dipped in and caught some sauerkraut in his fingers and ate it. "Take a taste, Sister, and see what you think."

She stared up at him while he chewed the sauerkraut and a droplet of brine glistened on his chin. He had a strong, forthright chin and a strong jaw, and when he tipped his head back and opened his mouth, she felt her own mouth water.

"Go ahead," he said, motioning for her to have some.

"Oh, I . . . no . . . no thank you, Mr. Olczak. I . . . um . . . that is, we'll be having supper soon, Sister Cecelia and I were just preparing it, and . . . well . . . it's . . ." Eating with seculars was strictly forbidden, *in writing!* Their Constitution made it *very clear!* And if sharing meals with non-religious was considered a breach of propriety, certainly dipping sauerkraut in a shadowy basement with an unmarried man must be a sin worthy of confessing.

He used the side of his hand to dry his chin, and she watched the simple action in acute fascination. Masculine allure was so new to her that it caught her by the viscera, undoing her recent promise to keep out of his proximity and avoid useless conversations. "I'm . . . I'm sure it's delicious," she finished, and bent to place the four boards across the crocks. When she picked up the first rock he jumped to her side and said, "Oh, here, Sister, I'll do that. They're heavy." He wrested the rock from her hands—a big round, awkward, fifteen-pound mass that had soiled her floor-length white apron—and in transferring it, he inadvertently touched her.

She jumped clear of him and grabbed her hand with the other, as if she'd been burned.

He looked up curiously, bent like an L with a weighty rock in his hands. "Something wrong, Sister?"

She shook her head wordlessly.

He glanced at her knotted hands and thought, *She's acting funny today,* as he finished his work.

The worst thing she could do was run from him, she thought. Then he would surely suspect what was going on in her head. So she waited as he put all four rocks on top of the boards, bending, reaching, lifting, his mucles bunching while he handled the weight as if it were nil. She watched him unbrokenly, forgetting she was not supposed to. When he finished he straightened slowly, then stood awhile, pensive, staring down at the fruits of his wife's labor.

"She'd be glad to know you got it, just like always."

Sister Regina, too, stared at the four crocks. "How many years has she been making us our winter's supply of sauerkraut?"

"I don't know, Sister. A lot of years."

"As long as I've been here, anyway." They stood in silence for a moment, missing Krystyna, recounting the many good deeds she'd done for so many. Then Sister Regina suggested quietly, "Shall we take a moment to say a thank-you, Mr. Olczak?"

She folded her hands and closed her eyes, and he did the same. Side by side they prayed in silence, to God and to Krystyna, whom they were sure had to be a saint, as good a person as she'd been. It was both healing and intimate, and for those few minutes while they stood motionless, they shared a bond of almost mystic quality. They were friends. They liked each other. They had both loved Krystyna. They were comfortable standing side by side, praying in the most unlikely of places—in the must and the cobwebs of the murky basement, with their elbows nearly touching.

It was as close to intimate as Sister Mary Regina had ever been with a man.

In the kitchen above, Sister Cecelia, ever on the alert for infractions to report to Mother Superior, cocked her head and sat still as a grouse off a pointer's nose. She listened for a long while but heard nothing. Setting down her paring knife and potato, she crept to the door. The basement was so silent she could've heard spiders spinning their webs down there. Stealthily she descended four steps and strained forward till she could peer below the rafters into the dimly lit storage room about twelve feet away. But all she saw was Sister Regina and Mr. Olczak with their hands folded and their eyes closed, silently praying.

*E*very year in late October the various parish sodalities combined their efforts to put on an autumn bazaar. It was held on a Sunday after the second Mass, in Paderewski Hall. The ladies cooked and served a hearty dinner, made of donated foods from the fall crop: chickens, pies, vegetables and breads. The St. Joseph Society ran a booth where fancywork was sold— doilies and dresser scarves and embroidered dishtowels, all displayed on wooden clothes racks. The Sacred Heart Society had a bake sale, and the Third Order of St. Francis put up a fishpond for the children. The Altar Society was in charge of the bingo game, most of the prizes donated by women who'd spent precious time making them. The Knights of Columbus operated a gambling wheel with bets placed on numbers laid out on the parapet next to the first-grade room. And on the west end of the school next to the boys' bathroom the K-C's also had a beer garden.

It was there that Eddie was drinking his second bottle of Glueks when Romaine found him. They stood among a crowd of men, most of whom had shed their suit coats but still wore loosened neckties and felt dress hats. Eddie had rolled up his white shirtsleeves but kept his tie tightly knotted. Several of the men were smoking cigars and talking crops.

"So, how goes it, Ed?" Romaine asked.

Eddie took another swig of beer and stared across the hall while lowering the bottle.

"Lonely, Romaine, lonely." He grimaced while answering.

"We're going to the dance next Saturday. Six Fat Dutchmen are playing at the Clarissa Ballroom. Want to go?"

"Nah. It's too soon."

"You could get a baby-sitter. Do you good to get out maybe."

"Nah. I'd rather stay home with the kids."

"Okay, but I promised Irene I'd ask."

"Irene?"

"Yeah, she said ask you if you were going, then she'd decide if she wanted to go or not."

Eddie's lips fluttered a little as he blew out a disdainful puff of air. "Irene," he muttered to himself, shaking his head.

"She's always liked you, Eddie."

"Yeah, I know." Eddie raised the bottle again. Above it he watched Irene place a kernel of corn on her bingo card on the other side of the hall. When he'd drained the bottle he set it on the table and said, "I don't want to encourage her."

"Irene's a good egg. She just wants to help."

"And she *does* help. Heck, I don't know what I'd do without her. She drives in every morning to get the kids ready for school."

For a while both men considered Irene. She'd had a new permanent and her hair was screwed up rather tight to her head. Her cheeks were florid and her breasts large, hanging over the table edge beside her pile of dried corn.

"You know, Eddie, she misses Krystyna almost as much as you do."

As if she felt his eyes on her, Irene looked up and caught Eddie watching her. The bingo caller announced, "N-thirty!" but she didn't even check her card. "N-thirty!" the caller repeated, and Eddie knew what she was feeling, from clear across Paderewski Hall. He turned away and laid down a coin for another beer.

"I just don't feel like dancing anymore," he said.

Romaine caught him around the shoulders and said, "Okay, but let us know when you do."

"Yeah, sure."

Romaine drifted away and Eddie stood in a cloud of cigar smoke, finishing his beer. Anne and Lucy came up, breathless, and asked him for more money to play the fishpond. He gave them each four nickels and they pranced away with a gang of their cousins.

There were tables set up throughout the center of the hall, and his gaze wandered over them. Diners shifted, finishing their meals and leaving their wooden folding chairs askew between the tables. Though the Knights of Columbus were supposed to take care of the tables and chairs, this was Eddie's bailiwick, and he reacted like a janitor, setting down his empty bottle and heading into the dining area, shoving chairs beneath tables as he went. In the far northwest corner, all the nuns were just seating themselves. They were invited as guests every year, getting their meal free and always occupying the same corner table nearest the door by which they'd entered.

He paid particular attention to Sister Regina. She'd been acting funny toward him for a couple of weeks now, ever since the day they'd put the sauerkraut in the basement. She was never in her room after school anymore when he went in to clean it, and he missed seeing her and chatting with her. Whenever they encountered each other in passing she refused to meet his eye, and once, when she'd seen him coming toward her down the hall, she'd done a quick turnaround and made a beeline for the girls' lavatory. More troublesome was that peculiar reaction he'd noted when he took the rock from her in the basement. If he didn't know better, he'd have thought she was afraid of him. Why else would she have jumped that way? And afterward, when he'd looked up at her she was clutching her hand and looked scared to death. The change in her had him absolutely befuddled.

Watching the nuns now as they carried their plates to their table, he noticed they were short two chairs. Sister Dora and Sister Regina were left holding their plates without seats.

Eddie grabbed two chairs, clapped them shut and headed their way.

"Here you are, Sisters. Two chairs coming up!"

"Thank you, Mr. Olczak," they all chorused as he seated Sister Regina first, then Sister Dora. When they were both seated, he asked the group at large, "Anything else I can do for you?"

Old Sister Ignatius, back from the hospital and enjoying this rare escape from cooking, replied, "Yes, Mr. Olczak, some coffee for me, if you don't mind." She tilted to the nun at her right and explained, "My hands were full."

"Coming right up, Sister. Anyone else?" Some had coffee, some had not. "Sister Gregory? Sister Regina?"

Though Sister Gregory smiled and replied, "Yes, please, Mr. Olczak," Sister Regina refused to look at him. She kept her eyes lowered and her chin on her chest.

"Coffee, Sister Regina?" he repeated, and she finally looked up.

And that's when he knew.

It struck him like a broadside how she was blushing, how very red her cheeks were against the pure, stiff white of her wimple, and how she could not hold his gaze. "Yes, thank you, Mr. Olczak," she nearly whispered, her glance skittering away self-consciously. She had always been demure in manner, keeping a proper distance, a soft voice and a retiring attitude. But today was different. Today she shied away like he'd sometimes seen Irene do. Just like that day in the basement. Just like a woman who's battling a case of lovesickness.

But that can't be, he thought. *She's a nun!*

The possibility rattled him so badly that he ran off to fetch their coffee, with his heart thundering in his ears. "Three coffees for the nuns, Tillie!" he ordered, butting into line and forgetting to excuse himself.

What if the others saw her blush and grow flustered, and suspected the same thing he did? What would happen to her? He didn't have any idea what they did to a nun if she got caught liking a man. Put into words, the idea seemed stupid. Preposterous! For of all the nuns he'd ever known she was the most prim and soft-spoken. She acted as if she was so happy with her life and at peace with herself—that's why he'd always enjoyed being around her.

Suddenly he started worrying that he'd made some unintentional remark or gesture that she'd misread. But, no, he had always treated her with perfect respect, staying his distance and keeping any conversation really light and impersonal.

When he took the three cups of coffee back to their table, he intentionally set hers down first, then moved around the table with the others so he could look back at her.

"Now, Sisters, if you want anything else you just whistle," he said, giving away none of the confusion he felt.

They all acknowledged him but Sister Regina. She kept her head averted, her eyes on her plate, and wiped her mouth on a paper napkin, as if she didn't trust herself to catch his gaze.

Something inside Eddie went *ka-wham!*

And it wasn't ego.

And it wasn't virility.

It was just plain fear.

Ten

Immediately after the Sunday of the fall bazaar Eddie began doing two things: avoiding Sister Regina's classroom until he was sure she was gone after school, and going to dances again. He hired a baby-sitter on Saturday nights and joined his brothers at whatever dance hall they were going to. Irene was always there. He danced with her occasionally, but mostly he stood by the bar with the men, drinking beer and comparing every woman he saw to Krystyna. They always came up lacking.

Sometimes on Sunday morning he'd have a headache, and it would be hard to get up in time to ring the early bells.

He thought about Sister Regina often and decided his suspicion was wrong. She couldn't have a crush on him. It simply wasn't in her nature. She was the most totally dedicated nun he'd ever known, almost angelic in her serenity, convincing him that she loved the life she led. That meant he must have done something to alienate her, and it bothered him considerably, wondering what it was.

One day, out of the clear blue sky, Anne asked him at supper, "Daddy, why can't nuns be mothers?"

He was so taken off-guard that he didn't know what to say.

"What's wrong, Daddy?"

"Nothing. Nothing. I was just . . ." He cleared his throat and wriggled on his chair. "Only married women can be mothers, honey, you know that."

"But why?"

"Well, because, to be a mother you've got to have a husband to be the father, and nuns don't have husbands."

"Why don't they?"

"Well, because, they're married to Christ instead."

"How can you be married to somebody who isn't there?"

"Well . . ." He scrambled through his mind for answers. "You see, it's . . . well, they aren't *really* married. Not like Mommy and I were married. But they wear a gold ring which means they've promised to give their lives to Christ, and not to marry anyone from this world."

"Oh." Anne grew thoughtful, picking at her food for a long while before she finally seemed to come to her own conclusion. "Then I'd never want to be a nun. But if I was, I'd want to be one just like Sister Regina."

He dreamed of Krystyna that night, the oddest dream. In it she said not a word, only stood in the stone grotto in front of the school, smiling at him with an expression of extreme peace upon her face. But she was dressed in a black habit of the Order of St. Benedict.

On November first, the Feast of All Saints' Day, there was no school, the perfect chance for Eddie to wash and wax the schoolroom floors. When he came to the open doorway of the third- and fourth-grade room with his electric buffer, he was surprised to find Sister Regina working at her desk, cutting out something made of brown construction paper. She glanced up as he appeared, then quickly back down at her work.

"Good afternoon, Sister," he said, pushing the machine inside and unwinding the electric cord.

"Good afternoon."

"Kind of a nasty day, isn't it?" he remarked, plugging in the machine.

"Yes, it is." Flurries of snow were pecking at the windows and the sky was the color of an overboiled egg yolk.

"Looks like we might get some real snow before the day is over."

She said nothing, but went on snipping, snipping with her scissors.

"It's a holy day of obligation. What are you doing working?"

"Oh, this isn't work. I'm cutting out a cornucopia for the bulletin board. This is . . . creativity."

He stepped closer and looked at what she was doing. "Oh, that's right, Thanksgiving's coming. It's going to be hard to be grateful this year without Krystyna." When she made no reply, but continued acting spooked and standoffish, he decided *something* had changed her, and he was going to find out what.

"You mind if I sit down a minute?" he asked.

She finally looked up, and he detected a blush she could not hide. But she spoke with total composure. "No," she said quietly.

He sat down on the first seat of the row of desks right in front of her. It had no writing surface, only the fold-down seat upon which he settled, with his knees poking up like Tinkertoys.

She finished the cornucopia and began cutting out an orange pumpkin.

"Sister, have I done something to offend you?" he asked quietly.

Her head snapped up and her hands drifted down to her desktop, with the scissors still catching the paper.

"No."

"I was just wondering, because you seem to be going out of your way to avoid me."

"No, I haven't, Mr. Olczak."

"Yes, you have, Sister Regina. Now what have I done?"

"You've done nothing." She spoke as reservedly as ever, but her cheeks flared redder than before.

"I used to come in your room after school and we'd talk about Anne and Lucy and how they were doing, and about Krystyna and all my feelings after I lost her. Now you make sure you're not here when I come in. I just wondered if I said something or did something that wasn't proper."

"I told you, you've done nothing."

He let his eyes settle on her and stay until she had no recourse but to look down and get busy with the scissors again.

"I miss that, you know?" he continued softly. "I suppose I could talk to the other nuns, but . . . well, they're different. I mean, I'm not as comfortable talking with them as I am with you. I always say to Romaine, 'Whenever I talk with Sister Regina I feel better afterwards,' and it's true."

She kept her eyes on the pumpkin and said, "You may talk to me now, Mr. Olczak."

He thought of the women at the dances on Saturday night who could not measure up to Krystyna. He thought of this woman who could. He'd never realized it before, but she was the only one whose company he'd actively sought since Krystyna died. Others only managed to repel him. Now that they were talking again, he didn't want to cut it short.

"So how is the sauerkraut?" he inquired conversationally.

"Delicious, as always."

"Yeah, that Krystyna, she knew what she was doing around a batch of sauerkraut."

Sister Regina said nothing. She put down the pumpkin and began cutting out a cluster of grapes.

"I dreamed of her last night," Eddie said. Still Sister made no remark. Her eyes remained on her work as he continued. "She was standing in the grotto wearing a habit like yours. I don't know why in the world I'd dream a thing like that." He hesitated, waiting for a response that never came. "I guess it was because Anne came home one day and asked why nuns can't be mothers, and I had to explain it to her the best I could. I told her it was because you are married to Christ."

"Yes, I am," she replied, carefully setting down her scissors and grapes on the desktop, then linking her fingers and hiding her hands on her lap beneath the kneehole of the desk. "And that's why conversations such as this are forbidden to me. Surely you know, Mr. Olczak, that in our Order conversation with seculars is strictly limited to necessity."

His spine straightened slightly and he felt a flush of embarrassment begin low and work its way up. "No, I never knew that."

She rose with great calm and dignity, and went to stand at the window, looking out, so she need not face him. Tucking her hands into her sleeves she explained, "The life of a nun is one of silence and reflection, which is all part of obedience. And obedience is one of the vows we take. Perhaps you're right. Perhaps I *have* been avoiding you, because I find that when I'm with you it's easy to forget to observe the rules about ordinary silence, and I talk too much."

"But . . . but what have we done wrong?"

"By your standards, nothing. But mine order me to confine my conversation to matters of duty, necessity or charity. I could recite you the chapter from our Constitution that states this."

"Talking?" he repeated, amazed, studying her straight back and the sheer black veil caught on her shoulders. He rose from the desk but remained near it, a goodly distance from her.

"You mean, Sister, that every time I come in here and talk to you I cause you to sin?" When she made no reply he insisted, "Do I?"

"Please, Mr. Olczak," she whispered. "I'm not allowed—"

"Well, *do I?*" He had all he could do to keep from approaching her and forcing her to turn around and face him. How could you read a person when she kept her face turned away like this?

"Our vows are perpetual, and the obligations they impose bind us under pain of sin, yes."

"Sister, would you please turn around?"

Her erect stature and utter stillness told him she would not.

"Why didn't you say something before this?" he asked.

"Because some of it *was* necessity, your necessity. I thought you needed someone to talk to, so I decided to be your listener, and since we as nuns are admonished to practice *the most cordial charity*—and I quote Holy Rule—

I thought, when is charity more needed than after a loss like you suffered? You and your girls. These last two months since Krystyna's death . . . these last two months have been . . ." She couldn't finish. There were tears in her throat.

"Sister," he whispered, horrified. "I've made you cry."

"No, you haven't." She dug a handkerchief from her sleeve and tipped her head down as she used it.

"Then, what is this?" He crossed the room and stood right behind her shoulder, his hands clenching and unclenching at his sides. "Please, Sister, turn around."

"No, I cannot." She sniffed once, and righted her head again.

"But . . . but, I feel terrible."

"It's me who has made me cry, not you. I've . . . I've been going through a personal crisis of sorts and it's . . . it's been a very difficult time for me." Her voice broke with emotion. "Please, Mr. Olczak, forgive me, but I must go." She wheeled around, avoiding him, and hurried from the room at a pace that made her veil fill and billow.

"Sister, wait! I'm sorry, Sister! I wouldn't . . ."

But she was gone, running from him, crying. Left behind in the empty schoolroom, his emotions in turmoil, he didn't know what to do, think, believe. He'd caused her to sin? And to cry? And to run from him? This nun who had always been so unshakably beatific? Jesus, Mary, Joseph, help me understand what I've done to her because she's the last woman on earth I'd want to upset this way.

He lay awake for over three hours that night going over and over that scene in his mind. Standing behind her today while she lost her composure, he had experienced an outpouring of feelings that in his entire lifetime he'd only ever experienced with Krystyna. Oh, how his heart and throat and mind had welled up with remorse for having caused her pain, and more—sin. It had been just plain awful not being able to touch her. He'd wanted to comfort her, to turn her around and hold her as she cried, the way he would any woman in distress. But the mere idea of it was jarring, given that she was a nun.

Hold her? In his arms?

You just get that notion out of your head right now, Eddie Olczack! She's a nun, and you treat her with the same respect you'd treat the Blessed Virgin Mary if she showed up in that schoolroom!

His whole life long, reverence for the nuns had been drilled into him under pain of punishment. When he was a kid in parochial school he knew that if he ever so much as looked at one sideways he'd get the living shit beat out of him at home. Nuns were representatives of God. They were holy creatures. They were as close to angels as it was possible to be on this earth. There was no man alive who revered nuns more than Eddie Olczak.

So what was he doing lying here in his bed thinking about holding one? And wondering over and over again what she had meant about going through a personal crisis since Krystyna had died?

Was it possible it had something to do with him?

She's a nun, Olczack! She took a vow of chastity, remember?

All right, all right. Then how come she blushed and got all flustered when I came close to her? Twice!

Watch what you think! This is a nun you're thinking about!

But she *had* blushed. He'd seen it. And she *had* been acting skittish around him.

You're getting mighty close to a sin here, Eddie boy. How'd you like to have to go to Confession and tell Father you've been thinking unseemly thoughts about a nun?

I'm not thinking unseen thoughts. I'm only trying to figure out what she meant by personal crisis. I mean, suppose, just suppose, that she does find herself feeling . . . well, you know, feeling something for me . . . that'd be about the scariest thing that could happen to a nun, don't you think? Wouldn't that make her cry that way?

Confessions, four o'clock Saturday afternoon, Eddie.

Lying in his bed at one o'clock in the morning with the first snow of the season dulling the streetlamp like a blowing curtain, he dropped a wrist across his forehead and tried to empty his mind.

He missed Krystyna, that's all. He missed her, and Sister Regina was the only other woman he felt comfortable with. It'd be a long time before he was over Krystyna. But if he was ever to marry again, it would be somebody like Sister Regina, he was pretty sure.

He was growing sleepy at last when he had the peculiar thought that he sounded just like Anne: *I'd never be a nun, but if I was I'd want to be one just like Sister Regina.* Anne was just crazy about Sister Regina. So was Lucy.

Half asleep, half awake, he pictured his younger daughter, running up to the nun and flinging her arms around her skirts, the way she had around her mother's.

Sister Regina . . . Sister Regina . . .

His thoughts were growing too muzzy to capture and hold.

Oh, Sister, could it be we all love you in a way that's not allowed?

When he tumbled into the abyss he wasn't sure if he'd had the thought or not.

The next day was All Souls' Day, on which a Catholic could get a plenary indulgence by going to Confession and Communion, in addition to saying a number of designated prayers for the poor souls in purgatory, and for the Pope.

Sister Regina pledged to herself she'd fulfill all the necessary requirements, believing it would bring about a remission of her temporal punishments for the sin she'd committed the previous day by once again talking to Mr. Olczak on such a personal level.

That morning after passing up Communion in chapel, she caught Father Kuzdek as he stopped in the front hall of the convent. "Father, may I have a word with you?"

The rotund priest lowered his bulk onto the small bench, where the piano students waited for their piano lessons, and pulled on his black rubber overshoes.

"Certainly, Sister."

"I'd like to go to Confession, please."

"Now?"

"Yes, Father, if you could spare the time. I don't want to put it off another day."

"Very well. Get your wrap. We'll go straight to church."

Outside the air smelled like fresh laundry and the sky was still blue-black at six-thirty A.M. Five inches of snow had fallen overnight, and flurries still drifted down in the light of a skinny western moon. Mr. Olczak had already been here and cleared a temporary path only one shovel wide between the rectory and the convent, for Father. There was no escaping the distraction of Mr. Olczak, for even now when Sister moved toward confessing her preoccupation with him, his shovel could be heard from somewhere at the front of the church, scraping away at the wide, tall steps before early Mass.

Mr. Olczak, Olczak, Olczak! His name was on her mind altogether too much. She knew his routine like a wife knows a husband's. How was she to get over her attraction to him when he was present in her world nearly every waking hour of the day? Even when she couldn't see him she could hear him—shoveling, hammering, drilling, whistling, gently teasing the children during recesses and school lunches. Even on her way to confess her excessive familiarity with him, she was thinking of him again.

Father entered the church through his own private door behind the left sacristy. He switched on some dim lights, found, kissed and donned his stole, and led her through the sanctuary, both of them genuflecting on their way to the confessional. Inside the cubicle it was murky and always seemed to smell of must with overtones of manure from the farmers' shoes. As Sister Regina stepped into the cramped space, the heavy maroon velvet curtains fell back into place behind her, stirring the two scents together. She knelt, hemmed in by the curtains that could not stop a chilly draft from circling her ankles. She heard Father settle himself in his chair before the partition between them slid back, and she saw the shadow of his hand make a cross in the air.

"In nomine Patris, et Filii et Spiritus Sancti, Amen."

She made the sign of the cross with him and began by rote the words she'd been taught as a child: "Forgive me, Father, for I have sinned. My last

Confession was two weeks ago. I've come to confess something of grave importance." She drew a shaky breath.

He heard it and said, "I'm here, Sister."

"Yes," she whispered, and after a pause, "this is very difficult."

"Remember that God is all-forgiving," he said, and waited.

She fortified herself with another deep breath before going on. "I've somehow managed to become friends with a secular, just friends, but in the course of our friendship I've allowed myself to speak too freely, and our conversations have sometimes bordered on personal things. I . . . I find myself tempted to speak to this person about nonreligious matters, because this person is caring and kind and in need of help right now. I know I'm breaking my vow of obedience by speaking to this person, yet it doesn't feel wrong when I'm doing it. How can this be so, Father?"

"This person is a man?" Father asked.

Her heart actually started racing with fear, and she answered meekly, "Yes, Father."

"And are you attracted to him?"

After several long beats she whispered, "Yes."

"Have you broken your vow of chastity with him?"

"In thought only."

"Not physically?"

"No, never, Father. I would not, nor would he, I'm certain. My attraction to him is as much to the pleasure of talking to him as anything else."

"Are these talks with him causing you to doubt your vocation?"

"No, father. I had begun doubting it before these talks between us began."

"Oh, I see."

The racing of her heart got worse and she realized tears had sprung into her eyes. It was a terrible, emotional moment, that one in which she admitted for the first time to someone else that her faith in her vocation was shaken. Until the words were actually spoken there was still time to recant, to tell herself she was wrong and these dissatisfactions were temporary and would soon pass. But the words were released, the stepping stone reached, and she recognized the momentousness for what it was.

Father took his time responding. She could tell he was shaken, and very probably aggrieved. He cleared his throat and shifted in his chair, leaning closer to the screen.

"Have you spoken to Mother Superior about this?"

"N . . ." Her voice failed and she began again. "No, Father."

"Do you feel that you should?"

"I'm . . . I'm afraid to."

"But Sister Agnes is your spiritual advisor. You must place your trust in her."

"I don't think she'll believe that this all started a long time ago, way before I ever spoke to this man about anything personal."

"What Sister Agnes chooses to believe is a secondary matter. What you know to be true is the primary matter. These are things that should be discussed with your spiritual advisor. They could affect you all the rest of your life."

"Yes, Father. I'll try. And, Father, there's something else."

"Go on."

"You must understand, Father, it's not just about this man. It's much bigger than that. I've begun finding faults with so much about my life within the religious community—the personal ways of all the sisters, their aggravating habits, and the fact that we are allowed so little freedom. Then there's Sister Agnes admonishing me not to get too wrapped up in the lives of the children I teach, and this makes me angry, yet I'm not allowed to discuss it with anybody. Holy Rule says my anger itself is a sin. More and more lately I've begun to question Holy Rule and our Constitution, how they repress everything natural, how they keep us in line. The very idea makes me angry sometimes."

"Anger is human. How we manifest it dictates whether it's a sin or not. Perhaps, Sister, you're being too hard on yourself."

"I don't think so. Time and again I've broken Holy Rule, and every time it happens I do penance, then go on believing I was right. It's like there are two people inside me, one telling me to stay and be obedient, hold my tongue. The other saying, 'They are wrong to repress you this way. Speak up.' It's been just terrible, Father, what I've been going through. It feels very much like purgatory right here on earth."

"Do you know what I hear in your voice, Sister?"

"No, Father."

"I hear anguish. That means that there's a strong, strong spirit moving within you yet, telling you that you are very much where you belong."

"Oh, it's true, Father. Sometimes I'm so at peace here, but those times grow fewer and farther between."

"Do you think, Sister, that there isn't a one of us who's doubted our vocation at one time or another?" She didn't answer, so he went on. "Sometimes when we wrestle with doubt and temptation and win out over them, we come through the test stronger than before, and more certain that the vocation we chose is absolutely the right one for us. Pray, Sister. Pray good and hard for the answers, and I know they'll come to you. Do penance. Meditate as much as possible. Pray to Mary to intercede for you, and to our Lord to grant you guidance through this troubled time. And do talk to Sister Agnes. You may be surprised at what you hear."

"Yes, Father. I will."

"Very well. And may I add, Sister, that I would hate to lose you here at St. Joseph's. You're an excellent teacher, and well liked by the children. I've always believed that a pupil who likes his teacher is going to do better in school than the one who can't stand her. I feel that your talking to Sister Agnes might avert a terrible loss, not only to you, but to your religious community and the students as well."

"Thank you, Father."

He gave her a remarkably slight penance: undoubtedly he knew that the struggle she was going through was penance enough for any nun who'd been dedicated to her vocation for as long as Sister Regina had.

They left church through the door they'd entered. Father took the left branch of the walk to his house. Sister Regina took the right, and halfway to the convent encountered Eddie Olczak widening the path through the snow. He stopped shoveling and stepped aside, resting one hand on top of the shovel handle.

"Good morning, Sister," he said quietly as she approached.

She kept her head down and one arm anchoring her knit shawl over her chest.

"Good morning, Mr. Olczak."

"Sister, wait."

"I'm sorry, I can't," she replied, and hurried on without looking back.

Everything in Eddie had seized up at her approach. What had passed between them the previous day created an unholy tension he could not ignore. He watched her until she reached the rear stoop of the convent and climbed the stone steps. Only when she opened the kitchen door and disappeared inside did he sigh and, with a leaden feeling inside, go back to work.

She decided against talking to Sister Agnes right away, thinking perhaps she hadn't prayed, meditated or done penance enough. She would do more of all three, and if that didn't work, *then* she'd talk to Sister Agnes.

The weather stayed as somber and joyless as her reflection, while November advanced toward Thanksgiving and she called upon Christ to let His will be known to her. She devoted herself to an intense period of soul-searching during which she prayed in a state of profound supplication many hours each day, often kneeling on a chain-metal doormat that left painful ridges in her knees. She routinely fasted from breakfast until supper, offering up her hunger as further penance for her doubtfulness. Meditation and reflection became a deeper part of each day, but they yielded little beyond continued confusion. She expected the answer to descend upon her in a nimbus of recognition, a shimmering knowledge that would suddenly light her from within and telegraph to her a certainty of which choice to make. She pictured herself, after making that choice, like a figure surrounded by fox fire, a nun yet—for that's what she thought her choice *should* be—but one who moved in a continual halo of contentment, like the pictures on holy cards. It would be, she thought, a saintliness that would suddenly lift all doubt and supplant it with such peace as only the souls in heaven know.

But this did not happen.

If Christ knew what he wanted her to do, He was keeping it to Himself.

During Thanksgiving week she wrote to her grandmother about the anguish she was going through. But the letter went unposted, because once again their Constitution dictated that all outgoing mail be placed, unsealed, on the superior's desk. Sister Regina put the letter away in her drawer, resenting the fact that she could never send it, adding yet another notch on her tally of repressions.

Her guilt over writing the letter and the subsequent anger over being unable to send it drove her into a state of renewed piety. Father had admonished her to do more penance, and perhaps if she did the ultimate penance she would find her answer.

The ultimate penance, as far as Sister Regina was concerned, was commonly referred to as "taking the Discipline," something she'd only once done and wasn't sure she believed in. "Taking the Discipline" was the genteel expression for self-flagellation. This was done in the bathroom on Friday nights, with a small weapon that looked like a coat hanger with lengths of finely linked chain hanging from it by an oval loop. She remembered the first time she'd seen one of these contraptions. She'd been a novitiate, a beginner, and as such it wouldn't do to ask questions. The general rule was, *what and when you need to know, you'll be told.* An older nun named Sister Serenity, the official rosary fixer, had been fashioning the metal spirals with a pair of pliers during evening recreation, and Sister Regina thought it was a wind chime of some sort. She asked Sister Serenity to hold it up so she could hear it. Later that night, Sister Serenity had drawn her to the side and, in private, told her it was called a "Discipline." Fridays, Sister Serenity said, were the days when each nun "took the Discipline." It was done in turn, in the bathroom after lights out, during Grand Silence.

Young Regina Marie Potlocki, fresh off the farm, had never heard of such a thing. She thought she'd misunderstood.

"Do *what* with it?" she'd said, horrified.

Sister Serenity had gently demonstrated, raising her sleeve and striking herself on her bare arm, where small red marks appeared between the pale blue veins. "The object is not to draw blood, but just to thwack yourself with it till it stings. But not usually on the arm. Back here." She indicated her posterior. "Underneath your nightgown."

Regina's blood seemed to drop to the soles of her feet. "B . . . but why?"

"In memory of Christ's passion."

She'd stared at the evil-looking thing again and muttered, "I don't understand. What good will it do?"

"It's a way of uniting our sufferings, both sought and unsought, with those of our Lord's," Sister Serenity explained. "It's a mystery how each tiny penance can gather to itself such meaning, and be joined to the infinite sufferings of Christ. But we believe this, that He suffered for us, so we suffer *for* and *with* and *in* Him, and that suffering touches the world, heals it."

The young novitiate, Sister Regina Marie, tried valiantly to believe this, but found only absurdity in the awkward physical act of administering pseudo self-torture. The first night she hoisted up her nightgown in the bathroom during Grand Silence and attempted to flog herself, she had not yet memorized the Miserere, which was to be recited, kneeling, throughout the taking of the Discipline. She tried propping the prayer book on a chair seat, but she needed one hand to hold up her gown, and one to hold the weapon, so the book flipped shut and fell on the floor. She tried it another way, but this time she flogged the chair instead of herself, and when she finally managed to strike her own backside she felt like a complete idiot. She could find no value in the mortification of the flesh.

Perhaps that's when her doubts actually began, for she had never again attempted taking the Discipline. Instead, on Friday nights when she took her turn in the bathroom, she said the Miserere prone on the floor. She'd spent many hours over the duration of her years as a nun examining and reexamining what Holy Rule said about penance. It merely stated that "the religious should esteem, love and practice penance according to their strength." Which threw the entire issue right back at her conscience.

Her conscience told her that while taking the discipline she'd felt as if she was caught in some miserable charade at which God himself was probably laughing. So she had never done it again.

It was a measure of Sister Regina's desperation that during the agonizing process of deciding what to do with the rest of her life, and in an effort to give her vocation every possible chance, she attempted to take the Discipline again.

But when she was closed inside the bathroom with the tool in her hands, the idea of applying it to herself seemed profane. She could not believe that a benevolent God wanted her to punish herself for something as human as feeling love for another human being. For if she truly was falling in love with Mr. Olczak, wasn't that love itself a gift from God?

The odd thing was, once she'd made the decision to set the Discipline aside without using it, she forgot to pray the Miserere. She remembered later that night, when she was lying in bed thinking of Eddie Olczak and reaching the conclusion that living as his wife would be as noble a way of life as this she was living: raising children and teaching them to be good people, being part of a union in which love was a driving force.

Oh, *Mr. Olczak*, she thought, *kind and good Mr. Olczak, what should I do?*

Eleven

❧

On Thanksgiving Eddie's mother butchered three turkeys she'd been raising all summer, roasted one herself and had a couple of her daughters roast the others. She peeled about a washtub full of potatoes, everybody brought side dishes, and forty-seven people piled into her house for dinner.

Hedy and Cass still lived on the home place east of town, where they farmed a hundred and sixty acres, milked a dozen cows by hand twice a day, raised about ten or fifteen pigs each year, had their own laying hens and put in a vegetable garden about the size of Horseshoe Lake.

When people asked Cass when he was going to slow down, he'd lift off his stained blue Osh Kosh B'Gosh cap by its threadbare bill, scratch his pure white head between the eight stringy hairs still there, and reply, "Hell, I don't know. Ain't had enough time to sit down and think about it." Then he'd settle his cap back in place, covering up the white and leaving a windburned red below.

Every year Hedy said, "I ain't puttin' in so big of a garden this year. My knees just can't take it no more." But the garden never shrunk, her knees always managed to hold up just fine, and at the end of the summer her root cellar was filled with about a thousand pounds of potatoes, and rutabagas and squash and a few hundred jars of home-canned jams, and jellies, and vegetables, and pickles, and relish and sauces of every kind imaginable. She also canned beef, pork and chicken, and ended up giving most of it to her married kids, because Hedy could never send anyone away from her door empty-handed.

Cass and Hedy's kids came flocking home for Thanksgiving on a day with lowered skies and a nasty wind. What remained of the early November snow lay in crusty bands between the rows of tarnished corn stubble. It stippled the tops of the new haystacks that hunkered near the oversized red barn with its immense gambrel roof. The farmyard had frozen in ruts, and the garden, which Cass had plowed under, looked like lengths of broad black chain, each bordered by white snow. The kids had all come home in mid-October and helped Cass put up his winter firewood. It stood in orderly rows halfway down the path to the outhouse. Woodsmoke rose from the chimney and blew eastward in fragrant ribbons as Eddie parked his green pickup among a half-dozen vehicles already there.

"Come on, girls," he said, swinging them down from the truck seat and slamming the door.

The kitchen door flew open when they were halfway up the path, and his mother leaned out, dressed in a flowered housedress, bibbed apron and black Cuban-heeled shoes. "Theeeere's my girls!" she yelled exuberantly. "Get in here before you catch your death, you two!"

"Hey, Grandma, guess what!" They barreled right at her and got hugs and kisses and told her, "Grandma Gaffke's teaching us how to make doll clothes on her sewing machine!"

Eddie came next, and got his hug in the open doorway with the cold swirling into the kitchen around him.

"There's my Eddie-boy," she said, softer, giving him a tighter hug than usual, and a kiss on the cheek. They both knew this day was going to be difficult for him, his first holiday without Krystyna.

"Hi, Mommo," he said and squeezed her plump waist.

He drew back and looked into her eyes, and neither one of them had to say it: each knew what the other was thinking. So they hugged hard, wordless, one more time before she backed up and wiped her eyes inside her rimless glasses with the skirt of her apron, and said, "Come on inside. Cold air's gettin' in."

Inside it smelled like turkey and dressing and roasting garlic, and there were people everywhere. Potatoes were boiling on the stove and the windows were white with condensation. The cast-iron stove was as big as a '49 Ford, and covered with so many kettles you couldn't see the top of it. Kids were running everywhere, their clothing still clean so early in the day. The grownups were drinking beer and at the kitchen table a foursome was already playing cards. On top of the woodbox a skinny striped cat nervously watched the hubbub with dilated pupils.

Lucy said to one of her cousins, "We brought doll clothes to dress Stringbean. Let's get 'er!" They dove for the cat and hauled her off upstairs.

Eddie's dad found him, and put a beer in his hand and gave him a slap on the back, then stood for a while with his hand there, between Eddie's shoulder blades, rubbing a little.

They might not be glib people, his family, but they had feelings, and understood his.

He'd needed a day like this, a gathering of people he loved who loved him. Play some cards, tell some jokes, eat Mommo's cooking, drink a few beers, and in the late afternoon go out with all his brothers to help Poppo with the chores.

That's what they were doing, Eddie and his brothers, helping with the milking late in the day just before dusk, when the teasing began. In the barn, where they'd all had to help as boys, they became boys again, tossing insults, ribbing each other, falling to the milking with nostalgic vigor.

"So, Eddie," his brother Vernon said from someplace behind Eddie while Eddie sat with his forehead against a black-and-white cow, sending pulsating streams of milk into his pail, "when you gonna give that little Irene Pribil a tumble?"

From down the line of cows came a wolf call. "Woo-woo! That Irene, she's waitin', that's for sure!" That was his brother Romaine.

"Who called Irene little?" came Clayton's voice from the other direction.

"She's little all right, a sweet little piglet!"

"You know what they say about the plump ones, don't you?"

About four voices chorused all together, "Yeah . . . warmth in the winter and shade in the summer."

Then Clayton's voice again. "Anybody know how you find the right place on a fat girl?"

"How?"

"Roll her in flour and look for the wet spot!"

Eddie laughed right along with all the rest of them.

"Hey, Eddie, you got any flour at your house?" his brother Bill called.

Romaine answered. "He buys it in hundred-pound bags."

A bunch of howling laughter, then, "Irene'll be at the dance Saturday night. Last one before Advent starts." Church tradition forbade dancing during Advent and Lent, so the dance halls closed down then.

"Who's playing?"

"Rainbow Valley Boys at Knotty Pine."

"Ruth and I will be there."

"So will we."

"Hey, Eddie, why don't you bring your flour and come?"

Cass's voice came next. "You boys lay off Eddie, now."

And Eddie's. "It's okay, Poppo. I know a bunch of jackasses when I hear 'em braying."

It was a sign of his healing that he could take their teasing this way, and everybody in that barn knew it.

————

On Saturday night Eddie hired Dorrie Anderson to watch the girls, and he got spiffed up in a white shirt and tie, and his brown wool suit, and went to the dance at Knotty Pine. A whole slew of his sisters and brothers were there, and so was Irene, with lots of curls in her hair, straight seams in her nylons and bright-red lipstick to match her bright-red dress.

His damned brothers danced with her, one after the other, and flashed him grins from the dance floor as if to say, You're next, Eddie, so you might as well give in. When Romaine led Irene off the floor they went right to the booth where Eddie was sitting with a bunch of others.

She was warm, her face shiny as she pushed back her hair and fanned herself with one hand.

"Hoo! Hot!" she said.

"Here, sit down, Irene," Romaine said and pointed to an empty space next to Eddie. Eddie jigged over, making a little extra space for her, and she sat down.

The waitress was there taking orders and Romaine said, "Buy you a drink, Irene?"

"Sure," she said. "A Grain Belt."

"Make that two. Anybody else?"

When the waitress went away the table talk continued quite loudly. Under its cover Irene said quietly, "How're you tonight, Eddie? You're not dancing much." She got out her compact, flipped it open and checked her face in the mirror.

Eddie said, "What is it about girls that they can't stand to see a man not dancing?"

Irene got out a Kleenex and dabbed her forehead, then flipped some curls into place and put the compact away in her pocket.

"Advent starts tomorrow. That means no more dances till after Christmas," she said. "Last chance for four weeks, that's all."

"Tell you what," he said. "If they play 'Goodnight Irene,' I'll dance with you." It was a popular song that year and you could hardly turn the radio on without hearing it.

"I'll make sure they do," she said, flashing him a saucy smile.

It was a crowded booth. Eddie put his arm along the back of it and Irene's curls brushed his wrist. Someone came and pushed into the open end, forcing her closer against his side. Their beers arrived, and everybody touched bottles and said, "Bumps," then took long swigs. Irene never went back to her own booth. She stayed and laughed at the Olczak boys' jokes, and visited with their wives, and remained hip-to-hip with Eddie.

The Rainbow Valley Boys saved "Goodnight Irene" until the very end. Truth was, Eddie had expected this, for the song had fast become the traditional last dance of the night, its words so simple everyone ended up singing along with it.

Irene was a good dancer without trying to be. She never made a misstep and followed so effortlessly she made a man feel masterful leading her. Dancing with her was a lot like dancing with Krystyna, except she was shaped differently. She smiled all the while they waltzed, staying her distance, enjoying the dancing for dancing's sake. They waltzed quite imposingly, taking wide, sweeping steps on every first beat. He liked that she didn't try any coy snuggling because if anything started between them, he wanted to be the one to start it. And stop it, too, as the case may be.

"Gosh-dang, I sure love to dance," she said. "I'd rather dance than play cards, and I *love* to play cards."

"I know. You've beat me enough times."

She laughed and asked, "You have a nice Thanksgiving, Eddie?"

"Very nice. And you?"

"We tried. It was hard without Krystyna. But just about everybody was home, and that helped a lot. All of your sisters and brothers come home?"

"Only about half of them, thank heavens. The house can't hold many more." They danced awhile, then he asked, "So who did you come with tonight?"

"Mickey and Dolores." Her brother and sister-in-law who lived in Sauk Center and were undoubtedly home for the holiday.

"So you riding back to your folks' with them?"

"I guess so."

They danced a few more steps before he suggested noncommittally, "I could take you."

She looked up at him. "You want to?"

The truth was, he didn't know if he wanted to or not.

The song ended and they stepped apart, dropping their hands. "Sure. Get your coat and I'll tell Mickey you're riding with me."

"Okay."

It was one o'clock in the morning when the dance ended. Dozens of cars pulled out of the parking lot at Knotty Pine, lifting dust from the gravel and dispersing to the north and south along State Highway 71. Eddie's truck was in the line heading north. Irene sat squarely in the passenger seat as he drove through the main drag of Browerville and out the other end—six blocks of sleeping village beneath a few dim streetlamps. The line of cars petered out the farther they got from town. He turned right onto County Road 89 and bumped over the railroad crossing where Krystyna was killed. Without looking at him, Irene reached over and caught his hand and squeezed it so hard his wedding ring cut into his finger.

"I'm trying real hard to get over her. To move on," she said.

"So am I."

"So I'm not going to cry right now, are you?"

"Nope," he said.

"Good for us." She tried to release her hand, but he held it there on the seat between them and could feel her thumb stroke his while she stared straight ahead at the dried weeds whipping past on either side of the gravel road. Up ahead they could see a set of taillights; behind them, none. He drove holding her hand, wondering if he was merely responding to his brothers' teasing or if he really wanted to start something with Irene. It had been nearly three months since he'd had any physical contact with a woman, and it was good just holding a hand. The movement of her thumb was so welcome it began to work its way into his vitals. The great swell of his loneliness was relieved by the knowledge that she had a crush on him and had for a long time. He realized he could probably do anything with her that he wanted.

Her parents lived up ahead about a half mile, around a sharp left-hand curve, and as they drew closer, the tension in the truck increased. He slowed down and released Irene's hand so he could shift into second before turning right onto a field access, where he stopped between a line of trees and a stubbled cornfield. The cornfield disappeared when he shut off the headlights, and as he killed the engine some bright autumn moonlight came streaming though the windshield.

Irene didn't say anything. Neither did Eddie. Something like this—loveless—he thought, was better done without words.

He turned and put a hand on the back of Irene's neck and they met in the middle of the seat, tilting to fit into each other's arms. Her lips were warm and plump and somewhat shy, and he sensed her tentativeness matched his own. He played with her lips awhile before nudging them apart and when he touched her with his tongue her breath issued in a gust against his cheek. He felt her relax and sensed that she was as relieved as he that they'd taken this first step at last, a step that everyone had expected from them.

He gave the kiss a chance to do its work, letting it grow deeper, then deeper still as he tested himself and found his body rising to the occasion while his emotions dragged behind. He wanted to have feelings for Irene, wanted very badly to, and perhaps they'd put in an appearance in the course of his seduction. He ended the kiss with feigned reluctance, keeping his face just above hers, testing the moment and her willingness to go on.

"Irene?" he whispered, his arm clear around her head, his fingertips kneading her cheek and jaw.

She made a mewling sound in her throat, half elation, half anguish, and drew him to her once more to resume what they had begun.

He knew—how could he not know?—all those years she'd banked her attraction for him. He was male, and human, and the knowledge floated on his mind and drove his hands to explore her. She was alive and passionate, and kissing her reminded him of the great sexual void in which he'd been living these past three months. Touching again, fitting himself against a willing body again, running his hands over another's flesh began to falsely fulfill him.

He twisted around with his neck to the moonlight and pressed her against the seat back at an angle to ease his access. He slid his hand inside her cloth coat and onto her abundant breast. So different from Krystyna's, so much fuller. But it lifted against his palm, acquiescing, inviting him one step further, one step further. In time he opened the quarter-sized buttons down the front of her dress and unhooked her brassiere. When he lowered his head and kissed her naked breast, her head fell back and her breath rampaged. He reared up, covering her mouth with his again, and they began listing and let themselves go until he half-lay upon her in the cramped space, with one leg pressing her red skirt tight against her girdle. Then he ran his hand up her leg, rucking her skirt up to her hips, lifting himself to clear the way. He explored the top of her nylons, her rubber garters, and the tight elastic girdle that was warm and faintly moist from all the dancing she'd done that night. He freed her two front garters and found his way inside her underwear, waiting for some inundating feeling of love to overwhelm him and carry him the rest of the way into this carnal act.

None came.

Only lust and a sense of wrongdoing.

And the realization that Irene was pushing on his shoulders, telling him to stop.

He let his hand flag and drift away from her moist flesh.

They lay a while letting their breath steady, then he pushed himself up. Their limbs were still tangled and her skirt still bunched at her waist, one arm was out of her clothing.

"Eddie?" Irene whispered.

"I'm sorry, Irene."

"You feel guilty? Like you're betraying her?"

"Something like that."

"Me, too."

She shifted her weight as if to free her leg, and he moved so she could do so. She covered her breast with her fallen coat. In the moonglow they pushed themselves upright and sat side by side, disheveled, feeling depleted and wrong.

He had tried her because it was expedient. She was the simplest answer to his loneliness, and his children's motherlessness, and his womanless house. She was what everyone expected him to do, and it would have solved so many of his problems if it had worked. But it hadn't taken him long to find out there had to be love in it first.

She had encouraged him because it was expedient. He was the simplest answer to her loneliness, and her childless life with her aging parents. Snagging him was what everyone expected her to do, and she maybe could have done it, even without getting pregnant, certainly *by* getting pregnant. But she was a good Catholic girl who had been taught the Seventh Commandment. Furthermore, she was Krystyna's sister, but she could never be Krystyna for him.

He slumped, and groaned softly, let his head fall back against the seat with his eyes closed.

"Oh, hell, Irene, I don't know . . ."

Disappointment settled between both of them, sitting there beside the ghost of Krystyna.

"I know," Irene commiserated—a meaningless conversation to anyone but them. A long time slid by while they did battle with their guilt over what they had almost done.

"Can I ask you something, Eddie?"

"Hm."

"You didn't stop because . . . well, because you found me repulsive, did you?"

He lifted his head to find her staring at the blue white corn stubble and the starlit sky.

"No, Irene. I stopped because it's wrong."

She looked at him squarely. "You sure?"

"Yes."

She sat in silence awhile, then said, "Could I tell you something, Eddie? Confidentially, I mean?"

"Sure, Irene."

It took her a while to get started. He knew whatever she had to say was difficult for her.

"There was this man once a couple of years ago. Doesn't matter who, just this man who said he'd drive me home from a dance at Bink's. I went with him, and he parked and tried to force me to do what you and I just started to do, but I fought him and told him no. He got real mad and called me a stupid fat *c-u-n-t*"—she spelled it out—"and said that I should be grateful to him for even trying to lay me because nobody else ever would. Then he drove me home like a maniac, only he didn't take me up to the door. He stopped clear at the end of our driveway and made me walk the rest of the way. He shoved the door open and said, 'Get out, fatso. The walk will do you good.' A girl doesn't forget something like that, Eddie, getting humiliated that way. That's why I'm . . . well, I'm grateful for how you treated me tonight, because all this time I thought that man was right."

Eddie's heart felt as if it would burst with pity. He put his hand on the back of her head, and her chin dropped.

"Oh, Irene," he said, and took her in his arms again.

She hugged him hard and burst into tears.

"Oh, Eddie," she said between sobs. "I've loved you for so long that I c . . . can't even remember when it started. I thought Krystyna was the luckiest w . . . woman on the face of the earth and you were the best husband and father. I w . . . wanted your children to be mine, but I know they c . . . can't be. I know you don't l . . . love me, Eddie . . ."

"That's not true, Irene. I do love you." He kept petting her head with his wide rough hand while she wept against his neck. "Not the way I loved Krystyna, but for your goodness, and your kindness, and the way you treat your parents, and how good you've been to me and the girls. You have so many wonderful qualities, Irene, any man would be proud to call you his wife. What that other man said—well, you just forget it, because it isn't true.

You just wait and see. One of these days one of these guys around here is going to open up his eyes and see what he's been missing, and you'll be raising a batch of kids of your own and you'll never pine for anyone else again."

"You really think so, Eddie?"

"Why, shucks, yes."

Her weeping subsided and she heaved a big broken sigh, still curled against him. He continued holding her, realizing everyone had their own private heartbreaks to go through; his wasn't the only life with sadness in it.

Finally, when the worst was over, he teased, "Hey, Irene, you making a mess of my suit jacket?"

She managed a single choked laugh and pushed herself from him. Her clothing was still awry and he was sitting on enough of it to limit her movement. "Reach me my purse, Eddie. There's a hanky in it."

He put her purse half on her lap, half on his, and she snapped it open, blew her nose and mopped her eyes and put the hanky away again. She rubbed her entire face with the length of both palms and drew an immense, shaky sigh.

"Feel better now?" he asked.

"Not exactly."

She looked up at him and they laughed at themselves, just once, quietly, the laugh of friends who've come through a bit of hell together and will have an even stronger friendship for it.

"Here, let's get you decent," he said, disengaging his legs from hers and making motions of helping her put herself back together.

"I can do it, Eddie," she said.

But he pushed her hands aside and replied, "I know you can, but so can I. I'm the one who messed you up, I'll put you back together again . . . that is, if you don't mind."

"You mean you really want to, Eddie?"

"Yes, I do. It's something Krystyna let me do now and then, put her clothes back on. And I enjoyed it just about as much as taking them off. So . . . well, heck . . . as long as we both have to go to Confession anyway, might as well get as much out of this as we can, huh?"

He couldn't get her garters snapped onto her nylons, but they enjoyed a chuckle over it while he tried and failed. She did it herself, and when her skirt was pushed back down he made her face away from him so he could hook her bra. Then he turned her around by the shoulders and buttoned her dress up the front and held her coat so she could slip her arm back into it, and buttoned it, too, all the time hoping she'd realize that a man who was repulsed by a woman's body would never do such a thing.

When she was all in a piece, she squared herself on the seat and he sat with one wrist draped over the steering wheel, looking over at her. The earlier tension was gone, in its place a friendship cemented.

"Hey, Eddie, one more thing," Irene said.

"What's that?"

"Don't get me wrong. Now that we know where we stand and there's no obligations between us, just kiss me once more as if it were real, 'cause that was the sweetest thing I ever felt in my life."

He took her in his arms, not too loverly but not exactly brotherly, and curved to her and kissed her as she'd asked, taking plenty of time and vowing he would never make jokes about fat girls again.

When the kiss ended and his hand remained on her shoulder, she said with a sad smile, "If you ever change your mind, Eddie, you just let me know."

He, too, smiled and said sadly, "I will, Irene."

Then he drove her all the way to her door.

Twelve

❧

The next day was the first Sunday of Advent when, by tradition, the Christmas crèche was put up in church, where it would remain until the Epiphany. After High Mass the trustees of the parish stayed behind to help Eddie carry up the statues, manger and canvas from the furnace room. At the left front of the church, they stood a backdrop of fresh green balsam pines. In front of the pines was erected a canvas cave that looked so much like real stone the children all believed it was, and wondered how it got there whenever it magically appeared, and where it went afterward, and who could carry stones that large and heavy. Inside the cave went electric lights and the manger scene itself—Mary and Joseph, the three kings, sheep and shepherds, and above the mouth of the cave a beautiful statue of an angel watching over the nativity scene, with a flowing ribbon in her hands and a beatific smile on her face.

Eddie had kept the girls with him while he worked with the men. There was a general rule: no talking in church, not even whispering. The girls were told to sit in the front pew and watch, and not get in the way. It wasn't long before they grew impatient and came over to whisper, "How much longer, Daddy? We want to go home."

"Not much longer. Now go back and sit down and don't get in the way."

They did as ordered, but soon Lucy returned, whispering, "Daddy, can Annie and me talk, too?"

"Not in church. In church you have to be quiet."

"But you're talking."

"Because I have to tell the men what to do. Now go sit down and stay out of the way."

She was back in a few minutes, saying, "Daddy, I'm hungry. When are we gonna go?"

"Not long, then we'll go to the Quality Inn for dinner."

Then Anne, whispering, "Daddy, I have to go to the bathroom." The church was old and had no public restrooms. He pulled out a ring of keys and handed them to Anne. "Here. This is the key for the school. Go to the west door—you know, the one you go out of for recess, the one the sisters use—and use the girls' bathroom. Come right straight back . . . and don't lose the keys!"

"Okay. Come on, Lucy."

As they headed down the aisle, he said, "And button up your coats and put your mittens on."

They looked incredibly small pushing through the tall swinging doors into the vestibule. Even though they walked to and from school together every day, watching them go away from him through the dim, vacant church filled him with protectiveness and love. He thought a quick prayer: *Lord, don't ever let anything happen to them. I don't know what I'd do.*

At the school building, Anne's nine-year-old hands had trouble getting the key in the lock. Plus, she had to go—bad. She was dancing around with her legs half crossed, and Lucy at her side telling her to hurry up, when Sister Ignatius saw them from the convent kitchen and supposed they were up to mischief.

She opened the door and stuck her head out. "Girls, what are you doing there? School building's locked up for the weekend!"

Anne and Lucy turned around. "I've got to go to the bathroom, and my daddy said I could go in the school. He gave me his keys to open it up, but I can't get it in the lock."

Sister Ignatius thought of her thick wool shawl hanging upstairs in her room, but she was in the middle of making gravy for Sunday dinner, and was disinclined to go out and help the children without her wrap, given her age and her rheumatism.

"Come on in here," she called, "you can use the bathroom here."

The children scampered along the sidewalk and up the stone steps into the warm, fragrant kitchen.

"Take your boots off and leave them on the rug," the old nun said.

They pulled their boots off and one of Lucy's shoes stayed inside. Anne helped her prize it out and put it back on. When it was rebuckled she turned to Sister, brushing a small side ponytail out of her eyes.

"Upstairs on your left. The door should be open."

They went upstairs with all the wide-eyed awe of souls entering the pearly gates. This place where the nuns lived seemed hallowed, invading their private quarters like being allowed to walk into the house of the Blessed Virgin Mary. What they'd seen of the convent was the waiting bench and music rooms where they'd had piano lessons, and occasionally the kitchen when their mom delivered food there, or when their dad was working there.

On their way up the stairs Lucy whispered, "How come it's so quiet, Annie?"

"I don't know."

"Haven't they got no radio?"

"I don't know."

"Where do you think they are?" In the upstairs hall all the doors were closed.

"Shh. It's probably a sin to talk about them. Come on."

They reached the bathroom and shut themselves inside. Anne went first. While she did so, Lucy looked around the spotless white room with its starched white window curtain, pedestal sink and clawfoot tub.

"Gee, it looks just like other people's bathrooms," Lucy observed in a whisper.

"But there's no perfume bottles like Mommy's."

"I don't think they can wear perfume. Only incense. Hurry up, I gotta go too."

Anne hurried and they changed places. During these minutes they were all eyes, examining the room for evidence that the nuns were mortal, for in their childish eyes the Sisters had dropped into their universe permanently dressed in habits that magically never needed changing; not from a world of parents and siblings and a childhood like their own, but from someplace that wasn't exactly heaven yet very much like it, someplace where nuns were created and stored by God and dropped down by Him whenever they were needed.

"Hey, Annie, do you think they use toothbrushes like we have to?"

"Well, of course, silly, they have teeth and they get cavities if they don't brush."

"They do not. Jesus wouldn't give them cavities. They're too holy."

"Well, Mommy used to take them to Long Prairie to the dentist, so there, smarty!"

Lucy, however, remained skeptical. "But they don't take baths, do they?"

"Oh, you're so dumb, Lucy. Of course they take baths, otherwise what would they be doing with that bathtub?"

Just then a handbell tinkled somewhere in the hall.

Both girls got big-eyed and scared.

"Oh-oh!" Lucy said. "Somebody musta heard what we were saying. I think we're in trouble."

"Hurry up."

She hurried and finished, and flushed, and they faced another quandary. Every adult they'd ever known had cautioned them to wash their hands after they went to the toilet—everyone from grandmas to parents to the nuns themselves.

"I don't think we should use their water," Anne said. They were both still whispering. It seemed the proper thing to do in this house.

"How come? We're supposed to wash our hands afterward."

" 'Cause it's holy water, and you shouldn't use that after the bathroom."

"Oh," Lucy said, always certain, as the younger of the pair, that her sister was right about these worldly matters.

When they got into the hall they could hear the murmur of the nuns' voices saying grace below. The smell of their dinner lifted up the stairwell, so wonderful it made their young stomachs grumble as they went down, sliding their palms on the waxed handrail all the way. At the bottom of the stairs the nuns' refectory was off to their right. They stopped, awestruck afresh by the sight of these holy creatures actually sitting at a table with food on it.

Mother Superior spoke first when she saw them. "Well, whom have we here?"

The girls said in unison, "Good afternoon, Sister."

Sister Ignatius explained, "They had to use the bathroom. Their father is putting up the nativity scene in church."

"Oh, yes, of course." Then Mother Superior asked, "Have you had your dinners yet?"

"No, Sister."

"No, Sister."

"Daddy says he's taking us to the *resturnt* after he's done."

"Well, I imagine you're hungry."

Lucy blurted out, "I'm starved," and got a nudge from Anne.

"Don't we have some extra cookies, Sister Ignatius? I'm sure the girls would each like one." As their eyes lit up, Mother Superior ordered, "Sister Regina, why don't you give the girls each a cookie to tide them over until their father takes them out for dinner?"

It was a new month, and Sister Regina's charge had changed. This month her assignment was to act as table server. She rose and smiled, as she left her place and led the two little girls away. As they went, Lucy smiled over her shoulder and waved goodbye, and got another bump from her older sibling. Behind her, every nun wore a smile.

Sister Regina got down a dun crock from a kitchen shelf, removed the cover and held it toward them. Inside were huge white sugar cookies with pink frosting. "Help yourselves," she said.

The girls each took a cookie. They had heard a story about manna from heaven in their Bible history classes, and Lucy figured for sure this was it. It had to be, coming from the nun's cupboard. She'd always figured manna for some tasteless bread, but—lo and behold!—it had frosting! She figured the food in heaven wasn't going to be so bad after all.

"Thank you, Sister."

"Thank you, Sister."

"And now you'll go straight back to church, won't you?"

"Yes, Sister."

"Yes, Sister."

"But, could you hold this first, Sister? I have to put my boots on."

She held their cookies while they sat down on the rug and tugged on their boots, inadvertently displaying their white cotton underpants beneath their Sunday dresses. Boots on, they stood and buttoned their coats and she handed them their cookies and opened the door.

"Goodbye now, girls."

They said goodbye and Anne led the way out. When Lucy was on the threshold, she obviously had an important thought, stopped and crooked a finger. Sister leaned down so Lucy could whisper in her ear.

"You don't have to brush your teeth, *do* you, Sister?" the child said with a knowing note. *"Annie says you do!"*

Sister Regina covered her smile with one hand, then bent to the child and whispered back, "I certainly do. And so do you. Don't forget now, when you get back home."

As she watched them go she was smitten anew, especially by little Lucy. This must be what it was like to have children, to be constantly amused by them, to award them with small treats and watch them scamper off, happy and unfettered by any concerns but their own. Lucy—darling unrestrained Lucy—she wished she had one of her own like that, a mixture of precociousness and sweetness wrapped into one adorable bundle. Why was it that fate seemed to put that particular little girl in Sister Regina's path so much more often than other children, as if to remind her of what she was missing?

When Sister Regina returned to the dining room the mood was unusually gay. The presence of any children in the convent, apart from piano lessons which went on all day long during school days, always elevated the mood of the entire religious community.

When Sister Regina resumed her chair, Mother Superior remarked, "Those are two very likable children, Mr. Olczak's. He and his wife have done a fine job of raising them so far."

Murmurs of assent rose in a soft chorus. Sister Mary Charles passed Sister Regina the meat platter, and while she took a piece of roast pork, Sister Regina told everyone, "Lucy wanted to know if we have to brush our teeth like everybody else does. I'm not sure she believed me when I said we did."

They all understood the sense of mystery that surrounded them as far as the children were concerned, and laughed quietly.

Sister Gregory said, "One of my first-grade piano students asked me the other day if nuns have mothers."

Again everyone laughed.

Sister Dora said, "I was asked one time how I could sleep in bed at night without bending my halo. He was talking about my coif, of course."

Mother Superior recalled a humorous story from her past. "I remember once when I asked my class if anyone knew what Lent was. One boy raised his hand and said 'Lint' was what sticks to your pants and your mother tries to brush it off."

It was Sunday, their one day a week with fewer obligations, and the afternoon to themselves, to do with what they wished, the one day a week that family was allowed to visit. The mood on Sunday was often more relaxed, and today was one of the best days Sister Regina had had in months.

This was what she'd always imagined communal life to be like among the religious. Camaraderie and a strong sense of belonging. Everyone agreeing and getting along with no underlying friction, and feeling a part of a bigger world family that would be there for each of them, whatever befell. Perhaps she was wrong to have had doubts about it. She was so safe and cared for here. And when the nuns were in such good moods she forgave them their foibles that had come to bother her at other times. Sister Cecelia wasn't telling tales on anyone. Sister Samuel wasn't sneezing. Sister Mary Charles wasn't whipping any children and even Mother Agnes was particularly amiable, joining in the mirth in an uncharacteristic way.

If only each day had this radiance and peace, Sister Regina thought, I would never ever think of leaving.

Dessert and coffee were in progress and Sister Regina was still reflecting on her present satisfaction with communal life when a knock sounded on the kitchen door. In keeping with her charge as server, she interrupted her meal to go and answer.

To her surprise Mr. Olczak stood on the stoop, wearing his good winter dress coat and felt hat, which he removed the moment he saw her through the storm door.

"Good afternoon, Mr. Olczak."

"Good afternoon, Sister. I'm sorry to interrupt you on Sunday, but the girls must've left my keys in your house."

"Oh, really?" She backed up a step. "Please come in and wait while I go upstairs and look."

"Thank you, Sister."

She found the keys lying on the bathroom floor and returned them to him. He thanked her again and apologized once more for both himself and for the girls' having bothered them earlier.

"It was no trouble at all. Tell me, did you and the trustees get the nativity set all up and in place?"

"Sure did. Smells just like the piney woods in there, and it makes you feel good just to stand in the quiet and look at it again."

"Well, perhaps I'll go over to church and make a visit this afternoon."

"You do that, Sister. Church is always open, as you know."

She gave the small nod he recognized as a polite dismissal but neither of them reacted to it. She stood smiling like the saints on holy cards, her hands in her sleeves, her veil caught in perfect symmetry on both shoulders. She should have returned to the dining room, and he should have opened the door and left. Instead they remained alone and motionless in the kitchen, gripped by some thoughtless force that had little concern for propriety. From the dining room came the soft clink of spoons stirring cream into coffee and from outside the voices of his daughters as they slammed the truck doors.

"Well," he said, breaking the spell, turning his hat around and round in his hands, his voice coming out quiet, deep and froggy in his throat, "better let you get back to your dinner. See you tomorrow, Sister."

"Yes. Goodbye, Mr. Olczak."

Returning to the dining room she wondered what had just gone on between them. Nothing. Something. It happened now each time they had the briefest private moment together. It was unspoken, but very much felt. Within their hearts. Within their souls, which seemed to reach out and yearn toward one another.

You stay away from him, she warned herself. *You make sure the two of you are never alone together and you strive for the reassuring sense of oneness you were sharing with your fellow sisters before he stepped into this house. Can't you see he is muddling up your mind? Leaving your vocation because it has not fulfilled you is one thing, but leaving it for a man is another. And it is* not *acceptable!*

The overall pacific temperament of that first Sunday in Advent was short-lived. A big snow came, followed by a period of intensely cold weather, so cold it was dangerous. The schoolchildren, shut in by the thermometer and relegated to playing in the gymnasium and the halls during recess and noon hours, became more and more rambunctious. Among the younger kids, running grew rampant. Among the older ones, bickering and fighting were common. Sometimes the younger ones got bumped into and knocked down by the bigger ones, and general mischief escalated the closer they got to the much-needed Christmas vacation. The older nuns especially began losing their patience and their tempers.

Sister Mary Charles took her strip of rubber flooring to a seventh-grader named Freddy Poplinski, and during the beating the sounds came quite clearly through the parallel doorways that connected the flower room to Sister Regina's cloakroom, and the cloakroom to her classroom.

She pictured what was happening and hated it. Her anger flared and she questioned who was sinning, herself for blaming Sister Mary Charles, or Mary Charles for venting her wrath on that boy. Sister Regina had a theory that Mary Charles was a frustrated old maid who'd never had a proposal of marriage and had grown more and more bitter over it as the years advanced. She took her bitterness out on the poor children.

The other nuns didn't hear the whippings as she did. The proximity of her cloakroom to the flower room made her more aware than even Reverend Mother of the brutal punishments being meted out to children who were, after all, only being children.

It was Monday of the last week before Christmas vacation that Anne Olczak got into a game of tag with some of her older cousins from the upper classes across the hall. Mary Jean was in the sixth grade, Lawrence and Joey were in seventh and eighth. They'd been racing around the parapets, zigzagging through a basketball game in the crowded gymnasium, and Sister Mary Charles had warned them a number of times to stop. They would slow down for a while, but soon the game would be going whole-hog again.

It was Anne who was unlucky enough to be hurtling around the stub end of the parapet toward the girls' bathroom hall, when she knocked off the brass handbell. It struck the head of a first-grader on its way to the floor, where it bounced with a resounding *clang*, only about a few feet away from the black shoes of Sister Mary Charles.

"Olczak, come here! How many times have I told you!" she screamed and latched on to Anne's shoulder like an eagle nabbing its dinner. "Now look what you've done!" Anne stared up at the nun, transfixed with fear. "Pick up that bell!"

Anne picked it up posthaste and deposited it back on the parapet. The first-grader was yowling with blood streaming from a slice in her forehead.

Sister Mary Charles pointed a bony finger at the floor. "You wait right here, and don't you move one inch. Do you understand, missy?"

"Yes, s'ster," Anne whispered as sheer terror swooped through her.

Sister bent to attend the younger child. "Come along, let's see what's happened." She took her away to her own teacher to be examined and bandaged. The bandaging was done, however, in the flower room which also doubled as the first-aid room, so poor Anne had to wait ten minutes with her terror mounting, until Sister Mary Charles returned for her. By this time her cousins had all disappeared and were watching from a safe distance while noontime play continued throughout Paderewski Hall.

Sister Mary Charles reappeared, sour-faced and bitter, with her hands stuck up her sleeves. "All right, young lady, march!"

Anne didn't have to ask where. She knew.

She was already crying when the flower-room door closed behind them. Through her tears she could make out the strip of rubber floor tile waiting beside the ferns. It was dark green and formidable. There was an empty space on the lowest tier of bleachers for misbehavers to lean over if their punishment was to be meted out on their backsides. The ignominy was nearly as bad as the pain. Through her tremendous fear she was trying to gauge which would be worse, having to lean over, or getting it on the palm of the hands, which was said to be as bad as when Jesus got scourged on Calvary.

"You are a disobedient little girl!" Sister said, rolling up her wide right sleeve, "and disobedience must be punished—do you understand?"

Anne tried to whisper, *yes, Sister,* but no sound came out.

Sister picked up the rubber strip. Her face was hard as cast metal, her mouth pinched with self-righteousness.

"All right. Hold out your hands. And don't pull them back, because every time you do you'll get one extra swat. And while you get punished you pray to God and ask him to forgive your sins, do you understand?"

"But I didn't si—"

"*Don't talk back to me!*" Sister screamed.

"But it was an acci—"

"*Silence!*" She screamed so loud her voice shook the fern fronds. "Now out with those hands or I'll give you five more!"

Anne's two sweaty hands, no bigger than wrens' nests, trembled forward in slow motion.

Sister raised her weapon and swung—and Anne couldn't help it, her arms retracted like window shades.

Sister Mary Charles's outrage magnified. "*All right! It was going to be five! Now it's six!*"

Lucy was sitting Indian fashion with her back against a hall wall, playing cat's cradle with the younger girls, when her cousin Mary Jean came tearing toward her and slid to a stop on her knees.

"Sister Mary Charles's got Anne in the flower room!"

"Annie? What'd she do?"

"She knocked the bell off the parapet and it fell on some little kid's head." Lucy knew *you didn't touch that bell.* "We were playing tag and running after Sister told us not to." Lucy also knew *you did not run in the hall.*

"Annie?" She looked toward the flower room and got a sick feeling in the pit of her stomach. "She's in there with Sister Mary Charles?" Lucy peeled the yarn off her fingers and was getting to her feet without realizing it.

Don't you hurt my sister, you big meanie!

"Hey, Lucy, wait!"

But Lucy was running in the hall, heading to the rescue, and she didn't stop till she got to the flower-room door. Inside, she could hear Sister screaming, "Don't talk back to me!" and her fear of the legendary persecutor overwhelmed her courage. She began crying and ran to the closest person she could think of to help.

"Sister Regina, come quick! Sister Mary Charles's got Annie in the flower room, and she's giving her a licking!"

Sister Regina had been sitting at her desk, supervising the noon-hour play in her room. She jumped to her feet so fast her chair tipped over as she headed for the cloakroom door.

"Go play, Lucy, I'll take care of this."

She flew through the cloakroom in a dervish of black veils and flung open the flower-room door.

"Stop that this instant!" she shouted.

Anne had taken four licks and stood sobbing, holding her striped hands out for more.

Sister Mary Charles spun around. "This child has disobeyed! She must be punished!"

"Not that way! Not with anger and cruelty!"

"She disobeyed me not once, but twice, and this is what she gets."

"No. I will not allow it."

"*You* will not allow it! Since when is it your place to allow or disallow it when I'm reprimanding the children!"

"This is not reprimanding, this is persecution, and that is not a naughty child. A stern talking-to would do."

"We teach them that disobedience is sin, and this is the punishment. It's no worse than hundreds of others've gotten over the years, and they're all better off for it."

"God punishes sin, not you. And I cannot believe one of those children is better off for it. Anne, come here."

Anne dropped her hands and ran to Sister Regina's side, flinging her arms around the nun's hips and crying against her black clothing.

"Mother Superior will hear about this!" Mary Charles promised.

"Yes, Sister, she will." More gently, to Anne who was still sobbing with her face a mess, Sister Regina said, "Anne, please go into the bathroom and blow your nose and wait for me there."

Anne ran out, leaving the two nuns alone. Sister Regina said, in her calmest voice, "I'm very sorry, Sister, but I simply could not tolerate it anymore. I've disagreed with your whipping the children ever since I came here, but it seemed to be a tradition, and everyone accepted it. Well, not me.

Never me. I see no reason why the children should be sacrificed to some bitter need you have within you. It is not the children who should go to Confession, Sister, but you."

Sister Mary Charles had thrown her strap aside and was rolling her sleeve down, muttering, ". . . young progressive know-it-alls they're turning out of the convent these days . . ."

"What are you so bitter about, Sister?" the younger one asked quietly.

"If it wasn't for people like me those kids would be running all over us, blaspheming in the halls, skipping Mass and who knows what else!"

"Is that what Anne was doing, blaspheming in the halls? Skipping Mass? No. What was it? Running? Like any healthy little fourth-grader is bound to do when she's cooped up for eight hours a day and can't even go outside for recess?"

"You overstep your bounds, Sister, and while you're doing it you break Holy Rule."

"Please, don't speak to me of Holy Rule. You might try relearning chapter six on charity, where it says teachers may not inflict corporal punishment of any kind on a pupil. What about *that* holy rule?"

Sister Mary Charles scoffed and headed toward the door through which Anne had run. "I don't have to stand here and take this from a nun who everyone knows plays favorites to those Olczak kids just because their dad is the janitor. I'm not stupid, Sister. Nor is Mother Superior. We know what's going on!"

She went out and slammed the door none too gently.

Sister Regina dropped her face into her steepled hand and collected herself for a moment. Tears stung her eyes. Nerves jumped in her stomach. But a sense of righteousness overwhelmed her at the knowledge that she'd finally stood up for the children and stopped Mary Charles's wholesale cruelty.

The bell rang for afternoon classes to resume, and Sister realized she was the one who was supposed to have rung it, and that Anne was still in the lavatory waiting. While her students took last drinks and shuffled toward the classroom, she went to find her.

The girls' bathroom had windows of stamped, textured glass, and woodwork as dark as molasses. Anne was standing with her face against a corner, crying her little heart out, and Lucy was nearby, vicariously miserable but too young to know what to do.

When their champion arrived, Lucy stated soberly, "She got 'er on the hands, Sister, and Annie won't stop crying."

Sister made Anne turn around, and Anne plunged against her, hugging hard. Sister's heart swelled with pity and love and she disregarded Holy Rule, and her own threatened vows, and returned the hug with one hand soothing the child's hair. Had Anne a mother of her own to go to for understanding, this would be a wholly different situation. What Regina had said to Mary Charles was true. This was not a problem child but a delicate one who'd been through enough turbulent emotions in the past several months. The ignominy and unjustness of today's whipping might leave a serious mark on her delicate emotions. What to do now—send her back to the classroom to face the curious stares and whispers waiting there? Or let charity rule, and give her a reprieve?

When Anne calmed somewhat, Sister drew back and looked at her tear-streaked face. "Here, dear, let's run your hands under cold water, and that will help."

Lucy stuck close to her sister's side, asking, "You okay, Annie? Do your hands hurt, Annie?"

Sister was touched by the younger sibling's fierce loyalty and recognized that the bond between them had grown even stronger since the death of their mother. This was not a day on which they should be separated.

Though she would have to answer for it, Sister made a decision.

"Come with me, girls. Let's go find your daddy."

They found him in the lunchroom, carrying out the luncheon garbage. The cooks, Mrs. Fisher and Mrs. Zapp, were sitting quietly eating their own meal before washing the dishes. Globules of tomato-covered macaroni dotted the floors and the smell of hamburger goulash permeated the room.

They could hear the garbage cans rattling in the rear hall, so Sister took the girls around the corner, out of earshot of the cooks. Mr. Olczak came in with an empty garbage can and stopped in surprise when he saw the three of them.

"What's going on, Sister?"

She stood with one hand on each girls' neck, holding them near her protectively. "I think it would be best if Anne and Lucy left school for the rest of the day. Is there someone whose house they could go to?"

"Sure. Aunt Katy's, but why?"

"Anne had an accident and knocked the bell off the parapet. It hit a child and Sister Mary Charles punished her in the flower room. I stopped her."

He pulled off his soiled gloves and went down on one knee, frowning. "Annie? Come here, honey." Both girls went, but he put his hands on Anne's hips and spoke only to her. "Tell me what happened."

"We were playing tag, Mary Jean and Lawrence and Joey and a bunch of us, and Sister told us not to run, but I was *it*, and I accidentally knocked the bell off the parapet and it hit this little girl on the head and it was bleeding, but it was an accident, Daddy. Sister said I committed a sin, but I didn't, and she hit me with the rubber strap on my hands . . . and . . . and . . ." Her chin was wobbling and fat tears filled her eyes again. ". . . I w . . . wish Mommy was still alive."

Sister Regina had never seen Eddie's face suffused with anger that way. She watched his expression set up with indignation as he listened to Anne's recounting of her punishment. She thought she could read his mind, and that what was on it must be what was on hers—how dare that bitter old nun perpetrate her viciousness on a little girl who hadn't a mean bone in her body, who was a model of comportment, and who had been through *enough* hell, having lost her mother!

"Come on. You, too, Lucy." He rose, stern-faced and decisive, taking both girls by the hands. "We'll go get your coats, and I'll take you over to Aunt Katy's. You can stay there till suppertime. And don't you worry about whether or not you sinned, Annie. You didn't."

He stalked so fast the girls had to run to keep up, back to the third- and fourth-grade room. While Sister returned to her students and began the afternoon classes with a prayer, Eddie went into the cloakroom to find the girls' coats. But before he left, he stuck his head into the classroom and motioned for Sister to come to the doorway. Then he whispered, "Thank you, Sister. Will you be in trouble for stepping in?"

"No, Mr. Olczak."

"Good. It's . . . I'm so . . ." She watched him do battle with an anger so immense that it knew no suitable expression. "Nothing. I'll talk to you later."

Thirteen

It surprised Sister Regina how calm she was now that the time was here. The misgivings from the past seemed to have vanished. Her doubts had dissipated with her abrupt decision to step in and stop Sister Mary Charles from whipping Anne. It was as if that moment galvanized her decision, for she knew with calming certainty that leaving was the right thing to do and now was the right time to set the wheels in motion.

She tried nothing so pointless as to beat Sister Mary Charles at telling Mother Agnes about what had taken place in the flower room; therefore, by the time she and Mother Agnes met at eight o'clock that night, Mother Superior was cognizant of it all.

Sister Agnes waited in the empty community room after all the others had retired to their rooms.

"Come in, Sister Regina," she invited in a kindly tone, "and close the door if you like."

Sister Regina did so soundlessly. Her shoes squeaked as she approached and knelt for Mother Superior's blessing. A whisper, a touch on the head, and she rose, seating herself at a right angle to the other nun on an armchair with a stiffly upholstered seat and a straight back. The house was silent, the knitting and crocheting of recreation time returned to the drawers. A single dim lamp glowed on a corner table between the two nuns, the forty-watt bulb their standard of poverty in illumination, and from a crucifix on the wall the tortured Jesus looked down upon their black-clad figures.

Sister Regina spoke first, so softly she might have been speaking to a student during study time. "Thank you for seeing me, Mother Agnes."

The older woman nodded wordlessly. There was a curious peace in the room, no rush, no urgency.

"I imagine you're aware of what transpired in the flower room this noon."

Mother Agnes nodded again.

"Undoubtedly you thought that's what I'd come to talk about, but I've come about something far more significant than that. What happened in the flower room is only one small manifestation of a much larger . . . I shall call it a problem that I've been praying about." Sister Regina spoke low and slow, certain of her course. "I fear, Mother Agnes, that I've been growing more and more dissatisfied with my life here within the spiritual community. These feelings have been growing for a very long time."

"I've been aware of it, Sister."

"Of course you have." Sister Regina smiled up at Jesus on the wall and went on quietly. "I cannot say exactly when it began, but not this month, not last, not even this year. These things don't start on a given day, but grow from some . . . some unknown moment and I don't know when that moment began. But I realize, Mother, that I no longer belong here and I wish to seek a dispensation from my vows."

Much to Sister Regina's surprise, Mother Agnes showed no sign of shock. She said quite calmly, "I imagine you've prayed and reflected long and hard over this before speaking to me about it."

"Yes, Mother, I have."

"And you've asked God's help in making your decision?"

"Many times."

"Good. Then let me start by saying that it's not a sin to doubt your vows."

"In my head I know that. In my heart I feel differently, because I knew from the time I was eleven years old that this was what I wanted to be. Everybody said I should be a nun, especially my grandmother, who was the most deeply religious person I ever knew. She, above all, gave me to believe that life as a religious was the epitome of service to God, and that I was cut out for it above all my other brothers and sisters. In school, of course, there were nuns who said the same thing."

"And now you think they were wrong?"

"What I think, Mother Agnes, is that I was so very young and malleable, too young to question their opinion. And, of course, I realize that it was part of the nuns' duty to foster vocations, just as it's now a part of mine. Time and again I heard it—'Oh, Jean Marie, you'd make such a wonderful nun, you're suited to it in every way.' When it's the people you love and trust the most saying it—your grandmother and your teachers—you tend to believe them."

"What about your parents? Didn't they want you to go into the convent?"

"Oh, of course they did. Every Catholic family wanted one of its children to become a priest or a nun. But there were so many of us at home—nine kids—that one wouldn't be missed so much, and I always felt that they were pretty much resigned to the fact that they'd lose one of us. It was their duty to let one go. But my grandmother never thought of it as *losing* me. She always believed I was blessed above all the others."

They let silence fill the room for a while, contemplating what Sister Regina had said. Then Mother Agnes, with her fingers laced over her round stomach, gazed at the crucifix and remarked, "Every religious I know has someone like that who inspired them. What has made you change your mind, Sister?"

Sister Regina had thought through her answer long before the question was asked. "I've come to the slow realization that I wasn't as cut out for it as they all thought. I'm sorry to say that community life has not lived up to my expectations, and though I've tried and tried to find fulfillment in my relationship with God, I can never disassociate myself enough from worldly concerns to be completely at one with Him. I've always had a great deal of trouble honoring my vow of obedience, and lately I've begun to question everything. Holy Rule most of all. Much of it I find senseless and counterproductive, and I break it so often that I live in a constant state of guilt and repentance. Sometimes anger. Today . . . when Sister Mary Charles took Anne Olczak in the flower room, it was as if everything finally became crystal clear, and I knew the time was here to make this change in my life."

Mother Agnes ruminated awhile, nodding. Then she asked, "May we speak of the Olczak children, Sister? Because I think they hold a very special place in your heart."

"Yes, Mother, they do."

"And I think maybe that when their mother died you wanted very much to make up for their loss."

Sister Regina chose her words carefully. "The death of Krystyna Olczak has had a more profound effect on me than I ever believed possible."

"In what way, Sister?"

"She was . . ." Sister Regina didn't know how to put it. "She was the most nearly perfect mother, and daughter, and wife and parish supporter I've ever known. When she died, I guess I began assessing what she had given to the world and comparing it to what I as a nun give to the world, and for the first time I began questioning what my grandmother and the nuns always said, that a life as a religious was the epitome of service to God. I felt . . ." Sister Regina's voice dropped to a softer note. ". . . I felt as if they had lied to me. For Krystyna Olczak served God in as noble a way as I ever did. Perhaps nobler, for she had to do it without a book of holy rules that automatically takes care of all the vicissitudes of life. I am convinced that Krystyna Olczak is a saint today."

"You may be right. Tell me, do you feel bitter about the years you've spent as a religious?"

"Bitter? No, Mother, not bitter at all. When I entered the postulate I felt dedicated to the way of life and believed it was God's will for me, that His voice was within me and it was important and true. Lately I've spent much time in prayer and meditation, and I realize that His voice is *still* within me, and it's just as important that I listen to it now as it was then. God isn't just . . . well, He isn't just out there somewhere . . ." She gestured to the world at large. ". . . He's in here . . ." She tapped her heart. "He *is*, Mother Agnes. And I believe He's guiding me in my present decision."

Mother Agnes sat calm and thoughtful for a long while. Her elbows rested on the arms of her chair, hands joined, thumbs slowly circling. Outside the night wind made a faint whistle around the downspouts, and upstairs the hall floor creaked as someone tiptoed to the bathroom. "Well," Mother Agnes said at last, the single word coming out on a soft gust of breath. "That's a very powerful argument, Sister Regina. And I am the last one to try to convince you otherwise. This is your life, you must live it as you see fit."

This was not at all the response Sister Regina had expected. Her surprise showed.

"Do you mean that, Mother?"

"Of course I mean that. But let me say just one thing that I hope you'll take to heart. There are very few nuns I've known who haven't at one time or another questioned that they made the right choice. All but two decided to stay, and I believe all are happy with their choice, including me."

"You considered leaving?"

"Yes, I did." The older nun looked at her lap while remembering, and decided to share the story. "It was at a time when one of my real sisters, the one I was closest to when we were growing up, had just delivered her third stillborn baby, a beautiful full-term dead baby girl, the last one she would ever conceive. Afterward she asked for me. I went home and saw her tremendous sorrow, and her husband's sorrow that they would never have any children, and I grew very angry with God." The old nun paused and gazed down at her knees. "And while I was there, I ran into a doctor at the hospital who had been a young, handsome man the last time I'd seen him, a boy I dated in high school. He had recently lost his wife, and he confessed to me that he'd been in love with me all those years ago and I'd broken his heart when I entered the convent. There were . . . shall we say, temptations."

In the small puddle of lamplight, surrounded by high shadows, Sister Regina waited, surprised by the older nun's story. Then Sister Agnes drew a deep breath, lifted her chin and went on.

"But I, like you, heard the voice of God within me. Only He told me He needed me here, so I returned. Having been through the trial and triumphed over it, I found myself more fully committed than ever, and I've never been sorry a day for the path I chose."

Sister Regina's expression remained quiescent, like the Madonna's. Her hands were linked loosely underneath her scapular, which tented to her knees. She thought about what Sister Agnes had told her, surprised that Mother Superior had revealed so much of her personal history.

"Tell me, Sister," the older one asked, "has there been a similar temptation for you? Does your vow of chastity play a part in this?"

Sister Regina wondered how to respond. "I don't know how to answer that. A small part, perhaps, but more as a catalyst to make me reconsider the religious life I've chosen. In physical terms there's been not a word spoken, not a touch exchanged, not a single indiscretion of any kind whatsoever. I believe it's been more of an examination of what I've missed—marriage, children and the home life that goes along with it. And the freedoms. Those have been beckoning strongly for some time."

"I, too, thought of all that when I faced the doctor."

"The freedoms, too? I would not have thought . . ."

"The freedoms, too. We are, after all, humans, Sister."

They let a thoughtful moment spin past, then Sister Regina said, "Father Kuzdek told me I should talk to you, and that I might be surprised at what I heard. I am."

"Ah . . . so you've already been talking to Father."

"Yes."

"It's come that far, then."

"Yes, I'm afraid it has. I would very much like to go home and tell my family about my decision, especially my grandmother. It won't be easy telling her in person, but I'd rather do it that way than in a letter. Christmas vacation starts this week. The timing seems providential."

Sister Agnes finally showed some dismay—a quick indrawn breath. "So soon? Perhaps if you take a little more time to pray and meditate . . . make a retreat."

"I've already done that, Mother Agnes. I made a retreat last August for exactly this purpose, and I've said so many prayers since, and meditated and done penance. I've gone through the whole agonizing process, searching my soul, asking myself and God what is truly right for me, and I believe that God and I have reconciled ourselves to my decision. Now I need to reconcile it with my family."

Sister Agnes continued nodding solemnly.

"Well . . ." She sounded sad. ". . . so soon. I thought maybe next spring, when the school term is finished."

"I understand it can take as long as six months for the paperwork to go clear to Rome and back."

"Yes, but . . ." Mother Agnes let her shoulders droop. "Oh, dear." She sighed and glanced at the crucifix again. "I suppose I'm resisting out of purely selfish reasons because I don't want to lose you, Sister. You're one of our best teachers, and in spite of what you think of life within a religious community, you have added much to ours."

"Thank you, Mother."

"Have you made plans for your life outside the convent?"

"Not yet."

"It's my duty to advise you that this step can be very difficult. What will you do to earn a living, and where will you live?"

"I'm not sure yet, Mother, but I can always teach."

"I must warn you, the Catholic Church frowns on letting former nuns teach in their schools."

"Not even in another town?" It had been Sister Regina's plan to become a lay teacher in another parochial school.

"It's very doubtful."

"You mean they'll blackball me?"

"Blackball is a very strong word."

"But that's what it amounts to, doesn't it?"

Mother Superior's voice grew understanding. "It's my duty to prepare you for your life after you leave us, and to inform you of the Church's stand on these things."

They'll deny me a job? When I'm a qualified teacher and Mother Agnes considers me one of her best? The news went zinging its way through Sister Regina like an electric current. What went unsaid, what she suddenly understood with amazing clarity, was that once she doffed her habit, the Church was afraid she might influence other nuns to quit; her presence would be a reminder that it was possible. She was still reeling from the news when Mother Agnes inquired, "Will your family help you get established?"

"I . . . I don't know. They aren't wealthy. Just ordinary farmers who work hard for a living."

"Yes, well . . . these things have to be considered." What Mother Agnes was saying was that a nun who received a dispensation left with very little, for all property was community property, even gifts that nuns might have received over the years. Their Constitution forbade the ownership of either cash or worldly goods by an individual.

"I'll just have to take this one step at a time," Sister Regina replied. "I thought I'd speak to you first, then my family, then whomever I must see to take the necessary formal steps."

"That would be the prioress, Sister Vincent de Paul at Saint Ben's. You would go to her and state your intentions and fill out a form requesting the dispensation of vows, and she'd forward it to the president of the congregation, who will then send it to the Holy Father in Rome."

"And then . . . while I wait? What then?"

"You return here and continue as before, until the Holy Father signs the paper and it's returned to you."

"And that takes six months?"

"Approximately."

"I see." *There's public school,* Regina thought. *I could always teach in public school.* But the idea was repugnant: teaching in a place devoid of prayer. She wanted to remain close to the religious structure much the way a child swimming over his head for the first time wants a life buoy floating along by his side. "So, after I see Sister Vincent de Paul is time enough to think about my future."

"Yes. I suppose so."

They seemed to have covered everything, but Sister Regina still didn't have one important answer.

"So, about my going to see my family during Christmas vacation?"

Mother Agnes's face had grown long and sad. Nonetheless, she found a weak smile and said, "You have my permission."

Sister Regina reached out and touched the older woman's sleeve. "Please don't be sad for me, Mother Agnes."

Mother Agnes put a dry hand over Sister Regina's and gave it a light pat. "Don't be hasty, Sister Regina. Just don't be too hasty. Make very, very sure you're doing the right thing."

"I promise." She smiled. "Maybe that's why it takes six months . . . to give people a chance to reconsider."

"Yes . . . well . . ." Their hands parted and got tucked away in each lap. "Please kneel for my blessing."

On her knees before Mother Agnes, Sister Regina felt the faint touch on her head. A moment passed. Was that trembling in Mother Superior's hand? Mother Agnes drew a breath and spoke in a voice that had thinned to a small whisper. "Good and gentle Jesus . . ."

And though her prayer invoked the deity to guide Sister Regina in the choice she would be making during the next couple of weeks, the truth was the choice was already made. Now that she knew exactly what she had to do, Sister Regina made up her mind that before she returned from Christmas vacation she would go to St. Ben's and sign the papers that would release her from her vows.

Fourteen

❦

School let out for Christmas vacation on Friday, December fifteenth, and wouldn't resume until Tuesday, January second. Since Eddie had to work throughout vacation, the plans were made for the girls to spend the first week at Grandpa and Grandma Pribil's, and the second week at Grandpa and Grandma Olczak's. After a dismal week putting up the Christmas tree at home and trying to make a joyful occasion out of one that dredged up painful memories of Krystyna, Eddie succumbed to the girls' pressuring, got one of his nephews to ring the evening Angelus and took the girls out to their Grandma Pribil's late Friday afternoon.

Krystyna's mother was doing a valiant job of keeping her chin up. She told the girls they could help her bake Christmas cookies and she'd cook them *pirohis* and *kolach* with lots of *psypka* on top, just like their mommy used to make. And out in the barn, she said, they had a mother cat with four new baby kittens, and they could choose one to bring in the house and make a bed near the woodstove for it, and maybe when they went back home they could ask their daddy if they could take it and keep it for their own.

Grandpa Pribil took them out to the barn and they chose a fluffy striped kitten with a tail straight as an asparagus sprout. Aunt Irene said it was the color of burnt sugar so the girls decided her name should be Sugar.

For Eddie, it was once again comfortable being with Irene. He gave her a hug and kiss on the cheek when he arrived, and felt free from the constraints of the past several months. He could be her friend again, nothing more. After a delicious home-cooked meal she helped her mother prepare, Irene brought out some homemade chokecherry wine and the playing cards, and said, "What do you say, Eddie, should we take on Ma and Pa in a few games of Smear?" So she and Eddie were partners, spending a long evening in the warm kitchen, playing cards and drinking wine. When Eddie decided it was time to go home, he left the girls tucked beneath cozy feather ticks with Sugar between them: there was no question of the cat sleeping behind the range.

The Pribil house had a small screenless back porch that jutted off the kitchen and held the washing machine in the summer and barrels full of frozen meats in the winter. Mary threw a misshapen blue sweater over her housedress and stepped onto the porch with Eddie as he was leaving. They paused at the top of the steps and looked out at Eddie's truck. A light snow was settling on its green paint, and in the sky a murky blue moon shone through the light flurries that fell lazily, like eiderdown.

Eddie put his arm around his mother-in-law's shoulder and gave her a hard squeeze. "Oh, Mary . . ." He sighed, dropping his head back. "How're we gonna make it through this, huh?"

"I don't know, Eddie. I just don't know."

"I put up a Christmas tree, but my heart wasn't in it."

"I know. I know."

He squeezed her again. "Appreciate your letting the girls stay out here this week."

"Oh, don't you say nothing, Eddie. That's about the best thing that can happen anymore is them two coming out here."

"You and Irene are gonna spoil them good this week, I know."

"You bet. As much as we can."

"And Pa, too."

"Yup. Pa, too. He don't say much, but he misses Krystyna something awful. She was always sort of his favorite, you know."

Behind them Krystyna's father came out of the house, shrugging on a frayed blue-denim barn jacket. "Better go out t'the barn, check the livestock one more time." His heavy hand landed on Eddie's back in passing. " 'Night, son."

" 'Night, Pa. Thanks for everything."

From down the path Richard lifted a hand without turning his head.

The two on the step watched him walk away, his back slightly stooped, while in the kitchen behind them Irene cleared away wineglasses and cards, and wiped off the kitchen table.

Mary said, "Richard and me, we sort of had hopes for you and Irene, but lately it seems like—well, something happened there."

"Yup. Something happened there. It wouldn't work, Mary."

"Forget I mentioned it. You can't fill Krystyna's shoes that easy, I know."

"Nope." Eddie sighed and dropped his arm from Mary's shoulders. "Well . . . better go. Angelus comes early."

They kissed cheeks and hugged goodnight.

"Take it easy," he said.

And she, mastering the urge to get teary-eyed, thumped him on the nape without another word.

From the window in the kitchen door, Irene watched Eddie all the while he walked to his truck, got in, started the engine and turned around in the farmyard. She watched with a yearning that filled her throat and eyes and made her heart feel like bursting. She was still watching when he rolled slowly out the driveway and headed off down the gravel road, leaving twin tracks in the snow.

he next day Eddie worked in the abandoned school building, taking down the Christmas trees from all the classrooms and burning them in the incinerator by Father Kuzdek's garage. With the help of Romaine's boy, Joey, he moved all the wooden folding chairs out of the storage room at the back of the gymnasium and washed and waxed that floor, then the gymnasium floor as well.

His workdays were filled with routine, especially in winter when the ancient furnace was running. Every day he oiled the water pumps on the boiler and twice a day checked the water level inside it, keeping it at ten feet, and also the boiler gauges, making sure they stayed below 130°. If the furnace started pounding, which it did frequently in extremely cold weather, he had to open the air cockpits on the radiators and bleed them. Near the end of each day he filled the coal hopper for overnight.

That's what he was doing when Romaine found him in the coal bin around quarter to four that afternoon.

"Hey, little brother, been looking for you."

Eddie stopped shoveling and pushed his blue-striped work cap back on his head. "Yeah? So what for?"

"Saturday afternoon, and I hear your kids are gone to the farm. Thought maybe you'd want to stop by the liquor store and have a couple of bumps."

"Yeah, sure. Why not? You grab that shovel over there and give me a hand with this coal and we'll get out of here a little faster."

They finished filling the hopper, Eddie checked the gauges and water pumps one last time, and they climbed into Eddie's truck and drove a block and a half to the liquor store. Outside it was one of those gray, murky days with the wind swirling up your pants legs and slapping your lapel against your cheek. Inside it was smoky and stale and lit by neon beer signs. The same drunks sat on the same stools they occupied every day. A desultory dice game was in progress at one end of the bar. On the jukebox Vaughn Monroe was singing *Ghost Riders in the Sky.* Clothespinned to a long drooping wire along the deep left wall were dance bills advertising New Year's Eve bands at all the dance halls around the area, as well as an advertisement showing Ralph Bellamy smoking a Camel. An outdated campaign poster had a picture of Slip Walter, who'd run for Sheriff. At the Clarissa Theater, Spencer Tracy and Katharine Hepburn were playing in *Adam's Rib* and at Long Prairie it was *Ma and Pa Kettle Go to Town*. But in the municipal liquor store it was the same depressing business as usual.

Romaine ordered a straight shot of whiskey with a water chaser.

Eddie ordered a bottle of Grain Belt.

Their drinks came, they made the senseless toast, "Bumps!" and wet their throats.

Romaine clapped his glass down and said, "So, how goes it, Eddie?"

"Horseshit," Eddie replied.

"It's that time of year. Tough."

"Yeah, tough all right. Who wants to play Santa Claus alone?"

"Rose thinks you and the girls ought to sleep at our house on Christmas Eve, then the girls can open their stockings with our kids. You could all come over after Midnight Mass and spend the rest of the night. What do you say?"

"I *think* the girls would like that . . . but you never know."

"Why don't you ask them?"

"I already know what Lucy would say: 'How will Santa find us at Auntie Rose's?' "

Romaine laughed. "That is a problem, I know, but I'm sure you'll dream up an answer."

The door opened and one of the locals, Louie Kulick, walked in. He perched on a barstool next to Eddie and said, "Where's Sister Regina going?"

"What do you mean?"

"Sister Regina's standing outside waiting for the bus."

Eddie perked up and glanced at the door. "She is?"

"Funny thing is she's all alone." The nuns always traveled with partners. Everybody knew this.

Eddie set down his bottle of beer and said, "Be right back, Romaine."

The wind caught the plate-glass door and set it back against the recessed entrance. Below the Greyhound sign on Dan and Mary Jonczkowski's restaurant next door, Sister Regina was standing on the sidewalk with a small cardboard suitcase at her ankle. She clutched a thick black hand-knit cape to her throat, with her veil caught beneath it and held from flying skyward. The veil nevertheless billowed to its limits, and she looked frozen in place, shuddering in the cold of the darkening afternoon as she gazed northward, hoping to see a bus approach.

"Sister Regina?" he said from behind her.

She spun suddenly at the sound of his voice and said breathlessly, "Oh, Mr. Olczak!"

"Are you waiting for the bus?"

"Yes. But it's late, it seems."

"Why don't you wait inside?"

She glanced at the window and offered him only a faint smile in answer.

"Oh," he said. "The beer." The Greyhound stop was a bar as well as a restaurant.

"I'm fine out here."

"You're freezing out here."

She only smiled and gazed northward again.

"Sister, it's . . . I mean . . . pardon me for asking, but where's your partner? Isn't anyone traveling with you?"

"I'm alone today, Mr. Olczak."

"Oh." His puzzlement showed on his face, so she decided to tell him the rest. "I'm going home for Christmas."

He broke into a smile. "Ah, isn't that nice? And home, if I remember right, is over by Foley someplace."

"My parents have a farm near Gilman, yes."

"Oh, that's right. Gilman." He did a quick calculation and guessed it was between an hour and a half and two away—that is, *if* the bus went all the way to Gilman. Generally the Greyhound didn't stop at every little burg on the side roads, but stuck to the bigger towns along the main highways.

If you considered stops, and possibly a change of bus in St. Cloud, she'd be lucky to reach her destination by ten o'clock that night.

"Will the bus take you all the way there? To Gilman, I mean?"

"Not quite."

"To where?"

"You needn't worry about me, Mr. Olczak."

"To where, Sister? St. Cloud? Foley?" She looked away to the north again, and her veil filled with wind. He stood at her shoulder, persisting. "And from there, how're you getting to the farm? Let me drive you, Sister."

"Oh no, Mr. Olczak." She spun to him, and he detected a note of panic in her voice. "I've already bought my ticket. The bus will be coming soon, I'm sure."

"I can take you right out to your folks' farm. Let me." His voice softened. "Please."

They stood in the gray dusk of near evening with the light from the restaurant window painting one side of their faces, she still clutching the black knit wrap with a black gloved hand, he with his hands stuffed into the rib pockets of a very old navy-blue wool jacket.

"Where are your children?" she inquired.

"Out at their grandpa and grandma Pribil's. And my house is so lonely that I don't even want to turn the Christmas-tree lights on, so I go to this liquor store and sit with a bunch of other lonely men who should be home with their wives, only they're too stupid to know what they've got, so here they sit getting drunk. Let me take you . . . please, Sister."

She wanted very badly to say yes, but could not. Glancing away from him she admitted, "I'm not allowed. Not without a partner."

"I'll use Romaine's car. You can sit in the back. I'll take you right to your mother and father's door."

With her hands wrapped inside her knit shawl she covered her mouth and chin, staring northward at the highway, where still no bus appeared.

"Are your parents expecting you?" he persisted.

He could tell from how she stared at the distance and refused to answer that they weren't.

"Do they have a telephone?" he asked. Still no answer, so he said, "They don't, do they?" Very few farmers did. In most of Minnesota the telephone lines weren't strung out into the country.

"I have an uncle in Foley," she finally replied. "I'm sure he would give me a ride out to the farm."

The streetlights came on and a patron from the liquor store stumbled out and went the opposite direction down the sidewalk.

Eddie's patience was growing thin. He'd never known how stubborn she was. "Pardon me, but this is stupid, Sister, that you should wait for a bus that's late, in weather like this, then wander around St. Cloud or Foley— maybe both—in the middle of the night, not even knowing when you'll get home. Would Krystyna have let you do that without trying to help? Well, neither will I. You wait here, I'll be right back."

He went back into the liquor store and told Romaine, "Got to borrow your car. Sister Regina needs a ride to Gilman and I better not take her in my truck. Will you ring the Angelus for me at six?"

"Sure."

"Thanks. If you need my truck, take it. Keys are in it."

Romaine's car was parked across the street with the keys in the ignition. Eddie made a U-turn at the corner, swung back to the curb and got out beside Sister. He put her suitcase in the backseat, let her get in beside it without so much as touching her on the arm, then slammed the door.

When he was seated behind the wheel again, he said, "I see there's a blanket back there. Better put it over your lap 'cause it'll take a while for the heater to warm up and even when it does, not much heat gets back there."

She covered her lap and watched the snowflakes parting like blown hair in the headlights, worrying all the while about giving the ticket money back to Mother Superior. She'd had to request money to buy the ticket in the first place; that's how it was done. Whenever a nun requested money for a special need, Mother Superior made a judgment as to whether or not the communal coffers should be dipped into. It had been embarrassing for Sister Regina to ask for money, given why she was asking—ultimately to enable her to leave her vocation. When she got back here at the end of

Christmas vacation she'd have to cash in the ticket and return the money to Mother Superior. Then she would have to admit that she'd ridden with Mr. Olczak, unchaperoned.

"How's the heat back there?" he asked. "Any of it getting to you?"

"Yes, it's warming up nicely, thank you."

"I thought I'd go to Long Prairie, then cut straight over east to Pierz, and south out of there toward Foley. How far is Gilman from Foley?"

"Just a few miles on this side."

"Good. Well, then you give me directions when we get closer."

After that he drove in silence.

She could make out the silhouette of his head against the windshield, the line of his cap, his right ear, right shoulder. It wasn't bad enough she was breaking Holy Rule with every mile they traveled; she was indulging in forbidden thoughts about him. The physical attraction he held for her, combined with his thoughtfulness, his loneliness, his very *availability* put a sharp pang up high beneath her ribs. It was a heady thought that in a mere six months from now such simple pleasure as riding in an automobile with a man she liked would be hers to enjoy whenever the opportunity arose.

What if he knew she was going to seek a dispensation of vows? What would he say? How would he react to the news? She experienced a spell of disembodiment, a floating feeling of unreality, as if it could not possibly be her riding in this car. As if it could not have been her who'd stood on the sidewalk only a short while ago and allowed him to make a decision for her that was sharply against all the vows she had taken. Obedience would have meant riding the bus as Mother Superior expected her to do. Poverty would have meant taking the less comfortable mode of travel. Chastity— ah, well, her adherence to the vow of chastity seemed to have been blown sky-high a hundred times since September when Eddie Olczak's wife had died.

The astounding truth was that she wanted to tell him why she was going home. But she was still a nun for at least another half a year, and during that time she was expected to comport herself according to the rules of the order.

She cast her eyes away from the view of his profile in an effort to keep her thought pure. He had a St. Christopher medal on the dashboard and she concentrated on it for a while. Then she found her rosary inside her habit, deep inside where it was warm and cozy from the blanket he'd so thoughtfully provided. She clung to the wooden beads, sleek beneath the fingers of her flannel gloves.

Dear God, silence me.

Don't let me tell him.

I must not tell him.

It would be wrong to tell him.

At Long Prairie they turned left and headed out into the flat farmland between there and Little Falls—twenty-five miles of darkness lit only by the headlights, the falling snow and an occasional yard light on a barn.

She had grown so accustomed to the silence that she jumped when he asked, "Sister, am I allowed to talk to you?"

"About what, Mr. Olczak?"

"That day you stopped Sister Mary Charles from beating Anne." He waited, but she said nothing, so he went on. "I mean, I don't want to make you sin again or anything, but you said you didn't get in trouble for stepping in, and I think you did. Are they . . . well . . . I don't know exactly how to say it . . . are they deporting you or something?"

"Deporting me?"

"You know—sending you away for crossing Sister Mary Charles?"

"Oh, gracious, *no*, Mr. Olczak! They don't do things like that."

"Then, why are you going home?"

"I told you, to spend Christmas with my family."

"I happen to know, Sister, that you're not allowed to go home but maybe once every couple years or so."

"Five."

"Five?"

"Five years. We're allowed to go home once every five years."

"Once every five years . . ." he whispered in horror. "Why, Sister, that's just terrible! They're your family!" He cleared his throat and sat up straighter. "Sorry, Sister. It's just that I don't know what I'd do if somebody told me I couldn't see my family for five years."

"My religious community is my family."

"It still must be hard. And I don't see any reason why they do that to you." He thought for a while, then asked, "Wasn't it about two years ago when Krystyna took you home for your folks' silver-wedding anniversary and Sister Dora went along with you?"

She said nothing so he turned the rearview mirror until he could see her in it. Her features were only suggestions in the reflected headlights, but the dots of light in her eyes told him she was looking squarely at the mirror.

"If you were home two years ago, what are they letting you go again for? This *does* have something to do with my kids, doesn't it?" he insisted. "You're getting reprimanded for sticking up for them, aren't you?"

"No, Mr. Olczak. I told you . . . no."

"Pardon me, Sister, I don't mean any disrespect, but I don't believe you." They rode for a while staring at what they could make out of each other in the rearview mirror. Then he righted it and they rode in silence once again.

She longed to tell him. But it was not allowed. Leaving one's religious vocation was done under a veil of secrecy, to protect the Church from the stigma, she surmised. There was a chapter covering it in their Constitution which she'd read many times this past year. It made quite clear that while waiting for the dispensation, Holy Rule and the Constitution were to be strictly adhered to.

They rode the remainder of the way with few words between them. In Little Falls they had to wait for a freight train at the Mississippi River crossing, and while it rumbled past, they sat in the glow of the headlights from the car behind them, the quiver from the speeding wheels trembling up through the car seats, adding to their unsettled nerves. They stared at the flashing stream of freight cars, at the loose snow whipped up by the wheels, and at the blinking red lights on the black-and-white striped yardarm that had halted them.

And sometimes they thought of Krystyna being hit by that train.

And sometimes they thought of each other.

And the weight of their mutual attraction for each other felt like those wheels were running smack across their chests.

This is it," she said after forty-five more minutes of silence broken only by her directions. "Pull right up next to the apple trees."

A dog started barking and a yard light came on.

Eddie pulled up where she'd told him to, killed the lights and engine, then turned around and looked at her over the seat. "Sister, look, I'm sorry."

"You have nothing to be sorry for, Mr. Olczak. I appreciate th—"

"Yes! I do!" She was folding the blanket, and he grabbed her arm through it. Even through four layers of wool the contact ricocheted through both of them. "Don't . . . don't . . . !" His eyes burned with frustration as he stared at her and tried to think of what to say. *Don't call me Mr. Olczak anymore!*

"Don't what?"

"There's something that . . ." He was so confused about what he sensed happening between them that he could not go on. There was no protocol for this kind of thing, falling in love with a nun.

"I must go in," she said in the calm, quiet way he'd always known, freeing her arm without making an issue of it. "My folks are wondering who's out here."

"Sister, please . . ." he said miserably. "I've never argued with a nun before, not with one I liked. I shouldn't have said what I did. I'm sorry."

She knew perfectly well the best way to handle this was to pretend nothing had happened at all, no attraction, no argument, no touch. "Thank you for giving me a ride all this way. I hope you'll be all right on the way home." She placed the folded blanket neatly on the seat. "I know you will, with Saint Christopher looking after you."

"You just tell me when, and I'll come back and get you," he offered.

"That won't be necessary. I have to stop at Saint Benedict's on my way home, and I'm sure my dad will take me."

"Well . . . okay, then. Merry Christmas."

"Merry Christmas to you, too."

He got out and opened the rear door for her, and reached inside for her suitcase. As they headed for the house the dog circled them, wagging and sniffing, and a woman's voice called, "Jean, is that you?"

"Yes, it's me, Mama."

"Oh my gracious me, it *is* you!"

And the man's voice, full of sudden emotion and disbelief. "Regina?" He used the Polish derivative, rolling the R in the old-world way, pronouncing it with a hard *g*.

Then they were leaving the shelter of the glassed-in back porch and hurrying down the walk. Eddie watched them hug, thinking over and over, *Her name is Jean. Her name is Jean.* Her father tried to wrest the suitcase from Eddie, saying, "Here, let me take that."

"No, sir, I've got it. I'll take it to the house."

"Well, who's this, then?" the older man said.

"This is Mr. Olczak, Daddy, our janitor at St. Joseph's. He was kind enough to drive me on this ugly night."

"Mr. Olczak." They shook hands. "We've heard your name."

The dog was barking. Her mother was crying. Her father said, "Enough of that now, Bertha. Better get inside before we all freeze to death."

Eddie planned to slip the suitcase onto the porch step and make a hasty retreat, but Frank and Bertha Potlocki would have none of it. Frank said, "Come on in here and warm up. Bertha will get you a cup of coffee before you head back."

"By all means, Mr. Olczak," Bertha said, remembering her manners before relapsing into surprise. "My goodness gracious, I can't believe this! Our Jean dropping in out of nowhere!"

The kitchen was as ordinary as field straw, but spotlessly clean. There was a cast-iron wood range, a table as big as a hay wagon, eight spindled chairs and worn blue linoleum on the floor. A water pail with a dipper, a white porcelain washbasin and a pantry, where Bertha Potlocki went to find coffee. She filled the pot from the water pail, while Frank stirred up the coals and dropped two pieces of firewood into the stove.

Then they all sat at the table and Bertha asked her daughter, "How long are you staying?"

"For Christmas."

With one hand Bertha covered her daughter's hand on top of the oilcloth. With the other she covered her own mouth. The tears that shot into her eyes told how long it had been since this had happened.

"You should have told us you were coming," Frank said.

"I would've made you some prune coffee cakes," Bertha added.

"We'll make some together, Mama. I'll help you."

"Wait till your grandma finds out you're here. Oh, Jean, how that woman misses you."

"How is she?"

As they talked, Eddie saw that Regina (Jean) Potlocki had grown up much like he, in this big drafty farmhouse, surrounded by people she loved. A mother with a face burned red from cooking on a wood range, and a father who, even in the dead of winter, sported a white head above his hat line, and a red face below. Somewhere on the glassed-in porch his overalls and boots must have been waiting, for the faint smell of the barn lingered even above the aroma of boiling coffee. Through a trapdoor in the kitchen floor, Bertha disappeared and came up with a quart jar of home-canned peach sauce. From the pantry came sauce dishes and a blue roaster full of home-baked buns. From out on the chilly porch, a bowl of butter and a pitcher of thick cream that had come straight from the separator.

Eddie wondered again how Sister Regina had tolerated being cut off from them.

She asked her mother, buttering a bun even before the coffee was done, "Do you have any chokecherry jelly?"

"Oh, how could I forget?" Bertha was up, lifting the trapdoor again to protestations of "No, no, Mama, you don't have to get it just for me!"

But she did. Up came a pint of chokecherry jam as clear and dark as wine, and Eddie watched the woman across the table fold her hands and say a quick prayer to the crucifix on the kitchen wall before slathering her bun with the rich memory of home. She took a huge bite, and looked up, with butter in the corners of her mouth, and saw him watching her with a smile.

She blushed.

And his heart thrilled.

And she remembered that she wasn't allowed to eat with seculars, but found her mother's homemade bread and chokecherry jelly too wonderful to resist.

At the door, when he was leaving, Eddie faced Sister Regina with her parents four feet away, hiding the things he was feeling. Here, amid her loved ones, she seemed like an ordinary person. He had met her parents. He had seen the house where she was raised. He had watched her eating a bun with butter shining in the corners of her mouth. Between a nun and a secular, these were intimacies. Saying goodbye to her felt like another intimacy.

"If you know what day you'd like to come back, I can come and get you."

"Oh, no thank you, Mr. Olczak. Daddy will take me wherever I need to go."

"You bet we will, won't we, Mother? All the way back to Browerville whenever she wants."

"That's for sure we will. Thank you so much for bringing her," Bertha added.

Frank shook Eddie's hand. "Now you have a safe trip back."

"I will. It looks like the snow's letting up."

Eddie glanced at Sister and felt the insane desire to hug her. He had the sharp impression that if he did, she'd hug him back. Instead, he dropped his head to put his cap on.

"Merry Christmas, Mr. Olczak," she said quietly, her hands once again properly tucked inside her sleeves.

"Same to you, Sister."

"And God bless you."

"You, too." He backed away a step, nodded, opened the door and said, "Frank . . . Bertha . . . nice to meet you."

"Same here," they said, and turned him out into the snow to drive home and wonder if it was a mortal sin to fall in love with a nun.

Fifteen

❦

The morning after Sister Regina got home, she went into town with her folks to St. Peter and Paul's for nine o'clock Mass. The snow had stopped and the sun was bright. The county plows had been through, but a strong wind lifted the surface snow and scalloped the edge of the road with it. The countryside was familiar, the silos forming the same constellations as when Regina was a girl. Riding in the backseat of her father's 1938 Ford, she wondered, *Will I live here again? Will they let me move in if I need to? And if so, how long will I stay?*

At church they sat in the fifth row from the front, the same pew they'd always used. They had just arrived and were still kneeling, saying silent prayers, when Grandma Rosella got there. Regina could tell that her grandmother had spotted her from behind because the old woman was breathless and glowing when she rose from genuflecting and slipped into the pew.

"Well for-*ev*-ermore!" she whispered, and

threw a bluff hug on her granddaughter, nearly pulling Regina's veil off its hatpin. "Where did *you* come from?"

"Hi, Grandma."

"You should have more consideration for an old woman's heart."

That's all she would say: Rosella Potlocki did not talk in church. To have said as much as she had was a measure of her elation at finding her favorite granddaughter home.

Once, however, in the middle of Mass, she captured Regina's hand and squeezed it long and hard, holding it firmly against her midsection. Her eyes remained riveted on the altar, but her love for Regina was as palpable as the soft black cloth of her winter coat.

Grandma Rosella lived in town, near enough that she could walk to church as often as she liked. Her husband, a retired farmer who spent all his days in a pool hall drinking and playing pinochle, had fallen away from Catholicism years ago. Regina never once remembered him going to church. She'd never been close to him, had, in fact, always held a modicum of fear of her Grandpa Potlocki, a crusty old man who shunned family reunions, always needed a shave, spit tobacco juice on the street, and called her "Girlie" the few times he'd spoken to her at all.

The result of Walter Potlocki's bibulousness and godlessness was a marriage that had rived years ago. He and his wife slept under the same roof, but in separate rooms. They occasionally ate at the same table, but had little to say to one another. For the most part they went their separate ways. Consequently, Rosella had learned how to drive; never gotten a legal driver's license, mind you, only learned how to keep a car between the ditches so she could go visit her children whenever she wanted.

When Mass ended that Sunday morning, there was no question she'd go straight out to Frank and Bertha's house and stay for dinner and the afternoon. She didn't even bother to ask, but announced as soon as they cleared the vestibule, "Sister Regina will ride out home with me. I'll bring the pork roast I put in the oven. Can I bring anything else, Bertha?"

"No, Rosella, the roast will be fine. I'm sure everybody else will show up with food, too. But I don't think you should drive on these roads."

"She's right, Mama," Frank spoke up. "Even though the plows have been through, the roads are a little slippery yet."

"Oh, bosh." Rosella pulled a red wool scarf from her coat sleeve and tied it on over her black felt hat, anchoring it in place. "You live two miles from church, Frank. If my car goes in the ditch, I can walk them two miles, don't think I can't!" She commandeered Regina's arm and descended the church steps with the wind slapping their clothes and shaking last-night's snow off the trees. They walked to Rosella's house through the blinding light of the unobstructed sun on the newly fallen snow, both of them with black missals pressed against their ribs, the older woman retaining her tight grip on her granddaughter's arm. The wind and chill bothered them little: they took their time. Being together again was precious in both women's eyes, a blessing, they believed, from God who had also given them this sublime winter's day, food for their table, family with whom to gather, and their good health.

"So, how have you been?" Sister Regina asked as they trod down the edge of the street.

"Busy getting ready for Christmas, baking coffee cakes, making doll clothes and sugar cookies for the grandkids."

"How's Grandpa?"

"That old fool. Never changes. Worthless as always."

"He's still not going to church?"

"He'll never change. Drunk three-fourths of the time and grouchy the other fourth."

"I pray for him every day."

"So do I, but it don't do no good."

"How many years have you been married?"

"More than I care to count. So how are you? How's things in Browerville?"

They veered onto a sidewalk that had been shoveled, and Regina stepped more slowly, grateful for this opportunity to speak to her grandmother privately.

"Well . . . things could be better with me, Grandma."

"How so?"

"I've come home to tell you something and I . . . well, I wanted to tell you while we were alone together. Actually, I'm glad we got the chance to be alone together so I *could* tell you."

"What is it, Jean? You sick?" Rosella stopped to examine her grand-daughter's face. "My goodness, if it's—"

"No, Gram, I'm not sick." Sister Regina moved on, forcing her grand-mother to do the same, Rosella's hand still clutching her granddaughter's elbow. "This will be very hard for you to hear, as hard as it was for me to decide, but . . . I'm going to leave the convent, Grandma."

"Oh no . . . and you liked it there so much! Where are they sending you next?"

"No, you don't understand, Grandma." Sister stopped walking and looked directly into her grandmother's eyes. "I'm asking for a dispensation of vows. I'm leaving my vocation for good."

Grandma Rosella's mouth opened, her face etched in lines of dismay. "Nooo," she whispered in disbelief.

"Yes, I am," Sister Regina assured her gently. "It's been a very difficult decision, one over which I've prayed many long hours and many long months."

"After all these years it took you?"

Sister nodded.

"And how hard you studied?"

"Yes."

"But . . . but why?"

"Because the life in a religious community isn't what I thought it would be."

"What does that mean—'isn't what you thought it would be'?" Grandma Rosella sounded piqued. "You were around nuns all your life! You knew what their life was like!"

Sister Regina tried to explain, but she could see her explanation was falling on stubborn ears. She touched upon many of the problems with which she'd been struggling—the difficulty of living with a bunch of women whose personalities sometimes clashed; the strict rules that often forbade worthwhile relationships and pursuits; the feeling of being isolated from some important aspects of life; the certainty that she'd made her decision at too young an age, before she'd matured enough to weigh the life of sacrifice against that of being a wife and mother.

"It's a man, isn't it?" Rosella asked, her expression pinched tight with disapproval.

"No. Although, in the future, I hope to have a husband and maybe even children of my own before I'm too old."

"It's a man," Grandma said conclusively, just as they reached her driveway. Sealing up her mouth, she marched ahead toward the house with censure in every step. She'd lived with a man she found odious for so long, it was beyond Rosella Potlocki how anyone could want to tie herself to one of the disgusting things.

"It's not a man," Regina called after her, "but it's his children, as well as all the other things I tried to explain! Will you listen to me, Grandma?"

"I'm listening."

"No, you're not. You're mad." Someone had shoveled Rosella's narrow driveway that went from the tiny wooden garage right past the kitchen door. Regina figured her grandmother had probably gotten up in the dark before church and done it herself. She was wiry enough, stubborn enough and independent enough not to expect anybody—including her husband—to do anything for her. She had learned years ago not to rely on him for much.

Rosella, visibly upset, entered the house, leaving Sister Regina outside in the cold.

Regina sighed and followed, understanding what a blow this was to her grandmother. Inside, she closed the kitchen door and said, "Grandma, I know it's hard for you to understand."

"You were doing what *I* wanted to do but my folks didn't have the money for—going off to study in a convent," Rosella said accusingly, for she herself had paid Regina's tuition. "I don't understand how you can give it up. It's the most esteemed way to serve God."

"No, it isn't. You always told me it was, but I'm convinced it's just as holy in God's eyes to be a good wife and mother."

Rosella swung around and held Sister Regina by both arms. "Jean, Jean, Jean," she said, "you were *chosen* by *God.*"

"No, Grandma. I was chosen by you. And by Mama and Daddy, because it was a great source of pride to have one of the family go into a religious vocation. You put the idea into my head from the time I entered parochial school, and I'm not bitter about it, but please understand. I gave it all these years and now I want some years for myself."

Rosella's eyeglasses had begun steaming up. She stripped them off, turned away from her granddaughter, and tossed them on the kitchen table. "I got to take my roast out of the oven."

Sister Regina's joy at being back in this familiar house was eclipsed by her grandmother's reaction to the news. She had expected disappointment. She had not expected anger. But there it was, marching around the kitchen in the form of this diminutive woman with the scarf tied over her Sunday hat, and her coat hem arching up to reveal brown cotton stockings when she leaned over the open oven door.

"Where's Grandpa?" Regina asked, hoping to melt her grandmother some.

"Sleeping it off. Where else do you think he'd be on a Sunday morning?" Rosella wrapped her roaster in newspaper which she tied on with a snow-white dishtowel. "Let's go," she ordered, and headed outside, making it clear she was still upset.

The garage doors were hinged on the sides. Together they folded them back and left them open while they went into the garage and got into a ten-year-old Chevy. Then Rosella backed out, scraping the left side of the car on the lilac hedge all the way to the street. She buried the back bumper in the snowbank across the street, unaware she'd done so, grinding the gears as she shifted into low and headed toward the church steeple and the country roads beyond. She drove sitting on a sofa pillow, gripping the wheel with both hands, with enough space between her and the seat back that she could have carried her roaster there. She asked one question on their way out to Frank and Bertha's farm, asked it without taking her eyes from the road.

"Well, if you ain't gonna get married afterwards, what you gonna do?"

Sister Regina answered, "I don't know."

The word had spread throughout the family that Jean was home, and the house filled with her sisters and brothers and their families. There were eighteen people around the table by the time the meal was served, and, with no formal planning, food enough for everyone.

Sister Regina led them saying grace, but the words of the prayer were the last that Rosella uttered. Twice during the meal Bertha said to her, "Mama, is something wrong? Aren't you feeling good?"

But the old woman kept her lip stubbornly buttoned.

Regina waited to announce her news to the family until the children had left the table and were playing with metal cars on the kitchen floor. When only the adults remained over the remnants of their pie, when the coffee cups had been refilled and the group had grown sated and lazy, only then did she speak. "I have something to tell all of you . . . especially you, Mama and Daddy."

The dining room was much quieter than earlier, and it grew quieter still. With every eye resting on her, Sister Regina spoke in a soft but resolute voice.

"Grandma already knows. I told her after church. Now I want the rest of you to know. I've decided that I don't want to be a nun anymore. I'm writing to Rome and asking for a dispensation of my vows."

Bertha's hand flew to her lips. Her eyes flashed to Frank's. His to her. They both gaped at Sister Regina.

Nobody knew what to say. Eyes met eyes all around the table, wives to husbands, husbands to wives. And every single person there thought, *It's a man.*

Bertha was the first to find her voice. "You don't mean that, Regina."

"Yes, Mama, I do."

"How can you *do* this to us?"

I'm not doing anything to you, Mother, she thought, but of course she didn't say it.

Then everybody started babbling at once.

"What will Father Whalen say?"

"Nobody quits the convent."

"But Jean . . ."

"Jesus, Mary, Joseph . . ." (whispered, accompanied by the sign of the cross).

"I knew it. I knew something was wrong when they let her come home for Christmas."

"It's that man who brought you home, isn't it?"

"Some *man* brought her home?"

"I'll never be able to face my friends again."

"After all that money it cost Grandma Rosella to send you through the convent?"

"Shh, keep your voices down! The kids will hear!"

The comments burbled on and on until Grandma Rosella stopped them by bursting into tears. In the midst of all that patter, without offering a word herself, she put her face into her hands and let loose with a bunch of noisy sobs that shook her skinny shoulders. This woman who claimed her place as the undisputed hub of the family, who was daunted by nothing, who had lived with a drunk for years and coped without his help and never felt sorry for herself for a day; this woman who had faith enough for the entire family, had they not had it for themselves . . . this woman was weeping.

Frank got up and went around the table to her. "Ma . . ." he said, dropping down to one knee with an arm around her shoulders. "It's not the end of the world, Ma."

"Oh y . . . yes, it is. Yes, it is . . . for me, it is." The words came out muffled into her hands. Finally she lifted her ravaged face. "That's all I ever w . . . wanted was for my little Jean to be a nun, and now what does she d . . . do but betray me."

Regina felt a bubble of anger pop inside, but she kept her voice meek. "I'm not betraying you, Grandma."

"God, then. You're betraying God. You made a vow to Him."

"With provisions for renouncing that vow."

"Are you talking back to me? What's got into you, talking back to your grandma that way?"

"I'm not talking back to you. I'm trying to make you understand."

Rosella raised her voice, angry, too. "You go ahead, then, and you tell the rest of them what you told me about why you're quitting! You see if they believe it any more than I do! It's a man—that's what it is! Nuns don't give up their habits unless there's a man involved!"

Someone else asked, "Can you still go to heaven if you do this?"

Her mother said, "If there's a man, Jean, you might as well go ahead and tell us. We'll find out sooner or later, anyway."

Her father said, "Now, Mother, give her time."

"Well, it was a man who drove her home last night!"

"It was?" one of her sisters said, surprised. "Is it him, Jean?"

Someone started reciting an Act of Faith and the hubbub mounted again.

Sister Regina Marie, O.S.B., who usually maintained a mien of composure that the saints themselves would envy, stood up and shouted at the top of her lungs, "Stop it, every one of you! Stop it right this minute!"

Their mouths shut like gopher traps and they stared at her, the soft-spoken nun with the gentle manner, who had finally reached the end of her rope.

She made a ball and socket of her hands and pressed them to her mouth. Inside, her heart was clattering. It had felt fantastic, shouting. Felt so horrid, being misunderstood. Felt so hurtful that they wouldn't consider her happiness first before their own. That they'd renounce her for her decision without asking with open minds what it was that made her change over the years. Without caring. They wanted her to be perfect for them, their perfect little Sister Regina, their own private conduit to heaven, the one they could mention to their Catholic friends and thereby imply they had an inside track to the golden gates. Oh, that was part of it, she knew. She'd always known, deep in her heart: those families with a professed religious felt a little more smug than others about the here *and* the hereafter.

But she wanted her family to be different. She wanted them to say quietly, *Sit down, Jean, and tell us why you're disappointed, and when your feelings started changing, and what happened to change them, and what you want to do with your future, and if you're sure this is the right thing for you. Let us commiserate with you and talk about your plans.*

Instead, they saw this as a disgrace.

Nobody had said a word since she'd shouted. They were all staring at her as if she'd gone daft. There was so much they didn't know about a nun's life. She decided to tell them some of it.

Her voice and stomach were trembling as she began. "I'm sorry I shouted, but that's something I haven't been allowed to do for eleven years, shout. There's a paragraph in our Holy Rule about it." She scanned the circle of faces. "Can you imagine your life without shouting? Or without touching other human beings? Or without being allowed to have one special friend of your own, or talking to acquaintances you meet on the street? Owning a wristwatch so you can check the time whenever you want, or buying your own bottle of shampoo, or sending a gift to someone when you feel like it? How about writing a letter to your own grandma without someone else reading it? I haven't even been allowed to do that—did you know that? Every letter a nun writes must be given to her superior unsealed. So I couldn't write to you over the years and tell you of my growing dissatisfactions. Perhaps if I could have it wouldn't have gotten to this point where I want so badly to be free."

They were all sitting with their chins dropped, staring at the tablecloth. She went on in the sweet seraphim's voice they had come to expect from her.

"Grandma asked, how could I not know what the life of a nun was like when I'd been around them my whole life. But there's a lot you don't know, a lot you'll never know about a nun's life. About the repression of emotion, and the amount of time spent in spiritual activities that might have been better spent on practical work. About living with a houseful of women with personality quirks that sometimes drive you mad, yet you can't say a word, because if you do, you break Holy Rule. About asking forgiveness for things that don't seem wrong. About obeying unquestioningly when you don't believe what you're doing is the best thing. About giving up your family and not being able to see them but once every five years. And yes, giving up the right to have children of your own when you love children so much and realize that you would have made a good mother, and probably a good wife, too.

"I made the decision to be a nun when I was eleven. Just think of that—*eleven!* I hadn't even grown to my full height yet, or had a say about how I wanted my hair cut, or been to the county fair without Mom and Dad, or paid for a dress with my own money. I hadn't had a boyfriend yet or a job. How can a child of eleven know what she's committing herself to when she says she wants to be a nun? Heavens, I was still entranced by their black habits.

"Mother gave me some old white curtains, remember, Elizabeth?"—she turned to the sister closest to her in age—"and a torn-up sheet, and I made a play habit out of white because there wasn't enough black cloth around the house. I dressed in it the way other children dress up for Halloween, and I danced around the orchard between the apple trees, and watched the wind catch my veil, and knelt and sang *Tantum Ergo* one evening after a spring rain when there was a rainbow in the east. At eleven I saw it all as a . . . a sort of costume drama. Everything at church was dramatic—the candles, the incense, the processions with banners, the beautiful chanting, and us little girls in our new white dresses and veils strewing flower petals for Corpus Christi. What little girl wouldn't be impressed by that? And the nuns were wrapped up in all of it. Besides that, they were teachers, and I revered them because I wanted to teach.

"So in our room Elizabeth and I played school, and she was always the student and I was always the teacher, and I'd take the wooden slat out of the bottom of a shade and use it as a pointer and tap the papered walls and pretend there were blackboards there and I was teaching her the alphabet. I wanted to be a teacher, and the only kind of teacher I had ever known wore a habit, so that's the kind I wanted to be.

"But I was eleven . . ." More softly, she repeated, ". . . eleven."

She glanced all around the table. Some faces were lifted, their expressions softening. "And everybody said what a wonderful nun I'd make. I should be a nun. Grandma said so, Mother said so, the nuns at school said so. And what child of eleven isn't going to believe the people she admires the most? Pretty soon I thought so, too. So I became one . . . and I *was* happy. For quite a long time, I was happy. So please don't think I'm blaming you, or that I have regrets. There are no regrets here." She crossed her wrists over her heart. "None at all." The gold ring on her left hand glinted in the light and her voluminous sleeve looped down. By now most of the family members around the table were watching her, and she stood in the motionless pose for several seconds before going on.

"There is so much I like about living in my religious community. There's the wonderful sense of belonging to this worldwide family that will always be there for me. There's a sense of purpose to every hour of every day, of doing good, and of changing the world in important ways. When we pray together, especially during Divine Office, realizing that every other priest and nun the world over is offering up the same prayer at the same time—why, I cannot tell you how powerful and rewarding those times are. And I love teaching . . . some of the children have grown very special to me, and their families, too, and the people of the town who are so good to us at Saint Joseph's.

"And, of course, from a much more practical standpoint, there's tremendous security to living in a convent. All my worldly needs are taken care of—food, clothing, shelter, company, a job, a place to go if I get sick, a home for me in my old age. All of those things *you* take for granted because you're married and you have children and you've always lived and worked here. You know where you belong. But when I leave my Order I'll have nothing. Not a home, or a job, or even clothing. Certainly not a savings account, because members of a religious order are allowed to own nothing for themselves.

"So . . . when I leave there, I'll be starting over as a . . . a displaced person. Maybe now you can understand what an agonizing decision this has been for me."

Nobody said a word, so she went on, beseeching them to believe her. "And I haven't missed the worldly things, honestly I haven't. But I want . . . I want . . ." Her voice had grown tender and yearning. "Most of all I want a friend. Somebody I could talk to about all of this." She paused and looked from one to the other, then her voice grew plaintive as she asked, "And if that friend were a man, would you forgive me?" She waited, but all remained silent. "Because I do have a friend who's a man, and yes, he's the one who drove me home. His wife died last September, and in his sorrow he turned to me. Oh, not physically. We talked, and prayed together, and on occasion wept, because he loved his wife so totally and richly and it seemed so unfair that God had taken her. He has two beautiful children, and I love them and feel such pity for them that . . . that holding myself apart from them has become a penance for me. I wanted to reach out to them when their mother died, and to their father as well. But this, you see, is forbidden to me. Because it is physical."

Her motionless hands were loosely joined on the table. Her voice landed on her family like rose petals on a lawn.

"I've taken a vow of chastity, so if I say to you that I love this man—and I think I do—you think he's the reason I'm leaving my vocation. But he came last. All the other reasons came first."

One of the children came to the doorway just then and stopped, gazing from one adult face to another. "What's wrong?" she asked. Another child joined her and said, "How come everybody's just sitting here? Aren't you going to do the dishes and play cards?"

Grandma Potlocki moved first: an easy escape. "Come on, girls," she said to her daughters, "Carol's right. Dishes are waiting."

———

*T*here was no card playing that afternoon. Instead, when the dishes were washed, Sister Regina's siblings left one by one, taking their families and empty roasters with them. When Grandma left, Regina walked to the car with her. The old woman gave her granddaughter a hard, prolonged hug and said, "I don't know, Regina. I just don't know. I think you should make a retreat, make sure you're doing the right thing. Will you do that for me?"

"I made one last August, for exactly this reason."

"Well, make another one. Promise?"

Regina sighed. "All right, Grandma, I promise."

In the house after everyone had left, Bertha tiptoed around as if there were a dead body laid out in the parlor. She seemed unable to meet Regina's eyes, said little, and finally disappeared into her bedroom, ostensibly to take a nap, which she'd never done in her life.

Sister Regina knelt in her room and recited Vespers and Compline, Matins and Lauds, and when dusk was falling, went out to the barn, where her father was milking. She had always loved milking time in the barn. Warmed by the animals' bodies, it was cozy and redolent of hay and bovine. Two dim electric lights spread a tarnished yellow dinge over the animals and the cobwebbed beams overhead. Her father sat between two holsteins, sending rhythmic streams into a frothy pail.

"Can I help you, Daddy?"

"Sure. Grab a pail."

She found a bucket and milking stool and settled down with her sleeves rolled up, her skirts forming a hammock, between the warm bulk of two cows who were noisily chewing their cuds. The knack came back immediately, and her arm muscles grew pleasantly hot. Soon she realized she and her father were milking in point/counterpoint as they had when she was young. He created a lead beat and she an afterbeat with their streams of milk.

Shtt.

Sht.

Shtt.

There was nothing like milking together to dissolve animosity. She sensed that his feelings about all this were different from her mother's.

"You didn't have much to say, Daddy."

"Been thinking."

"And what did you come up with?"

"That you're right. Your mother and your grandmother worked on you from the time you were old enough to blow your own nose."

"But *I* wanted to be a nun, too."

"Yeah, I know."

They milked some more. Thought some more. Enjoyed this time of closeness, which was rekindling many loving feelings between them.

After some time Frank said, "I'd like to know more about this man."

"It would be premature. When and if the time comes, I'll tell you."

"Fair enough."

Frank finished one cow and moved on to another. A cat came out of the shadows and preened her body against Regina's ankle, turned and did it again and again. She reached down and scratched the sleek black body, ran a cupped hand clear down its length to the tip of its curved tail, and murmured, "Hello, what's your name?"

"That one's Midnight," her father answered. "If you need to come home for a while and live after you quit, it's all right with me, Jean. I'll talk to your mother about it, and she'll come around. You'll see."

Regina's hand stalled halfway down the body of the cat, and she got tears in her eyes. She put her forehead against the hard, warm belly of the cow and sat so for some seconds, idle, thankful, filled with such emotion it felt as if her heart could not contain it.

Finally, she lifted her head and called softly, "I love you, Daddy."

She could not see him on the other side of the cow, but she heard him clear his throat. Then his milking stool scraped the floor. And though he wasn't a man who could say it, she felt as loved as she ever had in her life.

Sixteen

Christmas was as forlorn as Eddie expected. The pageantry and music of Midnight Mass, which usually filled him with joy and celebration, only left him melancholy. Not even the majestic pipe organ or the choir raising its *hallelujahs* could lift his doleful spirits. The nuns were present in the front right pew, but there was no Sister Regina to fix upon in an effort to cheer himself. The children fell asleep and when Mass was over he had to contend with two limp bodies all by himself. There was no Krystyna to prop up one of them and guide arms into coat sleeves, to bolster a slumping form and guide it down the aisle into the cold starlit air outside.

Eddie did as Rose suggested, slept at her and Romaine's house, doubling-up the kids in bed with their cousins and bunking, himself, on their davenport under a patchwork quilt. The worst was filling their stockings without Krystyna. He realized now that she had been the true spirit of Christmas in their family, and that he himself

made a poor substitute in that department. The toys he'd bought for their stockings seemed uninspired and lackluster; Krystyna's had always been inventive and exciting for the girls to find. He hadn't even thought to buy them a blackboard, in spite of the fact that they played school all the time. It was Rose who put a box of chalk in their stockings and stood a brand-new blackboard close by. It was Rose who gave them some toys for their new cat, Sugar, and remembered that Anne had loved playing marbles last spring and bought a bag of cat's-eyes for her. She'd made doll clothes for Lucy, and trimmed colorful gingerbread men for each of them, the way Krystyna always had. Grandpa Pribil had built them a doll crib and high chair, and Grandma Pribil had made special bedding for the crib, including a quilt that matched the one on their bed at home. Aunt Irene had embroidered them pillowcases with their names on them, and she'd mixed up a big batch of salt dough and given them a toy rolling pin and cookie cutters so they could make their own play cookies when they played house. Lucy's favorite doll had grown bald, so Irene and her mother had managed to make it a new wig out of fine yellow yarn that had only to be glued on to make the doll pretty again.

But the best gift of all came from their teacher, Sister Regina. She had put together a box of leftover worksheets, ends and scraps of construction paper, a couple of coverless, outdated textbooks, and some very well-used flash cards containing arithmetic tables. Also in the box was a 1948 datebook, with a page for each day of the year, few of them written on; and four partially used receipt books with carbon paper flaps in the front, the kind used by storekeepers to keep a running account of customers' charges. The uses for the treasures in that box were limited only by the scope of a child's imagination. Anne and Lucy and their cousins spent most of Christmas Day playing school, store and restaurant, and the truth was they were having so much fun they didn't miss their mother.

Eddie watched them enjoying their day and thought of what a perfect gift Sister Regina had dreamed up for them. Besides costing her no money, it found a second use for scrap materials, and it occupied the children so fully that it provided the much dearer gift of helping them forget their

mother's absence for a while. It was—he realized—exactly the kind of gift that Krystyna would have dreamed up herself.

The gift, of course, brought Sister Regina to mind. Eddie wondered what kind of Christmas she was having. He pictured her in that ordinary farmhouse, surrounded by her family, and wondered if they gave her gifts, and if so, what kind, for he knew the nuns had to turn over virtually everything they received from an outside source to their superior, to be shared by everybody in the religious community. A dozen times during the Christmas season he'd tried to think of something he could buy for her himself. He'd run lists through his mind: gloves, handkerchiefs, chokecherry jelly, Zagnut bars. But in the end he'd decided it wouldn't be seemly, so he'd gone into his workshop and cut out a bunch of scrap lumber into squares, triangles, columns—shapes of every kind—for her students to play with during the noon hours of these bitterly cold winter days when they couldn't play outside. No one would question the propriety of his giving such a gift to her students.

He wondered when she'd come back to the convent, and preoccupied himself for a long time on Christmas afternoon, stretched out on one of Romaine and Rose's easy chairs with his eyes closed, imagining himself taking the box of wood blocks to her, and the look on her face when she accepted it.

It never occurred to him that more and more often lately, such thoughts of Sister Regina were supplanting his lamentation over Krystyna.

Sister Regina's Christmas was odd. Parts of it she enjoyed: making prune coffee cakes with her mother; going to Midnight Mass at St. Peter and Paul's, where she'd attended as a child; living without the tinkle of bells telling her when to rise, to be at chapel, to be at breakfast; going out to the barn to find her dad at the morning milking; feeding the cats warm milk from sardine cans; watching her nieces and nephews opening gifts; going to her favorite sister's, Elizabeth's, for Christmas dinner.

But there were undertones. Everyone—with the exception of her dad—tiptoed around her, treated her as if she might be carrying some contagious disease they didn't want to catch. None of them sat easy with her and visited. No one teased her, asked her to help with dishes, or to set a table. Certainly nobody brought up the subject of her leaving her vocation. Ever since that announcement, they treated her like a pariah.

By the time she left, she was more than ready to go. Her mother hugged her at the kitchen door and tucked a five-dollar bill into her hand. "For everyone at your convent," she said. Then she took Regina by both cheeks and said, with hurt, tear-filled eyes, "Please make very, very sure you're doing the right thing before you quit."

"I will, Mother. That's why I'm going to Saint Ben's."

St. Benedict's Convent was situated in the sleepy rural town of St. Joseph, just west of St. Cloud. Her father drove her there and deposited her at the portal she remembered so well. It hadn't changed since Sister Regina had studied there as a novitiate. The open gate, the dormitory, the Sacred Heart Chapel were as familiar to her as if she'd never left. In that shadowy chapel, dwarfed by its Baroque granite arches and humbled by its stained-glass dome, she spent the next four days at prayer. Hours and hours of prayer, moving among others clad identical to her, slow-moving figures in black who sang Gregorian chants in a steady, sweet soprano drone that seemed to be coming from within the very walls themselves. She took her meals in the refectory, where the words of grace, recited in unison, were as musical as hymn, and slept in a spare cubicle devoid of worldly distractions. She attended Masses celebrated by Benedictine monks, and knelt in contemplative silence, open to her God, inviting Him into her heart and mind, inviting Him to change her will to suit His.

But by the end of the fourth day, nothing she heard, felt or sensed, asked that she remain a Benedictine nun. Instead, she emerged from her soul-searching feeling an unquestionable validation of her decision to quit.

Thus, she came that last afternoon to the daunting oak doorway leading to the office of the prioress, Sister Vincent de Paul. Of Sister Vincent de Paul she knew little, only that she was good beyond all goodness, and wise beyond all wisdom, and that it was from her she must ask permission to seek a dispensation of vows.

Sister Vincent was short on smiles, offering none when Sister Regina entered her bailiwick. She filled her white wimple so fully that her pudgy chin protruded from it in folds. Her wire-rimmed glasses rested on a bulbous nose with rather large nostrils. She sat behind a desk as big as a boxcar in a room whose dark woodwork seemed to leach the light completely out of the air. A statue of Our Lady occupied one corner. Books and comfortless wooden chairs took up the rest of the space.

"Come in, Sister Regina," the prioress said. "Praise be to Jesus."

"Amen."

"You're on a teaching mission in Browerville, if memory serves."

"Yes, I am."

"And Mother Agnes advises me that you haven't been too happy there."

"No, Sister, I haven't been."

"Would you like to talk about it?"

She did exactly that, realizing within very few minutes that Sister Vincent was a patient and attentive listener. She sat without fidgeting, her gaze level and unwavering on Sister Regina who, after delineating her reasons, said quietly, ". . . so I would like your permission to seek a dispensation of vows."

Sister Regina's heart was clamoring fearfully as she made the request. The prioress, however, reacted with the same calm thoughtfulness exhibited by Mother Agnes.

"I'm sure you've asked God for guidance on this."

"Yes, Sister."

"Prayed, done penance, made a retreat."

"Two retreats, yes, Sister, and many months of prayers."

"And you've spoken about it with your spiritual advisor."

"And with my priest. My family also knows."

"Well, then . . . your mind seems to be made up."

"It is."

"You're nervous, Sister Regina."

"Yes, I am."

"That's to be expected, I suppose. After all, this will bring a close to a major portion of your life. But let me say that I've known a number of nuns who saw fit to leave the Order, and every one of them made a strong ally for us as a layperson. Sometimes those without the habits take a hands-on approach to church work and charity work that we're not allowed to take, or don't have the time or funds to take, especially those of us who have a mission to teach as you do. So . . ." She found a form and passed it across the desk. ". . . all that remains is for you to fill out the official form, which I'll pass on to Sister Grace, the president of the congregation, and she'll send it on to Rome. You realize, of course, that the Holy Father himself will have to sign it?"

"Yes, Sister, I do."

Filling out the form took so little time it seemed ironic, after the years of study it had taken to become a nun. Several seconds to negate six years of preparation.

Sister Vincent added her signature and centered the form on her ink blotter, then rested her hands beside it and looked up.

"You undoubtedly know that it can take up to six months for a dispensation to come through."

"Yes, Sister."

"And during that time, be reminded that you are still bound by your perpetual vows, the same as always."

"Yes, Sister."

"One more thing . . . for obvious reasons it would be best not to disclose the fact that you're seeking the dispensation."

"Yes, Sister."

"Very well, then . . ." Sister Vincent rose, tucking her hands beneath her front scapular.

"May the Lord be with you, Sister Regina. And during these next few months, if you ever want to talk, I am here."

"Thank you. God bless you, Sister."

"And you."

The sense of irony continued as Sister Regina found herself leaving the grounds of St. Benedict's and walking down the street toward the bus depot, carrying her suitcase. How could something that had consumed and structured her life for all these years be brought to an end by so brief an exchange? She had expected to be put through the third degree by the prioress, to have to defend her decision the way a criminal defends himself under inquisition. Instead, the prioress deferred to her decision with the utmost respect and facility. She'd thought the opposition would be much stronger. Instead, there seemed to be an unwritten code at work that said, *We don't force anyone to stay who doesn't want to.*

When her father had dropped her off at St. Ben's for her four-day retreat, he had volunteered to come and pick her up afterward and drive her to Browerville. She was happy now she'd insisted on taking the bus. It gave her time to ruminate on the imminent changes in her life. Many of those changes, like being turned out penniless, were scary. Others, like being free to perhaps take up a correspondence with Mr. Olczak, filled her with joyful anticipation.

The Greyhound arrived in Browerville shortly after three o'clock on one of the dreariest of January afternoons. But it was Saturday, the traditional shopping day for farmers, so the town was busy. One block off Main Street, the feed mill was whining like a distant siren as it ground grain. On Main itself Pete Plotnik's sugar-maple fire was smoking Polish sausages in his meat market, perfuming the air. At Gaida's General Store farmwives were trading, their hair set in once-a-week pin curls and covered with knotted dishtowels.

As Sister carried her cardboard suitcase the short two blocks from Jonczkowski's to St. Joseph's, everyone she met greeted her by name. Every man wore a hat, and every hat was doffed as she passed. Children stopped pulling their sleds until she'd gone by. Every woman beamed a smile her way. She had lived here for nearly five years and knew their names as well as they knew hers.

It would be a lie to say she would not miss it.

When she arrived at the convent and opened the kitchen door, she was assailed by warm familiarity. Sister Ignatius was baking cinnamon cookies and someone was having a piano lesson in one of the music rooms. The aroma, the familiar plinking of the piano keys, the placid face of the old nun all combined to pull at her heartstrings and give her a moment of doubt. Could she truly leave all this when the time came?

She would carry away a heart full of nostalgia, but the answer, unremittingly, remained *yes.*

"Praise be to Jesus," Sister Ignatius greeted.

"Amen," Sister Regina replied, then stopped to visit briefly, ate a cookie and went upstairs to her room. She bowed to the crucifix on the wall, made the sign of the cross, unpacked her few things and heard the soft tinkle of the handbell calling her to supper.

The routine was back.

The reassuring, live-by-rote, make-no-decisions-for-yourself routine was back. And for the moment it was a relief to succumb to it.

Mother Agnes summoned her a short while later and inquired about her time away, her retreat to St. Ben's, and if it had changed her mind.

"No, Mother, it has not. I met with the prioress and filled out the forms. They're on their way to Rome."

Disappointment showed on the older nun's face.

"I guess I'd hoped for a different answer."

"I'm sorry, Mother."

The two sat in silence a moment before Sister Regina remembered. "Oh, I have some money for you." She took seven dollars out of a hidden pocket. "My mother gave me the five-dollar bill—a Christmas gift for our community, she said. And I only needed one-way fare for the bus because Mr. Olczak very kindly offered me a ride home. The bus was late and the snow was coming down pretty steadily, so I accepted his offer. I hope that's okay, Mother."

Sister Agnes stared with her watery blue eyes, disapproving, but weighing the fact that it was their beloved Mr. Olczak with whom Sister Regina had broken Holy Rule. If it had been any other man, Sister Regina would have gotten a talking-to. Finally Mother Agnes furrowed her brow, shook her head in bewilderment and folded the money away into the voluminous black whorls of her skirt.

Perhaps it's best that she's leaving, the old nun thought. *She never did learn true obedience.*

*S*chool resumed on Monday morning, and Sister Regina was in her room before the children arrived, writing a prayer on the blackboard when Mr. Olczak appeared at her door, carrying a good-sized cardboard box.

"Welcome back, Sister."

She had made herself a promise: no matter what, she would conform to her vows and obey Holy Rule until the day her dispensation was official. So whatever amazing response his voice set off within her, whatever cataclysm his appearance created in her heart, she would fight it, hide it, conquer it. She turned from the blackboard, showing only a remarkable reserve.

"Good morning, Mr. Olczak. What have you there?"

"Something to keep your kids busy when they can't go outside for recess." He came in and walked away from her to the rear corner of the room by the windows. Her eyes followed the blue-plaid flannel of his shirt and watched it stretch beneath the X of his overall straps as he set the box on the floor.

She went to have a look, not too close to him, bending over to peer into the box.

"Oh my goodness, how wonderful. Did you make them?"

"In my woodshop, yes, on my own time."

"Why, God bless you, Mr. Olczak. The children will love them."

She smiled up at him, but he offered no smile in return. Their eyes caught and held, and both of them remembered that the last time they'd been together they had taken a forbidden ride in his automobile, and had enjoyed it very much. They stood on opposite corners of the box trying to dream up more chaste and proper bits of conversation, anything that would be acceptable and not cause her to sin. All that kept coming to his mind was, *I missed you,* and he couldn't say that. All that kept coming to her mind was, *I'm going to get a dispensation,* and she couldn't say that.

Finally, when the seconds stretched long and bordered on indiscretion, she tucked her hands into her sleeves and gazed about the room. "I see you've polished the floors and washed the windows and made everything shipshape. Thank you."

"Well . . . you know . . . vacation. Good time for that." More seconds passed, while she felt his eyes on her and smelled some dressing he must have used on his hair. Something spicy like garden mums that made her insides seem to list pleasantly.

"Did you have a nice Christmas?" he asked.

Was it her imagination that he spoke to her differently than he used to? Subdued now, with an undertone of confidentiality.

"Yes, I did. Did you get back home safely in the weather?"

"No trouble at all."

"I want to thank you again for the ride."

"And I want to thank you for the Christmas gift you gave the girls. They haven't stopped playing school all week."

Her gaze returned to him and stalled on his keen dark eyes, and his straight nose and attractive mouth, and for that moment no habit, no vows, no rules could protect her from what she felt.

She loved him.

Be careful, a voice said within her, *you're not out yet.*

She turned away and walked to the front of the room, where she resumed writing on the blackboard. His footsteps followed, unhurried, and paused as he shifted a row of desks that must have been slightly out of line. Then he moved again, approaching. . . . and stopped behind her.

"Did your father bring you home?" he inquired.

"No, I took the bus." *Don't turn around, Sister Regina. Don't you dare turn around!* she thought. *You're not out yet!*

"You should have gotten to a phone and called."

"Thank you, but I got here just fine." *I came from St. Ben's, where I signed papers.* Having finished writing the short prayer on the blackboard, she invented a list of spelling words to keep her from facing him. But she'd used up space for an entire column and had nowhere else to write, so she remained facing the board, the chalk in her hand, motionless.

He watched her from behind, realizing she was no longer writing, wondering if he was right about why she refused to turn and face him. Though it seemed too incredible to believe, he thought she was doing battle with temptation. He wondered what she'd do if he touched her on the shoulder.

Thankfully, the first student of the day came to the door at that moment. "Morning, S'ster! Morning, Mr. Olczak!" he bellowed quite loudly, whisking through the classroom and disappearing into the cloakroom.

And the spell was broken.

They were saved from themselves.

"Well . . ." Eddie said, retreating, ". . . just about time to ring the first bell for Mass."

Only then did Sister set down the chalk and turn. Her cheeks were vivid and her expression a mixture of fluster and dismay. Eddie had reached the doorway, and heaven and earth could not keep their gazes from seeking. He noticed she had forgotten to hide her hands in her sleeves, but left one trailing on the chalk tray. She noticed his lips were open and his breathing seemed slightly harsh.

When he spoke, his voice came out in an taxed whisper. "It's good to have you back, Sister."

Belatedly, she hid her hands beneath her scapular and averted her eyes, biting back a personal reply and nodding silently instead.

Finally, he went out and she was left staring at the space he'd occupied, battling a body that had been denied its physicality from age eleven on, shutting her eyes and allowing her breath to escape in a sigh of relief.

*H*is children were exuberant and grateful when they thanked her for their Christmas gift. They also offered the news that their daddy had been sad and a little grumpy during Christmas, and that he said he was glad when it was over.

Anne made a thank-you card out of construction paper with macaroni rings pasted onto it, forming the words *To Sister Regina.* Inside she had written, in her rudimentary cursive penmanship (Sister was just teaching the fourth-graders cursive this year): *Thank you for are stuff to play school with. We play school all the time. I am the teecher and Lucy is the studint. Sometimes she is notty so I make her write on the blackboard I will not be notty. Thank you very much. You are a good teecher. Love Anne & Lucy.*

Lucy brought sister two cookies cut out of bright pink dough. They were shaped like hearts and looked streaked and dirty.

"You can't eat 'em," she advised, most seriously, setting down the toy plastic plate on Sister's desk, " 'cause they're not real. But you can look at 'em and pretend. Then I need my plate back."

Sister left them on her desk for five days until they looked like a pair of shriveled tonsils, then thanked Lucy and returned the plate.

*B*y now neither Sister Regina nor Mr. Olczak were denying to themselves that they had feelings for each other. But they realized that the near breach of good sense they'd experienced that first morning after Christmas vacation must never happen again. He knew nothing about her seeking a dispensation, so to him she was as inviolate as ever, and the sin of coveting her loomed over his daily life. She labored under the admonition of the prioress to keep quiet regarding her dispensation, thus she strove to keep out of Mr. Olczak's way, lest she be tempted to divulge the truth. Too, since she was still bound by her vow of chastity, loving him remained a sin for her as well.

Once again they grew wary of being in the same room alone together. When it happened, one or the other would quickly dream up an excuse to leave. They stopped stealing glances at each other. If dialogue was necessary between them, they made sure their hands were busy and their eyes were on whatever work was in progress while they spoke.

It was a peculiar time for Sister Regina in relationship to her religious community as well. She belonged there, yet she didn't. She followed Holy Rule yet felt exempt. She watched the other sisters, trying not to pity them, but sometimes pity prevailed, followed by excitement at the thought of the freedoms that awaited her. She counted the days, yet didn't know how many days to count. She longed to tell someone—especially Sister Dora—that she was leaving, for she needed to talk about it, about the scariness of striking out on her own and the uncertainties that waited. About the unthinkable delights of living in the secular world again. But, of course, it was the discussion of those very delights that posed a threat to the Catholic Church and the continuing population of its nuns. So her secret was her own . . . and Mother Agnes's.

Sometimes in the middle of silent prayers her thoughts would veer to the expected dispensation and never return to complete the prayer, not even if it was a required one. Maybe, she thought, it would be easier than she'd imagined to forsake the routine of the past four and a half years.

The big question was when, if ever, Mr. Olczak would declare his feelings for her. Doing so, of course, would be a sin before her dispensation. And since he knew nothing of it . . .

Even afterward, no former nun could withstand the stigma of beginning to date a man she'd worked with, within too short a time after her dispensation. Tongues would wag . . . that was, supposing Mr. Olczak declared himself at all. For all she knew, once she moved back to the farm he might very well forget her.

So she came to an important decision.

In late January, after reading up on funds available from the government, she applied to the University of Minnesota to enter graduate school, fall semester, and go for her master's degree in child psychology.

*E*arly February turned up a spell of warm weather and a letter from her mother which appeared at her place in the refectory, leaning against her water glass. It had been opened before being placed there.

Her mother had written:

> *Dear Sister Regina, (not Dear Jean as she'd always written before)*
>
> *It was nice to have you home for Christmas. Your dad talked to me about letting you live here after you get out, and where else would you go after all, so it's okay if you come back home to live. I can use the help with the garden and the canning my legs aren't as young as they used to be. I haven't got up the courage to tell anyone about this yet. Love, Mother.*

It struck sister that her mother was doing her best to accept the situation with good heart. It had taken her nearly six weeks to get around to writing this letter, and write it she did, complete with the offer of a roof and board.

But disgrace was still the footnote.

Seventeen

❧

The winter days rolled along, droll and dreary, with little to change the routine save Forty Hours Devotion when the church lights remained ablaze for forty consecutive hours of prayer and adoration. Guest priests came for the closing ceremonies, including a lavish procession.

It was just after Forty Hours that Eddie was uptown in Wroebel and John's one day buying some flannel for polishing brass. A couple of other local fellows were standing by the counter passing the time of day when John Wroebel remarked, "So we're going to lose Sister Regina. Too bad, isn't it?"

Eddie's entire body snapped alert.

"Lose her? What do you mean?"

"She's quitting. Didn't you hear?"

"Quitting what?" one of the others asked.

"Being a nun. Seems she's started the procedure to get out of it for good."

John was holding out Eddie's change, but

Eddie failed to reach for it. He couldn't have shifted a muscle if someone had lit a stick of dynamite under him,

"Who told you that?"

"Father Teddy." That was John's brother, Theodore, a priest at St. Mary's in Alexandria, Minnesota. He had been one of the guest priests here at Forty Hours Devotion.

"Are you sure, John?"

"That's what Father Teddy said. Here's your change, Eddie."

Eddie scarcely felt the coins drop into his palm. "Sweet Jesus," he breathed as he turned away, not knowing if he uttered a prayer or blasphemy. "Listen, boys, I've got to get back to work. Nice talking to you." He left them behind gossiping about the rare news, and made a beeline for St. Joseph's, wondering all the way, *Is it true, is it true? Is she really quitting? Wasn't she going to tell me?*

The foremost thought on his mind was getting it straight from her. He hurried up the driveway between the two buildings and entered the school building through her cloakroom door. When he peered into her classroom, she was strolling the rows with her back to him while the children bent quietly over their open books. The sight of her, combined with the possibility of her becoming a free woman, created a maelstrom within him.

He hid it as he tapped on the doorframe and said, "Excuse me, Sister, could I talk to you a minute?"

She swung around, meeting his eyes across the stuffy classroom. He saw the hint of pleasure she couldn't quite hide, followed by its quick containment that dimmed the radiance from her eyes.

From their desks Lucy and Anne sent him silent greetings that he returned, then Sister Regina tucked her hands into her sleeves and approached him.

"Yes, Mr. Olczack?" she whispered.

"Could you come into the flower room for a minute, please?"

She couldn't quite hide her surprise. Her brows lifted as if a tiny insect had bitten her during a recitation on a stage. She gave a quick glance at her students, but they were all quiet and engrossed in their work.

"Please?" he repeated, and walked away from her. Across the cloakroom, he opened the flower-room door and turned, holding it open for her, waiting.

She gave her students a last glance and gave in, keeping her eyes downcast as she passed him and entered the privacy of the flower room.

He shut the door behind them, then crossed the room and closed the hall door too. The flower room was quiet. A murky sun strained at the windows, and nearby Sister Mary Charles's whipping strap looked incongruous between the pots of blossoming violets.

Turning, Eddie caught Sister Regina adjusting the veil on the tips of her shoulders, then tucking her hands away afterward.

Arming herself.

He returned and stopped smack in front of her. Face to face. Closer than ever before. So close that she raised startled eyes to him.

"Is it true?" he said without preamble. "Are you leaving the Order?"

Once again he'd caught her by surprise. "Wh . . . where did you hear that?"

"From John Wroebel. Father Teddy told him."

She averted her head, unwilling to tell a lie, yet compelled to withhold the truth.

He touched her on the stiff white cloth beneath her chin, forcing her to lift it. There his finger remained, on the immaculate starch that he had never touched before and should not be touching now. "Is it true?"

"Wh . . . what are you doing?" she whispered. "You must not touch me."

He dropped his hand but refused to step back. "Just tell me if it's true. Are you quitting?"

Her mouth opened, struggled, found no words as she stared into his eyes, begging, with hers, for mercy.

"You're not supposed to know," she said at last.

"Why not?"

"Please . . ." She attempted to avert her chin but found it lifted again by his finger.

"Why?" he insisted.

She touched him deliberately for the first time: knocked his hand aside so she could escape. But when she tried to move he moved faster, gripping her thick black sleeves and making her stay.

"Do you know how scared I am right now?" His cheeks were flushed and a vein stood out in his forehead. "Do you think this is easy for me?"

"Don't!" She gripped his wrists and strained to push them away, but he was so tremendously strong it made no difference.

"Sister, please, talk to me."

"Don't!"

"If this has anything to do with me—"

"Don't!" A whisper this time with her eyes slammed shut. A plea.

"When did you decide to leave?" She refused to answer while the battle continued at his wrists. "When?"

"Please, Mr. Olczak . . . you're hurting me."

He released her as if God himself had happened by. "I'm sorry, Sister," he whispered, "but I need to know . . . when are you leaving? And why?"

"I must get back to the children." She moved toward the door, but with a single step he insinuated himself between it and her, a broad barrier of plaid flannel and striped denim that refused to let her pass.

"They're quiet in there. Please, just tell me—has this got anything to do with me? Because I think it does."

"I'm still a nun. This is forbidden."

"When will you get out? . . . *When?*"

"I cannot answer."

"Where will you go?"

She tried to veer around him, but he caught her by an arm once more, gentler this time.

"What will you do?"

She closed her eyes and began whispering, frantically, "Hail Mary, full of grace, the Lord is with thee . . ."

"I think there are some feelings between us, aren't there? Just nod, yes or no."

". . . blessed art thou amongst women and blessed is the fruit of thy womb, Jesus . . ."

"Do you have feelings for me like I do for you?"

". . . Holy Mary, mother of God, pray for us sinners . . ."

"Were you going to go without telling me?"

". . . now and at the hour of our death . . ."

"Sister Regina, open your eyes."

She did. They were wide and terrified.

"Amen," she whispered weakly. "Please, Mr. Olczak, you must not touch me. It's . . . I . . . please . . ."

"Just answer me one question then. Just one. When will you be free?"

Her mouth opened. Closed. Opened again. Against her wishes, tears shot into her eyes.

"I mean no disrespect, Sister, but I have to know," he said quietly. "When?"

For one horrifying moment, she thought he might kiss her. The look in his eyes said very clearly that he wanted to. He had both hands on her arms, gently, and one thumb was moving back and forth like a blossom in a breeze. His gaze dropped to her mouth and she knew if she didn't do something, temptation would win them both.

"It takes six months," she whispered. "Now let me go." He released her carefully and let his hands drop. "And if you have any regard for me, don't do this again . . . please."

"Very well. I'm sorry, Sister."

Able to avert her gaze at last, she did so, while smoothing and resmoothing her sleeves from elbow to knuckle, trying to rid her flesh of the reminder of the pleasure of his touch.

"I must get back to the children."

He stepped aside and gave her access to the door. She walked toward it briskly, but before opening it, paused and pressed both hands to her cheeks, found a handkerchief and dried her eyes, then tucked it away and aligned her veil on her shoulders. Without glancing at him again, she went out and returned to her classes.

*T*hey never mentioned what passed between them. Not he, to his brother and confidant Romaine, or to any of the rest of his family; not she to her confessor, Father Kuzdek, or to Mother Superior or even to her friend Sister Dora. They carried it with them like a burden they could not set down. Its great weight—retained in the form of guilt—brought along its own penance.

They prayed a lot.

He gave up meat for all of Lent.

She said a Novena to Our Lady, asking for special help, and sought a plenary indulgence by praying rosaries and fasting. And she was especially nice to Sister Mary Charles, her least favorite, offering it up for the forgiveness of her sins. And he tried to spend a lot of time with his kids.

But the memory of those two or three minutes in the flower room kept them awake nights. Sometimes, in the depths of Grand Silence, she would lie in her austere cell, imagining what it would have been like if he'd kissed her, and if he ever would, and when and where it might happen, and if, when it finally did happen, she'd be able to forget her inhibitions and act like a normal woman, or if she'd been barricaded behind this habit for so long that she'd lost the ability to allow herself any sort of sexual freedom.

Meanwhile, he too lay awake, wondering if he had anything to do with her deciding to quit. He thought about what she must have gone through to start the dispensation, the superiors she'd had to face, and how much mental anguish it must have taken for her to decide to do it. He wondered if they'd allow her to stay on here teaching afterward. He'd never known a nun who got out before, but he didn't think the higher-ups at the diocese would be that lenient with her. He supposed she'd be forced to go away. And then what? Would he lose track of her? No, he knew where her parents lived and he could go find her there. But people would talk, especially about an ex-nun and a school janitor, probably say there was some hanky-panky going on between the two of them while she was still here. Even after she was out, he had to be careful not to start ugly rumors.

A week passed. Two. It bothered him, how he'd confronted her in the flower room and tried to force her to tell him things she wasn't ready to tell, or maybe not allowed to tell.

He finally decided to apologize the safest way he knew how.

She discovered his apology one morning when she went into her empty classroom early, sat down at her desk and opened the center drawer, looking for a pencil. Instead, she found a Zagnut candy bar with a note: *I'm sorry.*

Emotions surfaced that she'd never felt before: it was the first love token she'd ever received. No boy, no man had ever had the opportunity to offer her affection, for she'd been too young when she first entered the convent, and afterward, of course, she'd been off-limits. She reached for the candy bar with a full heart, and held it in her hand a long time, tempted to peel the wrapper and eat it. But it was Lent, with fasting and abstinence in force, and more important, she was still a Benedictine nun, and forbidden to accept personal gifts from men.

So she tucked the Zagnut into the very rear of the drawer, promising herself that when she cleaned out her desk for the last time she'd take it with her.

That day at midmorning, as she was bringing her classes in from recess, she encountered Mr. Olczak in the hall.

He nodded and greeted her, low, reserved, "Sister."

She averted her eyes and said, "Hello, Mr. Olczak."

Not a word was mentioned about the Zagnut. But they both knew he'd left it, and they both knew she'd found it. So they had yet another secret they kept from the rest of the world.

*L*ent continued, mournful and seemingly endless. In keeping with the somber spirit of the season, Eddie and Sister Regina bore their feelings for each other like penances they could offer up: *I will practice patience. I will not succumb to my temptations. I will pray instead, and do good deeds.*

So if he had to clean her room after school when she was still there, they'd stumble through that hesitation step when he appeared at her door and came inside. She'd look up from her desk and say nothing. He'd stop inside the doorway and say nothing. Usually, she'd be the first to recover.

"Hello, Mr. Olczak," she'd say simply and return to work.

"Hello, Sister," he'd reply, then while he swept and emptied and erased and scrubbed, the two of them pretended an indifference that served only to make them more aware of each other. And if their hearts raced when they encountered each other in the hall, and if their breath shortened, they hid it well.

Passion Sunday arrived and tradition called for the shrouding of all statues and crucifixes in purple. Sister Regina's charge was once again to act as sacristan. She enlisted the help of two eighth-grade altar boys to help her with the job.

She told Eddie, "If you'll take the boys into the basement and show them where the purple shrouds are, they'll carry them up."

Eddie took the boys downstairs and unearthed the boxes of material—both slipcovers and drapes—plus the wooden curtain rods upon which the panels would be shirred. Though Sister Regina would have struggled through the job with only the help of the two boys, Eddie had no intention of letting her do so. Ladders were required to get the slipcovers over the life-sized statues on their high pedestals, plus a special garden rake that he had rigged with the teeth backwards, to place the wooden rods on the wall over the main crucifix.

The church had five altars and it took nearly two hours before all the shrouds were pressed and hung and the ladders put away. Working together all that time, Eddie and Sister were discretion personified. They exchanged not one untoward word or touch, they circumnavigated each other at every turn, keeping plenty of distance between them at all times. But whenever the boys weren't looking, whenever they could do so without being detected by each other, they stole glimpses.

She had tied a full-length black apron over her habit, rolled her sleeves to the elbow exposing her sleevelets, and had pinned the tips of her veil back between her shoulders. He worked bareheaded, as always in church, his usual striped overalls replaced today by khaki pants and a rough blue cambric shirt.

He imagined her in a housedress and wondered if she had any hair beneath her wimple and what color it might be.

She imagined him in a kitchen, bringing firewood in and asking, "What's for supper?"

He wondered about the shape of her arms and legs.

She wondered if he ever wanted to have more children.

Once she was up on a ladder, insisting she herself wash the statue of the Blessed Virgin before putting the slipcover on.

"Would you please hand me that wet rag, Mr. Olczak?" she asked.

She bent down. And he climbed up. And though their fingers touched nothing more than a soiled gray cloth, their gazes collided, and all within them willed summertime to hurry.

*P*alm Sunday arrived, beginning a week of the most intense activity to happen all year long in and around the church. If Jesus Christ was going to rise from the dead on Easter morning, he would be doing it in surroundings worthy of Him. The women of the various church sodalities gave the building a thorough cleaning, supervised by Sister Regina. Every altar cloth in the place got starched and ironed, every candle drip scraped, the floors scrubbed and waxed, and every crevice of the ornate plasterwork dusted. Stained-glass windows, radiators, light fixtures, organ pipes, kneelers, pews—all fell under the relentless probing of the cleaning crew. It was a tremendous task that happened, so thoroughly, only this one time a year.

There were other preparations as well. The same canvas that had served as a Christmas crèche was hauled out of the basement and outfitted as a sepulchre with a statue of the dead Christ. The children practiced for Easter Sunday's procession and the adult choir rehearsed its special music. The confessional was busy as Father heard the mandatory Confession of every member of the congregation. Add to all that the long and frequent ceremonies that took place between Maundy Thursday and Holy Saturday and the place was overrun with activity sixteen hours a day.

There was, too, an emotional buildup induced by the religious ceremonies themselves. From Thursday on, all candles were extinguished, no choir sang and no bells rang. Instead, only wooden clappers sounded through the Adoration of the Cross on Good Friday, through the kissing of the feet of Jesus on a large crucifix that lay on the floor, and through Friday night's somber procession led by altar boys carrying a cross that was still covered with a purple shroud.

Holy Saturday morning's ceremonies were long and somber: the blessings of the fire and of the Paschal candle, the reading of the prophecies, the blessing of the water, and of the Easter candle.

The somber mood lifted, however, on Saturday noon. Jesus had risen! Lent was over! Fasting was over! The children of the parish could eat the candy they'd given up for Lent, the adults could eat meat!

And Eddie rang the bells again.

He rang them and rang them, longer than at any other time of year, and with them he felt his spirits lifting.

The joyousness continued and even heightened throughout that afternoon, which was hectic for Eddie. The church building filled again for the annual blessing of the food when parishioners brought everything from coffee cakes to homemade horseradish for Father Kuzdek to bless. Eddie had to be on hand to ring the bells before and after the three o'clock service, and when the church finally emptied, it needed sweeping. The statue of the dead Christ had to be removed from the crèche and packed away in the basement, and a statue of the risen Christ hung in its place. Then the area surrounding the cave was decorated with Easter lilies. More lilies were placed on the altars and fern stands carried up from the storage room and filled with greenery. Also, throughout the church the purple shrouds had to be replaced with white ones before the evening service.

———

*S*ister Regina was there again with her two helpers.

It had been an exhausting week for both her and Eddie, and after the doleful stretch of Lent and the intense mourning of Passion week, the sudden elevation of mood affected them both. The church brightened with each white curtain that was hung. The vigil lights burned again in their little glass cups. The dozens of potted Easter lilies filled the nave with an overpowering perfume.

It was late in the afternoon when the last ladder had been put away downstairs, and the boys released to go home and dress for the evening procession. Sister Regina genuflected as she crossed the center aisle and smoothed the pristine white cloth that ran the length of the Communion rail. Everything so perfect—clean, bright, ready for celebration. Not unlike what it must be like preparing for a wedding, she thought.

She knelt in the first pew and made the sign of the cross, relishing the quiet and the cleanliness, the sense of accomplishment, even the weariness in her shoulders. She said a prayer, offering up the day's toil for the greater glory of God. Then Eddie appeared, workworn and soiled in his overalls and heavy boots. He genuflected, too, then slipped into the pew across the aisle from her.

The church was absolutely silent. It smelled sweet as a garden. The penitents' sins had all been confessed, and Father had closed up shop and gone back to his house for a respite before the evening's service. On the seats of the first five pews, candles with cardboard sleeves waited for the children to light them and join tonight's procession.

It had been an exhausting and rewarding week. And Eddie and Sister Regina had bumped into each other so often during all the work and worship that they'd begun to lose caution. As they knelt together one more time, the sense of wariness and disquiet were gone. Side by side they had prepared this house for their Lord, and they were quiet and peaceful as they awaited His resurrection.

A curious thing happened as they knelt, tired, reverent, silent.

He blessed them.

They felt it as surely as they felt the cushions beneath their knees, and the hard pew beneath their wrists. A benevolence descending upon them in unison, washing over them and filling their souls like sunrise.

Eddie turned and looked across the aisle at her, and she returned his gaze. Goodness flowed between them, and for once it felt untainted by guilt.

He whispered, "The church looks beautiful."

"Yes," she replied, "I love Easter."

"So do I."

They stayed a moment longer, then rose and genuflected. She left the nave through the altar boys' sacristy, and he followed, making no excuses for walking her out. In the curved passageway behind the altar, the late-afternoon sun angled through the amber and ruby glass, coloring the walls like Easter eggs. He opened the outside door for her and followed her out. When the door closed they lingered on a high concrete landing above a set of steep steps, enjoying an overview of the rectory, the playground, and, to their right, the convent. It was mid-April. Spring was freewheeling, and the smell of fecund, thawing earth lifted all around them. The trees surrounding Father's rectory wore fat brown buds, and beside his garage a volley of crocuses were splashing color.

During their time in church, Sister had prayed for Krystyna, and for Eddie's children. She remarked now, "The girls will miss their mother tonight, getting ready for the procession."

"I'm afraid you're right. It's their first one since she's been gone."

"She always took such pains with their dresses and hair and veils."

"That's for sure. But between Grandma Gaffke and me, we haven't been doing so bad, have we?"

"No, not bad at all. But tell the girls, if they need some special help tonight before the procession, they can come to me."

"Thank you, Sister. I will."

She descended the steps, then headed for the convent, her posture erect even after hours of labor. From his vantage point, he watched her go—the hatpin that secured her black veil on top of her head, the veil itself gently luffing with each step, her black shoes denting the hem of her dress as she walked away. He wondered what her feelings for him were, if he'd read her correctly, and what she'd think about the idea of being a mother to his children for the rest of her life.

Sister Regina's remarks about the girls almost seemed prophetic, for that evening, after weeks of getting along well without Krystyna, Anne cried for her. Earlier that day Grandma Gaffke had set her hair in skinny metal curlers instead of pin curls like Krystyna used to, leaving it abysmally kinky. Eddie tried to help her comb it and put her white veil on so that the whole arrangement looked satisfactory. But Krystyna had had a magic touch that Eddie lacked. His efforts looked sorry at best. He and the girls were standing in Eddie's bedroom before the vanity dresser, Krystyna's combs and brushes strewn on the dresser cloth, when Anne stared glumly at her reflection and got fat tears in her eyes.

"Do I have to go to church looking like this?"

"It doesn't look so bad."

"Yes, it does. It looks icky!" Her tears got fatter and her voice grew quavery. "I wish Mommy was here."

Eddie's heart suddenly hurt. Nothing hurt it so easily as the children's tears for their mother.

"So do I, angel."

As was often the case, when Lucy saw Anne get sad, she got sad, too. Her little pink mouth drooped like a ribbon in the rain and she looked ready for full-fledged tears. "And our bows aren't tied right, either. We can't do anything right without Mommy." Eddie had tried to tie the sashes at the back of their dresses, but, again, he'd been clumsy.

He went down on one knee and said, "Come here, both of you."

They fit themselves against his sides, trying to keep from crying, and met his eyes in the mirror.

"I know I don't do as well as Mommy with the bows and things, but the new dresses I bought you are almost as pretty as the ones Mommy used to make, aren't they?"

Anne nodded dismally.

Lucy did the same.

"And Sister Regina said that when you get there tonight, you look for her and she'll help you out with anything you need. Now how does that sound?"

"All right, I guess."

"All right, I guess."

They still sounded forlorn.

"She can help you tie your sashes and put your veils on—how's that?"

The two little girls tried to cheer up, but it didn't work.

Anne said, "If Auntie Irene would have set our hair it'd look like when Mommy did it."

"I know, but we can't rely on Auntie Irene forever. Come on, now," he cajoled. "Get your new coats and let's go. You can help me ring the bells. And don't forget—you get to carry candles tonight. That'll be special, won't it?"

"I guess so," Anne replied dutifully.

"I guess so," Lucy parroted.

But his efforts to cheer his children only left Eddie himself blue. He missed Krystyna tonight with an exceptionally sharp ache. He supposed it had to do with tradition—another one changed by her absence. Easter had always meant new clothes for all—dresses, hats, gloves and shoes for the children and Krystyna, and some years a new suit for him. The girls had their new coats—matching lavender ones with a row of pearl buttons down the front, ordered out of the Montgomery Ward catalogue—and new white gloves, and new white shoes, and long white stockings, and their crisp white veils for tonight's procession, and white straw hats with daisy trim for Mass tomorrow, but as the three of them walked to St. Joseph's in the cool damp of that spring twilight, the girls walked one on each side of Eddie instead of between him and Krystyna as it had always been before. The sound of their hard heels on the sidewalk brought such a lump to his throat he had to look up at the sky and force himself to think about something else to keep his eyes from welling up.

At church they helped him ring the early bell, and that cheered them somewhat when they got to ride the rope on the upswing. Then they went with him to flip light switches and illuminate the place to its fullest, and look up in wonder at all the purple shrouds turned to white, and peer into the stone cave and grow amazed at the appearance of all those lilies, and smell their sweet scent, and see the candles lying in wait on the front pews and realize with a touch of growing excitement that they would be trusted to carry burning flames in a very short time.

By the time they returned to the vestibule others were arriving. Mothers were spitting on their fingers and smoothing little boys' rooster tails, and clamping veils on little girls' heads. Fathers were collecting coats and carrying them inside as they found pews. Nuns were organizing the procession and shushing the children's whispers. Overhead, the organ started playing and the rumble could be felt through the floor. Inside, the altar boys were busy lighting candles.

Someone touched Eddie's elbow. "Hello, Eddie."

He turned. "Oh, hello, Irene." She looked quite pretty tonight, in a new soft pink spring coat and a hat with a fine veil that floated above her carefully curled hair. She wore eyebrow pencil and tomato-red lipstick and she'd darkened her lashes the way Krystyna always had. Eddie noticed that she looked quite a bit thinner, too.

"Happy Easter," she said.

"Same to you."

"Happy Easter, girls." She looked at their pathetic hair and hid her dismay from them, turning instead to their father.

"I thought you might send for me to help the girls get dressed for tonight."

"Grandma Gaffke helped."

"I would have done their hair like Krystyna." She looked hurt.

"I know, Irene, but I thought . . . well, you know."

"And who tied their bows? Girls, come here, let Auntie Irene fix you up a little bit."

The exchange between Eddie and Irene was observed by Sister Regina from across the vestibule, where she was lining up her students in preparation for the procession. She watched Irene touch Eddie's elbow, and Eddie turn to find her there, and the two of them visit. Then Irene knelt down to retie the children's bows. Irene was thinner and, since losing weight, bore a noticeable resemblance to Krystyna—same hair color, same makeup, same smile lines in her face as she turned the little girls to face her, took a comb from her purse and began performing magic on their hair. She produced some bobby pins, opened them with her teeth, drew their hair straight back, clamped it in place with their veils and showed them the results in a compact mirror. They both smiled and flung her a hug and a kiss. When she stood up, Eddie smiled at her, too, and touched her shoulder as they exchanged some conversation. For only an instant, a hint of coquettishness telegraphed itself from the angle of Irene's head and the slight tilt of her body toward Eddie's while she left one hand on each of her niece's shoulders.

A powerful and foreign reaction caught Sister in the region of her chest, a hand that seized and twisted for the passing of five awful seconds before she recognized it for what it was: jealousy. It spread an uncomfortable warmth, like a lightning bolt, up her neck and down her arms, and brought forth an insidious inner voice that said, *but I was supposed to be the one to help them. I'm the one who offered first.*

Appalled at herself, she turned away. But some truths were at work, and undeniable. Irene Pribil was more like the children's own mother than any other living being. She had the artistic knack to care for them with Krystyna-like flair that Sister Regina had never learned, living a life devoid of pin curls and bows and lipstick as she had. Irene could flirt, practice her wiles on her brother-in-law, comb her hair in a perky flounce, even lose weight in an effort to win him. She could demonstrate her abilities as a substitute mother, and—who knows?—maybe wangle a proposal out of him yet.

Sister Regina, on the other hand, was forbidden to voice a word of her own feelings. She was forced to stand aloof, beg his silence, and pretend she felt nothing for him. Maybe he was hurt by the fact that she hadn't divulged her plans to quit the order. Maybe he took that as an indication that he was nothing special to her. Maybe before her dispensation came through he would reconsider Irene and realize what a perfect stepmother she'd make for the girls.

That night, at evening prayers, she performed her daily examen, found herself guilty of jealousy and said one of the most fervent Acts of Contrition of her life. After lights out, she lay awake remembering with great chagrin what she had felt while watching Irene with Eddie and his children. How peculiar. She was twenty-nine years old and had never experienced jealousy before. Oh, maybe as a child, when one of her older siblings got a new pair of shoes or the last piece of pie. But jealousy over a man was different. It had been swift and nasty and thorough, and had left her with a sin on her conscience that must be confessed.

In the dark, she rested the back of one hand over her eyes.

Oh, she was so blasted tired of guilt. It seemed as if everything she'd done in the last six months resulted in guilt. She was tired, too, of the unorthodox irony of falling in love as a nun, being unable to speak of it, unable to verify that what she was feeling, he was feeling. How she longed to walk right up to him and say, I *do* love you, and your children, but I'm still bound by my vows until my dispensation comes through. Please be patient. Please wait. Only two more months.

But she could not do that, of course, under pain of sin.

Eighteen

❧

It was a warm sunny Tuesday, May eighth, and school had just been dismissed for the day when Mother Agnes came into Sister Regina's room and closed the door behind her.

They greeted each other as usual.

"Praise be to Jesus."

"Amen."

Then Mother Agnes said, "Your dispensation has come through from Rome."

Sister Regina's hand fluttered to her heart. It felt as though it had leaped to her throat from its accustomed place and pelted there like some berserk battering ram. "Oh! So soon? I . . . I was told six months."

"Three to six months. It's been five, I believe."

"Nearly . . . yes. It's . . ." Sister Regina stepped back and dropped into her desk chair, short of breath. "Why am I so stunned?"

"It's a step that will alter your life. And very final."

Sister Regina tried to conquer her emotions, but now that the time was here, the uncertainties of her future reared their heads like dragons. She sat in a state of fluster barely listening to Mother Superior.

"Arrangements have been made for your father to be here at five o'clock this afternoon to pick you up. He'll be bringing clothes for you to wear. In the meantime, you may strip your bed and remake it and pack your belongings."

"F . . . five o'clock?" That was prayer time when everyone would be chanting Matins and Lauds and would be unaware of anything happening in the rest of the house. "Am I . . . I mean, am I not to be allowed to say goodbye to the other sisters?"

"Under the circumstances, the prioress and the president of the congregation would rather you didn't." It was understood, of course, given the hush-hush methods of dealing with this issue, that preservation of the Order was a major concern.

"But . . ." What could Sister Regina say? *But some of them are my friends?* She was not supposed to have nurtured special friendships while she lived within the religious community. It suddenly seemed absurd that they would not allow a simple goodbye. What did they expect, a stampede out of here?

"Not even Sister Dora?"

A disapproving quirk of Mother Superior's eyebrow said she would brook no wavering on this issue.

If not Sister Dora, then surely not the children. Sister Regina glanced over her empty classroom. On the board some cursive writing angled uphill; her fourth-graders had put it there. From the book slots of some of the desks, the edges of papers protruded. On the back of one desk a worn pink sweater hung crookedly with one arm nearly touching the floor.

"But what about the children? Who'll be teaching them for the rest of the year?"

"One of our retired nuns from Saint Ben's will be coming to take over your classes for the last three weeks of school. If there's anything special you want her to know, you may tell me, and I'll relay the message."

The revelation that all these plans had been going on behind her back implied that Sisiter Regina was doing something wrong here, something that needed covering up. No matter that Mother Superior had told Sister Regina last Christmas that it was not a sin to question her vocation, now that the time had come for her departure, everyone was certainly trying to hush it up.

"I didn't get a chance to tell my pupils I'd be leaving," she said.

"I believe that's for the best, Sister."

I don't, she wanted to argue. Those children were not merely strangers who sat in these desks five days a week. They were individuals, with unique personalities and needs, young people she cared about in myriad ways, who brought to her something vital and important with each school day. Some, at her urging, had been slowly drawing out of their shells, others were learning to curb their negative tendencies. Some were being encouraged to read more, others to jabber less; some to do their adding and subtracting a little more carefully, others to be more kind or patient, others to brush their teeth every day. All were enjoying a book she'd been reading, chapter by chapter—*The Green Turtle Mystery*—and hadn't finished yet. And two special ones, Anne and Lucy Olczak, would think she cared so little about them that she hadn't bothered with goodbyes or explanations.

But the church saw every one of the youngsters as a potential priest or nun, and it would not do to be candid about a nun who was leaving the order. It might breed the dread question, *why?*

So she must depart without goodbyes. Not to the children, or to her friends, particularly Sister Dora, most certainly not to Mr. Olczak. Her eyes lingered on the box of building blocks he'd cut for her, but there was no time for dawdling.

Mother Superior was waiting.

"I'll show you where we were working in our reading and arithmetic books, and I've put a marker in the novel I've been reading them every Friday afternoon."

All the while she marked the pages and gave Mother Agnes verbal instructions to pass along, her heart grew heavier and heavier. She'd always assumed she'd stay until the end of the school year, and would have a picnic on the school grounds with the children on the last day, and watch them board the school bus, waving goodbye, ending the school year like any other.

But everything was orchestrated to keep this departure quick and clandestine. No time for reveries or goodbyes. No opportunity to speak of dissatisfactions or futures. Pack up the traitor and get her out of the convent without anybody finding out. Pretend she has gone anywhere but where she has: toward freedom.

The moment came to walk out of her classroom for the last time, and she requested, "Please, Mother, may I be alone for just a few minutes?"

"Yes, of course."

When Mother Superior was gone, Sister Regina opened her center desk drawer and found the Zagnut bar at the very rear. She tucked it into one of her deep pockets, shut the drawer silently and stood a moment, trying to force herself to go. She had not thought it would be this hard, but five years was a long time. Finally she made herself move as far as the doorway, but stopped and turned with tears in her eyes. This room felt very much hers—her writing on the alphabet that circled the top of the blackboard, her grades in the red grade book in the top-left drawer, her writing on the holy cards that were stuck in the pages of the children's catechism books.

Goodbye, children, she thought. *I will miss you so much.*

In the hall she found Mother Superior waiting, a discreet distance from her classroom door. From across the auditorium in the seventh- and eighth-grade room she heard Mr. Olczak whistling while he cleaned, but with Mother Superior waiting to accompany her to the convent, she had no opportunity to say goodbye to him.

I'll write to him, she thought, and explain why I left without a word. *Goodbye, Mr. Olczak. I'll miss you, too.*

In her room at the convent she stripped and remade the bed and packed her personal belongings in her cardboard suitcase. There were pitifully few—underclothes, the black shawl that Grandma Rosella had

knit for her, prayer books, rosaries, the crucifix she'd received from her p
ents when she took her vows, a black-bound copy of Holy Rule, shamp
toothbrush and toothpowder, a partially used bar of Ivory soap, and c
pictures from the last five years.

The pictures brought on a fresh onslaught of emotions. She drop
onto her ladder-backed chair holding the photograph from last school
on her knees. There was Anne, a little shorter than now, still missing
of her teeth, which had grown in beautifully this year. And herself, sta
ing dead center in the last row between all the smiling farm boys whose
was slicked back with Brylcreem for the occasion. She could still remen
the smell of them on picture day, perfumy like their dads on Sunday.
year's class picture included both Anne and Lucy. It had been taken she
after their mother died, and Regina thought she could see the sadne
Anne's eyes. Lucy was smiling foolishly big, so her eyes disappeared and
lips pulled flat.

What would happen to them? Would she see them again? Would
father come and find her? Or would he, too, believe she thought so litt
him she hadn't bothered with goodbyes?

She placed the pictures atop her personal items and the Zagnut ba
side them, then closed the suitcase just as the bell sounded for afterr
prayer time. Right or wrong, she opened her door and stood withi
frame until Sister Dora emerged from her room and passed by on her
to chapel. She stopped at the sight of Regina in the open doorway, witl
suitcase on the bed behind her.

"Oh, no," Sister Dora breathed. "I was afraid of this."

"I'm not supposed to tell you, but I've received a dispensation and
leaving today. They're trying to whisk me out without anybody finding
about it, but . . ."

Sister Dora looked stunned and saddened. She extended a hand
Regina took it, squeezing it hard between both of hers.

"Where?"

"To my parents' house for now."

"God bless you."

"And you."

"I'll miss you."

"No matter what Holy Rule said, I considered you my friend."

Sister Dora had tears in her eyes as she squeezed Regina's hand one last time, then continued along the hall toward chapel.

Moments later the chanting began. It echoed through the upstairs hall in one sweet, haunting, soprano note, ascending up, up, beyond the rafters and roof, carrying the Latin words to the heavens beyond. How displaced Regina felt, listening to unison voices without adding hers. She felt the urge to hurry, join them: she was late for chapel and would have to confess it at the Chapter of Faults on Friday!

But she was a nun no more. She would not chant the daily office again, or confess to anyone except a priest in a confessional.

A knock sounded below. She hadn't known Mother Agnes was still down there until her voice, chanting too, moved along the main floor hall from the rear of the house to the front. She stopped chanting before she opened the door, then Regina heard her father's voice. And her mother's—quiet, almost secretive. And Sister Agnes's low murmur, greeting them, telling them to have a seat in one of the music rooms.

Regina slipped inside her room, closed the door and waited.

Momentarily, Sister Agnes appeared with a packet of white butcher paper tied with store string.

"Your parents have arrived, and they brought these for you. And here are your dispensation papers, signed by Pope Pius." She offered a white envelope. "There's also a small amount of cash. It's not much, but you brought a dowry when you joined the Sisters of St. Benedict. They feel it's only right and proper not to turn you out without something to fall back on. Well, Regina, how do you feel?" Not *sister* anymore, just plain *Regina*.

"Scared."

Reverend Mother offered a benign smile. "No need to be. God will watch over you."

"Yes, of course."

"May I say again, Regina, that I'm sorry to see you go. I hope you'll teach again somewhere. You have too much talent to waste."

"Thank you, Mother Agnes."

"Now if you'll kneel for my last blessing . . ."

Regina knelt and felt the older nun's hands on her head for the last time.

"Good and gentle Savior, watch over Regina as she goes forth into the secular world to carry out Thy holy will in different but important ways. May she continue to practice obedience to Your commandments, and to offer up for Your greater glory whatever work she chooses to do in the future. May she practice charity to all, but especially to those less fortunate than she; and continue to espouse the cardinal virtues so that at the end of her temporal life she may dwell with You in life everlasting. Amen."

"Amen," murmured Regina.

She rose and faced Mother Superior, whose watery blue eyes looked a little more watery than usual.

"Remember His words—be not afraid for I am with you all the days of your life. Now, go in peace."

*A*lone in her cell, when the door closed behind Sister Agnes, Regina could still hear the chanting through the white stucco walls. She opened the butcher paper and found a short-sleeved white cotton blouse with buttons up the front, and a pretty spring skirt of periwinkle blue printed with tiny pink rosebuds. The skirt, she could tell, was homemade. Tears stung her eyes as she realized how much love it had taken for her mother to cut it out and stitch it for this occasion, for Bertha, she knew, remained heartbroken over her decision to leave the sisterhood.

Beneath the skirt she found a pair of white anklets, a very demure full-length cotton slip and a clean but used brassiere of unadorned white. Pinned to it was a note in her mother's hand: *I couldn't guess at your size, so this is one of mine. Hope it'll do till we can buy you some.*

For the very last time, Sister Regina undressed as required by their

Constitution, in the reverse order of which she'd dressed that morning. She kissed each piece and laid it aside with a prayer for each—veil, wimple, guimpe, scapular, the cincture with its three knots signifying her three vows, her sleevelets and dress. And, of course, the binding around her breasts.

Undressing felt indecent in broad daylight while the chanting of Lauds penetrated the walls. She hurried to don the brassiere, finding it too large, and extremely awkward to hook. The blouse was store-bought, size thirty-four, and fit her fine. The skirt was tight around the waist—how could her mother possibly guess?—but she got it buttoned anyway, and felt a first ripple of enjoyment at the feeling of the air on her legs. The white anklets looked silly with her black Cuban-heeled oxfords, but she had no other shoes, and promised herself they'd be the first things she'd buy, along with a brassiere that fit.

When she was all dressed, she removed from her left ring finger the plain gold band she had donned when she became the bride of Christ. Looking down at it in the palm of her hand she remembered that day, her gown of white, the bridal veil on her head, and the intense sincerity with which she'd vowed her fidelity forever: *"In toto corde."* With a heavy heart, she laid the ring upon her neatly folded garments on the chair.

"I'm sorry," she whispered. "It simply wasn't the life for me."

From her desktop she took the smallest of mirrors and a short black pocket comb and put them to use on her hair. So few times she'd openly studied her hair. It was cider blond, cut haphazardly by her own hand with a paper shears from her schoolroom. As she combed it, it lay in pathetic whorls against her skull, and she had a sudden fear of going out into public this way, unstyled and dumpy.

So much to learn.

But she would. She would.

When she was ready to leave, she paused in the doorway and looked back at her black and white clothing lying neatly folded across the chair and listened to the chanting from down the hall, which was nearing its end. Running her eyes over the barren, narrow room devoid of creature comforts, she felt a sudden craving for color. Wallpaper, curtains, rugs, clothing! Pinks, blues, yellows! She would not miss this austere cell, not a bit.

Downstairs in the music room her parents were waiting.

"Hello, Mother, Dad," she said. "Thank you so much for coming."

They sprang from their chairs as if caught in some illicit act.

"Sist—" Her mother shot a sheepish glance at her feet and began again. "Jean, dear. How did the clothes fit?"

"Just fine, Mother."

"I hope they were okay. I didn't know what to bring."

"They're just fine. So colorful," she added with a cheery smile. "Thank you for making the skirt."

"I didn't make it. Elizabeth did. She insisted, and she also sent a shorty coat for you. She wasn't sure what you'd have for outside wear."

"How thoughtful."

Her father hadn't said a word yet. He held the coat while she slipped it on, and for a moment she felt his hands squeeze her shoulders through the warm wool and shoulder pads of Elizabeth's coat.

"I'll bring your suitcase," were his first words.

Her mother said, "And I'll take that coat," reaching for her heavy black one.

They went out first, and she followed. Not even Mother Superior was waiting in the hall to say goodbye. She had secreted herself away and was chanting with the others, apparently following orders and letting the traitor slink out on her own. She passed the bench in the entry hall where she'd often greeted piano students, sometimes Anne or Lucy, who waited for their lessons with dimes wadded up in their handkerchiefs. From the glassed-in porch that ran across the entire front of the house she paused and looked back along the center hall where the shiny linoleum caught the light of the setting sun from the open music-room doorways, into the kitchen where something oniony and beefy was cooking for supper, and up the stairway where seven nuns were finishing up afternoon prayers with silent meditation.

I have no regrets, she thought, and went out into the spring evening.

h, the wind. The wind in her hair! And on her legs! And in her un-
covered ears! It sighed through the deep afternoon while the lowering sun clasped her bare head with warmth. Robins were singing, louder
than she ever remembered, so exquisitely audible without a layer of starchy
white cloth binding her ears. She caught herself attempting to stick her
hands up the sleeves of Elizabeth's coat, but the opening was too narrow,
reminding her she no longer need hide her hands.

Then she was in the backseat of her father's car and they were pulling
away from the curb, and she wondered if Mr. Olczak was on the opposite
side of the school building, cleaning her classroom, or if he'd gone home
already, and who would tell him she was gone, and if he would presume
she'd gone to her parents' farm.

Well, at least he knows where it is.

Her mother said, "Did you have supper, Sist . . . Jean?"

"No, not yet."

Her father said, "Your mother and I thought we'd stop at Long Prairie
maybe and eat in a restaurant, sort of . . . well, celebrate."

She noted her mother's abrupt left-face and the glare she shot at her
husband that warned she was not ready—might never be ready—for cele-
brations. Jean understood her father's attempt to inject some specialness into
this milestone, with its mix of bitter and sweet, for eating in restaurants was
as rare as missing Sunday Mass.

"I'd like that," Jean said.

At Hart's Cafe, they sat on one side of the booth, she on the other.
Sometimes she forgot she was allowed to look around at the Coca-Cola sign,
and the customers on the counter stools, and the candy bars in the glass case
beneath the cash register. A man with a beautiful voice sang "Mona Lisa"
on the jukebox. The waitress had wavy brunette hair, blood-red lipstick, and
called Jean "honey" when she suggested a malt to go with her hamburger.
When their food came she folded her hands, bowed her head and said a

fairly lengthy grace. When she put the straw to her lips her father asked, "How's the malt, Jean?" and she beamed and nodded with a mouth full. Then he said, "Oh, is it okay to call you Jean again?" and she smiled and took his rough hand on the tabletop, and took one of her mother's hands, too, and said, "Of course it is. Everything's just the way it used to be. I'm your daughter. There's no need to be uncomfortable with me."

But they were, and she knew it would take time to adjust.

When Anne Olczak walked into her schoolroom the day after Sister Regina became Jean Potlocki again, she balked at the sight of some stooped old nun with a fuzzy face and spotty hands sitting in Sister Regina's chair.

"Who are you?" she blurted out.

"I'm Sister Clement and I'm going to be your teacher for the rest of the school year."

"Where's Sister Regina?"

"Sister Regina was needed elsewhere."

"Where?"

"Jesus called her to another place."

Shock suffused Anne's face. "You mean *she died, too?*"

"Oh no, no, no. She's perfectly fine. Jesus just needed her there more than he needed her here, that's all."

"That's what they told me when my mommy died, but it isn't true! We still needed my mommy a lot! Why didn't Sister Regina tell us she was going?"

"Perhaps she didn't know."

"Is she coming back?"

"No, child, she isn't. What's your name?"

Anne's mouth pursed. She didn't want to tell this imposter her name, but she had no choice. "Anne Olczak."

"Olczak . . . mmm. The janitor's girl?"

"One of 'em."

"Yes, of course. I met your father. And I also have your sister in my third-grade group, I believe."

"She's outside waiting for her friend's bus to get here. We both liked Sister Regina awful much."

Sister Agnes came into the room then, and Anne used the interruption to make her escape. She went straight outside to broadcast the news to her arriving classmates as they stepped off the bus, that they had a new teacher who was very old and had a moustache.

That morning during Mass and classes, Anne studied Sister Clement with a jaundiced eye. The nun was boring, and lazy, and not a very good teacher at all. Mostly she told the kids to open their books and work on their own. At recess time, she didn't bother going outside with them, but assigned two kids as monitors and said everybody had to be good or they'd be reported. Recess was horrible. The boys aggravated the girls and took their jump ropes away from them and stole the rocks from their hopscotches, which never happened when Sister Regina was there. Back inside, Sister Clement assigned fourth-graders to team up with third-graders and give them arithmetic quizzes. Then she sat at her desk and just before lunch time started nodding off and looked as if she'd tip off her chair.

Long before Sister Dora rang the noontime bell, Anne knew what she'd do.

It had been a shock to Eddie as well when he walked past Sister Regina's room that morning and found someone else looking through her desk drawers. He had stepped inside and said, "Good morning."

The old woman and he exchanged pleasantries, and he found out in no time that she would be there for the rest of the year. However, she knew nothing of the whereabouts of the nun she was replacing. Nobody at either the diocese or the Mother House had informed her.

So she's out, Eddie thought, *her dispensation must've come through.* All morning while he worked he swallowed his disappointment at not having been told, and he wondered why Sister Regina hadn't bothered to say *something*. It would only have taken a moment; would that have been so hard for her to do, find him in the hall and say, *I'm leaving, Mr. Olczak, my dispensation has come through*, rather than leave him guessing about it?

It hurt, damn it! It hurt that she hadn't done that much. It hurt that she would disappear without telling him where she'd be or what she'd be doing.

That afternoon, needing a vent for his frustrations, he sought the heaviest work he could find. He was repairing rock heaves in the grotto with uncharacteristic ferociousness, manually rolling boulders that he should have moved with a pry bar, when Lucy found him.

"Daddy!" she called as she came bounding up the grotto steps. "Daddy, Annie's gone!"

He sat back on his heels and pulled off his soiled leather gloves. "Gone? What do you mean she's gone?"

"She didn't come back after dinner, and Sister Clement sent me to tell you! We don't know where she is!"

Alarm set his heart pounding.

"Did she say anything to you?"

"No."

"Did she eat dinner in the cafeteria?"

"I don't know. I think so."

"What do you mean, you think so?"

"I was sitting with my friends. I didn't pay no attention to her."

"Well, was she on the playground during recess?"

"I'm not sure. Maybe not. We were playing pump-pump-pull-away."

"And she wasn't there, playing with you?"

Lucy shook her head. Her face showed the first signs of fear as she thought she'd done something wrong.

"Okay, dumpling, let's get you back to your room, and I'll run home and see if she's there or at Grandma Gaffke's."

He walked her back inside and spoke to Sister Clement, but the nun was old and perhaps a little less than competent, as well as being new to the community. She had no idea where Anne might have gone. From what he gathered, she hadn't even known who was missing from the empty desk until Lucy had brought it to her attention.

He spoke to Lucy last. "Listen, honey, don't worry. I'll go check at home. Maybe she wasn't feeling well and went there to lie down. Now, you go back to your studies and be good for Sister Clement." To the nun, he added, "Thank you, Sister. I'll let you know when I find her."

It took him approximately two minutes to jump in his pickup and drive the block and a half to his house. Why he didn't check at Grandma Gaffke's first, he didn't know. Something told him Anne was at home, and he figured it had a lot to do with Sister Regina's leaving.

The front door was shut tight, so he passed it and went around back to the kitchen door, and sure enough, it was open. He stepped inside and let the screen door close soundlessly against his overalls. The kitchen was tidy, the spring sun flowing in behind him across the rag rug and the gray-and-yellow linoleum. A few bread crumbs and a buttery knife lay on the cupboard by the sink. From the girls' bedroom overhead he could hear the murmur of Anne's voice coming down through the heat register in the ceiling. He crept to the bottom of the stairway and listened. Though she was hovering at the age where she'd half given up playing with dolls, it sounded as if she was talking to one today.

"... wash your dresses and fix your hair and don't you worry, I won't go away and leave you. Every morning when you get up I'll be here just like I've always been. And I'll cook you oatmeal and sometimes French toast if you're really, really good, and on Sundays we'll all go to church together, and when you come home from school, I'll have your play clothes laid out and whatever kind of cookies you like best I'll have 'em baked for you. Now hold still while I tie this for you."

He thought surely his heart was broken as he started up the stairs. Though she heard him coming, she went right on fussing with her doll as he stopped in her doorway and looked in. She was standing beside the bed, wrapping the doll in a miniature patchwork quilt that Krystyna had made several years ago out of scraps from the girls' dresses. The doll had matted yellow hair and weighted eyes that were closed. Anne pulled down the chenille bedspread from her own bed, laid the doll on the pillow and covered her to the chin. She leaned over and kissed her and said, "There now, sleep tight, and if you have a bad dream I'll be right here."

She patted the spread around the doll's chin and, keeping her back to her daddy, began fussily folding some doll clothes that were scattered on the bed.

Eddie said quietly, "Does she have bad dreams a lot?"

"Sometimes."

"What are they about?"

"Train wrecks."

"You know, she can come to me in case you should be busy with your other dolls."

"She knows that."

"Then why doesn't she?"

"She doesn't want to bother you when she knows you have to get up so early every morning to ring the Angelus."

He went inside and touched her hair with his dirty hand that had been moving rocks all morning. "Oh, honey, is that what you thought? That you couldn't bother me?" He went down on one knee and turned her to face him. "Maybe I was having bad dreams, too." She hung her head because she was nine years old and nine-year-olds weren't supposed to cry.

"Everybody goes away and leaves me," she said with her chin pulled hard to her chest. "First Mommy, then Auntie Irene stopped coming over, and now Sister Regina's gone, too." Her first tears fell and she wiped her eyes on a flannel doll kimono.

"I know, honey . . ." He pulled her into his arms. ". . . I know."

"I hate school and I'm never going back there!" She gave up her stubborn resistance and flung both arms around his neck. "I hate that dumb old Sister Clement! She doesn't even know how to teach anything! She doesn't . . . m . . . make . . . the . . . b . . . boys . . ." The storm broke at last, and Anne's thin body shook with a rash of weeping. He held her and shut his eyes against his own tears, rocking them both, bumping the side of the mattress until at last Anne managed, "Why did Sister Regina go? Did she die, too, Daddy? I think she did and n . . . nobody wants to t . . . tell me."

"No, that much I'm sure of. She's very much alive."

"Then is she sick?"

He sat on the floor, leaning against the bed with Anne on his lap, petting her head with his rough hand and staring at the box-elder branches beyond the low south window.

"No, not at all."

"Then why didn't she tell us she was going? She didn't even say good-bye."

"Sometimes people have to leave suddenly and they don't get a chance."

"Like Mommy?"

"Yes . . . like Mommy."

They sat on awhile, healing, taking solace from the fact that they had cried together and felt better for it.

"Do you still miss Mommy?" Anne asked, still resting against him.

"Every day. But you want to know the truth? A lot of days get easier. I mean, at first . . . well, heck, I didn't even want to get up out of bed in the morning and go on without her. But I knew I had you girls, and you both needed me, so at first I did it for you. Then pretty soon, you know what?"

"What?"

"I was doing it for myself again. And now, I actually have some pretty good days when I can think about her without getting sad at all. How about you?"

He felt Anne shrug. "The same, I guess. At first when she was gone . . . well, I cried a lot, except when Auntie Irene would come over. I liked it when she was here. It was kind of like having Mommy here. Why did she quit coming, Daddy?" She looked up at him.

"Well, honey . . ." His hand moved off her hair and patted her shoulder blade. He thought maybe she was old enough to know the truth, this girl who was so close to giving up dolls. "I'll tell you what. Auntie Irene and I . . . well, she sort of liked me like a boyfriend, I guess you'd say. And I didn't feel that way about her, so we both thought it'd be best if I tried to get on with my life and not depend on her so much, you know what I mean?"

"Sort of." After a thoughtful stretch, she asked, "Did you ever kiss her like you kissed Mommy?"

"Once. But I missed your mom too much to enjoy it."

"Oh."

He smiled to himself as he watched her trying to piece together the why and wherefore of adult ways.

"So does that clear up your questions about Auntie Irene?"

"I guess so."

"Now, about Sister Regina and why she didn't tell you she was leaving. I'm sure if she'd have had the chance to tell you goodbye she would have, because I happen to know that we were very special to her, too. But you know what it's like when you're a nun. Sometimes other people tell you where you have to go, and when."

She nodded her head, knowing he was right. Still, he could tell she was sad.

"But I'll tell you what I'll do," he went on. "I'll see if I can find out from Father Kuzdek where she's gone, and then you can write her a letter. How would you like that?"

"Okay, I guess."

"I'm sure she'd love to hear from you."

They sat in silence awhile, then Anne said, "You know what, Daddy?"

"What?"

"I loved her. And I'll tell you a secret—sometimes I'd pretend that she was my mommy . . . after Mommy died."

"Oh, she'd love to know that." He gathered her up for one hard hug, then released her.

"Would it be okay if I told her that in my letter?"

"I think it would be perfectly okay. Now . . . what are we going to do about school this afternoon?"

"I *don't* want to *go!*" she declared stubbornly, and got up and left the room. He listened to her footsteps go down the hall, through his bedroom into the bathroom where she blew her nose, flushed the toilet, then came back to find him still sitting on the floor, with his arms outstretched along the edge of the mattress, ankles crossed comfortably.

"I'll tell you what," he said, slapping the mattress with both hands. "I'll make a deal with you."

"What kind of deal?" She came over and straddled his crossed knees, facing him.

"You can stay home this afternoon all by yourself. You're nine years old—I don't see why you shouldn't be allowed to have the place to yourself now and then. Spend some time writing to Sister Regina, or even to your mother if you want to, and I'll make excuses for you at school. But then tomorrow, and every day till the end of the school year, you'll go to school without complaint. Sister Clement or no Sister Clement. Deal?"

She hooked her wrists behind his collar and gave him a quick peck on the mouth.

"Deal."

He clasped her in one last spontaneous hug and said, "We're gonna be all right, you and I, aren't we, sunshine?"

"And Lucy, too."

"And Lucy, too."

"Now get off. I gotta get back to work."

They went downstairs together and she saw him to the door, just like Krystyna used to. But as he left her, he realized that for the first time the comparison brought no pain.

Nineteen

⤨

The peculiar thing was, she still felt like a nun, still awakened at five A.M. without the help of an alarm clock, still knelt and said lengthy morning prayers, still went to Mass each day, only now she drove into Gilman to do it, once again with Grandma Rosella as she had as a girl.

People stared at her when she went to town. *That nun who dropped out,* their curious eyes seemed to blame as they studied her face to make sure it was Jean Potlocki, whom they scarcely remembered. Few approached her and she supposed they didn't know what to say, so she remained as separated from friendships as she'd been in the convent.

With the exception of her sister Elizabeth.

Liz came out to the farm the first day, insisting she take Jean to St. Cloud shopping. They bought bras and shoes and cloth and patterns to make Jean some more skirts and blouses. They even bought a pattern for slacks. Liz apologized for acting *as stupid* as all the others when Jean had first announced her plans to seek a dispensation. Since then Liz had had time to reconsider, and she realized she was being selfish by concerning herself primarily with *what people would think.*

"Let them think what they will. You have a right to live your life the way you want to."

There was a tremendous sense of relief in having one ally at last, one person with whom Jean could talk about everything: her daily feelings of being a displaced person; her grave disappointment at how her departure was handled; her worries about the children thinking she had thoughtlessly abandoned them; her sadness at being unable to see her fourth-graders receive their First Communion after preparing them for two years; the way her mother continued to act hurt and embarrassed over the whole thing; her chagrin at being financially dependent on her parents once again.

And, too, she told Liz about Mr. Olczak.

"You mean he doesn't know where you are?"

"No. I wasn't given a chance to talk to anyone before I left. I'm going to write to him, but I thought I'd give myself time to adjust first."

"He'll find you. He knows where Mama and Daddy live."

"I've told myself a thousand times, I mustn't expect that. After all, we've never even spoken about our feelings."

"He'll find you."

"Even if he does, I couldn't . . . well, you know. People would talk even more if I took up with a man I used to work in the same school building with."

"Let them talk. You know that you were dissatisfied with *the life* long before you started having feelings for him."

"Yes . . . that's true. Well, what's the use in talking about it? Mr. Olczak hasn't even—"

"Doesn't he have a first name?"

"It's Eddie, but I've never called him by it."

"Well, let's hope you get the chance."

———

*T*hree days after she returned to the farm, the mailman brought a letter from Anne Olczak. Her heart fluttered with excitement as she read the return address, formed in the rounded, carefully written cursive penmanship she'd taught Anne this year.

Dear Sister Regina,

Daddy said it would be o.k. if I wrote to you because I was very sad when you left. I never thought you would go away too and now I hate school. Sister Clement isn't a very good teacher and she falls asleep on her chair all the time and its no fun to go out at resess cause the boys are meen to us and she doesn't make them behaive.

Daddy said the reason you didn't say goodby is that they make nuns go wherever they say and you have to do it. I don't think that's write so I've desided not to be a nun when I grow up. I was going to be a nun when I grow up but now I'm not going to be one. I hope that's o.k. with you.

Daddy says its o.k. if I tell you that I use to pretend you were my mother after my my mother dyed. I use to pretend that sometimes. That is why I felt bad when they said you were gone.

Lucy got 100 in her spelling test.

I hope you are fine Daddy says you are fine and you did not die too. Well I have to go and clean out sugar's sand box.

Love,
Anne Olczak

Her mother looked over when Jean finished reading and her hands drifted to her lap, still holding the letter.

"What's wrong?" Bertha said. They were in the kitchen, Jean sitting at the table, Bertha kneading bread dough on a floured board.

"Nothing." Jean dried her eyes with the edge of her hand and folded the letter back into its envelope. "It's from one of my students that I particularly liked."

"Oh? What'd she have to say?"

Jean gave a sniffle and a wistful smile. "That her new teacher falls asleep on her chair and the boys are mean on the playground. Very important stuff to a fourth-grader."

"I seen the return address when I brought it in from the mailbox. Is that Mr. Olczak's girl then?"

"Yes, it is."

"Hmph," Bertha said, and resumed her kneading.

Jean spoke to Liz about the letter. "It broke my heart."

Liz studied her sister closely and came to a conclusion. "Why, you love his children, too, don't you?"

"Very much, Liz. So very much."

"Then answer her."

"But maybe he'll think it's just a convenient way for me to let him know where I am."

"Well, isn't it?"

Jean laughed and dropped her eyes demurely. "Yes, I suppose it is."

"Well, anyway, you told me you were going to write to him."

"I know, but . . ."

"But what?"

"Maybe I shouldn't. Maybe it's too forward."

Liz said, "If I were you I'd write to them all! Tell them your superiors wouldn't allow you to say goodbye, so you couldn't tell them where you were going. While you're at it, tell them you miss them, too. I think they deserve that much."

"Actually, I do, too."

"Then, do it."

"Mama will—"

"Mama will just have to learn to live with the fact that you're not a nun anymore."

———

*J*ean waited until the last weekend in May, when Anne would celebrate her First Communion. Then she sent a holy card as a gift, and a letter to all of them.

> *Dear Mr. Olczak, Anne and Lucy,*
>
> *I shall address this to all three of you because you are all on my mind. I must first apologize for not saying goodbye and letting you know I was leaving. I certainly would have if I'd been able. Unfortunately, I had to leave in haste and goodbyes were not possible.*
>
> *Although you children will probably wonder why, I have made a big change in my life and I am no longer a nun. I requested a dispensation of my vows from the Holy Father in Rome, and it came the day I left Browerville. I am now living with my mother and father on their farm and am hoping to go back to college in the fall to get my master's degree.*
>
> *It's good to be back with my family again, but I certainly do miss all of my students. Anne, I was so happy to get your letter, though I felt very sad to hear that you didn't like school anymore. Next year will be better. Wait and see. You will be in Sister Mary Charles'. . . .*

(At this point in the letter Jean went back and started a new page, cutting out the mention of Sister Mary Charles next year.)

> *This Sunday you will be making your First Communion, Anne, and I'm so proud of you. I shall think of you in your white dress and veil and say a prayer for you that day. I wish I could be there at Mass with you, as I know it will be a glorious day in your life.*
>
> *Lucy, I remember last year when you were one of the angels for the First Communicants. Next year it will be your turn to receive the sacraments for the first time, so you must study your catechism hard during the school year to prepare for it. Anne wrote that you received a 100 on one of your spelling tests. Good for you!*

Mr. Olczak, I remember with fondness your face appearing at my schoolroom door behind a long broom handle. You are a good and kind man, and I always admired how much patience you had with the children when they'd come right behind your broom or your dustcloth and mess up the school building again. I continue to pray for you and for the repose of Krystyna's soul. I hope by now God has given you some solace in your life.

It would please me very much to hear from all of you in the future so that I may know you are doing fine.

God bless you all,
Jean (Regina) Potlocki

Eddie found the letter in his post-office box three weeks after Sister Regina left. It had been the longest, gloomiest three weeks of his life. He'd been in an agony of indecision about whether or not to try to find her, and he'd been a bear around the kids. But he had only to read her name on the outside of the envelope to feel his spirits soar. He tore the letter open right in front of the post office and stood on Main Street and read it two times. Then he reread the last two paragraphs three more times.

One part stuck in his mind: it would please her to hear from him in the future!

That night at suppertime, he read the letter aloud to the girls. When he finished, they stared at him agape.

"She's not a Sister anymore?" Anne exclaimed.

"No, she's not."

"But how can that be?"

"Yeah, how can that be, Daddy? She's *Sister Regina.*"

"Well, as she said, she had to ask the Pope himself to sign a paper letting her be a regular person again." He purposely avoided using the term *set free.*

"But why did she quit? Didn't she want to be our teacher anymore?" Lucy said, her young face showing disillusionment.

"Honey, being a nun means much more than being a teacher. I'm sure there were other reasons she left."

"Like what?"

"Honey, I can't tell you that because I don't know."

"You mean it's like a secret?" Lucy asked.

"Sort of, yes. Her secret. Her reasons are private."

Anne's face looked troubled as she tried to puzzle it out. "But, Daddy, it's . . . how come . . . I mean . . . I didn't think they could *do* that. I thought they had to stay nuns for the rest of their lives."

"Well, when they start out that's what they intend to do, but sometimes it just doesn't work out. Just like . . . well, just like . . ." He couldn't come up with an equation.

Lucy asked, a little sheepishly, as if doubting it was okay to ask questions about a creature who was only one step lower than angels, "Doesn't she get to wear her black dress anymore?"

"No, I suppose not."

"Or her veil neither?"

"No. I suppose she dresses just like other women now."

"But . . ." Lucy cocked her head to one side and thought for a moment, then beckoned with a finger so he'd lean down. Into his ear she whispered, "But nuns don't got no hair."

He hid his urge to laugh and asked, "How do you know?"

Lucy shrugged protractedly in reply, her eyes skimming other things in the room than him.

Anne spoke up again, more soberly than her sister.

"Won't we ever see her again, Daddy?"

He thought, *If I have my way, you will.* But he decided it was best to answer, "I don't know."

He counted the weeks since she'd left, cautioning himself that he must not rush. Three weeks and he got the letter. Another week and the children were out of school for the summer. Six weeks and the feast of Corpus Christi came and went. Seven weeks and the bare spots on the playground were beginning to fill in with grass. How long should a man stay away from a newly released ex-nun in order to keep her free from gossip? There was no protocol for this kind of thing. The minute he showed up at that farm, speculation would run rampant through her family and probably through the Catholic community as well.

He waited two full months, and on July eighth, a Sunday, he finally ran out of patience. But he decided it would look better if he took the girls along.

After church he asked them, trying to sound casual, "How about if we all take a ride this afternoon?"

"Oh *yeah!* Where to, Daddy?"

"Well, I thought we might go over and visit Sister Regina."

"Reeeally?"

"Now, we don't know for sure that she'll be home. We'll just drive over and take a chance."

He wasn't sure who was more impatient to see her, himself or his kids. He went home and recombed his hair, and debated about what to wear. In the end, he stuck with the dress trousers and white shirt he'd worn to church, rolling his sleeves to the elbow but leaving his tie and jacket behind.

The girls wanted to know how he knew where to find her, and he reminded them he'd given Sister a ride home at Christmas.

Halfway there Anne asked him to stop the truck so she could pick some wild roses *for Sister.* Then she corrected herself and said, ". . . I mean, for Jean."

It sounded foreign to all of them.

Three-fourths of the way there Lucy asked, all seriously, nearly whispering, "What if she doesn't have hair, Daddy?"

Less than a mile from her folks' house he found himself with a stomachache so mighty that for a minute he thought he'd have to stop the truck.

Horror of horrors, about a hundred yards from her folks' farm he saw that they were having a family picnic. Cars and trucks all over the place, and tables out on the lawn beside the apple trees, and people stretched out on their backs in the shade, and standing in clusters visiting, and kids in shorts splashing in and out of a washtub full of water.

Well, he couldn't stop now. Nor could he drive on past. Every eye at that picnic would look up to identify who was rumbling by on their quiet country road. Besides, the girls would raise a stink.

What could he do but pull into the driveway?

He couldn't identify her at first amongst all the strangers—too many people scattered over too much space. Some quit what they were doing and ambled over to see who it was as soon as the truck doors slammed. A horseshoe game stopped. Children stood in place and stared. Then a girl who was just getting ready to pitch a horseshoe looked over and saw the familiar truck and dropped the shoe on the ground at her feet. Waving exuberantly above her head, she hurried toward them.

"Hello!" she called, smiling as she came. "Anne, Lucy . . ." She reached them and squeezed both of Anne's hands, wild roses and all, then both of Lucy's, leaving dirt on each of them. "What a surprise! My goodness, this is just wonderful!" Her smile was brilliant as she continued to grip Lucy's hands, like a skater getting ready to spin. "You're both here. I'm so happy you've come!"

The girls stared at her, mesmerized, trying to equate this woman with the nun they'd known. Her hair was the color of a peeled apple left out in the air, neither gold nor brown, cropped rather short and left to its own slight natural curl. At her temples the hair was damp with sweat and stuck together in little spears. She was wearing a wrinkled cotton dress of pink and white lattice design, and over it a soiled white apron. Her feet were bare.

Eddie stared, too, and felt his throat knot and his face flush.

Finally she dropped Lucy's hands and centered herself before him. "And Mr. Olczak . . . how . . . how nice to see you again." She spoke much quieter to him than to the girls, offering her hand more sedately. He gripped it as if to exchange a handshake, but it never quite developed into such. Just a squeeze while she smiled up and he tried to catch his breath and get his fill of the look of her so he could remember it later. Quickly she spun and called, "Look, Mama and Daddy, it's Mr. Olczak! And he's brought his girls!"

Frank came over from the far end of the horseshoe court, and Bertha rose from a lawn chair, where she'd been visiting with some other ladies.

Frank gave Eddie a firm handshake. "Well, hello again, Mr. Olczak. Nice to see you."

Bertha lingered a step farther away, reserving her smile and enthusiasm. "Hullo." It was easier for her to be civil to the girls than to Eddie. "So these are the girls we been hearing about. Which one of you wrote that letter to Jean?"

Anne raised her hand, keeping her elbow clamped to her side. "I did."

"Well, that was some nice letter. Made her real happy, don't y' know."

Jean interrupted. "Come and meet some of the others. This is my brother George, and my brother-in-law Curt, and my mama's sister Bernice . . ." Eddie lost count of how many family members he shook hands with. One, with an especially warm smile and handshake, Jean introduced by prefacing, ". . . and this is my very special sister Liz. She's closest to me in age."

Liz said quietly, "Hello, Eddie. I've heard a lot about you."

She has? Eddie thought, but hadn't time to dwell on it, because just then someone said, "Have you eaten? We got more fried chicken, haven't we, Mother?" Then someone else said, "There's beer in the watering tank by the well. How 'bout a beer, Mr. Olczak?"

His kids stuck close and Jean paid them much more attention than she did him. She asked them if they were hungry and they both said no.

"Well, how about a piece of cake?"

They looked up at Eddie for permission, and he said, "It's okay."

"Come with me," Jean said, and took them off to a table in the apple shade where white dishtowels kept the flies off the leftovers.

The men occupied Eddie with talk after that, and he was taken down by the big galvanized watering tank, where a cold beer was plucked from the water and put in his hand. They talked about the crops, and Truman lowering the draft age, and all the Communists who were being indicted in

America, and about how Frank and Bertha's granary needed a new roof and they'd all get together and put it on in the fall after the crops were in.

Eddie tipped up his chilled beer and tried to pretend interest in all the man-talk, but his attention kept wandering to Jean, across the yard, while she accepted the wilted roses from his children, lovingly put them in water, then fed the girls and eased them into the established society of her own nieces and nephews. He couldn't take his eyes off her hair and shape. She had a waist now, like other women, and curves above and below, and legs that had a bit of suntan on them above her anklet line. And those bare feet! What a gol-dang surprise! Her face looked different, too, without all that stiff white starch around it. All in all, it was like looking at a different woman.

In an extension of how she used to play with her students on the playground, she organized the whole tribe of youngsters into some running game, and only when Lucy and Anne were happily involved did she find a moment to glance over at him. Discovering him watching her, she dropped her gaze to the grass, then began slowly crossing the yard toward him.

He wondered if he'd choke before she got there. It felt as if he might. She was careful not to act too anxious in front of her whole family. On her way past a table she grabbed a small empty glass, and reaching the group at the tank, said, "Could I have a little of your beer, Daddy?"

While her father obliged, she washed her hands in the tank, never looking at Eddie, then used her skirt as a towel.

"Thanks, Daddy," she said, taking the jelly jar from Frank.

Finally she turned her full attention on Eddie and asked, "Would you like to sit down and talk? I'd love to know how the girls are doing. Anne had her First Communion, and Lucy's taking swimming lessons out at Lake Charlotte, she tells me."

He didn't think all the color in her cheeks was from the sun alone.

"Sure," he said, following her, studying her spice-colored hair from behind, trying to get used to the fact that she was now as approachable as other women.

They sat on the grass in the shade of some birches, not far from where the children were playing and the women were talking gardening. She set-tled down Indian-style, tucking her feet beneath the latticed skirt of her dress, which now had patchy damp spots near the hem. They talked about his children, and Browerville, and the piano recital the last week of school, and she asked after all of his relatives, and if a permanent replacement had been found for her at the school.

He sat at her left, facing the same direction as she. She wasn't even look-ing at him when she remarked, quietly, "You're staring at me."

"Oh!" He snapped his attention across the yard and felt his face flare. "Sorry."

"It's all right. I guess I've come to expect it."

"Well, you *do* look different."

"Yes, I know. It takes some getting used to, doesn't it?"

He took a swallow of beer from his bottle and wondered just how ca-sual he could get with her. He decided to tell her, "Lucy wanted to know what we'd do if you didn't have hair."

She laughed and pulled a few blades of grass, then took a tiny sip from her glass.

"Now, there you sit, and not only do you have hair, you're drinking beer and going barefoot. Can you blame me for staring?"

"No, but my mother is watching us."

He glanced toward the women, and sure enough, Bertha was doing ex-actly that, and scowling to boot.

"Mama isn't accepting all of this very well."

"How about your dad?"

"Much better."

"And you?"

"It's . . . taking a while. I've lived in a convent of one sort or another for eleven years. Those are old habits to break." He couldn't resist studying her profile, whether her mother was watching or not. "At times I feel as if there's really no place for me anymore."

"Are you sorry you quit?"

"No," she answered without pause. "But, you see, that was my home.

286

That was my routine—and believe me, when you live in a convent your life is totally regulated by routine. But there's something very soothing about it. No decisions, just follow the rules and life flows on. Now I don't really have a routine anymore, or a home. I have my family, but I feel as if I'm here on sufferance."

"I'll bet they don't feel that way."

"No, I suppose they don't. It's just me. But it's odd to be a full-grown woman moving back into your parents' house."

He considered awhile, then said, "Your letter said you're going back to school in the fall."

"I'd like to. If the money can be arranged."

"I thought you'd teach."

"They won't let me, not in a Catholic school, and I'm not sure I want to teach in a public school."

"They won't *let* you!" he exclaimed in surprise.

"Bad influence, you see."

He bristled. "You? A bad influence? Who the hell makes decisions like that? Oh, sorry, Sister. I mean . . ."

"Not on the students. On the other nuns."

"Oh, I get it. Some of them might decide to quit, too."

"Preservation of the Order, it's called."

"Pardon me, but that's stupid."

"It's why there was so much secrecy surrounding my leaving. They didn't even give me any notice. Mother Agnes just came into my schoolroom that day and said I should go over to the convent and pack my things and that my dad was coming for me." She turned to meet his eyes. "I wanted to find you and—"

"Hello. Mind if I join you?" They'd been so intent on their conversation they hadn't seen Liz approaching. Eddie felt as if he'd jumped from a tree limb and caught his suspender on a branch. There he hung, suspended in midair with Jean's emotions only half-revealed.

She could do nothing but conjure up a smile for her sister and invite, "No, please . . . sit down."

Liz sat, bracing a hand on the grass and studying Eddie without pretending to do anything else. "So this is the man Jean talks about all the time."

Eddie and Jean both spoke at once.

He said, "Oh, I doubt that."

She murmured, "Liz, please."

Liz's eyes perked with interest as she watched them respond, then she added, conversationally, "I've been talking to your kids. They're delightful."

With the dialogue turned to a safer subject the tension eased. Liz stayed, and they talked and talked, and Eddie saw what it was that made Liz Jean's favorite sister. She asked questions, then listened attentively to the answers. You knew exactly where you stood with Liz because she didn't play games with anyone's emotions, including her own. She could praise herself and admit she was wrong with equal zealousness. Most important, she really loved Jean and wanted her to be happy, whatever it took.

In time some other family members joined the group, and before he knew it, Eddie realized the afternoon was waning and he should start for home.

Much to his regret, he and Jean never found time to finish their private conversation. When he rounded up the girls and headed for the truck, others were doing the same. Liz, her husband, Ron, and several of the children formed a knot that moved with them toward the parked vehicles. Frank came, too, and even Bertha, though Eddie suspected her motive was less to bid him farewell than to keep him from being alone with Jean. There was little chance of that anyway, with Anne and Lucy beside him all the time.

When they were inside the truck with the engine started, Jean's hands were the last folded over the window edge.

"Goodbye, girls. Say hello to everybody back home."

" 'Bye, Sister."

" 'Bye, Sister." They had forgotten themselves and called her by her old name. She merely smiled at the slip, then turned that smile to their father.

"Goodbye, Mr. Olczak. Please come again."

"I will. Goodbye." He, too, found it difficult to say *Jean* for the first time.

But as he put the truck in reverse and backed out onto the gravel road, he promised himself he would. And soon. As soon as he could get back here to pay a call on her.

Without the girls.

Twenty

◦⚬◦

One week passed, one hot, lengthy, impatient July week with the sun so intense it seemed to have faded the blue out of the sky. In the garden, the string beans grew so fast they needed picking twice a day. Morning and evening Jean picked them, and during the day, helped her mother can them.

And all the while she thought of Eddie.

In Browerville, Eddie passed the week sanding and varnishing school desks, dizzy from the scent of resin and alcohol, if not from his thoughts of Jean. He'd made up his mind he'd drive back to the farm and visit her the following Saturday night, though the girls were campaigning for him to go with them and watch the free movie under the water tower. Every Saturday night during the summer, the city put up a screen and sold popcorn from a popcorn wagon while every kid in town watched the Three Stooges or Ma and Pa Kettle, and scratched their mosquito bites until their ankles bled. Eddie could think of a lot better way to spend his Saturday night.

On Thursday he told his sister-in-law Rose, "I need a favor on Saturday night."

"Sure, anything, Eddie."

"I need to have the kids go to the free show with your kids, then sleep overnight at your house afterwards."

"Oh, really? Aren't you going to the show?"

Eddie cleared his throat and shifted his weight from one foot to the other. "No, I'm not."

"Oh, where you going?" Rose didn't mean to be nosy. It was just that life in such a small town was so predictable, it was the exception rather than the rule when someone broke with tradition. And the free movies under the water tower were tradition.

"I'm going to visit someone."

"Someone? Why so secretive?"

"Actually, it's . . . ah, Sister Regina."

"Sister Regina?" Rose repeated, her mouth and eyes widening as if she'd just inhaled gasoline fumes. "You mean *our* Sister Regina who isn't a nun anymore?"

"That's right. Only her name is Jean now. Jean Potlocki. She lives over toward Foley."

Rose said, "Well, I'll be damned."

Eddie shifted his weight back to the first foot and said nothing.

"How long has this been going on?" Rose asked, point-blank.

"What?"

"You. And our ex-nun."

"You mean the kids didn't tell you the girls and I went to see her this past weekend?"

"No! I didn't hear anything about it!" She sounded put out that nobody had slipped her such juicy news. "So what's going on? Are you *dating* her?"

"Aw, come on, Rose."

"Well, are you?"

"No. I told you, I'm just going over to visit her."

Rose pointed a finger at him and got a sly look on her face. "Eddieeee . . . Eddie, Eddie, you're blushiiiing." She ended in a singsong.

"Look!" he said, his patience growing short. "If I have to go through the third degree just to leave the kids here overnight, I'll find someplace else to take them!"

"Settle down, Eddie, I won't ask any more questions. Of course you can leave the kids here. Does Romaine know about this?"

"No."

"Well, I'm gonna tell him."

"I'm sure you will. And everybody else in town, too, I suppose."

"Well, is it a secret?"

"No. How can it be a secret when I took my own two kids along last Sunday?"

"Well, then . . ." Rose looked very pleased with herself.

Eddie walked out of her kitchen, shaking his head.

*H*e bought new clothes for Saturday night, a pair of pleated trousers, blue, and a nice light, cottony shirt with short sleeves and pale blue-and-white stripes. When the girls saw him getting dressed up they asked if he was going to a dance.

"No. No dance."

"Then where?"

It was harder to tell them the truth than Rose.

"Well . . . what if I said I'm going to see Sis . . . Jean again?"

"Without us?!"

"But I thought you wanted to go to the free show."

"Well, we do, but . . ."

He knew he had them because Browerville didn't have a theater, so those free shows were the most exciting that happened around here. Cars started pulling in with two hours to go before sunset, and every kid in town went early and goofed around. Sometimes the car horns started honking, demanding the show before it was quite dark, and the cartoons were so vague you had to squint to make out the figures on the screen. Add to that the novelty of buying their own popcorn, and he knew his kids wouldn't object too loudly to being left behind.

Lucy tried a new angle. "Why don't you wait till tomorrow, Daddy? Then we can go with you."

"Thought I was going to take you fishing tomorrow at Thunder Lake."

"Oh, that's right."

Another quandary, because he'd taken them fishing three times this summer, and now that they'd caught their first sunfish, they loved that, too. Also, he let them take their bathing suits along and go swimming for a while along the shore.

So, shortly after supper on Saturday night, he found them each a blanket to take to the free show, and walked them down to the end of the alley to the water tower, where cars were already starting to park around the perimeter, and kids in pajamas were running everywhere trailing quilts and army blankets. He gave them each money for popcorn, and left them with their older cousins with a full two hours of daylight left.

Jean recognized his truck coming down the road, raising a cloud of dust, and thought, *Oh no, oh no, why didn't I follow my instincts and take a bath and put on some decent clothes and let the beans go for just one night?* But she'd been afraid to believe he'd come again so soon, so she'd slipped on her dad's barn boots, tied a dishtowel on her head to keep the gnats out of her hair, and had gone out to the garden to pick the second batch of beans in the evening cool.

She stood there in the middle of the bean patch, straight as a scarecrow, watching his truck approach and flicker along on the other side of a tall, wide band of raspberry bushes that separated her from the road.

He didn't notice her there, but drove into the yard, parked and walked up to the house.

The garden was huge. She was fifty yards from the back door when she saw her mother answer his knock and point down at the bean patch.

He turned, searched, and she knew the moment he spotted her, for he didn't waste any time starting her way. She wanted to move, but couldn't. It felt as if her feet had taken root with the bean plants, and her heart seemed to be swelling faster than the doggone string beans themselves, which she desperately wished she would have forgotten till morning. Instead, there she stood, looking an absolute fright while the man she loved walked straight toward her between the vegetable rows.

He thought how cute she looked in the four-buckle overshoes that reached halfway to her knees and the white dishtowel flattening her hair. The dishtowel made her look more familiar, more like the nun he remembered, yet not enough to mar the realization that she was just plain Jean now. There wasn't the first hint of a smile on her face. She looked merely breathless as he continued toward her, forcing himself to walk when he felt like racing.

He stopped one bucket of beans away from her, his toe nearly touching the galvanized pail that sat between the rows, half-full.

There was so much to say, yet they thought of nothing, only to gaze at each other while the sun sat on the horizon and the shadows from the trees in the distant farmyard stretched clear down the sloping garden and painted it with gloaming. They had waited so long for this first moment alone, and had weathered so many repressed emotions that the burst of them, allowable at last, quite overwhelmed them both.

He spoke at last, only after the silence had become intolerable with yearning.

"Hello, Jean," he said, speaking her given name for the first time ever.

"Hello, Eddie," she replied, for the first time, too.

Their voices fell softly, in keeping with the twilight and the cabbage moths he had disturbed with his passing.

"I hope it's okay that I came back so soon."

"Oh, yes," she replied avidly, too honest, too ingenuous to try to hide her breathlessness.

"I would have telephoned, but . . ." He didn't bother finishing.

"And I would have taken a bath and gotten dressed, but . . ."

She shrugged, and they both laughed.

"I'm glad you didn't. I like finding you out here like an ordinary woman."

"A little too ordinary, I'm afraid," she said, touching the dishtowel on her head. "I look a fright."

"Not to me you don't."

She dropped her hand and her eyes, and said self-consciously, "No man has ever paid a call on me before. I didn't picture it happening with a dish-towel on my head and my daddy's barn boots on my feet."

"Actually, neither did I. Ever since last Sunday I've been picturing your hair the way it looked when we were talking under the birch trees."

She lifted her eyes. "My hair is very plain."

"I like the color of it. I wondered a long time what color it would be. Do you mind?" he asked, reaching toward the dishtowel.

Her stillness became acquiescence. He had to take one diagonal step spanning the pail and a row of beans in order to reach the towel. When he'd swept it from her hair they stood in place, letting him get his fill of her. She felt her color rising, but made no objection as he studied her openly.

Finally he said, "There are so many questions I want to ask you. Things I wasn't allowed to ask before."

"Ask me now. Ask me anything."

"Not here," he said, glancing over his shoulder at the house and pulling his foot back beneath him. "Can we walk?"

"For miles and miles," she replied and turned away from him, leaving the bucket of beans where it was. They walked side by side along two ad-jacent rows, in the opposite direction from the house. When they reached the end of the garden, she turned left along a fence line and said, "The mos-quitoes are coming out. It'll be better on the road."

As they reached the road, the sun disappeared behind them. They walked slowly to accommodate her feet in her dad's oversized boots, whose heels dragged with every step. She untied the knot from the dishtowel and slung it around her neck, holding the ends with both hands.

"What was it you wanted to ask me?"

"Last Sunday, remember when we were talking and Liz interrupted? You were about to say that the day you left Browerville you wanted to find me and . . . and what?"

"I wanted to find you and tell you that my dispensation had come through and I was leaving. I wanted to tell you goodbye. I wanted you to know where you could find me."

"I found you anyway, but I went through hell before I got your letter and realized that something prevented you from saying goodbye."

"I believe we've both gone through a lot of that since Krystyna died, haven't we?"

"Yes."

"How are you doing in that regard?"

"Without Krystyna? Going through some guilt since I started having feelings for you. How are you doing in that regard?"

"About the same. I loved Krystyna."

"Everybody loved Krystyna."

"I think both you and I will always love Krystyna, and I think that's a lovely note on which to start our friendship."

"Friendship?" he repeated and stopped walking. "Hey, come back here."

She turned around and went back to him, leaving heel scrapes in the road.

"I asked you this once before, but you refused to answer, so let's clear it up right now. Do you . . . do you have feelings for me?"

"Yes, Mr. Eddie Olczak, I do." She smiled and tilted her head. "I most certainly do. But it would have broken about a dozen holy rules, not to mention my vow of chastity, if I'd answered you then."

He took her hands off the ends of the dishtowel and held them. "Then there's one other thing I have to know. Am I the reason you quit?"

She considered awhile before replying. "No. You were a part of it, but certainly not what started it."

He released a breath that relaxed his shoulders. "I'm so relieved. I didn't want to be responsible for that."

He rubbed the backs of her hands with his thumbs and they averted their faces to study their joined hands. Hers were fine-boned and stained green on the fingertips. His were wide and coarse, his thumbs callused as they moved over hers.

"Then why did you quit?"

She told him, going clear back to a year before Krystyna had died, including the events surrounding Krystyna's death that had truly crystallized her decision to seek a dispensation. She spoke of all her misgivings with life in the religious community, and the anguish she'd gone through while making the decision, and the role his children had played in making her realize she wanted children of her own, and her fear of the feelings she felt herself having for him. She told him about coming home at Christmas and the scene at Christmas dinner when Grandma Rosella had burst into tears, and of going to St. Ben's in spite of her family's displeasure and being informed that the Catholic Church wouldn't let her teach in its school anymore once she received her dispensation.

"I was so afraid, Eddie."

In the midst of Jean's recital the afterglow of sunset had streaked the western sky like smeared fruit, but already it began to fade as he studied her downturned face.

"So was I. I told you so that day in the flower room. I'm still afraid."

She looked up in surprise. "Of what?"

"Lots of things. Starting rumors by coming over here too soon. That I still might not be over Krystyna's death. What my kids might say. Kissing a nun for the first time."

Jolted by shyness, she immediately dropped her gaze again. His voice fell to a softer note. "Tell me, how do I get over the notion that if I kiss you, I'd be kissing Sister Regina?"

"The last time I was kissed I believe I was something like ten years old, so you're not the only one who's scared, Eddie."

He put his hands on her face and beckoned her to lift it. When she did, he held it like a chalice, his rough fingertips reaching beyond her hairline which had been covered all the years he'd known her by a wimple. "Then let's get this over with," he whispered, lowering his head and touching his lips to hers with a pressure so slight they made no demands. Her lips remained closed, her body stiffly angled toward him from one step too far away. For the duration of the kiss, she held her breath, and he realized she didn't know any better.

He drew back only far enough to whisper, "Want me to teach you a way that's more fun?"

"Yes," she whispered, terrified, intrigued, eager and halting all at once.

"Open your mouth."

He showed her, placing his warm open lips over hers and encouraging her to enjoy it. She flinched when his tongue first touched her. He smiled against her mouth and waited patiently for her to lose her inhibitions.

He finally lifted his mouth and told her, "It's okay to breathe." Reaching between them, he captured her hands. "And it's okay to put your arms around me. There are no holy rules now."

He placed her arms around his neck and held them there as a new kiss began, and she became a willing student. When her tongue made a shy foray and touched the warmth of his for the first time, the pleasant shock rippled clear through her insides. She crossed her arms on his collar, and drawn by his arms, curved against him like the new moon against the eastern sky.

And at last the kiss flowered.

They stood beneath that rising moon ushering out the tired day with a ceremony as old as time. First kiss, standing between the ditches where the wild evening primroses opened their yellow petals and perfumed the air like vanilla. Second kiss, with his strong arms lifting her free of the road and her big black overshoes dropping off her feet to the gravel. Third kiss, ending when he lowered her down to stand on his shiny black shoes, and some frogs started croaking in a pond they hadn't noticed was there.

Standing on his shoes, she hid her face against his crisp, striped shirt, which smelled of factory starch.

"Oh, my goodness," she whispered, breathing hard, "it's much different when you're thirty."

"Is that how old you are? I always wondered."

"I was thirty in May." She looked up. "How old are you?"

"I was thirty-five in March."

They were comparing ages like people with serious intentions. To leaven the seriousness, she said, "Well, you know what they say, a person is never too old to learn."

He smiled and asked, "So what did you think of it?"

"I liked it very much. You're a very good teacher, Mr. Olczak."

"And you're a very good pupil, Sister Regina."

"Don't call me that."

"All right then, don't call me Mr. Olczak."

"I forgot."

"So did I."

"No, you didn't." She stepped off his shoes, back into the black boots. "You were teasing me because I'm so ignorant of these things."

"No." He joggled her up close and made her lift her chin. "I'd never tease you because of that."

"All right then, you're forgiven. For everything but catching me in my boots and babushka."

"I'm sorry," he said playfully. "What can I do to make it up to you?"

"Let me think," she said, turning westward and starting slowly for home. "I'll think of something." Her heels dragged with every step she took, rolling pebbles along the gravel. He smiled, watching her drop her chin and tie the dishtowel on her head the way it had been earlier. If he ever married her and they ever had kids of their own, it would be a great story to tell them, how their daddy had courted their mother and kissed her the first time in the middle of the road in her own daddy's four-buckle overshoes and her mother's dishtowel.

Full dark had arrived by the time they reached her driveway, and she informed him, "I thought of something."

"What?"

"You'll think I'm forward if I say it."

"No, I won't. Say it."

She drew a deep breath and told him, "I've never been on a date."

"You haven't!"

"Hm-mm."

"So are you asking me out on one, or do you want me to ask you?"

"Eddie! You promised you wouldn't tease!"

"Oh, sorry." He grinned in the dark. "Funny thing you should mention it, because I was trying to work up the courage to ask for one, but I didn't know what you'd think of me showing up here three weekends in a row. Seriously . . ." He caught her arm and stopped her from moving on while one of the apple trees shielded them from a view of the house. "I'd love to see you again next Saturday night, but what will your parents think?"

"My mama won't like it, but I'm thirty years old. I'll have to get used to disappointing her sometimes, won't I?"

He took her hand and said earnestly, "I don't want any talk to start, that's all. Your dispensation was only granted two months ago."

"The same goes for you. It's less than a year since Krystyna died. You and I worked in the same school until last May. What will the people in Browerville say?"

"We'll find out soon. I had to tell Rose where I was coming tonight. And the girls, too. Next Saturday I'll have to tell whoever baby-sits them. Three weeks in a row I drive clear over to Gilman to see you. They'll all guess why."

She said a most profound thing. "Our strength, Eddie, is in our truth, and our truth will render gossip impotent."

He did not kiss her goodnight—they were too close to the house—and although he was reluctant to face her parents, he remembered Irene's story about the jerk who dumped her at the end of the driveway. So he walked Jean clear to the door. Approaching it, he observed that only the front room lights were on. The kitchen, directly off the back porch, was dark.

They stopped at the bottom of two concrete steps, and turned to face each other.

"Seven-thirty, then, next Saturday night?" Eddie asked.

"I'll be ready. And this time I won't have my daddy's boots on."

A movement inside the kitchen doorway brought Eddie's head up, and in the shadows he sensed Bertha watching furtively. He could not see her, but he knew she was there, spying.

He took Jean's hand, a polite enough farewell. "Well, goodnight then."

"Goodnight."

The brief handclasp ended, and he turned toward his truck, wondering how to win over a mother who didn't fight fairly.

Twenty-one

❧

*E*ddie and Jean each did something that week that made them feel better about themselves.

He marched into Rose's kitchen on Monday afternoon when no one else was around, spread his hands defiantly at his sides and declared, "All right! Just so you'll know, I'm dating Jean Potlocki! I'm taking her out again next Saturday night, so you can tell the whole town!"

Rose surprised him by getting tears in her eyes and barreling into his arms. "Oh, Eddie, I'm so sorry. I told Romaine what I said to you, and he got so mad at me that he hasn't faced me in bed for two nights. He said it was none of my business who you dated, and he made me promise to apologize to you, so if you want to take Sister Regina out next Saturday night, I'll watch your kids again gladly."

He said stiffly, "Thank you, Rose, I accept. Only her name is Jean now. In the future, call her by it."

———

*F*or her part, Jean told her mother in her kindest tone, "I'm going out on a date with Eddie next Saturday night, and I want to make myself a new dress. Will you help me with it?"

Expecting plenty of pussyfooting in the dating department, Bertha was flummoxed by her daughter's directness.

"Me?"

"I'd really appreciate it, Mama. I'll work extra hard on the canning so we can find time in the evenings to do the sewing."

The tactic worked with some mysterious kind of reverse psychology. Being asked for help from a daughter who broke her back picking vegetables and canning all day long in the torturous summer heat, how could Bertha say no? And after helping Jean make the dress, how could she object to her wearing it out on a date?

*L*iz showed Jean how to put on makeup but dissuaded her from trying any elaborate hairstyles.

"They just don't suit you, Jean. If I had thick, lovely hair like yours I'd leave it plain and just give it a good fluff in the air after you wash it."

Jean did what Liz suggested, went outside with a wet head and hung it upside down, brushing it from the nape while the breeze blew through it. When it was half dry, she went inside and shaped some natural curls around her face. After it fully dried she was amazed at how flattering it looked in concert with the peach-colored lipstick and the hint of brown mascara with which she'd darkened her eyelashes.

She put the dress on and ran downstairs to find Bertha.

"Zip me, Mama, please."

Bertha did, wearing a displeased expression all the while Jean pressed her hands to her stomach, flat as a stovelid inside the gored dress with its beltless waistline.

"I've got butterflies," Jean said.

"Oh, for heavens' sake, Jean."

Frank lowered his newspaper and shot a warning glance at his wife.

"Bertha," was all he said, low, menacing.

"Well, she's thirty years old, for heaven's sake, and she's acting like a teenager!"

"Bertha!" More forceful.

"Oh, all right, all right, I know. She's never done this before."

"So slacken up!" he ordered, snapping his paper back in place, and Bertha finally shut her mouth.

*E*ddie got there ten minutes early and Jean was waiting on the back step. When he slammed the truck door and spotted her rising with a full smile on her face, his eyes refused to waver anywhere else.

Though he offered perfunctory greetings to Frank and Bertha, they could see they were only a pair of gray-haired obstacles in the way of a budding romance.

As Eddie and Jean got in the truck and drove away, Frank said, "Better get used to him, Bertha."

She grumbled, "Well, he's got brass, I'll say that for him."

*I*n the truck Eddie said, "Well, where do you want to go?"

"I don't know. I've never done this before." She was still smiling, sitting up straight as a striped gopher with her skirt spread over a petticoat that crackled.

"Well . . . do you want to go to a dance?"

"Oh, no," she said with a fleeting frown. "I don't know the first thing about dancing."

"Well, then, do you want to go somewhere and eat dinner?"

"But I already ate at home."

"Then how about a movie?"

"Yes! A movie! Oh, I'd love to see a movie. But it has to be a clean one. One that the Legion of Decency approves of."

"Absolutely. There's a theater in Little Falls. We could drive that way and see what's playing."

"Little Falls, great! Take me anywhere! I'm having the time of my life just riding in my new dress!"

He couldn't help chuckling at her and eyeing her askance. The dress had a V-neck, cap sleeves, and made her look thin as a buggy whip. "I thought it looked new."

"I made it," she said, pressing the fitted skirt flat against her stomach. "Especially for tonight. Blue, because that's your favorite color."

"How did you know that?"

"You wear blue suits a lot, and blue ties. Last Saturday night you wore a blue-and-white striped shirt. I forgot to tell you I liked it."

He was falling in love so hard it felt like a dogfight in his gut.

"Come over here," he said, catching her hand and tugging. "I'll bet you never rode in a truck with a guy's arm around you."

"No, I haven't." He could tell the minute his teasing flustered her, because she trained her eyes straight ahead and acted more prim.

"Well, now you have." He dropped an arm around her shoulders and let it lie lightly, rubbing her bare right arm. They turned westward and the sun got in his eyes. She lowered his visor and he said, "Thanks."

"You're welcome," she replied, then sat very still. He could tell she was absorbing the newness of having her arm very lightly stroked. It gave her goosebumps he could see on her bare skin.

When they were halfway to Little Falls he had the idea, but decided he'd better quit stroking her while he suggested it, otherwise she might think he was after more than either of them intended.

He removed his arm and told her, "There's a drive-in theater at Little Falls, too."

She wasn't *that* sheltered! She read the *St. Cloud Visitor!* She knew what happened at drive-in theaters and why the Catholic Church spoke out against them!

"A drive-in theater?" she repeated, sitting up more erectly and darting him a deprecating glance.

He squinted below the visor. A bright orange ray struck him in the eye. "Not long till sundown."

She didn't say a word, but he could tell she was tempted.

"Up to you," he said.

By the time they'd reached the edge of Little Falls, she still hadn't said a word, so he pulled over to a curb, put the truck in neutral and turned to her, resting his arm on the steering wheel. "Look," he said, "you know me. If you think I'd take you to a drive-in theater just to get you in some compromising position, you're wrong. It just . . . well, it just tickles me pink to see you excited, trying new things. I just thought you maybe never went to a drive-in before and you'd like to try it."

He watched her struggle with some remaining misgivings, but she conceded, "All right, then, I'll try the drive-in movie."

"If you'd like we can drive through town first and see what's playing there, and then you can decide."

"No, the drive-in is fine."

Nevertheless, they drove through town, but the marquee said Humphrey Bogart in *The Enforcer*, which put an end to that, since it was a story about killers for hire, which was sure to have a bad decency rating. So they went to the Falls Drive-in and watched Doris Day and Gordon MacRae fall in love and sing their way through a musical courtship in *On Moonlight Bay*. Jean's eyes glowed with delight all through the movie, especially when the two stars were harmonizing together. And when they sang "Cuddle Up a Little Closer" and kissed on screen, Eddie watched Jean's profile and wished he could kiss her, too. Her lips dropped open slightly and she stared at the scene, transfixed, as if she wished she *were* the one being kissed.

But he was as good as his word, keeping himself squarely behind the wheel, glancing at Jean only during that one kiss, or when she'd laugh or whisper a remark about Doris Day's pretty clothes and hair.

When the movie ended and the beams from a hundred car lights blanched the big screen, they stayed, discussing the story, and how much she'd loved it, especially the singing and the pretty dresses. Then she told him about how she'd asked her mother to help her make the dress she was wearing tonight, and he told her about his altercation with Rose, and pretty soon the second feature was starting. It was *On Moonlight Bay* again, so he turned down the sound and they kept talking.

She spoke about the worldly things she'd given up to become a nun, and how she was anxious to experience them now.

He asked if she regretted anything about her past.

They talked about Krystyna and wondered if she knew they were together on their first date.

It seemed there was no end of subjects they had to talk about.

"Do you want to go home?" he asked her once.

"Not yet," she replied.

Eventually, they grew tired and began watching the screen without sound. Then somehow they found themselves lounging with their napes caught on the top of the seat and her hand in his, and their eyes on each other instead of the screen, and they began to understand what the Catholic Church had against drive-ins. His thumb was rubbing hers hard enough to bruise it, but thumb-rubbing wasn't enough after the long week of waiting.

"Jean?" he whispered, and that single word tore them loose from their moorings. They met in the middle of the seat, kissing hungrily enough to scatter good intentions to the four winds.

"Oh, mercy, how I missed you," he breathed as the kiss ended in a powerful embrace. "I thought this week would never end."

"Oh, me too." She squeezed him hard. "Me too."

"When I saw you sitting on that step in your blue dress this is all I could think about, having you in my arms again."

"I never cut so many beans in my life, or filled so many fruit jars with tomatoes, and with every one I filled I just kept thinking, that's one more minute closer to Saturday night. One more minute closer to him."

They kissed again, running their hands over each other's backs, feeling the awesome power of temptation. It was a renewal for him, and a discovery for her who had been so afraid she was incapable of carnality.

When the kiss ended she said breathlessly at his ear, "Oh, Eddie, is this what I gave up when I went into the convent? I never felt like this before. Never."

"I want you."

"Shh, Eddie, don't say it." Her arms were doubled hard around his neck.

"But I do. I want more than just holding you and kissing you."

"Shh. No."

He kissed her jaw, then bit the cloth on her shoulder and kept it clamped in his teeth, crushing her so hard against him that he'd flattened her prettiest curves.

"If I say it, you'll know what you're up against. I wanted you when you were still a nun. Since that day I put the sauerkraut in your basement. I went to Confession and confessed it, but it didn't stop. And it's *not* just because I've been without a woman for a long time, and it's *not* because I'm missing Krystyna. It's you. I love you, Jean, and I'm afraid it's too soon to say it, but what else can I do? Wait until the rest of the world says it's okay for me to say it?"

She had dropped her head back to see his eyes, and he was pressing the hair from her face, speaking with fury and frustration. She calmed him with five words.

"I love you, too, Eddie."

"You do?"

"I've loved you since right after Krystyna died. Since that very day you talked about, the day you carried the sauerkraut into our basement. I went to Confession, too, but it didn't stop. And that day you nearly kissed me in the flower room, I thought I would surely die from want of you. After that I prayed and meditated and made Novenas, thinking maybe it would strike all unchaste thoughts of you from my head, but they persisted. And every day that went by I only thought of you more."

"Oh, Jean, I wish I had known. I was so miserable then."

"So was I."

"But not anymore."

"No, not anymore." Practicality interrupted, and he realized how late it was getting. "Okay," he said, "we're talking around in circles and it's after midnight, and by the time I get you home and drive back to Browerville, it'll be three-thirty in the morning, and I'll get about three hours' sleep before I have to ring the bells for early Mass. I can't go through this every Saturday night. It'll wear me right out. I love you, you love me, my kids are nuts about you and, if I'm not mistaken, you're nuts about them. Will you marry me, Jean?"

She let their embrace wilt. "And live where?" She waited a beat, then added, "In Browerville?"

He knew how preposterous it sounded, but what else could he offer? "I live there. My house is there. My work is there."

"I was a nun there. How can you expect people to accept me as your wife?"

He spoke with barely suppressed anger. "They're supposed to be Christians! Good Catholic ones! And what was it you said to me last week—our strength is in our truth, and our truth will render gossip impotent. Maybe it'll do the same to any of their . . . their *blame opinions!*"

"Let's think about it for a while. We've only been seeing each other for three weeks."

"But I've known you for four years—five, come September. I'm not going to change my mind."

"Nevertheless, let's think about it for a week. Now I think I'd better get home."

It was a difficult goodbye at her door. He didn't give a rip if her mother was watching through a telescope, he drew her to him, full-length, and kissed her with his throat already constricted from the thought of driving away and not seeing her for seven interminable days.

"Maybe I can get over here once in the middle of this week."

"No, Eddie. You need to be with the girls on week nights. You can't start running over here and staying till midnight on a work night. Please . . . just come next Saturday. Same time. I'll be ready."

He walked backwards away from her, his arm extended till their fingertips no longer touched. Only then did he turn away.

He hardly remembered driving home. He did so with a thumbnail jammed between his bottom teeth, glowering at his headbeams. Once he used the butt of one hand to angrily dash away some tears from his eyes. Then he jammed his nail between his teeth again and drove.

The first chance he got he talked to Romaine about it, because Romaine was an ally.

Romaine said, "Why don't you talk to Father Kuzdek?"

"Father Kuzdek! Are you crazy? After I caused one of his nuns to leave?"

"You told me you didn't cause it."

"Well, no, but that's probably not how Father would see it."

"You don't give him enough credit, Eddie. Maybe you don't give enough credit to anybody in this town. You *assume* they're going to say you and Jean had something going while she was still a nun. But, don't forget, they knew her then, too. Now, I ask you, who could know Sister Regina and believe she'd be anything but absolutely faithful to her vows? Tell me that, wouldja?"

Eddie grew thoughtful but made no reply.

Romaine repeated. "Talk to Father Kuzdek. That's what I'd do."

The suggestion worked on Eddie's brain for three days before he got up the nerve to act on it. He cornered Father in his study one afternoon after moving a heavy piece of furniture for his housekeeper.

"Could I talk to you a minute, Father?"

"Sure, Eddie, come on in."

Eddie closed the door and perched on the edge of a chair beside Father's desk.

"I'll come straight to the point, Father. I've been seeing Sister Regina since she left here, and we love each other and I want to marry her."

Father swiveled his extra-wide chair to face Eddie, his elbows propped up and his thumbs circling one another as they often did when he considered important matters.

"So you love each other, do you?"

"Yes, Father."

"Well, I saw it coming . . . oh, don't get all worked up, Eddie. I saw how hard you fought it. It's no picnic, falling in love when one of you is a professed religious. And I'm sure both of you must have agonized over it for quite some time."

"You're not upset?"

"Should I be?"

"Well, no . . . but . . . it's sort of a delicate matter, her leaving her vocation only two months ago."

"She went about it properly. She's free to live the life she chooses now."

"So you'll marry us?"

"I can't do that, Eddie. She'd have to be married in her own parish. That's St. Peter and Paul's in Gilman."

"Oh," he said, disappointed at the thought of such an important event happening anywhere else but here.

"Father Donnelly would have to marry you there."

"Oh," Eddie said again.

The room grew quiet. Father's thumbs kept circling.

Finally Eddie asked, "Do you think people would accept her here if she was my wife?"

Father's regard held steady on the younger man as he said quietly, "You really don't know how much you and Jean are respected around here, do you? And Krystyna, too. What she meant to you, and to the nuns, and to a lot of people around this town has a great bearing on how your marriage to Jean will be accepted. And to top it off, there are your children who already know and love Jean. I think it's a match made in heaven."

"You do?" Eddie couldn't contain his surprise.

Father only nodded. But his thumbs quit circling.

The next Saturday was only the fourth day Eddie and Jean had spent together. They stayed away from the drive-in theater and remained at her folks' farm instead. He said, when he got there, "Could we just sit in the yard and talk?"

She squelched her disappointment and replied, "Sure, if that's what you want."

" 'Cause I hope that before I leave we might need to have your parents come out here so we can talk to them, too."

They sat on a pair of weathered Adirondack chairs out near the apple trees, where Bertha could watch them to her heart's content from the windows. Eddie related to Jean the conversations he'd had with Romaine and Father Kuzdek during the past week, and he asked her again, "Will you marry me, Jean?"

She got tears in her eyes, pressed eight fingertips to her lips and nodded repeatedly, until she could get control.

"You will?" he said, amazed that no further wheedling was needed.

She nodded again, for she still couldn't speak.

Eddie let his eyes sink shut and whispered, "Thank you, God."

Their chair arms were angled close together. He bent forward and took both of her hands. She tried to say, "Oh, Eddie, I'm so happy," but little came out, so he leaned forward and kissed her softly.

When their lips parted she said, smiling through her sniffles, "Just think, I get to be Anne and Lucy's mom."

That old dogfight started up in his belly again.

"You mean I can tell them at last?"

"Oh, yes."

"And maybe we'll have a couple more someday. What would you think of that?"

"Just thinking of it makes me happy. Imagine . . . having your babies."

"What about going to college?" he asked. "Will you be disappointed you can't do that?"

"I never did find the money for it."

"Well, then . . ." He fished in his pocket. "I have something for you." He came up with a modest diamond ring and put it on the finger that had once held a plain gold band.

"Oh, Eddie . . ." she said, admiring her extended hand. "Oh, Eddie . . ." She leaned forward and hugged him the best she could, considering the awkward juxtaposition of their lawn chairs. "I love you so much."

"I love you too, Jean."

They sat like that awhile, as evening cooled the yard and the frogs started a pulsating serenade down in the ponds. Their temples touched, but beyond that their embrace remained meager, mainly a hand of each rubbing the other between the shoulder blades while they rocked a little.

In time he asked, "Should we go get your parents now?"

She nodded against his shoulder.

"All right. How soon should we tell them we want to get married?"

"Soon. Please." Her voice was muffled as she continued rocking with him.

He smiled, and rubbed a hand down her hair, caught the back of her neck in an affectionate squeeze, and whispered, "Let's go, then."

*J*ean told Eddie later, "My dad must've given my mother a good talking-to," for their announcement had brought a stolid acceptance from Bertha, and a statement from Frank: "You can have the wedding reception here. No daughter of mine is going to get married without a proper send-off. Mother will butcher the chickens and your sisters can come over and help with all the cooking. It's no less than we did for every one of them."

So the law was laid down.

When Eddie kissed Jean goodbye beside his truck, she said, "Drop me a postcard and tell me what Anne and Lucy said. And tell them I can't wait to be their mom. Or should we say stepmother?"

"Mom will be fine. It doesn't take anything away from Krystyna."

They kissed again, starting out pretty politely, but in the middle of it he cast an eye at the house, then swung Jean around so her spine curved against the truck door, and pressed her against it with his body. "I have to admit, I liked going to the drive-in movie better," he whispered. "More privacy."

His hands slid from her waist up her ribs.

She stopped them just shy of her breasts and said, "Goodnight, Eddie."

"Wait till our wedding night," he warned. "Just you wait, lady."

"That's exactly what I intend to do," she murmured in her soft Sister Regina voice, then slipped from beneath him and opened the truck door for him.

When he told the girls he was going to marry their ex-teacher, Lucy's face scrunched up in delighted surprise.

"You *are?* Then can I wear my white dress and be your flower girl?"

"Well," he chuckled, "I hadn't thought of that. Maybe."

"Annie could be one, too, couldn't she?"

"Maybe. If she wants to."

"Is Sister Regina gonna live with us, then?"

"Her name is Jean now, and yes, she's going to live with us."

"And take care of us like Mommy did?"

"And take care of you like Mommy did."

Lucy clapped her hands and said, "Goody." Then she whispered in his ear, "Will she bring her old nun clothes along so we can play school in them?"

He tried very hard not to laugh.

"I don't know if she's got them."

"Well, ask her," Lucy whispered. "Pleeeease, Daddy?"

Anne told him, matter-of-factly, "I knew you were going to marry Sister Regina."

"How did you know?"

" 'Cause you were flirting with her at her picnic."

"I was not. I was being a perfect gentleman."

"I saw you."

"Doing what?"

"Just sort of . . . I don't know . . . looking at her. Kind of like you used to look at Mommy sometimes."

"Well, maybe you're right. Maybe I was flirting with her." He rested a gentle hand on Anne's back. "So is it okay with you if I marry her and she comes to live with us?"

Anne moved closer and nestled against him. "If I can't have my real mommy, she's the next best thing."

With a lump in his throat, he kissed Anne's forehead. Then Lucy's. And they both stood beside his kitchen chair, folded close to him while they all thought about Krystyna.

Twenty-two

~

The banns were announced for three weeks, and they were married in St. Peter and Paul's on a sparkling Saturday in late August, one week shy of the anniversary of Krystyna's death. Half the town of Browerville was there, including Father Kuzdek, and so many Olczak relatives it looked like a family reunion. All of Jean's family attended, too, including Grandma Rosella, who still wasn't convinced her granddaughter was doing the right thing but brought a clean hanky along anyway, because she always cried at weddings. Richard and Mary Pribil came, too, but not Irene. Irene, they said, wasn't feeling well that day and had decided at the last minute to stay home.

Anne and Lucy did, indeed, act as flower girls. They were outfitted in their first long dresses ever, petal-pink and pouffed over crinolines, lovingly stitched by their Aunt Irene who sent a little note via her parents telling the girls how sorry she was not to see them march down the aisle, but that she'd be thinking of them all day long.

The bride wore a white dress . . . for the second time. And a white veil . . . for the second time. But today her betrothed waited at the front of the church, a real, flesh-and-blood, beloved man, withheld, at her insistence, from viewing her until the moment she appeared at the foot of the aisle and moved toward him.

She did so while the pipe organ shook the floor with Mendelssohn, and his children strew flower petals grown in their grandparents' gardens. Ahead of Jean, Liz moved—step-point, step-point—gowned in homemade pink a shade deeper than the children's. Beside Eddie, Romaine waited with two rings in his pocket.

Eddie, in a new blue worsted suit, waited with his hands joined, his feet spraddled, stiffly motionless but for one knee that kept locking and unlocking nervously. His face bore a telltale flush beneath its summer tan as he watched his bride approach, her face screened by a shorter veil while an immense one trailed behind, rolling rose petals into cylinders.

As she neared, he made out her eyes—seeking his, eager and happy and nervous all at once. A shot of adrenaline jolted him and prickled his scalp. *How can this be? How can I be so lucky twice in my life?* he thought. Philosophers said love comes only once in a lifetime, but to him it had come twice.

Jean's father squeezed her hand and passed her to Eddie. When she touched his sleeve, he covered her hand, felt it trembling, looked down at her and smiled. He did not remove his hand from hers until the ceremony forced him to.

"*In nomine Patris* . . ." Father Donnelly began, and Eddie had to make the sign of the cross. But the minute it was made, he covered Jean's hand again.

He wanted to look at her some more, but stood as he must, facing the priest.

She wanted to look at him, too, but had to content herself with the constancy of his hand over hers. It seemed the entire nuptial ceremony was masterminded to keep them from gazing at each other. They stood, they knelt, they bowed their heads, they were prayed over, and all the while they stared at the priest's white vestments.

Finally, he murmured instructions for Liz to help Jean turn back her veil, then to the bride and groom, "Would you join right hands, please?"

And the two in love at last cast unfettered gazes upon each other.

She was radiant beneath a halo of white tulle, lifting eyes filled with certainty.

He was splendid in a fresh haircut and white, white collar that made his skin appear copper.

With hearts in one accord, they heard the words, "Repeat after me . . ."

"I, Edward Olczak, take thee, Jean Potlocki, to be my lawful wife, to have and to hold, from this day forward, for better, for worse, for richer, for poorer, in sickness and in health, until death do us part."

By the time he finished, Eddie's heart was clubbing so fiercely his collar felt tighter than it had been.

Then she spoke in the sweet, calming voice he had sought so many times when he was troubled: "I, Jean Potlocki, take thee, Edward Olczak . . ." Her grip on his fingers tightened in earnestness and in her eyes a hint of tears reflected the surrounding candlelight. She felt the tears form while she repeated the phrases that tied her to Eddie for life. ". . . until death do us part."

Father made a cross in the air and sanctified their union. "I join you in holy matrimony in the name of the Father and of the Son and of the Holy Ghost, amen." He raised his silver aspergillum and holy water rained blessings on them. He asked for the rings, blessed them as well, and Eddie repeated: "With this ring, I thee wed." Holding his wife's thin hand, he slipped the band where another had been only four months ago.

She, too, whispered, "With this ring, I thee wed," and slid his new ring over the place where Krystyna's used to be.

The others to whom they'd been wed were with them in that moment as surely as the guests filling the pews behind them, blessing this union and granting it peace.

The church allowed no kisses in the midst of this holy sacrament. Instead, they knelt side by side through the lengthy High Mass, trying to pay attention to the prayers, but distracted time and again by more mortal concerns—the touch of an elbow, thoughts of tonight, the realization they were actually married, the wedding reception that waited, the children fidgeting in their pink dresses, Krystyna, Grandma Rosella. They were married! Married! Tonight they'd be alone, and tomorrow morning they'd attend Mass together in Browerville.

It finished at last.

The organ boomed.

They strode from St. Peter and Paul's and burst into the sunlight where, at last, on the high church steps, he kissed her, politely, reserving his ardor for later, but smiling in jubilation as their mouths parted and their smiling eyes met.

"Mrs. Olczak," he said.

"Oh, the sound of it!" she replied.

Then they turned and submitted themselves to six hours of social obligation.

They tried to find private moments to duck out of sight and kiss, but there were just plain too many people and too few places to hide. Obligations never quit: receiving line, dinner in the farmyard, hugs from well-wishers, perusing the gifts, thanking the gift-openers, spending time with Anne and Lucy and giving special attention to Grandma Rosella, making sure to thank all the relatives who did the cooking, and hauled tables and chairs, and picked their flower gardens bare, and brought the ice blocks and chilled the beer and cleaned the farmyard and set the tables and served the food and cleaned up afterward.

Perhaps the most touching moment of all came when Richard and Mary Pribil congratulated them as they were preparing to leave. Mary captured Eddie and, with an arm around his neck, began to cry. He shut his eyes and held her fast, warding off many emotions of his own, while Richard stood with an arm around Jean.

Lucy, who was departing with her grandparents, pulled on Jean's hand and said, "Why is Grandma crying, Jean?"

Jean bent near the child and answered, "Because she's both happy and sad."

"But why is she sad?"

Jean cupped Lucy's sunburned cheek and said, "Because she misses your mother, and so do I." Anne, too, stood close by. Jean beckoned her over and took a hand of each child in her own. "I was very proud of you today, and I want you to know that I love you both and I will be the best mother I know how. I don't have much experience, so sometimes you might have to help me and tell me what I'm doing wrong, but you had the best teacher of all in your own mother, so I'm quite sure we'll muddle through. Now you be good at Grandpa and Grandma Pribil's house and say your prayers at night, okay?"

"We will."

"And if you want to come home before Wednesday, you just tell them to bring you." The plan was, they'd come home Wednesday afternoon, giving the newlyweds a four-day honeymoon, only they'd be spending it at home in Browerville, where Eddie could settle her in the house and be on hand to take care of the last-minute janitorial duties before the new school year began next week.

Mary had broken free from Eddie and turned to Jean. She opened her arms and hauled Jean close. "My dear . . . have a wonderful life, just as wonderful as you deserve. And always remember, anything you need, you or the kids or Eddie . . . we're always there."

"Thank you, Mary. God bless you."

"That goes double for me," Richard seconded.

"Thank you, Richard. God bless you, too."

"Well, Grandma, come on," Richard said, "let's get these kids in the car and get home to chores. Them cows can't milk themselves."

After seeing the children off, there were final goodbyes and thanks to Jean's family, and while she changed clothes, and her mother stuffed some favorite recipes into her hand, and Eddie's brothers loaded the wedding gifts onto the bed of Eddie's pickup, he stood by impatiently, trying not to pull his pocket watch out every sixty seconds and check the time.

She came out of the house at last, wearing the pretty blue dress she'd made for their first date. He put her in the pickup and somebody stuffed her wedding dress and veils in after her, pushing her to the center of the seat, then finally . . . finally . . . Eddie was starting the engine and they were waving goodbye as they pulled out of the driveway and raised a dustcloud down the road.

It was around six in the evening, the sun still high and the red-winged blackbirds bobbing in the marsh, their songs whistling in the open truck window. Eddie and Jean's responsibilities were behind them and they had the rest of the night to themselves. He peered at her, and she peered back, and they laughed for their freedom.

"I thought we'd never get out of there," he said.

"So did I."

Suddenly he had an idea. "Well, wait a minute. Wait just one gosh-darned minute here," he said, pulling the pickup to the side of the road. He braked, shifted to neutral and said, "Come here, Mrs. Olczak."

She went gladly, into his arms, into his kiss, into the mushroom of white wedding veil where they stayed a good long while, until some de-parting wedding guests came roaring past them on the road, honking their horn and cat-calling out the window. It was Romaine and Rose and a car-ful of kids.

"Hey, Olczaaak . . ." Eddie heard, like a train whistle going past, as he swung away from his new bride. The rest he missed as Romaine's dust rolled in his open window.

He laughed, put the truck in gear and said, "Let's go home."

———

*H*e parked in front of his yellow brick house beneath the box elders, and said, "Leave your dress, would you?" Somewhere between the farm and here their playfulness had disappeared, replaced by a reserve that hid plenty of jitters.

She slid beneath the steering wheel, leaving the froth of white behind, and he walked her to the house, holding her elbow. He decided to take her in through the backdoor, which was out of sight of the street, giving them more privacy. The door was never locked. He swung it open and said, "I thought I'd do the honors," then picked her up and carried her inside.

She had never been inside his house before: they'd been extremely careful to observe every propriety. From his arms she surveyed the kitchen— wood range, white cabinets, running water, and the table and chairs he'd made for Krystyna.

"Put me down, Eddie," she requested quietly.

He stood on the rag rug while she moved about the room, examining it in silence. The chairbacks, the white sink, the angled cabinet doors above it where Krystyna had checked the back of her hair, canisters shaped like apples, the coffeepot on the cold stove, the ice box, a wringer washer crowded behind the door, which brought her full circle around the table, back to him.

Looking up into his face, she said, "It's a very nice kitchen, Eddie. Did you make all this?"

"The cabinets and the table, yeah."

"I thought so. Show me the rest."

The sun was setting through the west living-room window, and the neighborhood children were playing running games outside. Their voices drifted in when he opened the front door, and she took in the maroon horsehair furniture and the upright piano, too big for its corner.

"There's a sewing machine out here," he said, pointing to it in the tiny front entry. "You're welcome to use it anytime."

She passed near him, went to the machine and touched it lightly with her fingertips, giving him the impression she might have said a word to

Krystyna while doing so. She remained facing it for quite some time before turning back to him.

"And there's an upstairs, too."

"Yes." It was clearly visible off the opposite end of the entry. He let her precede him, and when she mounted the bottom step the metal washer bumped the wall on the end of its long string.

"What's this?" she said.

"It's a string so the kids can turn on the light before they go up to bed. Krystyna put it up."

He chided himself for mentioning Krystyna, while Jean pulled the string and looked up as the light came on in the upstairs hall ceiling. She started up the steps and he followed.

"This is the girls' room," he said at the top. She stepped into the sun-lit room and smiled as her eyes wandered over the wallpaper and the rosettes on the window frames that Krystyna had painted white. Sugar was sleeping on the bed, woke up and stretched all four feet straight out in front of her, squint-eyed and stiff.

"This is Sugar," he said. "I'm sure you've heard a lot about her."

"Hi, Sugar," Jean said, giving the cat a cursory scratch before Eddie led her to the other end of the hall.

"And this is our room."

They stood just inside the doorway.

"Oh my, it has a door to outside . . . isn't that lovely."

"We sleep with it open a lot in the summer." He realized too late that he'd said *we*.

"May I?" she said, unfazed, glancing up at him.

"Of course."

She crossed the linoleum and opened the east door, letting in the sound of the children again and the green whisper of the box-elder trees which were much taller than the house. She gazed out over the black tarpaper roof of the porch and put her warm face toward the gentle breeze blowing in.

"There's a bathroom," he said. "I put that in, too, and the hot-water heater."

"I think I'll be lucky, married to a handyman." She came near him and peered into the bathroom. "I don't think there's anything you can't do, Eddie."

"There's a dressing table. I cleared it all out for you, and two dresser drawers, too. The closet's awful tiny, but whatever you have we'll make room for."

"Thank you, Eddie."

He took off his suit jacket and hung it in the closet, then stripped off his tie and looped it over a glass towel rod that Krystyna had screwed onto the inside of the closet door to hold all his Sunday ties. "Well, you know what?" he said. "I'd better get those wedding gifts inside in case it rains."

"Do you want me to help you?" she asked, but he was already heading for the stairs.

"Naw, I'll take care of it. If there's anything you need, just open doors and look."

She went into the bathroom and opened a pink cupboard to find a clean washcloth. While he pounded in and out of the house downstairs, she washed her face and looked inside the medicine chest. His razor and shaving mug were inside. She picked up the soft brush and ran it over her jaws and beneath her nose, recognizing a scent he carried on his skin early in the day, or late in the day if they had a date.

The doors closed downstairs, first the front, then the back, and his footsteps returned: everything was closed up for the night.

But it was barely eight o'clock, and the sun hadn't even dropped below the horizon. It streamed through the west bathroom window, straight through the doorway and across the blue scatter rug beside their bed.

She was standing uncertainly near the dressing table when Eddie reached the doorway, bearing with him her suitcase.

"I brought you this," he said, and put it on the foot of the bed.

"Thank you." She went to it and snapped open the cheap metal locks, folded back the top and took out a white plissé nightie while he hovered nearby, at odds with the time of day.

"Eddie, there's something that I want to say." She turned and found him close behind her. "I understand that this was Krystyna's house, that she lived here with you and shared your life. And it's okay when you mention her name, and when you tell me this was hers, or that was hers, or that she did whatever for Anne and Lucy. Memories of her will be here for many years to come, but because I love you, and because I know you love me, it takes nothing away from our marriage. So, please, Eddie, don't look so guilty when you mention her name."

In the beat before he scooped her into his arms she saw relief flood his face. "Dear God, how I love you," he breathed, clasping her as he might a child he'd just plucked from in front of a runaway team.

"I love you, too," she told him gently.

"I think, Jean Olczak, that you're a saint."

"Oh, no I'm not. I'm so very mortal that I'm scared out of my wits right now."

"Don't be scared . . ." He eased his hold and repeated, softer, into her eyes. "Don't be scared."

"What should I do?" she asked.

"Go into the bathroom and put your nightgown on."

There were precedents being set here; she didn't want to live like her Grandma and Grandpa Potlocki. So she left the door open but slipped behind it to change clothes.

When she padded back into the bedroom, her suitcase was closed on the floor, the bed was turned down, and Eddie was wearing nothing but trousers, leaning against the doorframe with one shoulder, looking out at the twilight. The children's voices had disappeared. Purple shadows were stealing over the town. Mosquitoes buzzed futilely at the screens.

Sensing her return, Eddie sent a glance over his shoulder and opened his free arm. It closed around her when she reached him, then he shifted her over and settled her comfortably against his front. She liked his ways, felt soothed by the length of him warming her back, but stirred by this first intimacy with a man. His scanty clothes, her nightwear, both of them barefooted—all innocent, but more than she'd ever experienced. It was hard to believe that what she wanted to do with him was no longer a sin. All those years she had striven to put all thoughts of carnality out of her mind; now she strove to put them in, to know what to do, and when. But, of course, she knew nothing.

She reached back and rested her hands on his trouser legs, and he started kissing her neck, his right arm clamped firmly across her collarbone.

"I'll tell you something . . ." he said, nuzzling her earlobe. "I'm a little scared myself."

"Why?"

"You have to ask me that? An ex-nun?"

"But it isn't new to you."

"Oh, yes it is. It feels new."

So she thought she'd do her part, what little part she knew. She turned in his embrace and kissed him, tucking her elbows to his ribs and folding her arms up his bare back, following her instincts. His back was warm and long, the ridge up the middle inviting beneath her fingertips. While she explored it, he drew away from the doorframe and coiled more sharply into the kiss, opening his mouth. Touching him, tasting him was the best thing she ever remembered being allowed to touch and taste. It grew easier and easier while minutes stretched on and she acquainted her hands with his shoulders, and ribs, the hair on his chest, and the beltline of his trousers.

In time he fell against the doorframe again, hauling her with him and wrapping one bare foot around her calf, forcing her body into an arc against his.

They fit exquisitely, and she experimented, rising against him.

Abruptly, he lifted his head, found her hand and whispered, "Come with me." To the bed he led her, and sideways across it so they could see each other. He kissed her eyes, cheeks, nose, mouth, and covered her breast with an unhurried caress.

She fell still beneath it, wonder-struck by discovery. Through half-opened eyes he watched her face, the lips fallen open, the breath shallow and quick while he moved his hand, pleasuring her through the soft puckered cloth, gathering it and her in his hand as if picking tender fruit from a tree. He lowered his head and closed his eyes, his lashes sweeping against her nightgown as he kissed her through it, on one breast, then the other, rolling her gently to her back.

She murmured once, his name he thought. "Oh, Eddie . . ." before sensations silenced her again.

He lay on her, let her feel his weight for a while, and learn the movement of an aroused body. He gave her time, easing her through the rudiments of early sensation, showing her without words what was yet to come. He reached behind her, ran a hand the length of her longest, smoothest curve—twice, thrice, and yet again before finding the hollow behind her knee, and finally he felt her hip and leg relax. Then once again he made a space and spread a hand on her stomach, feeling it palpitate with each short, stressed breath she took as the hand remained, firm, idle, open. Soon it pressed, stirring the soft cloth of her nightie into a whorl to match that within her heart.

And at last, at long-awaited last, he touched her through the wrinkled cotton.

She held her breath and lay unmoving. She might have been a carving, so still she remained, tensed, arched, expectant.

But no carving was this warm.

He whispered something to her, something to calm whatever fears she held, called her Jean, darling Jean, put your hand on me, too, Jean, you can, it's all right, let me take this off, Jean, Jean . . . ahh, Jean . . .

He taught her things he'd learned with Krystyna, and there, in the lessons, Krystyna brought them another gift. For it *was* a gift, and wondrous, and deserved. They had waited, done the pure, right thing, postponed every pleasure till they'd earned its right through marriage. And when that marriage was consummated, there in the dark of that warm August night, they emerged resplendent, loved and loving.

———

$\mathcal{S}$he said, afterward, with wonder in her voice, entwined with him, still, "Isn't God wonderful . . . thinking up such a thing?"

Eddie kissed her forehead and rested his cheek against it. "I think he's pretty wonderful for giving you up to me."

"I do, too," she said, and fit her foot into the snuggliest place on him, and her hand, and one bent knee. "I hope you like sleeping all snuggled up, because I know I'm going to want to be like this a lot. I've slept alone too long."

He wriggled deeper and spread his hand wider on her flank. Down the hallway the caramel-colored cat walked silently. At their doorway, it stopped and listened, unseen.

Jean said, "Eddie, could I ask you something?"

"Sure."

It took her a while to work up the courage. "How often . . . I mean . . ."

"How often—?" he encouraged.

"Nothing. Just forget it."

"No, you were going to ask, so ask."

"Well, how often do men and women—um—do this?"

He laughed heartily and rubbed her bare hip and said, "Ah . . . my adorable virgin bride."

"You promised me you wouldn't laugh at my ignorance."

"I'm not laughing at you, darling, you just tickle me. You're so perfectly innocent."

"All right, then, how often *do* they?"

He decided to have some fun with her. "Well, let me see—tomorrow is Sunday and once Mass is taken care of, we've got the whole day to ourselves, so we could do it, say, thirty, forty times. But then on—"

"Thirty or forty!"

"But then on workdays we'd have to cut that down some. Let's see . . . I ring the first bell at seven-thirty. Say we do it at six-thirty A.M., then I could run home before the noon Angelus and squeeze one in then, but at the supper Angelus it'll be tougher, because the kids will be around then, so we might have to wait till bedtime. Then, after bedtime, why, heck, I'd say we could manage seven, eight times before we fell asleep if we—"

"Oh, Eddie, you're teasing." She gave him a punch through the soft bedspread.

"No, no! Look, we got seven more times yet tonight. Will that satisfy you? It better, 'cause, I mean, I've got to get *some* sleep. A man can't live on sex alone."

"Oh, Eddie, are you always such a tease?"

"When I love a woman, I am. And I sure do love you, my little petunia." His voice lost a lot of its teasing, got soft and seductive. "I suuure do love you."

They kissed, and afterward he told her, in the voice of a patient teacher, "We can do it every day if you like. Usually at the beginning, when people first fall in love, they want to do it more than once a day, then after they're married awhile they do it less often. Maybe a couple times a week, maybe more, maybe less. When women get pregnant they don't feel much like doing it, then toward the end they're not allowed to do it at all."

They thought about that awhile, and she said, "Just think . . . I could be pregnant right now."

"And what would you think?"

"I said a Novena asking that it would happen soon."

He reared back and looked down at her, surprised. "You did?" In the dark he could scarcely see a rim of light on her hair.

"Yes, I did. I'd take as many of your babies as I could get."

"Oh, Jean . . ." He hauled her up from the crook of his shoulder and kissed her softly, then rubbed a finger over her lips time and again. "I'm so lucky."

They thought about the children they might have, the ones they already had, and a future of loving them all, working hard for them, and for each other. At the foot of the bed, they felt Sugar jump up and pick her way tentatively up the bedspread.

Eddie's hand went down and found the cat. "Hi, Sugar, you miss the girls, huh?"

"Hi, Sugar." Jean's hand joined his, scratching Sugar's soft fur. She hadn't had a cat since she lived on the farm as a girl.

"I like cats," she said.

The cat started purring. They were getting blissfully sleepy, their thoughts fraying.

Suddenly Jean sat up and threw the covers back. "Oh my gosh, I forgot my prayers."

She scrambled from the bed, got to her knees and joined her hands, naked as a jaybird, while he grinned to himself in the dark. He didn't interrupt her, but neither did he join her. He'd had enough prayer for one day during their long wedding ceremony. Besides, what they'd done together seemed like a prayer to him.

Pretty soon she finished and climbed back in. He held back the covers for her, and she found her old spot on his shoulder, with her knee once again across his midsection.

"Do you kneel down and pray every night?" he asked.

"It's an old habit, hard to break."

"Ah." He understood.

"Eddie?"

"Hm?"

"I'll need to get a driver's license, but first I'll have to learn to drive. Will you teach me?"

"Of course. Why?"

"So I can take the nuns to St. Cloud or Long Prairie when they need their eyes examined, or their teeth filled. Like Krystyna did."

"Oh. Like Krystyna did."

"Yes."

"And maybe we could ask your mother or Krystyna's mother if they've got enough cabbage in the garden that we could make up a big batch of sauerkraut for them like she always did. Oh, Eddie, we loved that sauerkraut so much, and we waited for it every year."

He smiled and thought what a curious subject to be discussing on his wedding night: sauerkraut for the nuns.

But he understood, there would always be a little touch of Sister Regina left in his wife, Jean. But that was okay with Eddie. After all, it was the nun he'd fallen in love with.

When he was growing woozy he mumbled above her ear, "G'night, Sister."

But she was already asleep, dreaming of having his babies.